# THE ITALIAN TEACHER

Also by Tom Rachman

*The Imperfectionists*
*The Rise and Fall of Great Powers*

# The Italian Teacher

## Tom Rachman

Doubleday Canada

Doubleday Canada and colophon are registered trademarks of
Penguin Random House Canada Limited

First published in Great Britain by riverrun, an imprint of Quercus Publishing

Library and Archives Canada Cataloguing in Publication

Rachman, Tom, author
The Italian teacher / Tom Rachman.

Issued in print and electronic formats.
ISBN 978-0-385-68960-1 (hardcover).—ISBN 978-0-385-68961-8 (EPUB)
I. Title.
PS8635.A333I83 2018          C813'.6          C2017-904912-7
C2017-904913-5

Designed by Amy Hill
Jacket image by photominus/Getty Images

Printed and bound in the USA

Published in Canada by Doubleday Canada,
a division of Penguin Random House Canada Limited

www.penguinrandomhouse.ca

10 9 8 7 6 5 4 3 2 1

Penguin
Random House
DOUBLEDAY CANADA

*For Alessandra*

# Childhood

OIL ON CANVAS

68 X 160 INCHES

Courtesy of the Bavinsky Estate

# Rome, 1955

## 1

Seated in a copper bathtub, Bear Bavinsky dunks his head under steaming water and shakes out his beard, flinging droplets across the art studio. He thumbs a bolt of shag into his pipe and flicks a brass Zippo lighter, sucking hard to draw down the flame, tobacco glowing devil-red, smoke coiling toward the wood-beam ceiling. He exhales and stands. Beads of water rain off his torso.

His five-year-old son, Pinch, hoists a thick bath towel, arms trembling under the weight. Bear runs his fingers through receding reddish-blond hair and—hand on the boy's head for balance—steps onto newspapers previously used for wiping paintbrushes. His wet footprints bleed across the print, encircling dabs of oily blue and swipes of yellow.

"That's final!" Natalie declares from across the studio, chewing her fingernail.

"Final, is it? You certain?" Bear asks his wife. "Not the slightest doubt?"

"All I've got is doubts."

He proceeds to the iron front door and shoulders it open, dusky light from the alleyway pushing past him, glinting off glass pigment

*3*

jars, illuminating abused paintbrushes in turpentine and canvases drying along the bare-brick walls. In the early-evening air, he stands in place, a fortyish male animal, naked but for the towel twisted around his neck, his shadow narrowing up the studio, hurdling the tub, darkening his wife and their little boy. "Absolutely positive then?"

Natalie yanks a strand of black hair over her eyes, wraps it around her baby finger, whose tip reddens. She darts into the WC at the back of the studio and closes the warped door, her head bumping the bare bulb, which alternates glare and gloom as she consults the mirror: emerald ball gown cinched at the waist, box-pleated skirt, polka-dot overlay. It's as if she were wearing three outfits at once, none of them hers. She tucks her hair under a cream beret but it hardly helps, the same gawky twenty-six-year-old looking back, all elbows and knees, a manly jaw, deep-set black eyes, as uncertain as if drawn with smudged charcoal, the worry lines added in fine-nib pen.

She joins Bear, who remains naked in the doorway, a puff of smoke released from his pipe. "I'm not even acceptable," she tells him, and he rests a rough palm against the swell of her bosom, firmly enough to quicken her pulse. He strides to his leather suitcase and plucks out neckties, one for himself, one for their son. Bear raises the louder tie, holding it up as if considering a mackerel. He sends Pinch to fetch the canvas shears, with which he snips one of the ties in half, twirling it around the boy's neck. "What do you say, kiddo?" Bear grins, the beard rising to his eyes, which disappear into slits. "Natty, I love the hell out of you. And I listen the hell out of you. But damn it, sweetie, we are going."

She clutches one hand in the other. "Well then, hurry!" she responds, quickstepping past her husband, nearly stumbling as she crouches to knot their son's tie. Natalie touches Pinch's forehead, her hand throbbing against his brow, jittery fingers like a secret message: "We waited all this time, Pinchy, and now he's *here!*"

Bear, who moved in only weeks earlier, approaches his son, mussing the boy's fine sandy hair (quite like Dad's), playfully flicking the kid's nervous chin (like his mother's), while Pinch's blue eyes (with an urgency all their own) gaze up, awaiting his father's command.

## 2

High above the cobbled streets between Trastevere and the Vatican, a cloud of starlings swings back and forth like a black pendulum across the sky. The three Bavinskys are speed-walking from the studio toward the center of Rome, with Natalie clasping Bear's arm and pulling Pinch to her other flank. She raises her husband's sleeve to read his scratched wristwatch.

"Don't fret, Natty," he tells her. "Nothing but friends tonight."

"Yes, your friends."

When she was living here with Pinch alone, Natalie heard from nobody. Then Bear moved to Rome and the invitations gushed in. He avoids soirees but agreed for her sake—there'll be fellow artists, and she needs to circulate, to find collaborators for her own work. This is her night, promised and planned, minutes away. "They'll be busting to meet you," he insists.

Natalie has spent six years in Rome—an astonishing stretch given that there were days she scarcely endured, crumpling from isolation, especially after giving birth alone, a disastrous delivery that ruined her insides, meaning Pinch will be her only child. From the start, she clung to him, yet was clueless about child-rearing, rescued by Italian neighbors around whom she played the free-spirited Canadian lass, awaiting her famed American painter husband (even if she and Bear weren't technically married at the start). He turned up each summer, painting compulsively, Natalie sitting for him in the sweltering heat, their son dozing by the wall. At summer's end, she would pack his suitcase, bereft at the sight of Bear dragging himself back to New York again, where three daughters and a spouse wouldn't let go. All that is done now. He pledged to move here for good, and proved true to his word.

As they hurry over Ponte Mazzini, Bear leans over, smushing their boy between, and kisses his young wife flush on the mouth, smearing her lipstick. "Listen to me, rhubarb: I love you, and they will too." As long as his gaze holds, she believes it.

They arrive at a palazzo overlooking the weary green Tiber, and Bear thumps on its vast door with both fists, a syncopated jazz beat. The footman bursts forth, hurrying them in—late! late!—conveying the Bavinskys past a drizzling Renaissance fountain, up a marble staircase lined with ancient Roman statuary, into a ballroom of soaring ceilings frescoed with Mars and Venus in various stages of marital discord. At twin grand pianos, maestros in tailcoats tinkle Debussy while scores of revelers chortle and slurp from champagne coupes, their cigarettes leaking gray ribbons before rococo murals and avant-garde artworks by Guttuso, De Chirico, Burri.

In attendance are sculptors, writers, and composers; Anglo women who married Italian nobility (gals from Wisconsin once, now princess-something); plus all the expat businessmen: the Procter & Gamble guy, the Aramco fella, the Coca-Cola man, alongside wives who, when their dearly beloved cracks a joke, either tilt forward uproariously or just sip a drink. "Well, he sure has your number, Joan!"

Natalie can pick out the artists from their outfits—baggy suits, scuffed shoes—while the socialites wear shiny silk numbers, yanking up long gloves and yanking along portly menfolk in three-pieces, gold watch-chains swinging. The groups can also be distinguished by topic of conversation: The moneyed all speak of art, the artists all speak of money.

"Wait just a second," the middle-aged party hostess says. Squinting into pince-nez as if through peepholes, she sashays over, waving a clutch purse designed like a pink lobster and holding down a hat shaped like a high-heeled shoe. Mishmish Shapiro is an art collector of Californian provenance who, years before, escaped a bout of ennui by hurling herself into the beauty of Rome, landing in the arms of Count Ugobaldo, a shabby aristocrat who paints surrealist landscapes and cries. If she has an ulterior motive (and Mishmish always keeps a few handy) for having pressed Bear to attend, it's to convince him to sell. She owns a couple of early Bavinskys, but he disavows those as juvenilia. His new paintings are the prize—they are truly something else, it's said, and diabolically hard to lay one's hands on.

"I was scared half to death that your mob wouldn't make it," Mishmish says cheerily, clasping Bear's hand and touching Pinch on the head. "Oh, what an adorable scamp! You found him in some dark *vicolo*, did you?" She nods to a butler, who has been hovering, to add this ankle biter to those already stashed in a distant nursery. Once the boy is dispatched, Mishmish appraises the big-boned young wife of Bear, from her shoe straps to her beret. "Well, you sure are a tall drink of water," Mishmish concludes. "Speaking of, who's thirsty?"

"Oh, I would *love* a drink," Natalie answers.

"Patience," Mishmish replies acidly. "You're not speaking to the barman."

A flush rises up Natalie's chest. She apologizes but is hardly heard: Guests keep noticing the celebrated painter in their midst and push closer, among them an oak of a man, branches aloft. "Well, if it ain't big old Bear! How in the Sam Hill are you?"

"Holy smoke! Rod, old man! What brings you to the Holy Roman Empire?"

Natalie swipes two glasses off a waiter's tray and hands one to her husband, who clinks distractedly, the crystal *ting* vibrating till her lips meet the rim. She holds her nose above the liquid, hiding herself in its fizz. As the scrum jostles her, strangers converge around Bear. A wall of backs closes before her.

## 3

Bear reaches through the crowd, dragging Natalie to his side. "My miraculous wife, a serious talent in her own right," he says. "Tell them, sweetheart."

A mass of eyeballs turns to her.

"Now listen here, Bear," someone interrupts. "You've simply got to explain how . . ."

Nobody came to meet an unknown lady potter. They're here for Bear Bavinsky, creator of expressionistic masterworks, wild colors crashing across each composition, a bare throat filling the huge canvas, or a roll of tummy fat, or a pricked shoulder. His detail portraits are *too* intimate—uncomfortably penetrating despite never once including a subject's face.

In 1953, when *Life* magazine trumpeted Bear Bavinsky as "tomorrow's action painter, conjoining twentieth-century dynamism with classical forms," what it meant was, "Here's an artist who doesn't drizzle paints, as your kid could." But what drew most attention was the photo of Bear's New York studio with, in the foreground, the long leg of a female sitter, presumably undressed. And not just "presumably," for the snapshot inadvertently included a mirror reflection of the woman's right breast, the first occasion on which that eminent chronicle of Americana had featured a distaff nipple. Discovering its calamity, *Life* pulled the issue, turning a modest profile into "that notorious piece," establishing Bear as the archetype of immoral Greenwich Village artist—precisely the type this expat crowd is itching to meet.

"What you got brewing, Bear?" asks the saucy wife of a Chicago adman. "How's about a show for us yokels here in the provinces?"

"I fear you won't get far," Natalie warns her. "My husband never talks about his work."

But the crowd's attention remains stuck on Bear, who makes a nearly identical comment to hers, prompting stern nods all around. "Fact is, I burn most everything," he continues. "Maybe six canvases a year make the cut. Mishmish, you won't like this, but I never painted to get on the walls of some palace."

Natalie adds, "Bear's art is intended for the public—for museums, for places where regular people can see them."

"Regular people at museums?" Mishmish responds. "If *they* start turning up at museums, what possible reason would there be to go anymore?"

Everyone laughs, after which Bear addresses the crowd. "My advice, folks? Don't waste your time on a dope like me." A wink, a half smile, a puff of his pipe. Everyone is beaming.

Natalie knocks back another glass of champagne, bubbles burning her throat. She's queasy, as if about to tumble. Everyone here is so much older and so sophisticated. On a passing tray she deposits the glass and steps back from everyone, clasping both hands atop her beret, cramming it down as if to stub herself into the marble floor. She watches these people yet sees only herself—big ugly hands, knobbled from making ceramics that nobody cares to see. Actually, the idea of them viewing her work fills Natalie with shame. She stops a passing man for a cigarette. He doles one out and moves on, never offering a match. Her unlit cigarette raised, she casts about, ignored. Cackles of laughter emerge around her husband. He may deplore these events, but he's so skilled at them. Everybody solicits his views—about art in the Soviet bloc, about Ike's health, about rival painters. "What I'd like know," one gent says, "is whether you understand Señor Picasso's work. I mean *truly* understand it."

Natalie wishes herself erased. Looking to a far wall, she glimpses something, her eyes narrowing. She stoops to see better. Among dangling purses and wobbly knees, Pinch is there, reaching up to a silver bowl, bringing down fistfuls of peanuts, gobbling them from cupped hands. He must've escaped the nursery, wanting away from his peers, much as she wants away from hers.

She moves through islands and eddies of people, and Pinch sees her approaching. His expression brightens, matching hers. Natalie opens her skirt pocket, and he deposits the peanuts for safekeeping. He points to her ear, which she lowers to his height.

"Mommy, can we go?"

Out in the courtyard, they sit on the lip of a burbling fountain, Pinch recounting adventures from when lost in this palazzo, that he found an old man asleep in the library, and a staircase in the wall, and a giant marble foot in the basement. She deposits another peanut into his hot palm—the hand closes fast, snaffling it to salty lips. From above, the party echoes, cries of amusement jabbing at her. She drags a strand of hair from under her beret, pulls it, straining the roots, her neck stiffening, jaw clenched against the pain.

The five-year-old reaches into her dress pocket. She squeezes him around the middle, trying to mimic Bear's rough cuddles, almost tight enough to crack a rib. "You saved me," she tells him, nose to Pinch's ear.

Confused, the boy pushes back, looking at his snipped tie.

Rebuffed, Natalie takes out that unlit cigarette, holds it out as if for a waiter—then crushes it, sprinkling tobacco in the fountain, brown threads bobbing on the frothy surface. "Don't worry," she tells Pinch. "Your father will get here soon. He'll save you soon enough."

4

Bear's studio was once a grain depot at the walls of a sixteenth-century prison, but today is a cave of a workshop, dingy because Bear prefers it that way, seeking extremes of shadow in his paintings. It's also where they live, Natalie having first posed on the drapery at the back, then moved in, now raising their son here. The only sources of illumination are three scorching metal spotlights that Bear picked up from a props guy at Cinecittà, plus whatever daylight sneaks through the iron door. When it swings open late one Sunday morning in December, Bear stands there, fresh from his favorite bakery near Campo de' Fiori, which he visited after a late night out.

"Hello, my reptiles," he calls to them, lobbing a warm *bignè* toward his wife and another to the comic-reading Pinch, who fails to catch it, stumbling from bed to chase the bouncing pastry, which skitters down the paint-spattered stone floor. Bear quick-steps over and captures the custard-filled treat in a snatch, slapping it into his son's hand, then flopping onto the boy's narrow bed, the crunch of comic pages underneath. Grinning, Pinch stands by, stuffing in *bignè*, allowing Dad to poke him playfully in the ribs.

Before all this commotion, Natalie was enjoying a rare tranquil morning to work on her own art. She persists with her efforts but this proves challenging, especially with Bear now tickling Pinch, who shrieks and rushes off, only to return for more, giggling madly. Natalie preps clay, lines up sponges and turning tools and scrapers, fills her battered wooden bucket with fresh water from the drinking fountain outside, and plonks it by the potter's wheel. She massages her neck, imagining sculptural forms, clay squeezed into mad shapes, lunatic glazes slapped on—*what I want to make. Am I capable?*

Turning from her two males, she kicks the potter's wheel into action, willing its motion to spur theirs. Bear promised to take their son to the Christmas fair in Piazza Navona today. *Has he forgotten?* Stomach tensed, she centers a lump of wet clay, hearing them horsing around, hunting missing socks and orphaned shoes. But gradually, Natalie grows beguiled by the wheel's rotations and the shape rising under her hands. She torques around, a beseeching gaze at her husband.

He raises his right hand, then hurries to the back of the studio, looking for something, dragging out a blank canvas on stretchers. "Stay how you are right now, Natty. That right there."

"I was doing work," she implores him. "Bear?" She clasps a beige sponge, which dribbles down her wrist. The potter's wheel slows, off-kilter rotations chafing her inner thigh.

Bear apologizes as he circles Natalie, doing preliminary studies and contour drawings in a sketch pad, his charcoal stick cracking, carbon dust in the air. "Just a second. I swear. You're too tempting— it's your own goddamn fault!" he says as if joshing, but frowns, backing off, leaning in, alternating between her and the oversized canvas, whose front side he hasn't marked but on whose back he wipes his hands, impressing black fingerprints and tobacco strings into the weft. He darts away to drop the gramophone needle. A record hisses, then wails. He needs a racket to work, a rhythm to his elsewhere thoughts. The jazz single lasts a few minutes, and he's still laboring. Pinch crawls over, rowing both hands on the paint-thick crank of Dad's portable Telefunken, cautiously lowering the diamond tip, which undulates over the wonky 78, one of a stack of records Bear purloined from the Armed Forces Radio Service during the war. *Hiya, fellas. This is Gene Krupa. My trio and I are going to knock out a little jazz for you on this V-disc.* A ruffling drumroll, vamping piano, hooting sax.

Bear mutters, mixing paints, his forehead creased, pebbled with sweat. He glowers at the blank canvas, teeth edges grazing.

"My clay is drying out," she says.

"No, I'm done here." But not quite. Almost. Nearly. He flings on colors with the palette knife, buttery oils trembling. He drags a hoghair brush across the support, ferrule scratching the canvas raw. "I'm finished," he reiterates yet is still working, with bare fingers now, fingernails raking the image. "Don't move. I'm finished. No, wait."

After the same record has played for the twenty-seventh time, Pinch prepares to drop the needle again, looking to his father for approval. Bear is occupied, cursing this bastard of a painting, especially when he achieves something sublime, as if it's him against the picture and he just slipped something past his foe. He works on all parts of the painting at once, adjusting harmony, refining, obliterating— the pain of it being wrong, fucking *wrong* still. "A minute more, sweetie."

She clutches her bare knees, shivering. (Bear never closed the front door.) A magnified part of her body takes form on the other side of the canvas, but she doesn't know which—his sitters are never allowed to know, lest they become self-conscious and adjust.

Abruptly he halts, jotting something in the sketch pad. He tears out the page and summons Pinch, who is sent back to his mother with the folded note. She opens Bear's letter, mailed from across the room: "To my Natty, loved more than paints can say." What strikes her is that Bear signed it, his full name, underscored with a flourish.

"Bear, please."

"Finishing up. Need you there one second. One more. Just." His voice trails off, gaze alternating between her and his canvas, capturing something essential about her, and failing to hear one word.

# 5

Natalie was barely twenty, he nearing forty, when they met. It was July 1949, and Bear was browsing around a cramped art-supplies store near the Pantheon, searching for rabbit-skin glue. Natalie, in Rome that summer to study drawing, recognized him immediately, and with a flutter, because this man had been featured in newspapers. What was he doing here? Eavesdropping on his bungled attempts at the local language, she held her breath and stepped forth, addressing the clerk in French, which was as close as she got to Italian in those days. *"Colle de lapin, peut-être?"*

"You're a magician," Bear told her, scratching the thicket of his beard. "And you just earned yourself lunch."

"For that?" she asked, unable to hold eye contact, wondering if he teased. These had been lonely weeks: a room rented at a convent where she pretended (with diminishing success) to be Catholic, and struggling through art classes conducted entirely in Italian.

"Young lady, I've fed people for less."

"Lucky I didn't do anything truly useful, or who knows what you'd owe me."

"I'd be buying you dinner too, maybe breakfast besides. Alas, it's only lunch for now. What say you? I'd tell you I could eat a horse, but one of these locals might hold me to my word." He winked, twinkling at her.

Minutes later, Bear was leading her down a narrow, urine-scented Roman side street, laundry fluttering overhead, a tomcat scampering before them. The best lunch joint in the city lay straight ahead, he promised, his orotund American tones booming off the shadowed medieval walls that hemmed them in—until she emerged, dazzled by sunlight, on a tiny piazza, his promised restaurant across the way.

Bear chose a table in the far corner and queried Natalie about her art, listening with genuine curiosity, conferring with her as if before a venerable colleague. She sat on her sweaty hands, sliding down in the chair to diminish her height to match his, while slowing certain responses to imply gravity—only to lose nerve and rush out the line, as if she were ever scrambling up a heap of words that kept collapsing beneath her. For safety, she moved the discussion back to him.

Without airs, he recounted his dealings in the New York art milieu: quirky collectors, avaricious dealers, boldface-name artists she'd read about but whom he knew personally. In each story, he downplayed his role, as if he were a bumbler among the greats. At Franz Kline's softball game, Bear struck out five times and chucked a ball at Harold Rosenberg, knocking out the critic's tooth. "I was not asked back." He drank homebrew cider at the de Koonings and threw up in their sink, earning the lifelong enmity of Elaine. When Bear visited Pollock's barn in East Hampton, Jackson was drunk and threatened to "knock that wiseacre look off you." He slapped Bear twice, left and right.

"Were you hurt?" Natalie asked.

"What people don't realize about me is that I boxed in college," Bear responded, smile forming. "Unfortunately, it was art college."

She laughed, confidence rising. "Plenty of painters slapped you around, have they, Mr. Bavinsky?"

"Plenty would like to." He explained that his paintings bothered that milieu. They scorned his jaunts around Europe, considering it hoity-toity that he dwelled in the pulverized Old Continent years after its most renowned artists had escaped to New York City, rendering *that* the capital of art, a metropolis suited to mammoth canvases and mighty brushstrokes.

"So the Europeans are more welcoming?"

"Not especially," he admitted. "Pablo Picasso nearly took a swing at me one time." At the time, Bear was in liberated Paris with a gaggle of fellow U.S. infantrymen, artistic souls stuck in uniform who called on the master's atelier in Rue des Grand Augustins. "A pigeon is to blame, as so often it is," Bear joked. "Nobody but the great man was to touch this pet of his. Certainly not some lowlife such as yours truly. But I'll be darned if that bird didn't up and land on my shoulder. Is it my fault? Poor Pablo was torn up with jealousy. Watching me stroke that bird, he gets hotter and hotter, finally shouting, 'All yous, outta here!' Or however they say that in French. He marched up, grabbed my lapel, and shoved me halfway to the door."

"Did you fight him?"

"What do you take me for? I've seen how that guy rearranges faces!"

She grinned at that, cheeks burning, looking a smidgen too long. It was hard not to stare. The famous are compelling up close, like big game.

A waiter in bow tie and waistcoat arrived, his eyebrows raised at her.

Natalie hadn't considered the menu—come to think of it, she hadn't seen one.

"Me, a *piatto di* Gillardeau oysters," Bear interceded, to buy her time. "Then *rigatoni alla amatriciana*, and the roast *vitello* with that mushroom sauce. As for liquids, what are you selling in the way of *vino rosso?* Something we can wade through; surprise us." The waiter nodded humbly and swiveled back to Natalie, hanging over her like a bat.

She felt a fool to replicate Bear's order, as if broadcasting that she had no ideas of her own. So she delayed, a blush spreading up her chest. She glanced at other diners' choices, her toes curling under the table. "I'm keeping everyone waiting."

"Everyone who?" He beckoned her closer for a little friendly advice. "Would it offend you, my new friend, if I had them bring you what I got? You won't regret it. Best dishes in the place. That's a promise."

So they took the same meal, and Natalie raved about each plate, eager to affirm the senior artist's wisdom. She matched him in glasses of Barbaresco too, the room growing warmer, louder. When the roast veal arrived in thick dry slices, Bear pointed to a shared gravy boat. She dripped a dot of this sauce at the edge of her plate—after which Bear deluged his meat, the steaming porcini sauce oozing everywhere.

"There are folks that drip their gravy to one side," Bear commented, "and there are folks that pour it right over everything."

"I'm always worried about ruining what I already have," Natalie said. But the truth was more complicated. Sometimes she had lurched into rash decisions, and suffered regret—the kind that deepens, its pang worsening over time. This defect made Bear especially appealing: His cavalier style safeguarded her; he emboldened Natalie to *try*. So, she upturned that gravy boat right over her own meat, watching him. He reached out, touching her cheek with fondest familiarity—for the sauce was all gone but for one drop, which hung off the lip of the inverted crockery, straining to fall.

In Natalie's life, few men had touched her face with romantic intent, typically during civilized conversation, when a fellow's lips smushed clumsily into hers, his eyelids ardently shut, hers fluttering. But Bear was different—not a schoolboy in Montreal, nor one of the self-serious chappies from art college in London. She wasn't even panicking this time, though her pulse raced. It was as if she had walked onto a property and knew uncannily: This is my home. This is where I'll live.

Claiming a need for the ladies room, she stood, feeling the booze as she edged across the raucous dining area, shifting her broad hips at each red calico tablecloth, all presided over by Italian business-men, many pausing to ogle the foreign girl. Natalie kept her gaze down, stepping over napkins and toothpicks, her eyes smarting from the rising cigarette smoke. Outside, she inhaled deeply, the *sanpie-trini* cobblestones rubbery under her heels. She walked fast around that small piazza, halting at the limestone facade of a church, against which she pressed her overwarm face—only to leap in fright when a bicycle juddered past, its rider gesticulating to his fiancée on the back as they trundled by a torn movie billboard. Under the restaurant awning, a hangdog waiter waited, surveying her.

*Does he see that I don't fit here?*

When Bear was busy tangling with Pablo, she was still in high school, a pretender even there, unable to tell anyone about home, where her father was sick, and worsening. In Natalie's mid-adolescence, her father shot himself in the face. He survived, disfigured, nursed up-stairs, his moans coming from that room. Back then, she confided this only once, to her high school art teacher, Mr. Fontaine, a failed sculp-tor who introduced her to abstract art and to pottery. "Could there be abstract *pottery*, Mr. Fontaine?" she inquired, when they were alone in a classroom after school. He answered by thrusting his tongue into her mouth, edging her hand to his groin. Behind his smock was the dusty blackboard, marked from a history class, obliging her to read "The Diet of Worms" throughout that jerky first sex act, after which Mr. Fontaine slumped and tucked in his shirt, treating her frigidly ever afterward.

Standing tipsily in the piazza, she experienced a surge of vindica-tion: *I'm in Europe, dining with a proper artist.* She glared at the hang-dog waiter, causing him to slink back inside. Legs wonky, she strode toward the restaurant. *A painter who will go down in history is waiting for me. Right this instant.* She covered her mouth, saying to her hand: "I'm an artist."

As she entered the dining room, Bear summoned her urgently. Red-cheeked, she settled across from her future, ignoring the fresh boat of gravy but daring under the table to touch his hand.

6

She has been posing for hours, listening to that same jazz record. "Bear, I can't." Words struggle from her throat. Minutes more pass— until he throws his paintbrush across the studio floor, threads of ultramarine spitting, causing Pinch to leap from the gramophone.

Bear kicks his easel, which shakes, and he wipes his hands on a discarded *Herald Tribune*. He leads Natalie from her potter's wheel, around his canvas, so that she may finally view the portrait: the paint thick and wet and glossy, scratched off in parts by his fingernails, a convulsion of colors. The image is enlarged almost to abstraction, yet it is distinctly her: just hands, nothing more, her fingers knotted as when she speaks, fearing herself dull, fraudulent. And he sees that.

Bear opens his shears into an X.

"What are you doing?"

He stabs the canvas, slices diagonally, paint accumulating up his hand, a lip of fabric gaping.

"Bear! Why are you doing that? Can you say something to me? Bear?"

"It's not right. I can't remain in the same room with this fucking insult." He drags the ripped canvas into the alley, crams it into the oil barrel that he keeps for this purpose, and slops the painting with kerosene. He clacks open his Zippo, flicks the wheel, flame swaying. He calls over Pinch, places the lighter in the boy's hand, holds him around his midriff, and lifts him toward the picture. "Flame steady, kiddo."

"Don't," Natalie pleads. "That's my whole day, wasted. Please, Bear. Could you consider—"

The painting ignites. Bear pulls their son back to safety, depositing him on the cobbles, stroking the kid's head in thanks. Apologetically, Bear approaches his wife, nestles his face against her neck.

Destruction is a relief as completion never can be. But it's *his* completion, *his* destruction, *his* relief.

# 1961

## 7

The eleven-year-old flattens both hands against their giant building door and pushes, exchanging suffocating heat for the cool mosaic-floored lobby. His parents follow, the three Bavinskys racing for the elevator cage, which is so small that Bear must suck in his gut—only to swell it once the door closes, mushing his wife and son, both in hysterics. "Dad, you're making me hit the buttons with my head!"

Not long after Bear settled in Rome, they moved to these swanky lodgings, a nineteenth-century apartment last occupied by the futurist poet Filippo Marinetti that retained the man's chintzy wallpaper, faded rectangles marking where paintings once hung. Years earlier, Mishmish Shapiro bought the property to loot its art and left the place vacant until hearing that "the Bears," as she calls them, were shacked up in an art studio. So the Bavinskys upgraded to Prati, once meadowlands north of the Vatican walls, now insurance companies, advertising offices, bourgeois residences. If this area has gone up in the world, so has the country since those tough times after the war. All down Via Veneto, cabarets are packed now, film producers disporting themselves alongside wasp-waisted coquettes, while ancient

Roman sites are flush with playboy tourists leaning on columns, their diamantine laughter echoing through the ruins.

As for Pinch, he attends a private international school aimed at kids from the United States—Bear prefers his son to grow up American. The student body consists of diplo brats from the coasts, army brats from the South, business brats from the Midwest, plus the children of assorted oddballs who landed in Rome for the cheap living. Even though many of his classmates were born in this city, the prevailing mood is scorn for Italian ways. Everyone returns from summer vacations with Sears Tower postcards, Yale pennants, Hawaiian tans.

As for Pinch, he has never traveled. Natalie, who tends home year round nowadays, would happily venture abroad. But Dad can't give up a day of work, weekends and holidays included. Also, he's occupied with an admiring coterie of junior painters, students, artists' models—Bear is beloved by them all. Just when Pinch worries that he's nowhere near the top of his father's list, Bear will pick him out: "Forget school today, young Charles," he says using Pinch's proper name. We're going to the movies, me and you. Far as your teachers are concerned, you got a fever. What say you, old man? We on?"

On such occasions, Natalie could use her husband's studio for her pottery. When Pinch and Bear arrive home, however, she is busy with household chores, mending torn shirts, turning up trousers, bad-tempered because of this endless burden—although it's she who adds more duties. When her toils are complete, she grows impatient, obliging Pinch to accompany her somewhere, perhaps inventing a task: "Come grocery shopping. I need help with the bags." Together, they evaluate the market stalls, boycotting those who fiddle with the scales, knowing she's a foreigner. On weekends, Natalie takes her son to Porta Portese, the vast outdoor flea market, where they fill out his latest collection: old maps lately, coins before, medals next. They ride bikes too, tracing the city walls, Pinch veering dangerously into traffic, looking back to ensure that she is suitably scared.

He hardly resembles his mother—she, large and dark; he, small and sandy-haired. Yet even strangers find a similarity: how they walk, each footstep tentative, as if treading across a moving carpet. Their manner of speech is similar too—slow and fast to a metronome sounding only in their heads. He finishes Natalie's sentences, and she knows what he's about to say (though he denies it, changing course to prove his point). Pinch passes so much free time with her because his schoolmates find something amiss about him. At an age when boys in the same grade look five years apart, he is near the bottom of that scale. He stands too close, jabbers too fast, claiming miracles. "Yesterday I looked out my window, and Marilyn Monroe was there, sitting in a car!"

"She was *not*."

When refuted, he falls silent, which makes everyone laugh. He is caught mumbling to himself a few times, and is taunted for it, so tries to stop. Before entering the school doors each morning, he avoids eye contact with Natalie—she knows how he dreads each day.

As for sports, Pinch considered himself good for a while. Until it became incontrovertible that he was not. Other kids hurl baseballs in vanishing arcs; he throws out his arm. "Sorry, Ronnie!" he hollers across the playground, shoulder throbbing. "I slipped on this dumb mud!" In the street with Italian boys, he rushes toward the soccer ball, his weight invariably on the wrong foot once he reaches it. He must reset or miss, and does both, slicing air, walloping ground. *"Scusate, ragazzi!"* he tells the departing stampede of boots. His knees bloody and encrusted with dirt, he tries not to mind, and runs after the others, who are too far downfield ever to be reached.

He watches Natalie prepare dinner, just the two of them because Bear is always working late. She cooks appallingly, which Pinch realized from dining occasionally with Roman neighbors who had invited him when Natalie was faring poorly with her nerves, as happens now and then—always presaged by explosions of anger about nothing. When Pinch perceives her plummeting, he talks fast, attempting to do something, not sure what, so recounts facts learned in class or makes up astonishing coincidences. "I passed these people on Lungotevere, and they were all talking about you, Mom, saying how much they like you."

Natalie grabs him.

"What?" he asks in fright. "What, Mom?"

She holds on to him, almost violently. He pulls back in embarrassment, looking at his shoes.

When Bear returns, Natalie transforms, striving to mirror his mood. If he battled a painting at the studio, he enters in silence, a quiet that exudes across the apartment. On the other hand, if he completed a work, he marches in with a holler of "Where you reptiles at?" Doesn't matter what time or who's sleeping. And he's right: They prefer to be awake for this. He tackles and tickles his son, hoisting and lowering Pinch like a squealing barbell in pajamas. More often than not, Bear recalls a flaw in his just-completed work, which compels him to rush back to the studio, leaving the scent of pipe tobacco and Natalie to sedate their hot-faced, wild-eyed boy. She races around until catching Pinch, who is forcibly soothed by the imprisonment of her embrace, his muscles twitching, then asleep

8

Pinch waits beside his mother on the steps of their building, until she leaps up, shading her brow, waving to a malnourished fiftyish

Englishman in tweed who lopes closer, hands clasped behind his back, supporting the weight of his canvas rucksack. Cecil Ditchley was her favorite instructor at the Central School of Arts and Crafts in London, which she attended straight out of high school, wanting to study among the British, who took pottery seriously. What she found were classes of chilly young men brooding over form. English pottery of the period, a critic remarked, had the elegance of "the tree trunk, the boulder, the flint block, if you like, the turnip." But Natalie longed for more than turnips: to spin and raise and score in clay those expressionistic passions that had already transformed painting, sculpture, music. Why should art be beyond ceramics? But her classmates' interest in her derived either from the hope of a cheap seduction or to request that she decorate their work—"Add something airy, Natalie." It was Cecil who saved her, the solitary instructor to encourage that she throw her own pots. She loved Cecil for this, a connection without any hint of sex but only a wish (on her part, at least) to vault all intermediate stages and be devoted. They've corresponded in the dozen years since, growing closer in longhand. He was always too destitute to visit. But Bear intervened, sending a ticket.

Pinch runs toward their guest—only to turn shy upon reaching him. The potter presents a bony hand and Pinch shakes it, his grip sliding down long tapering fingers, yellowed at their tips from roll-your-own cigarettes. "You are Charles," the Englishman notes, sweeping back blond bangs that flop over his brow and give him youth, or did so from a distance.

Natalie leads her friend inside, showing him around their grand shabby apartment. Pinch trails after, buzzing at the precise frequency of his mother's high. She is proposing a thousand outings for Cecil and querying him about his trip here on various third-class trains, while Pinch interjects rapid-fire questions about the life of a hermit (he expected a graybeard in rags).

"Activities are somewhat lacking in my parts," Cecil explains with surprise, as if only noticing this deficit. London artists who are aware that Cecil Ditchley today inhabits a stone cottage in the Eastern Pyrenees (snowed in for weeks each winter, no electricity) mull over this image, pondering whether the man is tragic. On balance, admiration wins out. Careerists always salute those who lack ambition.

Long ago, Cecil was a beautiful youth and celebrated for it, passing through the arms of various lovers, of various sexes. After Cambridge, he dedicated himself to sculpture, influenced by Archipenko and Epstein and Moore. Pacifism turned him against muscular sculpture, and he moved to St. Ives in Cornwall, taking up residency at the Leach Pottery. To his surprise, he found himself a natural craftsman. Art required explanation, converting the maker into a talker, and he found it deathly embarrassing to profess what anything meant. Pottery, by contrast, meant only itself: A pot is for honey, a jug is for water.

These days, at his isolated home on the French side of Catalonia, Cecil digs his own clay and fells timber for the wood-fired kiln, barely subsisting off the sale of domestic pottery to local peasants, even though a dozen Ditchley ceramics would constitute a modest show on Bond Street. An enterprising London dealer once drove to Roussillon to procure crates of Cecil's work for a pittance. But the potter's location proved so remote that the dealer merely wasted petrol, returning home with a trunk full of wine and a foul mood.

Whatever the cost, Cecil sticks with his French exile, like those Cambridge spies who traded dreary postwar Britain for Soviet paradise, only to find themselves condemned to being irrevocably English abroad. Except that Cecil drinks gallons less liquor than Guy Burgess et al. For him, the beverage is Assam tea, whose loose leaves he keeps in a suede drawstring pouch that he pulls apart with chipped front teeth, inhaling India, distracted for a moment—he lived in Bengal as a child—then here again, back among them, even if Cecil is never entirely among those he is with, his sight line skimming above their heads, as if someone else were expected presently.

9

As Natalie and Cecil tramp through the scorching city, Pinch tags along, either scurrying a few steps ahead or lingering a few behind. "Nothing is like the sky in Rome," Cecil remarks, causing Pinch to look heavenward, wondering what is special about the bright blue and the brushstroke clouds, the only he has known.

Beforehand, Natalie spoke to Pinch about how desperately she sought Cecil's advice on restarting her art after all these years. She has lost any idea of what her peers are making—and they have no knowledge that she exists. Pinch waits, seeing his mother nearing the subject, then backing away. Cecil himself hardly speaks of pottery, as if it were vulgar to mention one's vocation. He inquires about life in Rome and life with Bear Bavinsky, whom he hopes to know better. Natalie claims that her husband is occupied with students, yet Pinch heard her telling Dad that the guest himself prefers time with her alone to discuss pottery.

As they wander across Piazza San Cosimato, Pinch stoops to a public drinking fountain, his rosy face under the gush of the spout. Cecil is checking if they'll see Bear this evening, which is the Englishman's last in Rome. How fascinating it'd be, Cecil remarks, to hear of Bear's art.

"You're not even going to *ask* what I'm doing," Natalie blurts. "This whole time you haven't."

Pinch looks over, fountain water spattering gently. His mother's neck is blotchy, flushed in patches as happens when she is rattled. Mom regrets this, he knows, but she can't reel back her outburst.

"Suppose I didn't want to intrude," Cecil responds stiffly.

Natalie observes Pinch, his bangs soaking. She tells Cecil, "I was only joking. Ignore me."

The two adults walk on, a step farther apart. Occasionally, Cecil veers away to peek through the dark doors of a church, not calling her to join him. They arrive back at the apartment and separate to wash for the big meal.

Bear, who barely had a chance to greet Cecil, has promised to treat their guest to a farewell banquet at the best trattoria in town. On the walk toward Largo Argentina, Bear raves about the pizzas. "Nothing better outside Napoli. I'm telling you: Got to try this." They bundle inside, each ordering one of the much-touted pizzas—except for Bear himself, who opts for "*il* fried *di* fish."

"Dad!" Pinch bellows, smiling. "You *always* do this!"

"*La frittura di pesce, signore?*" the waiter confirms. "*Ottima scelta.*"

Bear taps the boy's chin playfully, asks the waiter for a couple of "*bottiglia di* bubbly *vino,*" then tells Cecil: "No matter how I try, I cannot learn this damn language. Something missing in this nut of mine," he says, rapping his temple. "Thank God for my translator here." He gives a cheek kiss to Pinch, who is lobster red from sun and pride. Dad does this—spreads his mood, the man's pleasures clapping you on the shoulder. Even Cecil approaches jollity and confesses admiration for the painter's work. Bear claims the same of Cecil's pottery (though Pinch heard Dad say before that he hadn't seen a single piece).

"What in hell are you doing living on a damn mountain?" Bear demands. "Move here to the Eternal City, brother!"

The merriment only increases when Bear solicits Cecil's expert opinion on the recent ceramics by Picasso. The little Spaniard doesn't even make his pots, Cecil says, but merely "adjusts" those of true artisans. Nothing delights Bear more than the disparagement of his overpraised rival. "Pablo hasn't a drop of your talent," Bear professes, slamming his open palm on the table for emphasis, causing the Englishman to cough in mortification and insist on his own mediocrity.

"What you're producing is *art*, Cecil. Art to the highest degree," Bear persists, grabbing Natalie's hand across the table, pulling her into this estimation.

She withdraws her fingers, as if to fetch something from her purse, fumbling in there for cigarette and lighter.

"You're not doing some second-rate craft!" Bear reiterates to Cecil.

"Oh, I don't know. Potters get so exercised about art versus craft. But the older I get, the more I prefer craft. With craft, you know if a piece is right. Is the pot so cumbersome that the farmer's wife couldn't lift it? Is my glaze poisonous? A pot is either correct, or it is not. Whereas art is never quite good or bad. Art is simply a way of saying 'opinion.'"

The notion that art is never good or bad is so alien to Bear that he fails to hear it. "Here's the real problem," he resumes. "Soon as a piece has a use, then the blowhards won't accept it. If I took three Botticellis and hammered them into a side table, the critics would look at those exact pictures and call them second-rate. The same damn pictures!"

"Please don't hammer Botticellis into a side table, dear man."

"I'm telling you, there's nothing critics hate more than a hinge," Bear says. "And you, out there in the countryside, fighting that wood-fired kiln! Natty tells me it's a ton of timber for each firing. That can't be true."

"Two tons actually. The real struggle is stoking for three days, round-the-clock."

"I won't stand for it! I'm forking out for a proper kiln, state-of-the-art. Picasso has one, I bet. Can't picture *him* stoking a goddamn thing!"

"You're far too kind. I couldn't possibly."

"Couldn't you?" Natalie mutters under her breath. "Why you came here, no? Broke."

Cecil looks over, pained.

"What's that, sweetie?" Bear asks his wife, calling to the waiter for a bottle of red now. He returns to Cecil. "I'm warning you. You don't let me help, and there will be dire consequences. For a start, I tell Romolo to cancel your pizza—and Romolo listens to me." Affectionately, Bear pokes his son's gut. "Cecil, I'm determined on this point. You are going places, and I want to say I helped."

"If I were going places, I'd be there already, I daresay." Cecil looks into his lap, as if a map rested there. "You know, I did want to sculpt once, and would've cut off my left arm merely to be adequate. But my drive just went." He looks up. "To tell the truth, I've felt better ever since."

"Hear that, Natty? Take a page out of this man's book."

"A page?" she responds, smoking hard. "You're saying I ought to give up on making art?"

"What in hell you talking about, sweetie?"

"I never gave up," Cecil clarifies. "Merely that I stopped trying to impress people I didn't even care for."

"Why impress *anyone*, if not the people you don't care for?" she responds.

"Point is," Bear intercedes, clasping her forearm, "can't let the bastards get you down is all Cecil's saying. But sure, the business ain't for everyone. It's a foul mess, art is. Am I right?"

Cecil nods wistfully. "Can be, yes."

"You are a talent, my Natty. If you want to be. All it takes is a bit more oomph. But who says you've got to?" He takes a drag off her cigarette, then stubs it.

"I was still smoking that."

"You hearing what I'm saying, sweetheart?" He takes her hand, his other on Cecil's chest, gripping the man's tweed jacket, as if unifying two comrades. "It's not just me saying so. Your teacher agrees. Ain't that so?"

Cecil's eyebrows rise in confirmation.

"You're humiliating me," she tells Bear.

"I'm saying you're swell," he corrects her. "Who cares what others think! Oh, for crying out loud." He drops her hand, releasing Cecil too, and fills his own glass too high with wine.

"On what basis might I be decent?" Natalie asks, hope in her voice.

Pinch realizes that, oddly, it's Bear's *dis*approval that stirs his mother.

"Crazy girl." Bear pulls her chair closer, grabs the back of her neck. "I love the hell out of you, Natty. *That* is what matters." He pulls an abandoned pizza crust from her plate, stuffs it into his mouth, and pokes her ribs till she's in hysterics. Only Pinch sees that his mother's laughter isn't pleasant—she's nearly in tears, pushing her husband back.

Finally, Bear returns Natalie's body to her control.

Wiping sweat from her upper lip, she holds her own throat, glancing around the trattoria, as if everyone noticed, though the only person watching is Pinch, who pretends to busy himself by gobbling the leftover *fiori di zucca*. Bear and Cecil resume their sloshy conversation about art versus craft, and Pinch turns his attention there, as if spectating a sporting contest from the stands, most of the action in Dad's favor.

Bear runs his hand repeatedly through thinning shiny hair, holding the floor as he recounts tales of his failures of long ago, each of which renders his current glory all the richer. When the bill comes, he insists on snapping it up. "No wrestling me for it, Cecil. You'd probably win, and how would I live that down?

The four promenade home down Via del Pellegrino, which is dark and deserted, punctuated by conversation from apartments above. Bear—to emphasize points—keeps stopping, taking Cecil's forearm, declaiming to his new pal (rather too loudly for this hour). The modest potter chortles, and Natalie steps away, idling outside locked storefronts, Pinch beside her—until a mouse runs over his shoe, causing him to kick the air in fright. The center of Rome is unnerving at night; Pinch has heard of knifings. When a teenager barrels toward them, Pinch tenses, tracking him, watching the kid stop at a decaying pastel-red facade, then holler to a high floor, whose closed shutters crank upward, revealing a little sister, who darts from sight, the glow of light within, the tick of forks.

Bear takes Cecil's shoulder, leading him forth, and their convoy sets off again, right down the roadway. A distance back, Pinch feeds his arm under Natalie's, both mimicking Dad and trying to speed her pace, lest they be stranded here.

"Not once," Natalie mumbles, lost in an argument only she can hear. "All night."

Pinch looks at his mother, contemplates her, almost asking what she meant—then he slips free, sprinting ahead to join the men. As they turn the corner onto Via dei Banchi Vecchi, Pinch glances back: his mother on distant cobblestones, allowing herself to drop farther and farther behind. On they walk until Natalie is lost from view.

## 10

Cecil stayed only a week, but he lingers in Bear Bavinsky lore as the comical stoic: "You walked here in the hail with no umbrella? Why, Cecil would've loved that!" At any mention of their departed guest, Natalie finds reason to leave the room. Nightly, she works on an apology letter to Cecil and reads various versions to Pinch. Yet she cannot send one; she's too angry still. Meanwhile, Bear—who was kept away for much of Cecil's trip—extends that absence, at his studio constantly now. Nobody questions this until another guest appears.

Birdie is a fifteen-year-old with short dirty-blond hair, an elephant-footed gait, pudgy pubescent curves. She's also Pinch's half sister, although he never heard her named before. The arrival is a merry occasion for Bear, who lifts his youngest daughter off the ground, swings her around, her saddle shoe hitting the mahogany bureau with a *thunk*. "Birdie, little buddy!" Alas, her timing is not the greatest, with Bear right in the middle of a sitting. "You'll be your big sister's tour guide for a few days," Bear tells Pinch, who is on summer break. "How about it, kiddo?"

Pinch always longed to meet his relations in America, of whom he's heard only vague mention. This fogginess allowed him to invent them, concocting a clan of best friends, the kind of pals Pinch reads about but never finds at school. Still, it's peculiar to have an unknown girl in the apartment who happens to be a blood relation. "I want the grand tour of Rome," she says, but Pinch has no clue what this involves. So Birdie buys a guidebook and takes her little brother along to interpret.

They stroll around the Forum, forging through weeds, high-stepping over a fallen marble column. "So crazy: a treasure like this, left out in the open, nobody guarding," she marvels, approximating the view that local males hold of her, they sizing up her shorts, cocking their chins beckoningly. Birdie is pinched on the bus, fondled in churches—there's a palpitating sexuality in the city that summer. With aplomb, she bats away each hand yet claims to enjoy the attention, which confuses Pinch. Romance is the embarrassing part of every movie, the part that drags on with no purpose. Still, he likes that older boys approach him for information about his sister. He wants Birdie to like them, so that he may be their personal translator.

"Tell him my husband's about to turn up," she instructs Pinch, when a fresh contender addresses her in the Pantheon.

"Aren't you too young to be married, Birdie?"

"Fine, then. Tell him my fiancé is on his way."

The Italian lothario, a spotty adolescent, gazes down long black eyelashes at Pinch. *"Allora? Che t'ha detto?"*

*"Che è già fidanzata."*

*"Ma che m'importa a me? Sarà in America, 'sto fidanzatino. E mica è bello come me, vero?"*

Pinch reports to Birdie: "He's saying, 'He's not as beautiful as me, right?'"

"Who isn't as beautiful as you?"

"Not as beautiful as *he* is."

"You lost me, Charlie."

"Your fiancé isn't good-looking enough."

She rears on her suitor in mock outrage. "Don't *dare* talk mean about my fiancé who doesn't exist."

The adolescent responds in English: "You no 'ave boyfriend?"

"Hey, you're not allowed to understand. I will not abide a cheater, cute *ragazzo*." Off she stomps, little brother hurrying after.

Birdie is equally likely to sass grown-ups. As if measuring her target, she narrows her eyes, lips twitching sardonically. Snarkiness has already landed her in heaps of trouble—it's why her mother dispatched Birdie here in the first place, unwilling to tolerate a full summer with this hellion. But her boldness is a hit with Pinch. He has developed into a boy who must prep everything he says. By the time he's ready to speak, conversations have moved on, causing him to blurt. By contrast, Birdie can't hesitate—just out with it. When Bear returns from his studio late each night, she is often snarky, such as when Dad summons Pinch for a bit of roughhousing, and Birdie calls him back, saying, "You don't *have* to go, Charlie, just because the dog barks." Regarding Pinch's mother, Birdie is dismissive of the new wife, who busies herself with domestic chores, ironing sheets, making meals. That's nice and all, Birdie tells her half brother, but when is Dad taking me out? He promised. You heard him.

She and Pinch sleep head-to-toe in his bed, whispering in the dark, she asking about Italian boys and he asking about Chicago, where she resides with her mother and stepdad plus two elder sisters who—scandalously to Birdie—don't share her fascination with horses. The eldest is marrying next year; the middle won't ever leave home, she's such a stick-in-the-mud. But what her brother longs to hear are tales of Dad when he used to live in America, a time that verges on the mythical to Pinch. Birdie loves to dish, claiming privileged knowledge, although her reports are often based on merest rumors.

"Which is when she caught Daddy in bed with that dancer."

"Why was a dancer in his bed?"

"Do I got to explain everything, Charlie?"

Not necessarily. But Pinch finds ways not to understand—to hear aspersions about Dad feels like betrayal.

"Everything's always about his art," Birdie complains. "He doesn't hardly care about his actual creations."

"What do you mean?"

"The human ones."

"What do you mean?"

"Don't be an imbecile, Charlie. I mean you, me, Dina, and Kelly. Actually, you know what? Let's *please* stop talking about Daddy."

## 11

"Ready?" Bear shouts.

Pinch—on the living-room floor, sketching with Birdie—stills his pencil. He turns to his sister, as if to reiterate Dad's question, which was addressed to her. She remains fixed on her drawing, heel of her hand against chubby blemished cheek, fingers straight upward, blocking her peripheral vision. "I'm still drawing Thunderclap," she says, referring to her horse.

"Birdie?" her father says. "I rushed over to get you, sweetie."

This is her last day before flying home, and Bear promised they'd spend it together, wanting to make up for how busy he'd been. Alas, he was detained by work this morning; couldn't be avoided. Pinch understands. Natalie has explained how every one of Dad's brushstrokes is the intersection of him and that instant—the slightest interruption, and art is obliterated from the record. Nobody hates this bullying fact more than Dad himself, who'd rather be horsing around here.

Bear walks from the room, and his daughter looks at the empty doorframe, then anxiously at her brother. On her behalf, Pinch sneaks into the hallway, listening hard: the back-and-forth squeak of floorboards in the master bedroom, where Dad must be pacing, his indignation seeping down the hallway. Pinch wants to warn Birdie that their father has important work, that he interrupted it for *her*, that he can't be made to wait. "Birdie," he says tentatively.

"When I'm ready!" she snaps, pushing the air to reproach him, returning fiercely to her sketch, though she tucks her hair behind her ear, listening desperately for Bear.

Another squeak of the floorboards. And another. In this direction now. Dad is coming back.

Both kids look up. He stands there. "Well, one thing's for sure: My rivals don't suffer foolishness like this!" Bear says, as if light-hearted. "Honey, I can't be wasting time." He taps his watch face. "I took the day off."

"You did not. You said you would."

"What am I doing here?" he responds, frustration rising. Now I'm slave to a teenage girl?"

Pinch holds still, muscles tight.

"Last chance," Bear says.

"For what? We were supposed to have a *whole* day."

"It didn't work out that way. But I'm still looking forward. Or trying to. Don't you want your painting lesson?"

She pretends not to hear.

"Well. That's that."

"Wait, Daddy!" Birdie exclaims, clutching the pencil against her chest. "I said I was almost done."

"If I knew you didn't want my company, I'd have gone straight to the art store instead of wasting this trip home."

"Why are you getting sore, Daddy?"

"I'm not getting anything. Except the hell out of here."

"But we're supposed to eat ice creams!" She leaps to her feet, fighting back tears, and storms down the hall.

"Oh, come on now, Birdie. You're off for a sulk?" Bear shrugs to his son. "I will never understand. Well, Charlie, it's just the two of us. Now, I need supplies, and you look like a first-class translator. What do you say—you and me, off to Poggi's?" He gooses his son in the thigh, causing a squeal of joy.

Pinch darts to the front door, adding nervously, "Should we ask her too?"

"I asked twice already. She doesn't like us fellas today."

Birdie must've been listening, for she slams the door of Pinch's bedroom.

In silence, father and son walk past the second-century ramparts of Castel Sant'Angelo, over a reconstructed Ancient Roman bridge lined with marble angels bearing whips and nails and lances. "What choice did she leave me?" Bear asks belatedly. "Played it the only way I could. That fair, Charlie?"

Pinch can't find the right answer, so nods fast, hating to forsake his best friend of these past two weeks—yet hating even more to imperil a rare outing with Dad. All morning, Birdie was saying how she'd give Bear a piece of her mind. *But*, Pinch wonders, *for what?* She only wanted this; precisely what he is guiltily enjoying.

Dad slaps his hand on Pinch's shoulder, and they walk the rest of the way like that: Bear guiding the boy, stopping him before traffic, leading him via a diversion to admire the elephant obelisk in Piazza della Minerva, explaining the wizardry of Bernini's chisel work with such exaltation that Pinch forgets his guilt. When they find that the art store is closed until four, Bear promises his son "the best lunch place in this whole damn city," grabbing Pinch's waistband, lifting him off the ground for a few steps, plopping him down, which sends the kid into wild giggles.

At lunch, Bear feasts on course after course, until all that remains on their ravaged paper tablecloth are tomato-sauce specks, a finger-smudged bottle of purple vinegar, and a single slice of bread, which

Bear flings into his mouth as they leave, munching as he points them toward "the best coffee in Rome." On the way, they pass the Chiesa di San Luigi dei Francesi. "Won't find much better art in the world than in that church," Bear says.

"Could we go in?"

Bear leads his little son through the doors, down the nave, under gold medallions, glinting starbursts, and muscly sculpted saints who behold the frail human worshippers below with pity. Bear—of Ukrainian-Catholic stock, but a dedicated idolater—directs Pinch to three paintings in a back corner: Saint Matthew the Evangelist's calling into the faith, his inspiration by an angel, and his martyrdom. "Look at this church, made of money and *schifezza*," Bear says, loudly enough that people glance over, frowning. "But these paintings here? When Caravaggio painted a saint, he never modeled from nobles or clergymen. Those are street bums. Hobos and whores. Imagine what the cardinals said!"

Pinch adds Caravaggio to his list of "the best artists," composed entirely of those his father admires: Sickert and Elsheimer, Dürer and Rembrandt, Degas and Toulouse-Lautrec, Mantegna and Soutine. By the same token, Pinch reviles Correggio and abominates Renoir, his father's second-worst painter, outmatched only by that clown Picasso.

At length, Pinch ponders the three paintings by Caravaggio. "The shadowy parts," he attempts, having readied this comment for several minutes, "are like your paintings. Dad?" He turns to Bear, fearing that he erred.

"Good eye, Charlie!"

"But which of those men is Saint Matthew?"

"It's all him. There. And there. And there."

"He looks different."

"He gets older in each painting."

Pinch looks from Matthew to Matthew to Matthew, but cannot process three ages as the same man.

When they emerge into the roasting sun, "the best art store in Rome" has reopened. Colored chaos reigns within: paint sets for beginners and stacks of oil crayons; sable brushes—brights, flats, and rounds; and canvas rolls, down the walls like Doric columns. "This is where you come in handy, old man," Bear tells Pinch and beckons for the clerk.

When father and son leave, laden with supplies procured by Pinch's own words, the child is emboldened to ask: "One time, Dad, would you like to paint me? Starting with me right now, then me later when I'm bigger, and me when I'm old?"

"I'll go one better. How's about I show you to do it yourself?"

"To paint?"

Ever since they moved to the fancy Marinetti apartment, Pinch has been allowed to visit the art studio only by invitation, and he is forbidden to approach Dad's supplies. This is a spectacular treat— and it was supposed to be for someone else. After a few minutes of walking, Pinch forces himself to ask: "Does it matter about Birdie?"

"What about her?"

"That she's waiting?"

"You saw, kiddo. She didn't want hide nor hair of me. Tell me if I'm wrong."

Pinch stops, lips parting. But the boy must hasten along. Dad is striding away, and Bear Bavinsky does not slow his pace.

## 12

Birdie sits outside the art studio, chin on her knees, having rightly guessed that her father would end up here. She claims to want nothing to do with Bear and Pinch, yet follows them in, plonking herself on a spattered stool, unhappily fiddling with a plumb line.

"You joining or not?" Bear asks, stuffing tobacco into his pipe. "Pouting like that, you don't hurt anybody but yourself."

Pinch wants to intercede, to warn her that Dad won't say sorry— just come over, please.

Instead, Bear is talking again, mouth to the boy's ear, "We can't make her, if she wants to be that way." He places a charcoal pencil in Pinch's hand, takes out a sketch pad, swishes to a virgin page. In full voice, he begins the lesson: "Charlie, I need you to extend your arm. Now, look at your hand from a distance. Okay, bring it close again. Same hand, but not the same object. Question is, kiddo, how to capture it, its essence. People talk about accuracy, but what's that mean? There's a gap always between what the object is and what the picture isn't. And that gap, Charlie, that's where the art is. Too hard?"

Pinch, uncomprehending, shakes his head.

"Good boy. Now, see that kettle? Close one eye and use your pencil to measure out its parts. Like so. The handle in relation to the underside now. Copy it in simple lines, concentrating on the dimensions. Once you've got the proportions, step back, then in. Remember: Look far, draw close."

Birdie burps.

"I'm showing your brother something."

"I'm the one who's visiting."

"You could've taken part, Bird. But you can't disrupt. Those are the rules."

Pinch glances up at their father, willing him to include her.

"Charlie, an artist doesn't see as normal people do," Bear resumes. "When normal people look, they see events: a bus stop, a pretty girl waiting, the rain. When an artist looks, he sees geometry. Everything is a shape. And within each shape, more shapes. We teach ourselves to overrule what the eyes tell us. Like Cézanne said, 'Treat nature by means of the cylinder, the sphere, and the cone.' All right now, shut your eyes and describe the studio."

"Right now?"

"Not yesterday."

When the boy finishes, they check his recollected inventory, chuckling at all the oversights. "That bathtub, right there! Son of mine—I ought to disinherit you!" He kisses Pinch's cheek, as if only the two of them were here.

Pinch says, "Can you try, Dad?"

Eyes closed, Bear describes for more than four minutes, adding dozens of items that Pinch hadn't seen, excluding only one major object: Birdie herself. "The shears, kiddo. Where are my shears?" He cuts into a roll of preprimed canvas, slicing freehand but perfectly straight, a piece as large as Pinch's mattress. With a carpenter's speed, Bear hammers together stretchers and crossbars, tacks the canvas to the frame, mallets the corners into true, pulls the canvas taut with pliers, gently taps in wedges, and lifts it onto the easel, erecting a wall between them and her. He and Pinch pass minutes drizzling linseed oil onto pigments, swirling the muller in a figure eight to achieve the desired paste, adding drips of turpentine to thin it ever so slightly, Bear explaining that he seeks a roughness on the side of strokes, an uncooperativeness, a slowness.

Bear demonstrates how to square up sketches and map out a canvas, how to choose a ground, how to do grisaille underpainting, how to vary skin tones. Pinch loses track of anything beyond—except when Birdie makes snide remarks.

The studio door squeaks and Natalie enters, halting as if interrupting holy rites. She lifts away Pinch's jacket, whispers something to Birdie, who shakes her head defiantly. Natalie returns an hour later with food. All four sit on the mildewed couch, Birdie grumbling about the meal.

"Goddammit, Elizabeth," Bear snaps. "Natty prepared this, special for you."

Eyes wet, Birdie clutches her fork tighter.

Bear returns to the canvas, nodding for his son to join, turning the boy away from the others. "Not everyone is an artist," he says under his breath. "But for those of us that are, it's war. You get me, Charlie? Total war, or you're dead from the start. There is a reward, though. Out of this—" He holds up a paintbrush. "And that—" He jabs the bristles toward the canvas. "*We* get to live forever."

Birdie drifts around to their side of the canvas, spilling forward and falling onto the picture, smearing paint everywhere. "Oopsy," she says.

Forearms flexed, Bear faces her. Natalie watches, hand over mouth, as Bear drags his daughter by the elbow to the studio door. "What are you doing?" Birdie cries. "What are you doing, Daddy?"

Still clutching her, he gathers himself. "Bird, you can kick me as much as you like. But not them. Hear me?"

Birdie struggles to open the iron door, battling the mechanism, finally shoving it wide, blinking at the light. She runs outside, clanging the door shut, her weeping muffled in the alley. Natalie hurries after her. The crying fades as Birdie is led back toward the apartment.

Bear avoids Pinch's gaze, mixing pigments. He opens the studio door. There's only empty cobbles. "You should go back too."

"Are you coming?"

"I don't figure Bird wants *me* around too much!"

As the iron door closes him out, Pinch hesitates by Dad's oil barrel. After a few minutes, the boy stealthily pushes at the door, opening it just a crack, and peeps into the studio where his father drags

Tom Rachman

out an unfinished painting. Bear stands before it, pulling his thin hair. He reaches for his pipe—then glimpses the spy. "Your father is a lousy sonofabitch," Bear says, staring at Pinch. "Not because he wants to be. I don't want to be. Understand me? Do you, kiddo?" He approaches, hand extended. Bear closes the door.

That night, Pinch and Birdie lie head-to-toe, the only illumination a bar of light under his bedroom door. Pinch shuts one eye, attempting to flatten everything, turning her toes into geometry.

"We're like two dogs, supposed to fight it out," she says.

"Is that the name of a song, Birdie?"

"Sometimes, Charlie, I wonder if you're all there."

If Bear doesn't come home soon, Birdie won't see him before her early-morning departure. But time runs short: Natalie is already closing up the apartment for the night. Her heels click nearer.

The hallway light goes out.

"But we *don't*, right?" Birdie whispers to her little brother.

"Don't what?"

"Fight it out," she says, voice cracking. "Do we, Charlie." She pushes him. "We won't."

## 13

At the end of that summer, Bear departs for work in New York. Pinch finds out only after his father has left. Whenever he inquires into Dad's return date, Natalie grows irritable. The school year starts and weeks pass. One evening, Pinch notices that his mother no longer wears a wedding ring. He hastens away from her, into the living room, and stands over the record player. She joins him, needing to explain—but he drops the needle, leaning his face into the dusty gramophone trumpet, the noise deafening him.

Soon thereafter, a representative of Mishmish Shapiro appears at their door, explaining that this apartment, sadly, is no longer available—it was previously offered to support an artist, but that man is no longer in residence. Natalie and Pinch return to living in Bear's studio. The space seems so different; everything does.

At school, Pinch boasts of his father's travels, saying he's away temporarily, dragged abroad because of grand exhibits—such lies that the boy expects traces of them upon returning home: newspaper clippings or letters from afar. Instead, he pushes open the studio door to the stench of his mother's cooking; strange soups, peculiar herbs. She crowds him, talking incessantly of pottery, which she has resumed.

Before, they managed with the one tiny WC here. Now that he is older, Pinch is appalled to hear her pee in the middle of the night. And she seems hardly to sleep. In his cot, he wishes for daylight so he can escape this jail cell. But morning arrives, and he hides under the covers, dreading school.

Early one Sunday, she plonks herself at the end of the couch, devouring a breakfast apple in her dressing gown, which hangs carelessly open, the gap between her two loose breasts visible, obscured by a black-bead necklace over freckled skin. "Get up, Pinchy!" She has become so obtrusive, mobbing him with cuddles, cavalier about her job search, and turning up with unwanted presents—a cat, for example, which immediately escaped down the alley. When he fails to share her highs, she lashes out, spitting fury for a minute, then prodding him to converse.

Natalie settles at her potter's wheel and kicks it to life, wetting her hands in muddy water from the bucket. Shoulders taut, arms rigid, elbows planted in her thighs, she forces the clay to comply, asserting herself over this gray lump, transforming it into a smooth puck, perfectly round, glistening—until she touches a finger to the spinning form and opens it up, raising the walls into a cylinder. His mother is so good at that. It astonishes Pinch, who hasn't properly watched her working in years. Yet he does not praise Natalie, instead launching into a silly dance to draw her attention, an intrusion he'd never have contemplated when Bear was painting. Her clay cylinder pirouettes on the wheel. She slices a metal wire under its base. "Your turn." Standing, she points to her wooden seat.

Instead, he walks away, meandering toward the once-prohibited easels in the far corner. He gazes the length of his arm, then at the fruit bowl—everything evokes paintings now, as if the world existed to represent art, not the reverse.

"You listening?" she repeats.

"Not really."

"At least look, Pinch. I need an opinion. The show is soon." Recently, she marched into a tiny gallery off Via del Babuino and asked if they'd consider exhibiting her work. When she gave the last name "Bavinsky," the gallerist looked up. After years of inactivity, Natalie labors constantly, amazed to see that all her output is outstanding. Impulsively, she decides to show a series of intentionally broken jars, with radical glazes that she'll wipe by hand onto once-baked clay.

"I don't care about stupid pottery!" he snaps, imitating the defiance of Birdie. But Pinch cannot pull it off—penitent, he looks to his mother. "Sorry." In the alley, he sits on cobbles, pondering the foreign address on a letter he's been composing for weeks, pages and pages in his head with little written down. He wants to ask about New York, about whether it's better than here, about whether he'd like it (and could I come see you soon, Dad?).

A month later, he still hasn't sent the letter. But life at the studio has changed. Natalie is never at the potter's wheel, hardly goes out, hardly talks to him.

"When is your show happening?" he asks.

"It's over; it happened."

"What?" he snaps, to mask his guilt. "Why didn't you say something?"

"You were interested? Since when?"

"I *said* I wanted to see it," he lies. "Did people like them?"

She clears her throat. "I don't know."

"How many sold?"

"They didn't."

"What? *None?* It's that stupid gallery's fault—they must've put the prices too high."

"Nobody asked for prices, I'm told. Now I have to go in there and disgrace myself, carrying it all out again." She covers her face. "They were all so very helpful on the way in; nobody will see me when I go back there. I'll be an embarrassment."

"No, you won't. They should apologize to you."

"Maybe I never pick them up."

"You have to, Mom. Or people will hear."

"What possible fucking difference would that make?"

He flushes.

She says, "I'm not going back. It's a humiliation."

"Could I go and get them?"

"That'd be even worse: sending my kid."

"Could I come help at least?"

"I'll seem so pathetic." Brow furrowed, she lights the umpteenth cigarette, looks to him for a twelve-year-old's assurance. Fast, she walks away.

That weekend, Pinch lugs boxes of unsold pottery to a waiting taxi, taking utmost care, wishing to treat her work with kindness. His pussyfooting causes Natalie, who waits outside the gallery, to slam the boxes into the back of the cab. "I don't mind being reminded that I'm second-rate," she says shakily. "It's useful. It's good." As they pull away, she stares out the taxi window, kneading her stomach, hurting herself. The city passes, Romans streaming by. "Having people looking, staring at my things. It's ridiculous."

"Don't you do art for people to look at, Mom?"

"Apparently not. The wife's show—that's why the gallery gave it to me. How disappointed they were. Didn't I have more friends to come by? And where was Bear Bavinsky? They figured your dad would come, and how grand that'd be."

"Who cares about those stupid idiots? Anyone that didn't buy your stuff is dumb!" Pinch blusters. He studies the taut side of her face, believing he's gaining momentum, that he is helping. His eyes burn—a surge of emotion, remembering how he sniped at Natalie these past months *because* she was determined to raise his spirits. "Who even walks into that dumb gallery, Mom?"

She touches his hand once, to silence him.

"You can't care what idiots think!" he persists. "Aren't I right?"

She turns sharply to him. *"I'm* right and the world is wrong? No. I am not good. And I *should* feel sick. Very, very fucking small."

"You're just sad."

"I see clearly when I'm sad. The only time anything is clear." She picks at dry skin on her lower lip, a dot of blood rising, and fumbles in her purse for a cigarette.

"That's just how you're feeling, Mom. It's not true."

"Why not? Why does everyone have the right to tell me what I'm *really* feeling?"

"I wasn't."

"People always are," she flames back. "Telling me: 'You're only sad. You're just low. You're only upset. It's because you're hungry. Or tired. Natalie, it's just in your fucking head.' What isn't in your head? What isn't?" She struggles to light the cigarette, ranting to the window now: "But, yes, yes: Discard any opinions of mine that are sad. Call me deluded."

"I never said that."

"Deluded because it's not nice to hear. I'm not here to be nice and pretty and nice and pretty and nice and pretty."

"Mom, I didn't say any of that." His pulse races, a sickening flutter, for Natalie doesn't hear him anymore, as if his statements and hers were out of sync by minutes. "I never said that."

# 1965

## 14

After quitting pottery, Natalie takes a full-time secretarial job at Olivetti, and socializes with a group of expats, none in the art world, mostly childless couples, the husbands old, the wives a younger version of old, perhaps with a parrot that'll outlive them all. It's a boozy circuit, so Pinch is often alone at night, when he takes to experimenting with Bear's leftover art supplies. When Natalie returns late, she is often struck by his efforts. "You really are good," she marvels, turning from the sketches to Pinch, as if he were someone new.

By age fifteen, he is painting seven days a week. Her potter's wheel is heaped with paint tubes and spattered rags, as it was during the occupancy of Bear (who has given Natalie his old studio for as long as they care to stay). Outside their home, the warren of alleys is still inhabited by the same push-and-shove Roman working class, housewives, and boisterous kid gangs that don't consider Pinch, a weedy blondish teen, one of theirs, much as their parents don't quite get his Canadian mother. Beatnik tourists sometimes wander through their quarter, talking loud English searching for street signs. Pinch wants to intervene and show that he knows their language—only to dash back inside, taking refuge among his paints.

Most evenings, he studies *The Materials of the Artist* by Max Doerner, a book of Dad's that has become gospel, including revelations on intermediate varnish and underpainting, on the weight of pigments in Cremnitz white, sap green, Prussian blue. He mixes paints at length, deferring that frightful instant of decision. (As Bear once said, "What is art but decisions?") Pinch hesitates at the brink—then kisses color to canvas, first a peck, bristles probing as he stoops to the easel, which he has not yet raised to his new adolescent height.

"Should I keep my bad pictures too?"

"Of course," Natalie replies, a trifle forcefully, rising from her seat on the couch. "Sorry—I know I promised not to look. But it's hard."

"Why?"

"I'm excited. You pick up techniques so fast, Pinch," she says. "So, yes: Keep everything. People will want to know how your style developed."

"Oh, come off it, Mom!" he scoffs. "Art historians will be dying to see another painting of our door!"

"Maybe they'll be researching the early years of Charles Bavinsky." She grabs him. "Pinch?"

Chuckling shyly, he pushes back—then scans her face for reassurance. He is a wary teen, assuming that everyone mocks him. Kids at the international school, even in younger grades, treat Pinch as if he were toxic. Partly because he hasn't once left Italy (poor?). Because his parents aren't married anymore; a deadbeat dad who flew the coop, a kooky mom who smells of garlic and wears chunky colored jewelry. In gym, Pinch doesn't sprint so much as lollop breathlessly after the pack, his fine hair always greasy, his chin and forehead pimpled constellations. He speaks little, so they think him dim. But it's because silence is safer. Once, last year, he bumped into three boys from the grade above larking around Piazza Farnese. They knew a secret entrance to catacombs, and led Pinch down, all of them scouting for skulls while sipping from a bottle—risqué because wine is a peasant beverage for the locals. The excursion was memorable, unforgettable, and Pinch had friends! Later, when he approached those boys at school, one kicked him hard in the shins, pinned him, and burned his eyebrows with a match, while the others stood there, laughing away, ridiculing remarks that he'd made underground. ("Imagine you were trapped down here, Eric, but you weren't really dead, but they closed the opening, but you were alive and nobody knew!") As for artsy kids at school, they have nothing to do with Pinch either, because they meet after-hours, sculpting soapstone or silk-screening or nailing together the *Guys and Dolls* set under teacher supervision. But Natalie keeps her son away from all that—she mistrusts schoolhouse art instructors, who remind her of Mr. Fontaine. Her child can paint at home, safeguarded by her.

Before a canvas, he disappears, eliminating school indignities, even sweeping aside Natalie. He smirks in mumbled dialogue with Vincent van Gogh, as portrayed by Kirk Douglas in *Lust for Life*, which Mom took him to see at that cinema whose roof opens during the intermission; Pinch gazing skyward, expecting a swirling starry night, finding slate clouds. Ever since that movie, Pinch sees the red-bearded Dutchman overseeing every paint stroke, offering advice in Bear's American accent.

Pinch and his father exchange letters now and then, Pinch trying to sound grown up, with all sorts of questions about New York and artists and baseball. Never does Pinch mention his own attempts to paint. He is saving that, a surprise for when they meet, when he'll say, "Remember that lesson you gave me, Dad?" Meantime, Bear's letters are warm and jovial, even if they rarely connect to his son's questions. Bear mails a postcard whenever somewhere exotic, marked with a colorful stamp and his manly scribble across the back: "Write me soonest, Charlie boy!" So Pinch does, sending off an exuberant letter the next day, waiting months for his next snippet of Dad.

Their telephone calls are rarer still. The Italian state monopoly phone operator refuses to run wires into the studio, so incoming calls must be arranged at the apartment of neighbors, a family of carpenters who, for generations, carved ornamental altarpieces but whose sons are now selling West German vacuum cleaners. On the rare occasions Pinch hears that voice down a crackly phone line, he is so overexcited that he can barely think what to say, allowing Bear to lead the conversation. Then it's over: Pinch is back in Rome, in the neighbors' living room, and he failed to ask about anything: When might he visit America? Will Dad be coming here again?

"Enough of my lollygagging—I'll leave you to it," she says. To forget, Pinch hurries back to his easel, with Natalie lingering behind him. "I keep wanting to know what you're thinking, why you did that bit. But, yes—I should get out of your hair."

He considers the tip of his brush, which tickles a purple blob on the palette.

"Yes, yes," Natalie mutters, and out she goes into the alley, without coat or destination. Pinch keeps working, until his mother pushes back inside. Three hours have passed, which seemed three minutes to him. She recounts her jaunt around the city center, how she stood on Ponte Milvio, watching the Tiber flow underneath. "Like a liquid forest."

"A liquid forest, Mom?"

"That's what it was like!" Natalie is thrumming again of late, that intrusive buzz. She speaks unguardedly about her job, how she hates everyone at Olivetti, how they are the idiots, not she.

"Why are you out of breath?" he asks. "Did you run back?"

"Yes, why not?" she answers, laughing, and wipes sweat from her upper lip, hastening to his side, studying the progress in his picture: a view out the studio door into the alleyway. "You," she says. "Are really. Very! Good!" She pulls his shirt collar, yanking his neck. "Save *everything*, Pinchy. Even your so-called bad paintings. Or let me keep them. They'll be worth a fortune." Still the taller, she kisses him hard on his forehead, hugging him tight. In a whisper, her voice changes, normal for a moment: "You're banned from throwing away anything. Please, Pinch?"

Back when he started painting, Natalie's praise, her clasped hands and glee—they plumped his hopes. Yet fervor has dwindling worth. Soon, he cared less for her approval, craving others', painting primarily for those who snub him, teachers who never remember his name, classmates who'll be shocked when it's known that Charles Bavinsky is someone important, and always has been. In daydreams, he discusses art with his father, grinning at the scene. It's better, he decides, that we lived apart—saved me from embarrassing myself by showing lousy early work. But I'm ready now. Aren't I? Only, not this picture. He drags the canvas to the empty oil barrel in the alley, returning for Natalie's matches.

"Pinchy, I was asking you to keep it. Please."

Bear destroys paintings that he deems unfit, however, so Pinch must do the same. He stuffs it in the barrel, runs a matchstick down the wall, holds it for an infinity against his canvas, which finally smolders. Pinch blinks at the rising smoke, turning away, glimpsing his mother through the open iron door. Natalie stands behind his easel, looking toward the very view that he just painted and that now burns, curling submissively before him.

Into the heat, he looks, imagining Dad's face: that crinkly grin, the booming voice, a thick hand clapped on Pinch's shoulder. "Well, I never, kiddo! Charlie Bavinsky! Well, I never." Pinch shuts his stinging eyes, beaming.

## 15

Motorbikes buzz down the bumpy roadways of Rome, riders hopped in air and thudding back onto their tailbones. Before today, Pinch never rode a moped. The boys at his school—in raptures over pictorials of Mustangs and Cadillacs—snigger at the piddly horsepower of Italian vehicles and the effeminacy of these wops who cling to another man on a rinky-dink *ciclomotore*. If anyone from school were to see Pinch on the back of this Italian boy's motor scooter, it'd be excruciating. But Pinch climbs on anyhow—to be invited by a fellow teenager is too rare an offer, even if Vittorio just wants to show off the neighborhood American to his friends.

The dented white Vespa coughs to life, shuddering as it merges into traffic, all the sputtering vehicles edging toward a robin-breasted traffic cop at the intersection, who feigns blindness as a dozen scofflaws squirt past. The obedient motorists remain in place, fixing hairdos in side mirrors, revving in a rising growl until the lights change.

Outside a café-bar in Parioli, Pinch dismounts, queasy from motion, sicker from anxiety at joining these unknown Italian kids cavorting here, including girls. He switches to Roman dialect, adopting their syncopated *pip-pop* cadence, their salty slang, hearing himself become coarser and bolder, as if previous speakers had chewed these phrases and his lips assume their swagger. The teens flirt and they howl, small groups ebbing away for conspiratorial sidebars, flowing back together. A boy in pink cashmere cuddles his eyeliner-blinky girl, their foreheads pressed together, necklaces swinging, the chains entwined for an instant, crucifixes clinking. They are sentimental and showy, acting out lovers' tiffs as if soap-opera cameras rolled: girl with arms folded over small chest, her beau tugging at his sweetheart's sleeve. *"Ti voglio bene, amore! Smetti di piangere, ti prego!"*

Pinch is a source of fascination because he is a proper American. Or so they believe. By passport, he's a Canadian like his mother. Anyway, when he utters English words, it sounds exotically American to them.

"Jets!" a girl echoes when he mentions "jazz."

"BROOK-leen!" another cries, contributing the only English word that enters her mind, then hiding against her boyfriend's shoulder.

"Man-AT-tan!" someone adds.

His celebrity increases when he claims intimate knowledge of New York City. This is not strictly true, but he *is* visiting there soon—a fact that makes him smile uncontrollably. The invitation came during his last phone call with Dad, who said casually, "Why in hell don't I ever see you, kiddo? I'm busting for a bit of Charlie around these parts!"

"Could I come out there one time?"

"Nothing would make me happier, old man! Tell your mom to arrange it. On me, naturally."

Pinch has barely slept a full night since. At lunch break he pores over the school copy of the *New York Herald Tribune* to prepare himself: gleaming astronauts, President Lyndon B. Johnson, humble sportsmen doffing caps. Even the stock tables signify something now, pulsating beneath black print.

Speaking to these Roman teens, he fixes on one girl—overweight, pimply—who watches him with viridian eyes, though he is seeing her in black-and-white, a photo of Jayne Mansfield in a cleavage-exposing blouse, his pulse quickening, casting ahead to Manhattan bohemia. He intends to kiss a girl during his New York trip, and hears himself confiding to the Italians what he has not dared tell his mother: He won't be returning here. Rome is a backwater for the modern artist. Crumbled ruins, crumbled careers. He is moving to New York for good.

"*Magari, un giorno leggerò il tuo nome sul giornale,*" the girl says, impressed.

Blushing, chuckling, he looks down at his shoes, in love with this young woman whom he'll never see after today. He thrills at the self-sacrifice of this. The first of many loves, he thinks when lying in bed that night, impatient for the future.

### 16

Wearing blazer and tie, Pinch is sandwiched between two business-men who squash him without compunction. Never having flown before, the boy lurches at each shudder of turbulence, scanning other passengers for panic. To calm himself, he visits the toilets, splashes water on his face, his fleshy pink lips gnawed, greasy blond hair short, a neat side-parting swept across, a few pale chin whiskers.

He's not the baby of the family anymore, and has younger siblings to meet in America. Pinch intends to take a big-brother role with them but is unsure what this entails. All he knows about his extended clan comes from Birdie, who is in her early twenties now, apprenticing at stables in Kentucky. (Her teen love of horses wasn't just a phase, it turns out.) She stayed in touch, writing every few months since that summer, often to bemoan their father. With a chill, Pinch recalls her trip to Rome, a previous kid from a previous family, meeting the new Bavinsky clan. He cannot blunder, won't crowd Dad, nor argue. Recently, Birdie was driving to a horse farm in Upstate New York and she dropped by Dad's, meeting his new wife then writing Pinch a catty letter about the woman. "Just Daddy's type, in the worst way," she said—which has resolved Pinch to like the new Mrs. Bavinsky.

At the airport arrivals, Carol spots him and waves. A big-boned blonde in her early thirties, she folds her chewing gum into a paper napkin, then smiles. "So pleased to meet you, son!" They drive and drive, ignoring each turnoff for Manhattan. Pinch always assumed that Dad's mailing address of "Larchmont, New York" was a neighborhood of New York City. Instead, they motor deep into Westchester County.

"I was so sorry we never met in Rome," Carol remarks.

"Oh yes," he says, perplexed. "I didn't really know you lived there."

"Oh, sure. That's where me and your pop met. It'll always feel so romantic to me: Bear's studio by the Tiber. Makes me swoon still."

"You were there?"

"Was I? How many hours I sat posing in that cave of his! But don't you *adore* Italy?" she continues. "What I wouldn't give for those Roman meatballs!"

Hazily, Pinch gazes through the station wagon window. He orders himself to be charming. "Yes, meatballs are neat," he agrees. "I guess that, um, guess I never thought of them as especially Roman. They make me think of Sweden."

"Where's Sweden again, honey? Is that in Switzerland?"

He turns to her. She looks back guilelessly, then at the road. "Gee, I sure love Europe."

He heaves his luggage into their sprawling suburban home, craning around for Bear, whom he expected at the airport. Pinch wipes his clammy fingers on the tie, chest thudding beneath.

"Well, well, well—see what the wife dragged in. Put it there, kiddo!" Bear, not seen for four years, shoots out his hand as he strides toward Pinch. His youngest daughter, Widgeon, hugs to her father's leg, a six-year-old goggling up at her own personal giant. Following is Dad's eight-year-old, Owen, who lugs a thick medical textbook.

Before thinking, Pinch charges to his father, causing the man to tuck his visiting son (suddenly little again) against his chest, kissing his temple, a big loving smack. "Been *busting* to see you!"

That phrase—"busting to see you!"—fills Pinch nearly to busting. Yet he shrinks back, fearing he's done something stupid and has deflated their affection. Scratching his beard, Bear grins down, admiring this half-grown little man. He grabs Pinch's suitcase and lugs it upstairs, everyone tromping after. Pinch follows so close as to inadvertently step on the back of his father's slippers. Owen keeps tapping his new stepbrother on the shoulder, and when Pinch turns, the kid holds up his medical book, open to an image of burn victims. Unaware, everyone continues to the guest room, where Bear tosses his son's suitcase on the bed.

"What *I* can't figure," Bear says, "is why it took you so damn long to come out here! It's a helluva trip, I guess. Are we ever tickled to have you! We got some times ahead, Charlie! You on board?"

"Yes, sir!" In Rome, he sometimes wondered if Bear really was so splendid. But love sluices through the teenager just to stand before Dad, who grabs Pinch in a roughhouse cuddle, leaving the kid determined to upturn his whole life, to speak his mind, to denounce those who deserve it, to adore those who require it, to paint sublimely— suddenly certain that he *will*. Shy to be smiling like this, Pinch looks anywhere else.

"I started to think," Bear adds, "that your mother would turn up here with a pitchfork if I didn't send you a ticket. Good old Natty!"

Pinch tries to dismiss this—hearing Mom's name jars him.

Then Bear winks, immediately restoring his son's smile. "Young fella," the man says, poking Pinch's ribs. "You need a little shut-eye." He nods to the others, and everyone makes their way out.

Abruptly, Pinch is alone, alert to any sound in the house, their voices downstairs. He looks through the window down at the backyard, a long lawn, a swing set backed by maples. Momentarily, he's distracted by arithmetic. If that funny kid Owen is eight and Widgeon is six, both were born while Dad was in Italy. Is that possible? Dad and Carol weren't even married then. Bear was often away from the Marinetti apartment, working late. Pinch banishes the thought—I'm *here.*

He unbuckles his suitcase, pulse quickening: A rolled canvas lies there. He lifts it out with trepidation, unfurling it on the bed, his knee planted on a corner. The leg survived—that's what this painting depicts, his bare left leg. Pinch is too timid to ask strangers to sit, and it feels dopey to keep painting Mom, so he depicts his own body. Also, that's how Bear learned to draw, sketching himself in enlarged detail after he leaped from a window as a little boy for kicks and ended up in traction. Pinch snorts with amusement—what a card, Dad, even then!

Summoning courage, Pinch makes himself consider his painting. Sometimes, it has seemed excellent; other times, awful. But his attention is too fractured to evaluate it now. He sniffs pipe tobacco from downstairs and steps onto the landing, marveling that his father is Bear Bavinsky, who is a floor below and will be taking Pinch everywhere these next two weeks, showing him the life of a famous painter in New York. Standing at the banister, Pinch imagines enduring in history, a major painter, he and Dad recalled together. And he cannot restrain himself, bolting downstairs, finding a raised newspaper in the den, Bear on the other side, smoke rising behind the page. "Dad, could I show you something? When you get a minute."

"Weren't you resting?" Bear lets the newspaper page wilt. "Shoot, kiddo. What's on your mind?"

"Just, there's a painting I did that I brought for you to see. Remember how you showed me all that stuff in Rome? I've been painting since then. I paint all the time. I never said it in my letters because I was lousy before. Maybe I still am lousy." He looks up, pursuing a denial—then hurries out more words. "Maybe you could tell me if it's okay. Or if it's no good. I don't mind. Either way. Dad?" He scrutinizes his father's expression. "Only if you have time."

"You are painting pictures? Chip off the old block! Hell, I'd love nothing more than to see what you put together."

From euphoria, Pinch's voice leaps in register. "Can I show you now? I could get it from upstairs?"

But Carol enters with a tray of peanut butter cookies. "Widgeon made these, you guys. I only helped, got me?" She gives a stage wink. "Ain't that so, Widgey?" The little girl—fingers jammed in her mouth—clings to Carol's leg under the woman's dress, peeking at this overgrown boy in their house.

Bear grabs three cookies, pops one in his mouth, uttering all manner of approving moans, the crumbs accumulating down his beard, the little girl clapping in excitement. Bear leans to Pinch, raising one eyebrow, whispering through crumbling cookie: "We can't properly cut out right now, with the little darling like this. You understand."

"Absolutely."

"I am *busting* to see what you did, kiddo. We'll find the right moment. What say you?"

Before Pinch can respond, Bear has grabbed his squealing daughter with one arm, hugging her lovingly, flinging her in the air.


## 17


Every day, Bear drives to his barn in North Salem to paint, come hurricane, war, or the visit of a child. He is going to show Pinch the messy old place as soon as he finishes a major work currently under way.

While waiting, Pinch spends his hours with Carol, who treats him to a matinee showing of the *The Sound of Music*, takes him around the World's Fair in Flushing Meadows, brings him on suburban shopping trips, the hi-fi panel in her Oldsmobile playing doo-wop, radio broadcasters' patter flooding through the boy. He hasn't adjusted to hearing English everywhere—still thinks of it as the language of school or home, but not a sound of passersby. Each afternoon, Carol picks up Owen and Widgeon from day camp. Pinch tries to be the big sibling Birdie was for him, but neither child buys him in this role, Widgeon bolting if left with her half brother, Owen talking back in gibberish. "Oh, baby," his mother says indulgently. "Don't do that, baby."

After dark, Bear comes home, sometimes near midnight. When possible, Pinch finds excuses to stay up, claiming he was reading or listening to the radio. But it's so late that Pinch has time only for a bit of clumsy flattery before being bundled to his room. He sits on the bed, painting ready in case Dad passes the open door. At his window, Pinch contemplates the rustling darkness out there, the guest bedroom reflected back, himself in pajamas, forehead against the pane, which mists at each breath. He wonders what time it is in Rome, which seems like another planet, one he was never meant to inhabit. In the fogged window, he writes his initials, thoughts wandering back to the Roman studio, his mother. But an artist can't worry about other people. Think of the middle-aged French stockbroker who left his wife and kids to paint in the tropics, never bothering to see them again, scarring them forever. Who doubts Gauguin was right to go? Yes, you must act, if you are to become someone. Pinch's innards contract at the thought of telling Natalie, she taking the call in their Italian neighbors' living room, returning to the studio alone.

The next night, when Carol is fixing her husband a whiskey sour at the cocktail trolley in the den, Bear sits at the kitchen table, leafing through the newspaper, Pinch watching, needing to take advantage of this rare moment alone. "There was a man on my plane, Dad. I forgot to tell you," Pinch says, too loudly, then lowering the volume. "He was talking about your paintings the whole flight."

Bear lets the page flop like a dog's ear, chuckling at this yarn. "That so, Charlie?"

Caught out, Pinch looks away, persisting with the fib, his voice dwindling. "He was saying how the Museum of Modern Art wants to buy more of your paintings."

"News to me."

"Yes, he said that."

Bear flaps the newspaper upright again.

There was so much time for this vacation, but Pinch is hurtling toward the final days now. And Pinch hasn't worked up the courage to ask his father. He planned to explain everything at Dad's barn: how strange Mom has become, how she talks to strangers, how people nod to shut her up and look past the foreign woman, staring at her son.

"You think there's still time to maybe see your studio, Dad?"

"I cannot *wait* to show you, kiddo."

"You do recollect," Carol says, handing over his tumbler, ice cubes clinking. "You recall that Charlie here leaves in three days, right?"

"He's got a week or more! Ain't that so, Charlie?"

"I leave on Monday."

"Well I never!" Ben casts aside the paper, pages flying across the carpet, and he focuses on his son. "Now I'm really mad: You, about to go, and I got this nonsense in the city!"

"You're away tomorrow?" Pinch asks, panicking.

"Should be back Sunday, kiddo."

"Oh, honey," Carol interjects. "Bring the poor boy, why don't you?"

"To the Petros opening? I wouldn't wish that on my worst enemy. Charlie, you'd go blind from boredom."

Pinch nods fast, then shakes his head faster, then stops, flushing.

"Can I come? Please?"

"Not sure we can arrange it this late," Bear responds, tapping his pipe into the ashtray. "Aw, hell—why *can't* I bring my own son? To hell with those people!"

"You two boys could stay the night in the city," Carol suggests.

"Carousing till all hours," Bear adds, jabbing Pinch's ribs. "What do you say, Charlie boy? You and me, kiddo. We on?"

## 18

On the Larchmont train platform, Bear spreads himself across a bench, placing Pinch alongside him, one hand on the teen's head, the other flipping through *Partisan Review*, a wreath of pipe smoke expanding from him. Pinch—tingling where his father's fingers press—views the tracks, filling them with the night ahead. Painters and sculptors. Modern art itself, into which he'll walk this very night. He leaps to his feet, earning hardly a glance from Bear, who returns to his reading.

After boarding, Pinch dithers about his seat. Across from Dad or beside him? Finally, he inserts himself next to his father and, in sidelong glances, contemplates the man's face, the lines across his stony brow, crinkles bracketing determined blue eyes. Pinch is caught looking and turns away.

From his blazer pocket, he fishes a folded page full of technical questions about painting, amassed these past years of studying *The Materials of the Artist*, jotted in careful fountain pen, all for this precise moment. Yet Pinch is rattled by other thoughts—about living here, painting at the barn, apprenticing with Dad. *Might I?*

"I hope you're not too disappointed with me, Charlie boy," Bear says, rolling up his magazine, swatting his son's knee. "This damned picture refused to get finished. That's been lousy for you, I know. Me coming home late, mind elsewhere. It can be like that when I'm working: I'm not really where I'm at. You follow?"

"Oh yes. That's fine," Pinch says urgently.

"Some folks would sit here tut-tutting."

"No, I understand, Dad. I didn't mind."

Bear squeezes Pinch's fingers, shakes his head. "Events like tonight—I got to put up with them." Pinch doesn't know whether to clutch his father's hand back or stay limp. Bear, noticing the page on his son's lap, reads aloud the heading: "Questions for My Dad." He smiles, clearly touched. "Well, your dad is right here, Charlie. Ready and waiting. Fire away, my one and only."

Pinch scans the questions, too anxious suddenly to understand his own handwriting. He stammers out a query about that lesson in Rome, how Bear taught him traditional methods like mulling paints and squaring up, yet Bear himself doesn't necessarily apply such old-fashioned techniques. "Did you show me that because," Pinch ventures, having prepped this line, "because an artist should know the old ways so he can forget them, and go forward freely?"

"What is this, an interview?" He ruffles his son's hair, pulls him close. "You're a smart one. Know that? You could explain a thing or two to these bums we'll meet tonight, I promise you."

Gaining momentum, Pinch dares another question about when people sit for you. "Should *I* talk and get them when they're reacting? Or should I say nothing and let them grow bored, then get them when they're distracted and not thinking that I'm watching? Because I can't really talk and draw at the same time. Mom says you're like that," he adds, having posed this question chiefly to cite a trait they share.

"Charlie, let me tell you a story about me and portraits. After art college, I got this commission to paint some couple's little daughter. When I tell you that the only notable thing about that gal was the ears, you better believe me! Immense, they were, like an elephant's. I set up my easel, pose the little darlin', and I paint her. The parents, they see the finished product, and they're speechless. The lady, she goes, 'Can't you do *anything* about the ears?' I say: 'Why, sure: Pay a doctor to pin them back, and I'll paint her fresh!'" He pinches Pinch's thigh. Unsure of the point, Pinch grins. His father continues: "*That* is all you need know about portraits, Charlie. Are you accurate or are you cruel? That is the difference between a good painter and a great one. Because it's impossible to be true *and* kind. Not been done."

"But if you'd painted her without elephant ears, the parents would've complained too, wouldn't they? They'd say she didn't really look like that."

"Oh, Charlie. You should know by now: Nobody sees themselves." Bear raps the window, bothered suddenly. "What can I tell you, kid? What's there to say about making paintings?" He looks hard at his son. "My real life, it's when I'm working. It's entirely there. The rest—everything—is flimflam. And that's tragedy. Because what am I really doing? Wiping colors across fabric? Tricking people into feeling something's there, when it's nothing? When I'm doing the work, I *almost* think it adds up. Then they drag me to some farce like tonight, and I'm reminded what my job really is: goddamn decoration. Understand?"

Pinch, stabbed by his father's virulence, replies softly, "I don't know." For if this is tragedy, then Pinch wants his share: a mission like Dad's, a trapdoor through which to pass, on whose other side is real life, making everything on this side fleeting and void. "Dad, can

I stay here? With you and Carol? And— and work on my painting? Is that something that—"

"You give me hope, Charlie. You know that? We will make this so special tonight, me and you. We'll show them, hey? Buddies. You hear?" He shakes his son's hand, a tight grip. Bear rests the crumpled copy of *Partisan Review* in his son's lap, throws his arm around the boy's shoulders. Pinch, fighting back tears of relief, stares hard out the window, hardly breathing. He clutches the magazine all the way to Grand Central.

## 19

The Checker taxi trundles south past Houston Street, passing industrial buildings and punctured garbage cans, whose pungent ooze trickles onto the sidewalk. The cab halts before a cast-iron facade, six stories of fire escape, the doorway defaced in spray-paint scrawl. Out front, a delivery truck idles, its clicker blinking. Bear and Pinch get out, father leading son up a rickety staircase to the second floor, where a tin sign—"Heights Manufacturing (Dresses) Inc."—designates a previous tenant. Pipes run down the soaring ceilings of the newly converted gallery, machine parts and fabric bolts still heaped on the floor. A workman in overalls makes pencil marks on a wall, hammer jiggling on his tool belt.

The opening tonight features younger artists than Bear Bavinsky, including three who are already present, sharing a bottle of Schlitz: a tall black woman in a Mondrian dress and orange bead necklace, and two jittery white guys, whom she teases, both in velvet jackets, leg-strangling black jeans, and Beatle boots. Nobody notices the middle-aged painter at the entrance, with his adolescent son in tie and blazer.

The artists' giggly banter sounds across the room, names drifting mystifyingly into Pinch's ears: "Henry Geldzahler" and "Barry Goldwater" and "Lee Strasberg"—worryingly, he hasn't heard of any of those artists. On a far wall, two blue fluorescent beams are mounted into an X. Beside this hangs a collage of Heinz ads. The largest work, however, is a plywood board stenciled with pink and yellow speech bubbles that contain no speech. Unsure how to react, Pinch turns to his father.

"Planning to buy?" the black woman asks, approaching Bear. "Or just looking?"

"Neither, if it's all the same to you," he replies.

Smirking, she asks what brings him here, and looks most entertained to hear his name. "Shit, I've heard of you. But you're not on tonight."

"Lovely lady, if I had something on these walls, nobody would look at anything else," Bear tells her, charm turned up. Dad loathes these occasions, Pinch knows, yet he masters a room so effortlessly. He's not even friendly to people, but they seem to like that. "Which is you?" he asks her.

She points to the speech-bubble artwork. "Plus a few more to come—I'm waiting on a delivery man."

"You're not the ketchup lover, I take it?"

"That's my friend René. You don't dig that?"

"If I was in the market for a hamburger, I don't doubt your friend René would have all kinds of useful advice. Till then, I suggest he quits pretending to do anything more than drivel."

"He's right there. You can tell him yourself."

"More than happy to." Bear lifts a bottle of beer from her hand and places it into his son's. "Now, *this* young man," he informs her, clutching Pinch's shoulder. "*This* is an actual, proper painter. Right here. He's the one you should know. Not this hooey on the walls."

She cocks her head at Pinch, noticing him for the first time. "What's your name, young man?"

"Charles," he replies faintly and offers his sweaty hand to shake. Instead, she takes back her beer, sips it, then returns the bottle, her eyes sparkling. "You gonna be famous, big guy?"

Smiling, he glances at Dad.

"You don't know his work?" Bear responds, slinging an arm protectively around young Pinch. "Ain't heard of Charlie Bavinsky? And you call yourself an artist?"

"Wait one minute. You saying this is *the* Charlie Bavinsky? In the flesh?"

Pinch laughs, blushing.

She takes her beer full-time now, summoning her friends and elaborating on the prodigy in their midst. One of the men touches Pinch's head for benediction, saying, "You are the future." As more people turn up for the hanging, each is introduced to "Charlie Bavinsky, artist of tomorrow." With every introduction, the fanfare grows, each new entrant hearing another layer of grandiosity: "The world-famous genius, Charlie!" and "Charlie B, master of all forms, spiritual and sexual!" and "Charlie Bavinsky, visionary!"

Pinch—casting wild-eyed looks at his father—is pulled from one side to another, these artists pawing at him, sharing beers with him, asking kooky questions for the others to overhear. "Everyone knows," the black woman says, "that age is just a number." She plants a kiss on Pinch's lips, causing his legs to shake and everyone else to buckle with laughter. Pinch stands there, knowing—for the first time in his life, *knowing*—that this is his setting, and these are his people.

Gradually, conversations bubble elsewhere. The mob disperses. Pinch spins about, seeking someone else to question him.

The black woman is against a wall, prodding at the chest of Bear, who mock-falls back a step. "I know you," she says, waggling a finger at him. "You're one of those guys still got paint stains on his sneakers. I didn't think they made your kind no more."

"Nah, what they make, sweetie, is shit. Which is everything in this gallery today."

Everyone laughs. They think he's joking.

"See?" the woman teases. "This is why you folks in such a bad mood. You *used* to be in charge."

"I'm out of date, you're saying?"

"Baby, you're old! But don't take my word for it. Let's find you a mirror."

The sharper their exchange, the more Bear chortles—until everyone turns at the arrival of a portly man around sixty, Victor Petros, owner of this gallery, who is gasping from one flight of stairs, cigarette scissored between hairy middle finger and brass signet ring, sandalwood cologne emitting from large pores. He sloughs off his overcoat, allowing it to slump onto the floor, and he greets a few young artists, caressing an arm of each. He reaches Bear finally, taking both of the painter's hands, leading him away for a private chat.

Pinch—tipsy from beer, overheated, unsure of what to feel or where to stand—follows after his dad.

"You approve, fine sir?" Petros is asking Bear, wiping his mouth from side to side, nostrils twitching. "Departing our home on Fifty-Seventh Street was not without bitterness. But walls must be had, my dear Bear: meaty walls for meaty masterpieces such as yours—those lunatic Bavinsky glories, hanging above the chasm of disaster, only to pull back at the last!"

In a spurt of tipsy irritation, Pinch almost denounces this stupid description.

Petros continues: "I know, Bear, I know. It's not your style tonight. Nor mine perhaps. But that's the market, alas. I trust you'll be in attendance for the big splash later? There'll be scribes and sausage rolls and sensational dames."

"I got the youngster in tow."

Pinch stands higher, presenting himself to the famed dealer for appraisal, a trifle defiantly—then hastily dabbing sweat from his upper lip.

"What do *you* think of it all?" Petros asks. "You're young—can you see any value in these works?"

"I think it's drivel," Pinch declares, glancing at his father, then back at Petros, the boy's neck flushing.

"Youth speaks!" Bear says, chuckling.

This prompts Pinch to push onward. "Nobody who has taste could like this junk. Why would anyone put this on their wall? It's for idiots." Noting the glare of Petros, Pinch falters. "It isn't . . ."

The dealer contemplates this spotty adolescent, as if struggling to discern a feature of minimal worth.

Pinch is desperate to maintain poise yet wracked by his childish outburst, having shown off so stupidly, having insulted this important man, who Pinch has dreamed might someday represent him alongside Dad. Suddenly, Pinch glimpses himself: a little nothing among adults, who see how stupid he looks, a schoolboy in suit and tie.

Petros takes a puckery drag of his cigarette. "When do I get a studio visit, Bear?"

"That's why you pulled me down here, Vic, to try that on again?"

"I invited you to see our new dwelling, dear man, that I might receive your blessing for the move. But, naturally, I'm ever hopeful that you have fresh work for me. Been a long while! As I say to all my artists, popularity is a tan. It fades when out of the light."

"What is that supposed to tell me?"

"That you *must* have pictures at your studio I could discreetly place with a few choice collectors. If only to keep your name among the living. Bear?"

"When I'm ready is when you get something. But if you're planning to push my paintings to some of your rich know-nothings, you won't see anything ever."

"Don't tell me you're *still* insisting on museums. You know how needlessly complicated this makes my life."

"Vic, if you don't like my terms, tell me so. Tell me. Play whatever games you want with these twerps you got showing tonight, but I'm a grown man. You don't bring me all this way into the city for this."

Petros goes into backstroke, recasting what he just said, lavishing praise on "the unique vision of Bear Bavinsky," even while gently scolding Dad for not making work like everyone else. It's the market, he claims, conspiring against us both! Pinch wants to ask, But aren't you, Victor Petros, part of that market?

An awkward young woman in glasses sidles up, whispering to Petros about his meeting with Alfred and René at MoMA. "*So* glorious to have shown you our new cathedral," Petros concludes. "It means the world to have your blessing." He looks again at Pinch. "Everyone tells me that you are an artist too, and with great promise. Not to mention strong opinions. We'll get properly acquainted tonight, agreed?"

Pinch nearly leaps. Instead, he nods. "Yes, thank you. Thanks."

Bear watches, a little chuckle, arm around his kid, leading him away. As they descend for the street, Petros hurries to the top of the stairs, calling down a final thought to Bear. "Red, yellow, and blue! Primary colors make collectors happy! Keep that in mind!" He waves an unlit cigarette and returns to younger clients.

Bear walks fast away with Pinch matching his pace, not sure

where they're headed but ready to sprint there, barely able to suppress his drunken tongue from blabbing about all that transpired. He aches for Dad to speak, to say whether that was triumph or disaster, if Pinch conducted himself acceptably.

They walk in silence, Pinch buttoning and unbuttoning his jacket, armpits damp and itchy. At Washington Square Park, a college kid is playing the banjo, wailing Pete Seeger while Old World retirees hunch over chessboards. The metal railings are laden with paintings for sale: tawdry sunsets and Picasso knockoffs.

"Those people showing at the gallery," Pinch begins, watching his father, "it's like they weren't even doing the same *profession* as you."

His father keeps walking up Fifth Avenue, until leading Pinch through a revolving door into a hotel lobby. "You have a room for the young man?" he asks the front desk.

"Get ya fixed right up."

Pinch goes cold. He's being left here, and can't object—he saw Birdie remonstrate with their father, and it never ended well.

"Here's a buck for the bellboy," Bear says, slipping his son a dollar, turning back to the revolving door.

"But will Mr. Petros mind if I don't come back?" Pinch asks, suppressing desperation. "I was supposed to speak with him later, I think."

"Get anything you want, Charlie boy. Room service, anything. On me, kiddo." And he's gone.

Up in his room, Pinch stands in bewilderment, still muzzy from the booze, mouth dry. He punches his thigh, hammering it three times, tears welling up. In confusion, he keeps flashing to before: Dad telling everyone I'm an artist.

Once calmer, Pinch toys with the radio in the headboard, tunes into a ball game—he's never heard one before. He leans out the window, scanning the concrete far below, seeing his father in every thick-shouldered guy who plods toward the hotel. Drowned out by car horns, Pinch states his name to the smoggy summer air, as if encountering real artists again, telling them about his influences. He replays those interchanges—except that he kisses back when the black artist pecks his lips. Pinch leaps onto the bed, landing on his knees, then darts back to the window, studying the sidewalks. As hours pass, the concrete below turns darker gray until the street lamps pop, coating the asphalt white, passing yellow stripes of taxicabs, red dots from a traffic light down the next block.

Only at breakfast does he see Dad again: there, at the back of the hotel restaurant. Across from Bear is the black woman from yesterday, wearing the same Mondrian dress, a little rumpled this morning. She is caressing Bear's open palm. He clasps her fingers, brings them to his mouth, a playful bite. Bear notices his son, nods, not calling the boy over.

## 20

Bear sleeps on the train back to Larchmont, with Pinch watching. Lightly, he rests his hand on his father's upper arm, which rises and falls with the man's heavy breaths. Stirring, Bear utters a peaceful sigh, draws his son closer, as if pulling a bony little cushion under his arm. "What a time!" Bear mumbles. "Told you we'd turn that place upside down." His eyes remain shut, crow's feet deepening from amusement. "And what an impression *you* made. They loved the hell out of you, Charlie."

"At the gallery?" Pinch says, needing to hear this again.

"We made a scene all right! But not for talking about, hey?" He opens one eye. "You got that, kiddo?"

"After the gallery, we ate hamburgers for dinner at the hotel," Pinch responds, as if recounting to Carol.

"With plenty of Heinz ketchup," Bear adds.

The boy laughs, recalling that idiotic collage. "And baseball on the radio."

"*You* are a solid customer," Bear says, touching his forehead to Pinch's temple, before settling back to sleep.

But Pinch still awaits an answer about moving here for good. As the train slows into Larchmont, passengers stand, smoothing suit jackets, collecting hats from the overhead racks, adjusting brims. Bear leaps to his feet, lifting Pinch as if he were a brown-paper parcel. "Back in the suburbs, young man," he says. "Time to adopt our disguises, Charlie boy. Ready?"

Carol waits on the platform, talking a blue streak about Widgeon's tonsillitis. Back at the house, Pinch runs to his room, opens his suitcase with the rolled-up painting inside. He darts to the top of the stairs, calling down when Bear passes along the corridor. "Could I show you that picture I brought? Would that be okay?"

"Be right up, Charlie."

Chilly with sweat, Pinch sits on his bed, leg jiggling. The murmur of his father's phone conversation downstairs drifts up, punctuated by Bear's thunderous laughter, each bolt of which hits Pinch with such love for this man. The call ends. Bear clomps upstairs. "Well, kiddo, what you got? I know I'm gonna love this."

Pinch unrolls the canvas and swallows. "Remember you told me in Rome to 'paint close, but look far'? I always do that."

Bear's gaze flits expertly across the painting, absorbing a hundred details an instant. "Tell you what, Charlie. I will tell you what." Bear packs his pipe, shaking his head. He looks up. "*You* did that, son of mine?"

Swelling with pride, Pinch nods.

With his knuckle, Bear pins down the edge of the curling canvas. "That is one hell of a leg."

Pinch grins. "It's mine. Like how you drew your legs when you were in the hospital as a kid."

"Sure, sure." Bear continues to scrutinize. "Young artists show me their work all the time. I can tell right away if a guy's got something."

Pinch commands himself to act like a professional. He'd give up his remaining life to hear Dad's admiration for this picture. Pinch blurts: "Dad, did you think I could stay here? Here at the house?"

"You just did, Charlie."

"For longer, I mean. To live." His chest thuds. "If it's okay with everyone."

"You serious, Charlie?" his father says.

Pinch nods.

Bear pauses. "But is that fair to Natty? Doesn't she need you there?"

"Mom isn't like when you were with us."

"Aw, come on—Natty never changes. Sweet girl. And a kid ought to stay with his mother." He grabs Pinch's arm. "Son of mine, I think the world of you. You know that." He nods toward his son's painting. "So I got to tell you, kiddo. You're not an artist. And you never will be."

# Youth

OIL ON CANVAS

78 X 124 INCHES

Courtesy of the Bavinsky Estate

# Toronto, 1971

## 21

He stuffs a bolt of tobacco into his pipe, sucks a matchbook flame to the bowl, and coughs discreetly, browsing the art section of a used bookstore on Bloor, paging through old catalogs, obscure pamphlets, dusty Dadaist treatises that make him sneeze. He crouches to peruse a work on Pop Art, finding color plates of works by now-celebrated artists, a few of whom he encountered years before at the Petros Gallery with his father.

That night, Pinch cooks a lavish dinner for two, having procured the necessary Italian ingredients on College Street: cans of peeled San Marzano tomatoes, *guanciale*, black olives, *pecorino romano*, capers in sea salt—every ingredient except someone to eat with. He prefers a test run before inviting a date, just to ensure that everything works, from the saucepans to the conversation. "You come from Toronto?" he asks the empty chair, reading off a sheet of questions resting beside his plate of steaming rigatoni. He tries again, with different intonation. No, that sounded perverse. Anyway, he'll presumably know where she's from by the time he asks her out. Pinch crosses off that question and proceeds to the next: "Do you like music?" But everyone does. He scribbles this out, printing over it, "What type of music?" Then, "Is the record too loud/soft?" And, "The other day, (HER NAME HERE), I walked past a protest against the Spadina Expressway. What is your position on that?"

Smirking, he shakes his head. Poor girl! We'd better hope the food comes out well. Pinch stabs another forkful, raising it to his lips, his mouth watering. There *was* an interesting question here. He reads down the sheet: "I notice that you"—blob of red sauce—"yourself." He dabs the stain, touches it to his tongue. *Too acidic?* "I notice that you"—blob of red sauce—"yourself." *You* what *yourself?*

He jumps at the noise of an engine coughing and looks out the window over a tree-lined street of the Annex, watching a Volkswagen camper van disgorge record crates and shaggy students. His fellow University of Toronto freshmen are another species to Pinch. They're mere months from high school—one summer since lunch bells and locker smells, testing their new adult privileges, trading rock 'n' roll albums and philosophizing. By contrast, Pinch is a grown man of twenty-one, and presents himself as such: his receding blond hair side-swept, a tweed jacket and tie, corduroy bell-bottoms ironed with a sharp crease up the middle. Only his thick sideburns are unkempt, and this is less about fashion than incompetent shaving.

He hasn't had a classmate since age sixteen, when he returned from visiting his father in Larchmont. Upon arriving back in Rome, he told Natalie that he wasn't going to paint anymore, intending to wound her as he had been wounded. Her entreaties only pushed him to burn his best efforts, then his supplies; in the end, everything. What remained was the two of them in a cramped art studio. His aim succeeded: He had hurt her badly. And she had stopped trying with him. She decided to move back to London to resume her own art. He could come if he wanted. He didn't, but had no alternative. So, by correspondence from London, he completed his remaining high school courses, a minimal burden that left him most of each week free in a dark cold city. He haunted the museums, watching other visitors, confabulating their lives, wishing for the courage to address someone.

At first Natalie roared through a frenetic period of work, pulling overnighters at a pottery cooperative in North London, talking immodestly about her art—until, with crashing clarity, she saw herself: These pots were desperate, botched; she possessed nothing. Natalie struggled to sleep, grew paranoid, thin, smoking constantly. Once he came home to find her seated in the kitchen, a bread knife resting on her thigh. "Just need to go to bed for twenty-four hours," she said. "Then I'll get on with things." Two days later, he watched her being led down a beige hospital hallway. Several spells in psychiatric wards followed.

After Pinch received his diploma in the mail, he found work as a guard at the National Gallery to bring in a little money (though Bear helped out with fat but irregular checks) and also to escape home, where Pinch found himself insufferable, having assumed the role of nagging parent to his mother: "Open your mouth, so I know you took them." Every workday at the National Gallery ended with a plunge in spirits as he walked over the Churchill mosaic and out the portico entrance to Trafalgar Square, tensing further as he stepped onto the Tube train and rigid by the time it clattered into Belsize Park, their home stop. No matter how fine his day, it was dashed as he walked into their basement flat, hearing her smoker's cough from the kitchen, Natalie barely responding to his greeting, he yearning to tell of a famous museum visitor, say, or a stupid new policy, or the guards from Mauritius who were teaching him Creole.

Each night he cooked their dinner, lest Natalie go without—left to herself, she consumed only coffee and smokes, a regimen that alone could set off another manic-depressive episode. He tried to replicate dishes tasted in Rome, struggling to recall (and to find) the ingredients, apologizing when his experiments ended in catastrophe.

Sometimes Natalie *was* still loving—and he spurned her then.

"I think you hate me," she said.

"I don't."

"Is there anything you like about me?"

He changed the subject, never explaining the source of his anger: that she had encouraged him, had adored his painting, had stoked his hopes, telling him, "You are *really very good*." Yet he wasn't. He couldn't forgive Natalie for that. In secret, he wrote to her estranged mother, asking about Canada. Pinch dreaded telling of his contact with Ruth in Montreal. But she responded unexpectedly, hugging him, holding on tightly, whispering, "So pleased you're doing this," as if she were his mom again. Pinch turned formal, showing her the course catalog, a map of campus, where he'd be living—a collage of information plastered over his guilt.

"The funny thing about having a child," Natalie told him, "is that it's really about *not* having the child. That's what raising one is. Doing everything possible so they're able to leave you. Not that it's a credit to me. You raised yourself, Pinch."

"That's not true," he said, hurrying her attention back to his upcoming studies.

Now Pinch explores his large new home in Toronto, owned by Ruth and lent for his time at university. Previously it was a student flophouse. Four bedrooms bear the scars of former occupants, with psychedelic pen doodles on walls and the stench of wet dog. He ventures into empty rooms and floorboards creak. In darkness he stands there, hands on hips. *I must do well here.*

In class the next morning, he hunches over a small desk, taking copious notes to avoid stray gazes from the surrounding students, all women, which turns out to be the case in most of his art history courses, though nearly all the professors are men. Here, a middle-aged academic in a leather jacket lectures to his pretty favorite, who fiddles with a bouncy pendant. When the prof poses questions, Pinch shoots up his hand, answering in a rush, his throat constricting.

"Well . . ." the professor responds, stretching out the pause. "You are correct in point of *fact*."

Pinch didn't think there were points other than fact. Chastened, he resumes his febrile note-taking, throat blotchy. In bed that night, he replays his classroom blunders, burning with self-scorn, tugging at his hair. Barefoot, he opens the refrigerator, plucking pieces of cold rigatoni from a bowl. "Come here often?" he says, smiling at a red-sauce spatter on the linoleum. "It was dinner. But is it *art*?"

## 22

His emaciated grandmother wears penciled eyebrows that rise in skeptical arcs, her short yellow hairdo pasted down, giving Ruth the impression of a shriveled lemon. On her dining table in Montreal, she places a sweet loaf, candied cherries and almonds glistening, and she urges Pinch to eat, then to eat more (it's awful). She touches none herself. "I'm on a diet."

"Oh, you shouldn't be," Pinch responds, wishing to please the only relative he knows in this country, who is also paying his tuition.

"Since 1926."

"What is?"

"My diet."

He laughs—Ruth meant this as wit yet she appears annoyed at his response. She returns from the kitchen with two china teacups tinkling in saucers, each containing perfectly clear hot water. He sips, unsure if this too is a joke and whether he's allowed to smile.

Instead, he thanks her. Much of that afternoon he is expressing gratitude. She wants this, expects this—and repudiates it when offered.

Pinch always worried that involving himself with Ruth risked awakening hostilities between her and Natalie. The two women never communicated by phone, only the rarest letters, which Natalie read in a fury, one hand clasping the writing paper, the other hand clasping her shirt. Seated across from Ruth, who is supporting him, who is acting far more like family than Natalie has for years, Pinch feels poignant kinship for his absent mother. "What was Natalie like when she was little?"

Ruth fails to offer a portrait so much as a case study, telling of crippling anxiety, intense friendships that ended in fiery breakups, a girl who was insufferable in adolescence. Pinch attempts to broaden this account, adding his mother's subsequent accomplishments, how she set herself up overseas, raised him alone in Italy.

A framed photo of David sits on the mantel, and Pinch expresses regret that his grandfather died before they could meet.

"That's what she told you? Before you were born?"

Pinch—distressed to learn of his mother's deception—nevertheless claims that he must've misunderstood. But Ruth pursues the topic, seeking the safety of anger. She speaks as if having wanted to state this for years, to correct what her daughter has lyingly fed her Italianized grandson, who wasn't even brought up remotely Jewish, who knows nothing of David, nothing of our past or our lives in Canada. "Did she tell you David put a gun to his head? That he shot himself?"

Pinch nods.

"Did she tell you that he didn't die? That he didn't do us that favor. Couldn't even get that right. He went on for years. And who had to nurse him?" She jabs her own chest.

"Why did he, Ruth?"

"He was miserable," she says unhelpfully. "Kept telling everyone how decrepit he was. What's funny," she adds with an inauthentic smile, "is to *shoot* himself! You never saw a less violent man. They didn't even let him fight in the war. He was a man who went around on a bicycle, for God's sake! He lay upstairs for years, brain half removed. But he was too healthy in body—wouldn't fade away, not for years. How does a wife say she prefers her sick husband to die? I'll tell you how: 'It'd be a mercy.' Meaning, 'a mercy' to me."

"And to him," Pinch says.

"You weren't here. Someone never brought you." Ruth allows her cigarette to leak a gray curlicue, never inhaling. "Here's the strange part: I was broken up when David did pass away. Why?" She scrutinizes Pinch.

He looks to the man's photo: wiry, bald, stern.

"Of everyone, it was your mother who was closest with him. Why else run so far away? Not because she hated me—well, not only that."

After the subject of David exhausts itself, any other topic seems frivolous. She doesn't dismiss Pinch, though—it's as if she can't face his leaving, so will sit here, saying *"Mmm . . ."* to his dull accounts of classes. Abruptly she stands. He gets to his feet, pledging to return. She tells him to write first. He does so, almost every two weeks, asking about her daily life of which she revealed so little. At first he proposes a return visit. But she never writes back—unless he falls slack in his correspondence, whereupon a two-line letter arrives, containing neither salutation nor her name, just "Do you need stamps?"

# 23

Toronto is swallowed beneath clouds. As the plane shudders, Pinch grabs an armrest, nervously flicking the ashtray, peering in at elbows of cigarettes there. It's summer break, and he is flying back to

London. As a freshman, he performed well but not so superlatively as to gain notice, instead dissolving into the blinking ocean of survey-course undergrads. His letters to Natalie described fellow students, told tales of camaraderie, all fabricated. His was a solitary year; he counted down until today.

In the rail carriage from Heathrow, he studies English feet: scuffed dress shoes, bandaged pinkie toes (the first week of sunshine, sandals still tight). At Belsize Park, he steps into the morning, blinking. Minutes later, he's in her doorway, Natalie before him, only her hair different, shorter now, a black bob haircut with strands of white. He wants to apologize or thank her or cover his eyes and think for a minute. She lives in the same garden flat they shared for years, and Natalie herself seems mostly the same. But Pinch finds himself different, realizing only as he steps through the door.

She offers a packet of Maltesers. "Still your favorite?"

"I don't often eat sweets in Toronto." (When he unpacked on his first day in Canada, he found packets of Maltesers secreted throughout his luggage.)

"You must get back into the habit, Pinchy. I bought you lots."

"Let me start then." He opens the packet, tosses a few into his mouth. "This place smells *exactly* like before."

She leads him through the kitchen, past her small-press cookbooks and jars of carob and sticks of dried rosemary, past her stubby cactus that never takes water and grows measly defiant spines. Out on the patio, they sit at the bistro table, she shading her brow from the sunlight, steam curling from the cups of mint tea. Natalie has an unreal aspect: She is Pinch's most familiar sight, viewed since before his clocks started. Yet she isn't as he expected—not quite his mother today but a middle-aged woman.

"It's so lovely to have you here," she says. Natalie speaks of her current pottery, jokes that she works far better without him around.

She speaks of colleagues at the craft shop, denouncing them so scathingly that Pinch hears himself defending strangers.

"I'm doing better now," she protests. "Can't you give me credit for that?"

"I do."

"Doesn't sound like it."

He mentions Ruth, speaks of her frailty, urging Natalie to travel back to Canada after all these years.

"You're taking her side now?"

"I didn't know there were sides."

In less than an hour, they have regressed. While apart, each remembered their fondest version of the other. But the Natalie who wrote him loving letters is absent, replaced by the Natalie of hospital courtyards, hands shivering, struggling to pluck another cigarette from her pack, biting it out with her lips.

Pinch tries to force back those recollections, saying, "I don't even know what we're talking about." Citing fatigue, he retreats to his old bedroom, drags his suitcase in. He so longed to be here. Now he longs only to hide again under Toronto textbooks.

Over the following weeks, Pinch claims a more urgent need to study than exists. He also claims to want long walks on his own, but instead takes the Tube to view Old Master drawings at private galleries. He is obliged to knock on locked doors, his face appraised through the glass, whereupon he is admitted by a fawning clerk, who says with head tilted, "Let me know when I may explain." Pinch, applying the thickest Canadian accent, responds: "Such neat drawings. Where's the price tags?" After a few minutes of playing the heathen, he poses questions pointed enough to expose the ignorance of the snobbish clerk, whereupon Pinch leaves, flushed with pleasure, stepping into this jostling city—and empty to have nobody to tell this anecdote. What is mischief if not for retelling?

Every minute that summer is tense, he and she stepping around a quarrel that won't explode but simply exudes. "But what is your life like there?" she asks, smoking, though he's still eating a lamb chop. "You never give me a picture I can see in my head."

"You know which classes I take."

"Look, we can change your plane ticket if you'd rather fly back sooner."

"I never said that."

"You certainly don't want to be here."

Then, two days before departure, everything changes. They regress further still, becoming the best friends they were, perhaps are. They sit side by side at the kitchen table, scanning the *Guardian* for plays, exhibits, restaurants—suddenly there's too much to fill the dwindling time. They hasten out for dim sum on Gerrard Street, seated at a vast table by themselves, taking opposite sides of a lazy Susan, each spinning the last dumpling away when the other's chopsticks close in.

"Shall we get more?"

"More! More!"

"Tons more!"

On his final morning, he is buckling the straps on his suitcase when she appears in the doorway, saying, "I hardly slept last night."

"Why?"

"You." She wrinkles her nose. "Going."

## 24

A preposterous young man swans into the lecture hall, ludicrously late for class and wearing a long Russian coat with ermine collar, froggish eyelids fluttering as he seeks a free seat, only to flop across three in a heap of pastel scarves. Pinch recognizes him as Marsden McClintock, a twit enrolled in two of his sophomore-year courses—that is, they have six hours in common each week. Failing to acknowledge this fool requires effort, which Pinch is fully prepared to make. But today, Marsden has plonked himself right beside Pinch, reeking of liquor, though it's morning. Pinch leans away but Marsden's long arm probes ever closer, bearing a note in purple and yellow crayon: "Are YOU a Bavinsky like HE'S a Bavinsky?" Beneath is a clothbound volume, *Modern Art in the Americas*, opened to a plate of "Shoulder XXVII, 1951."

In fine ballpoint, Pinch jots a perfunctory "yes the same" in tiny lowercase, as if to make a point about restraint. Inwardly, he is overjoyed that somebody here knows. In their next shared class, Marsden again settles next to Pinch. "Terrible thing this morning," he whispers, as the professor rambles. "I woke up, looked around, and I'm in fucking Queen's Park! I had to run all the way here. Could I still be drunk? Is that possible? By the laws of physics, could I be?" He drifts to sleep, susurrating through the early Renaissance, snorting to wakefulness as everyone else is donning overcoats and mittens.

Outside, the tall young man bounds after Pinch. "Something about Donatello?" he guesses, by way of recollection. "Then I lost consciousness."

Pinch summarizes the class, leaning into the hard wind as if impatient for his next engagement, although he has nowhere next but home.

"You know everything!" Marsden exclaims.

"I'm just repeating what he told us."

"No, no—you are a genius. How would you feel if I copied?"

"Copied what?"

"Everything. For the rest of my entire life."

## 25

Whenever Pinch trudges up the slush-slimy steps of the Sidney Smith building, Marsden and his foppish entourage call to their grouchy new acquaintance. As if reluctant, Pinch joins them, frowning, moving from foot to foot in the subzero morning. Back when Marsden first buttonholed him, Pinch hastened to his house on Major Street, hung his coat on the rack inside, and ran whooping up to the third floor. Weeks later, Pinch has a distinguished role in Marsden's clique of aesthetes: He is their sourpuss scholar, the future critic of renown.

Marsden—who hails from a patrician Ontario clan, his father a leading Conservative member of Parliament—has styled himself a bohemian since age ten, at considerable personal cost. For this, he is resentful of the slovenly interlopers who have tied on bandannas and acoustic guitars in recent years, claiming *his* countercultural turf. A group of flower children straggle down St George Street, bandying signs for an antiwar protest while caterwauling Country Joe and the Fish lyrics about the fighting in Vietnam.

"Vietnam?" Marsden heckles them. "Your war zone is the shower!" Back to his friends: "It's like these people emerged from three decades in a yurt. Civilization is *not* about getting closer to nature. It's about getting as far from nature as possible!"

"What's a yurt?"

"I'd tell you, Nigel, but you'd have nightmares." Marsden looks away, saying "Now I've lost my train," which makes Pinch see a locomotive rushing past, a heap of pastel scarves piled up in second class.

Shortly thereafter, rumor circulates that Marsden has fallen seriously ill, bedridden at his Trinity College dormitory. Pinch buys an orange and sets forth to brave contagion—only to discover that Marsden's infirmity consists of a middling case of the sniffles and a serious case of sloth. He is treating this condition with a combination of Gitanes and sentimental French records about *la vie de bohème*.

"Why are you in bed? You don't seem ill."

"I'm comfortable here, and have yet to hear a persuasive case to leave." On the wall is a reproduction of Egon Schiele's *Self-Portrait with Arm Twisted Above Head*; on the floor, a hillock of cigarette butts. Most startling is what scurries beneath his bed: a squirrel that climbed in from the ivy. Marsden claims to have domesticated it, with powerful evidence to the contrary. Starved of admirers, Marsden talks and talks to his surprise guest, catapulting among subjects, lingering on slanders, especially of the bully boys in this residence whose romantic misdeeds he satirizes. "Sex," Marsden comments, "is proof of the futility of mankind."

"How?"

"Because the sex drive is never quenched. It keeps rising, as it were. And never does one accomplish anything with sex."

"Well, children."

"Not the way I do it," Marsden responds, describing himself as "a homophile," a term Pinch has never encountered, though he knows enough Latin to understand. It strikes him as sophisticated to take this admission in stride, and he wishes to match it with a revelation of his own. All he can confess of his own sexuality is virginity, which is entirely the wrong direction. So he resorts to ribald anecdotes about his father. "Once, Bear got his schedule mixed up about when he was supposed to meet his wife—long before my mom—at his studio in Greenwich Village. By mistake, he'd also invited his mistress at that exact same hour. Both women turn up, see each other, and go berserk. It's, 'Either *she* goes or *I* do!'"

"What did he do?"

"Well, he had them wrestle."

"What?" Marsden sits up in bed.

"Yes, he made them wrestle for his affections."

"That's incredible!"

"Another time," Pinch continues, registering this success, "Dad was painting my mother, and he started complaining that her hair was in the way, that he couldn't capture the form of her head. He got a pair of scissors, gave it to her, and said, 'Cut it all off, right now.'"

"And she wouldn't," Marsden says in hope.

"Not at first. But he kept on about it. Finally, she couldn't fight anymore. She gave in. And then—as she's raising the scissors, nearly in tears—he snatches them away! 'I only wanted to see if you would,' he told her."

"I hope you don't mind me saying this, Charles, but your father is a monster," Marsden says approvingly.

Pinch beams with pleasure, even if both stories are lies (the wrestling promoter was Picasso; the barber, Giacometti). Encouraged, Pinch drops the names of other art stars whom Bear knows. And he tells of his own visit to New York at age fifteen, when he attended the opening of the legendary Petros Gallery in SoHo, where Dad jokingly introduced him around as an up-and-coming artist.

"You're an artist, Charles?"

"No, no. I might've *wanted* to be. I dreamed of it back then, in a stupid childish way."

"Oh," Marsden responds, pondering the scene. "Isn't that a little cruel then? Building you up, then packing you off to the provinces?"

"You're missing the spirit of it. It was quite a memory he gave me."

"I suppose." Still in bed, Marsden reaches under the mattress for a bottle of warm retsina, jams the cork into the liquid with his thumb, splurting a puddle of white wine onto the floor, which encircles the pile of cigarette butts, making a squalid desert island.

"You're definitely not wicked enough to have been an artist," Marsden comments.

"Aren't I?"

"You suffer the fatal flaw of being quite lovely, Charles. And every great artist has to end up in hell. Then again, imagine how beautifully it'll be decorated." He passes the bottle. "What disturbs me is that you aren't more twisted, given your papa. I, by contrast, never saw a single nude besides statues. Yet I end up an inveterate pervert."

"You're hardly a pervert."

"How dare you deprive me of my finest trait? Though, frankly, homosexuality is a simple act of reason. The male body is far more beautiful than the female. That much is indisputable."

"Consider yourself disputed." Pinch takes a glug of the wine, a shudder of well-being passing through him. He contemplates the lips of this person. But no—Pinch cannot muster physical attraction, much as he'd like to. "If men were beautiful, Marsden, why is beauty always portrayed as a woman?"

"Because artists are servants of the rich, and the rich are men. They've always wanted their pinup girls."

"Great art is *not* a matter of sex."

"My dear friend! What else would it be?"

As they guzzle the wine, Pinch hears himself admitting to his paltry record in matters romantic—a few flirts as a guard at the National Gallery; a girl or two he fancies in classes, each of **them** cold when he addresses them, as if Pinch might just launch himself on them.

"Well, that's your error: failure to launch."

Pinch speculates that it's his undeniable ugliness and is slightly hurt when Marsden fails to contradict this. So he shifts to that favored subject of the lovelorn: personal ambition. His current aspirations took shape while at the National Gallery. Employed to view the crowds, he viewed the walls instead, imagining a Bavinsky there among the Holbeins, Turners, Gainsboroughs. During breaks, Pinch explored the basement reserve, inspecting once-worthy art now relegated to the racks: unfashionable Mannerists, devotional works, pictures by dead apprentices of greater dead men. In his ill-fitting guard's jacket and polyester slacks, he visited Zwemmer's art bookshop on Charing Cross Road, happening across a biography of Renoir by the artist's son—a volume of aggrandizing rubbish about that mediocrity. Even Renoir could be made important! What if a sublime painter got that treatment? *What*, Pinch began to think, *what if I wrote the biography of Bear Bavinsky?* A rush of optimism as he foresaw Dad's approval, not to mention the hours they'd talk and debate. *What if I even become famous for it?* He skimmed artist biographies in the bookshop, finding no more sons but plenty of professors. So that is what he decided to become.

The needle reaches the end of a Jacques Brel record. Embarrassing snippets of Pinch's confessed ambitions echo in his ear. He pulls out his pipe, stuffs it with tobacco. "That's not for telling anyone, Marsden. Just a stupid idea of mine. Don't say that around. If you wouldn't mind."

"You brought me an orange, Charles. I consider that an act of heroism. And you spoke in confidence. I hold to privacy as does a cat."

"Do cats hold to privacy?"

"Have you heard one talking? And there's too much talking," Marsden says in an unfamiliar tone, sincere for the first time in their acquaintance. "You can pull this off, Charles. I'm *sure* you can. Absolutely certain. If it's what you want, my friend." With this, Marsden emerges from bed, shoeless but otherwise fully dressed, in his Russian wool coat over white fencing knickerbockers. For encouragement, he touches Pinch's forearm then turns and whistles for his squirrel, Balthazar, to no good effect, before standing at his sash window, gazing into the dark quad.

Never does he refer back to Pinch's needy ambitions, as if words in alcohol should remain suspended in that liquid. This sensitivity prompts Pinch weeks later, when the Trinity College residence expels Marsden because of the squirrel, to offer him a room. Fortunately, he leaves Balthazar behind.

After sixteen months of monastic solitude, Pinch begins to go out by night, walking across the underbelly of Toronto, chaperoned by the protective Marsden, who diverts any bid to lure his earnest scholar into debauch. Pinch even engages in a few trysts with women whom Marsden introduces. These are affairs with boozy beginnings, sober endings. But they win him confidence—he didn't realize how little he had until it materializes, changing everything, from his posture to his voice. Love affairs also reveal a quirk in Pinch's tastes: He is oddly unattracted to any woman he finds beautiful.

As for Marsden, his preference runs to rugged older men, typically married, prompting undignified couplings in city parks after nightfall. In contrast to Pinch, he experiences chest-crushing tenderness for beauty, whose sole consummation is physical, brief, incomplete.

## 26

Cohabitation, like foreign travel, presents the risk of getting to know one's friends. But sharing a house only brings Pinch and Marsden closer. At times, Pinch finds his shirts ironed or his shoes polished at the bedroom door. When he cannot reach a jar on a high shelf, his lofty housemate retrieves it. If Pinch struggles to open it, Marsden pops the top, neither of them interrupting the conversation.

"You're talking absolute pumpkin," Marsden exclaims. "Art is too hung up with this right-on politics and dreary conceptualism. My tragedy, dear Charles, is to have been born in this age of brutes."

"I thought you were going to say 'this age of ugly feet.'"

"If I had feet like those philistine hippies, I'd probably like bad art too, from moral shock alone," Marsden says, ignoring the ringing telephone. "Artists *used* to strive for beauty. Now they all want to 'say something.' Have you heard artists saying things? Bless their little hearts, they're unintelligible!" To punctuate this, he flings the *Philosophy of Aesthetics* textbook over his shoulder, which is his way of dropping a class.

Perceptive, opinionated, highly educated, Marsden suffers from fast-fading passions, the results of which are strewn about this house: unread volumes by Sontag, Isherwood, Gide on the staircase; Jan Garbarek albums still in the cellophane; half-finished embroidery on the kitchen table. That which falls behind Marsden ceases to exist, as if it were his duty to start, another's to finish. "My life is a flurry of inactivity," he once said, and his degree prospects are indeed flurrying into the distant horizon. "What thrills *me* about pictures is the opposite of 'saying something.'"

"What then?"

"Licking a painting," he says, by way of example, "as I so famously did to a rather succulent Philip Guston at the Janis Gallery in New York, very narrowly avoiding arrest."

"Are you going to get that, Mars?"

Finally, he snatches the phone. "Let me give him a shout." Marsden covers the receiver, mouthing: "Your mother."

After Pinch's visit to London last summer, he and Natalie agreed to talk regularly. Given the expense of long distance, they limit themselves to ten minutes per week. When it's her turn to call, the phone rings exactly on time. When it's Pinch's turn, he sometimes fails, humbled by a hangover or lost in schoolwork or in a swirling conversation with Marsden and cohorts. The following week arrives, and Natalie places her call, never reproaching Pinch for his oversight.

But this is not a day that either of them was expected to call. To his roommate, Pinch shakes his head.

"Seems that he's not around, Mrs. Bavinsky," Marsden reports.

Shunning Natalie only transports Pinch directly to her kitchen. He knows precisely where she's sitting. He waves his arms to stop Marsden from hanging up.

"When I say he's not around, Mrs. Bavinsky, I mean that he is. Or has just come around. Not in the sense of unconsciousness. In the sense of—"

"I'll take it upstairs." Pinch leaps two steps at a time and dives onto his bed, phone receiver flying from its cradle. He catches it. "I can't really hear you, Mom. You need to speak louder."

"I'm sorry."

"No need to apologize."

"I just wanted to hear how you are. Been ages."

"Not ages. Has it?" Lately, he dreads these conversations, fearing that oddness creeping back into her voice, something wrong again, requiring urgent travel there. She is fragile, but so is his current existence: classes in which he thrives, and a friend. The possibility of returning to what he was before—that pimply boyish self, issuing gale-force words when he met someone—it terrifies him.

He exerts himself to converse as if Natalie were normal, speaking of his essays and of the snow but bypassing his social life. To tell of happiness feels disloyal. Both he and she watch the clock, counting down the ten minutes, each for opposite reasons.

"I think of you so often, Pinchy. With such warmth."

He puts down the phone, harrowed, needing to restore himself to this house, this city. Then he dials Arizona, where his father lives with a new wife, Charlene, and their toddler, Johnny boy. Bear is always happy to hear from his Canadian son. Pinch, before speaking with his father, fetches his pipe, sparks it up, grinning at that boisterous booming voice: "Son of mine! What news from the true north, strong and free?"

Versed in art history now, Pinch dares raise topics of his father's expertise, occasionally earning ticks of respect, even stirring Dad's pleasure, which redoubles inside the youth, who presses the receiver hard against his warm ear. Above all, he quizzes Bear on the subject of Bear, his views on life and art, to which Pinch can listen for hours.

"Honestly, Charlie, I look at my work sometimes and think, Is that *really* what I meant?" he says, an echo on the line. "Or is it what I painted because that's the limit of what I can do, and I'm not as good as I need be?" When Bear is among strangers, he presents himself as one who'll freely tell tales against himself, immune to pomposity, stumbling through the nutty art world. But in private with Pinch, he is far more shrewd. Culture, he explains, is a pyramid: a few on top, many squashed under. You don't say this aloud, he adds, because people want to believe that art is holy, crafted by a clergy of sinners. Pinch smiles, and Bear chuckles. "You like that, kid? "There is an unfunny subtext to this, however, because Bear's work is increasingly overlooked. He is drifting from the history of art, replaced by those who are objectively worse. Yes, *objectively*. For Pinch deems artistic merit as fact, not opinion. His fury flames that Bear is subject to idiots, to peons who spurn transcendent work, leading the public to mediocrities and condemning a master to darkness. Pinch would hurt someone to correct this.

"Dad, I know about your new art going only to museums. But maybe you should rethink that. If you let a few go privately again, might that—"

"The market is a sewer. It needs to be there, but don't make me go look. Okay?"

"No, you're right. Remember that absolute shit we saw at the Petros Gallery? I never witnessed such worthless junk in my life."

"Charlie, every piece from that show—every piece—is worth more than anything I ever did."

"It won't last."

"Says?"

"Hey, Dad, I've been meaning to tell you something—this idea I've been playing at. Pretty much my whole university career actually." His hands get clammy, mouth dries out. "Just, obviously, I'm a nobody now. But I had this idea, Dad: how I could become a professor, and write books eventually."

Bear takes a drag on his pipe, which prompts Pinch to relight his own, puffing hard.

"Pete's sake, kiddo, finish your story!"

"So, okay, so I was planning something. That you concentrate on your painting while I get into academia. Eventually, I end up somewhere influential, in a position where I can affect opinions." Stated aloud, the conspiracy sounds deluded to Pinch. He rushes toward the end, to mask his doubt. "If I got your art even a *bit* of what it deserves, that'd be worth a huge amount. To me. Or. Don't you think? I know great art rises in due course. But maybe it can do with a lift sometimes."

"Who said great art rises naturally?"

"That's what I mean." Gaining momentum, Pinch wonders if this might really be a good idea. "One can't let idiotic criticism take its course, Dad. We've seen its course." He opens his palm, as if pleading in court, the phone cord wrapped around his forearm, briar pipe gripped in his hand.

"Listen. Listen," Bear interrupts, adding nothing, holding the floor, smoke audibly blown from his nostrils, Pinch able to imagine that gray cloud twisting around his beard. "Edvard Munch once said, 'Paintings are my children—they're all I got.' But here's what *I* say. You, Charlie boy, are a helluva man. I think the world of you. You know that? We got work ahead."

"I could pull this off, you think?"

"We're fighting the same war. Comrades at arms," Bear responds. "So it's back to work, I say. For the both of us."

After placing down the receiver, Pinch opens the door to the bedroom balcony. He walks out there in his socks, which are instantly soaked and freezing. Breath clouds dissolve as he mutters in the various foreign languages he studies. He shoves a line of snow off the wooden balcony edge, the flakes glimmering as they sink before the streetlight glow. "I'm actually doing this. I'm going to do this."

# 1975

## 27

She pulls the marked Latin exam from his hand and carries it away. "Hey! Hang on!" Pinch calls out, hurrying to catch up as she disappears down the stairs. "What are you doing?"

Even once they're outside the building, Cilla Barrows—his main rival in the art history master's program—hasn't answered. But she does stop, scanning his answers while lazily chewing the collar of her burgundy roll-neck, the fringes of her suede jacket swishing. "Hold it up for me," she says when Pinch reaches her.

"Hold my own exam for you?" But he does so.

She runs her hands through her hair, pulling it tightly back—looks painful—a deft twist into ponytail elastic, all while surveying his answers. She lights a long thin white cigarette and holds a loose lock of bangs under her nose, smelling it.

A recent arrival on campus, Cilla Barrows moves around with more consummate assurance (and a better sense of direction) than Pinch, even though he completed his entire undergrad here. Since their first master's seminars, she has made herself known, standing over the classroom garbage can, sharpening pencils and peeling a grapefruit too, devouring it instead of a midday meal while making comments from the doorway, the professor so dumbfounded that he permits it. More than a few instructors have taken to delaying class for her arrival, shuffling papers, glancing down the hallway, until: "Oh, fine, here you are." As for her comments, they're well-reasoned and startling in equal measure, such as when she dismisses the oeuvre of Piero della Francesca.

"You're ruining all my favorite artists," a fellow student whimpered.

"You'd prefer to live in a dream world?" she replied.

The student's crumpled expression suggested that, yes, she would.

Pinch, still displaying his exam for her, asks, "Why are you smelling your hair?"

"Expensive shampoo." She holds out the strand for him to sniff, but he demurs.

"The university trustees would be thrilled that your scholarship money is going to cosmetics."

"They'd be pleased to know that I steal this shampoo from my roommates," she counters. "Scholarship money is strictly for cigarettes and whiskey. You beat me by two, bastard."

"Ninety-three is still excellent."

"Not as." She lifts the corner of his exam to her mouth, bares her teeth, and bites it, giving a quiver of a smile that holds till she turns, striding away down the frosty sidewalk.

## 28

Soon, Marsden has heard too much about Cilla Barrows, so he precipitates a meeting at the small library atop Sidney Smith Hall, where she works part time, collating prewar German art journals and alphabetizing yellowed leaflets on archeology. Within moments, he makes her laugh and lures her downstairs for a cigarette. It's Marsden who bypasses her icicled first name in favor of "Barrows," which pleases her because it evokes her parents, with whom she communicates rarely and opaquely. She is redeemed at the sound of their name, meaning her.

From an oil town in northern Alberta, Barrows was blessed in childhood by the proximity of an eccentric librarian who introduced her to the works of Dorothy Parker, Rebecca West, Hannah Arendt. In high school, her education expanded further when several of her father's friends made passes, proving themselves hairier versions of boys in her class, talking just as tediously about hockey and reckoning that any statement from her must be dubious. She toyed with a few grown men but disliked the results, including a memorable fistfight between two contenders, one's hand slamming onto her icy windscreen, which didn't shatter—*ingenious engineering*, she marveled, seated inside the vehicle, cratered glass inches from her face. She drove around the rutting males and resolved during a gentle black-ice skid that she would live in New York as an adult, never marry, and produce one daughter, her brainy accomplice. After the University of Alberta, Barrows proceeded to grad school in Toronto, where she shares a ramshackle house in the Annex with seven fellow Albertans.

Her budding friendship with Marsden—the first of many such bonds with urbane gay men—provides Pinch with close glimpses of Barrows. When he enters his living room, she is often there, drinking black coffee and smoking, with *Songs of Leonard Cohen* on the record player. She quizzes Pinch about deponent Latin verbs and presses him on comments made in seminar.

"When did you first know you were clever?" she asks him once, and Pinch bumbles out a nonanswer. He never considered himself clever until this instant. Thrilled, he wonders now.

Barrows—after a night of rye-and-Cokes with Marsden—excuses herself to the bathroom, then explores the house. Upstairs, she knees open a creaky door to a bedroom that, it transpires, contains a Latin speaker.

"Hey, I'm in here!" Pinch yelps.

"My apologies," she replies, entering anyway, knocking on his door from the inside. She sits at the desk chair, her hands slid between the thighs of her flared jeans. "Are you gonna try to get me in?"

"In where?"

She points to his bed.

Pinch lies under a duvet, which he yanked to his neck upon her appearance. Below, he wears coral-red pajamas with white piping. "Convince you?" he stammers. "Why don't you convince me?"

She pulls her hair back, eyebrows yanked higher. "Tell me something interesting. About yourself."

"I don't know."

"Liar."

"I wear red pajamas."

She smiles. "Right now?"

He juts a leg out from under the covers, flannel on display, his socked foot cold from nerves.

"You." Pointing at him. "You are going places." She smooths down her jeans and returns downstairs.

## 29

When Marsden flunks out of university, his politician father pulls strings for a position at the Royal Ontario Museum, where the errant son becomes a research assistant to the world's leading expert on eighteenth-century Canadian schooner paintings. Oddly this fails to captivate Marsden, who drifts into employment at the Pilot Tavern, an artists' bar in Yorkville. He and Pinch see less of each other, their schedules pulling apart, Marsden carousing till dawn, snoring as Pinch fries his morning eggs. They communicate via notes on the Frigidaire, each following the other's day by plates in the sink.

When they do cross paths, it's usually because of Barrows—Pinch is studying late and hears her voice. He tidies himself and makes an appearance, hastening gruffly past, as if motivated only by a need to fill his water glass from this particular faucet. "I'm a big drinker," he notes, taking a gulp.

"Nobody drinks more water than I do," Barrows responds.

"You are sorely mistaken there."

His provocation sparks the water-drinking contest. The rules are as follows: Talk normally while matching each other glass for glass; whoever runs to the toilet first is the loser. After two gallons, Pinch rises, fake casual—then sprints. While peeing, he commends himself for not being competitive. But that's untrue. It's because he is competitive that Pinch concedes, just as he quit every sport he ever tripped through. To give up asserts that this contest doesn't count, that the real battle is elsewhere—in his case, the war over taste. Because taste contains everything else, from morals to who you love to who you'll vote for. And taste *is* a matter of life and death: One artist gains ground, another vanishes from the record. There's only so much wall space. That's Pinch's battle. That is where he'll triumph.

"Nobody drinks me under the table," Barrows says. "What do I win?"

"Everlasting glory."

"I'll boast of it to my grandkids. In the meantime, Italian lessons?" She's preparing doctoral applications and pondering a thesis on Sofonisba Anguissola, a student of Michelangelo deemed by Vasari to be the finest female artist of her time. Barrows hopes to get a book from it, but must read texts in the original. "So," she concludes, "you get to be my teacher."

For her introductory lesson, Pinch arrives at a Hungarian diner on Bloor, greeted by the whiff of stewed meat and paprika. He sits at a window table and watches the waitstaff sail about. A cook's hand juts through the kitchen cubbyhole, thrusting forth a bowl of steaming goulash. Pinch looks outside, picking at a sticker on the window. From the other side, a tapping: her chewed fingernail.

To begin, he explains basic Italian grammar. But she grows impatient. "Yes, I get that part." Her chair screeches back and she moves to another table, not asking his opinion, although she's right: It was drafty by the door. A half hour later, she ends the lesson with equal brusqueness, and Pinch is left with his cooling crimson soup. He takes this lesson to be their last. But Barrows solicits another. He accepts every further invitation, no matter how ill-timed. And gradually, he comes to know her, even identifies a frailty, the first he's discerned in Barrows. Languages: She has no ear for them.

"You can't hear the double consonant?"

"It's the same sound!" she insists.

"It's not. Listen: *freddo*. Not: *fredo*."

"Why can't I get this?"

By their next lesson, she has labored at "*freddo*" for hours—she does not accept blundering twice. Still, she hears no difference. When he reads aloud a passage from Vasari, she says, "I'll never say a single phrase of Italian like that. I hate you, Charles."

That night in bed, when he is poring over *Les Mots et les Choses* by Michel Foucault, his door creaks open again. "What color pajamas?" she asks.

He wriggles up in bed. She approaches his bedside table, turns off the banker's lamp: blackness. "You could say any color now." A bed-spring squeaks where she sits.

Pinch—willing his eyes to adjust—fumbles for the light chain, but touches her knee instead. "Sorry," he says, pulling back. But she doesn't retreat. He reaches out again, returning his fingers there.

"Still just a knee," she tells him.

"I can't see what I'm doing," he says, raising his arm. "This?" He rests his fingertips on her collarbone, the heel of his hand against her chest, which sets his own to thumping. He draws her closer, thumb parting her blouse, top button straining in its eyelet. In darkness, he cannot see whom he kisses, which intensifies the sexual blur—until a half hour later his bedside light clicks on, cigarette smoke rising under the bulb, and he is altered, amazed that this is he and that is she: Barrows, undressed on his bed. And that's what her body looks like, and her slender hand atop his sheet, the chipped polish on her nails. He just kissed those fingers; he'd be allowed to do so again now. She rolls over, sighing peacefully, the softness of her backside against his bare hip. Only his pajama top remains on. She casts back her long chestnut hair, which cascades ticklishly over his face. He blinks through the strands, inhaling the scent of rose-patchouli shampoo and the distant musk from between her thighs.

After that night, Barrows and Pinch become a combined force, the stars of their program, already talking of where they'll live together in New York next year when doctoral students at NYU. Marsden fades into the background, his views on art silly, conceived chiefly to shock. And rarely does Pinch call his father anymore. As for the weekly calls with Natalie, he keeps missing them, stung with guilt when he thinks of it. Everything is moving at rocket speed: He and Barrows roaring through final assignments, reading voraciously when not talking voraciously, finalizing proposals, consulting prospective PhD advisers—not to mention nightly beer and pretzel sessions at the Blue Cellar Room, and morning sex that erases every other consideration.

Pinch lies awake before dawn, her warmth nestled into his. Blips of disbelief pass through him that she finds him kissable. Her roommates let it be known that Pinch is a puzzling choice—balding and decked out like a high school math teacher, so shy as to appear witless. But her priority is a man intelligent enough to keep up. And it doesn't hurt that he cooks Italian.

He places before her a plate of *osso buco*. "This," she says, "is the life."

"I just realized. You don't want a man, you want a servant."

"That's not fair." Tasting, a long *mmm*, devilish smile. "Why can't I have both? A man servant. Or how else am I to get anything done?"

They hardly consume that meal, however, because the phone rings. It's her pregnant roommate, screaming. Barrows takes control of the situation, flagging down a taxi on Harbord Street and dragging Pinch along to help. On arrival at the hospital, Pinch questions the expectant mother in a show of vast ignorance about premature labor. But this is what Barrows wanted him for: to help distract the petrified mother until her twenty-year-old husband reaches the maternity ward.

Upon the breathless arrival of the prospective father, a nurse tries to calm him: "Don't look so worried, my dear. Once the baby arrives, you'll fall in love."

"Hopefully with the baby," Barrows quips, earning a stifled laugh from Pinch, a frown from the nurse.

On their way out, Barrows grabs Pinch's hand, slaps it to her hip. They proceed down the hospital corridor, her flank purposely bumping against him every second step. "Wondering if I could suggest something," he says.

"I'm all ears."

"Go to bed with me?"

"I need your application essay and proposed topic of study."

"In my defense," he says, "romantic spontaneity is a bit tough given our present location."

"How about this location?" She hip-checks him into a visitors' bathroom and locks it after them. Pinch kisses her neck and breasts, struggling for passion in this setting. When he glances up, her hand is clapped over her mouth, eyes giggling. She strokes the back of his neck, looks into his eyes. He presses his forehead against hers. Barrows hugs him. "We need to stay together," she whispers.


## 30

When Marsden is fired for giving away too many drinks at the Pilot Tavern, a customer hires him at an edgy Yonge Street gallery, where his first assignment is babysitting the artist Temple Butterfield, a strapping Californian ex-marine so polite that no one can tell if it's humility or sarcasm.

Temple's exhibit opening is packed, the sizzling disco beat punctuating crowd babble. Women in floppy hats wave to friends, purses smacking into displays, while mustachioed men slurp from beer bottles, admiring each other. Now and then, someone notices the art, points a pinkie, and explains as those around nod gravely.

Through this sweaty throng, Pinch and Barrows edge, intrigued because Marsden—normally scornful of contemporary art—raves about Temple. The first piece they encounter is *Moment O' Mori*, a pink vanity mirror in which the viewer is supposed to look and ponder death. Next is *Beethoven*, a whoopee cushion on a chair. There are a couple of performative works too: one featuring male strippers who offer fruit punch from pitchers labeled "Urine"; the other is two nude women covered in blue paint doing interpretive dance, first bunny hops, then dropping to their knees and humping the floor. Temple's most celebrated piece, however, is *Piss Shit Fuck*, a large electric freezer. The artist statement explains the title as a tribute to Duchamp and Manzoni, the former having signed a urinal in 1917, the latter having canned his feces in 1961 and sold them for their weight in gold. Temple joins such esteemed company by offering frozen vials of his semen for $500 each, encouraging collectors to inseminate someone with his seed. He has pledged to sign any resulting offspring.

Pinch reads this to Barrows, widening his eyes at her, shaking his head. He adds over the pulsing music: "From politeness to Marsden! Let's say nothing too mean until after we leave!"

"Agreed!"

Marsden approaches with a man of thirty, blond hair to his shoulders, wearing train-engineer dungarees: Temple Butterfield himself. Marsden looks at his two friends. "So?"

"Isn't it incredible what one can do with art!" Barrows says ambiguously.

"Hey, man," Temple responds gratefully, raising his hand before her. "Gimme five."

With an ironically soft slap, she obliges. The artist holds on to her fingers, adding, "Your support means a lot."

"Do you even know who I am?"

A stoned smile. "I do now." He speaks as if watching each word float to the ground, belatedly releasing her hand. "My practice is still so young, you know? So that means a lot."

"Don't be so modest!" Marsden tells the artist, explaining to his friends that Temple was already a huge star while studying at CalArts.

"What's it like there?" Pinch asks. "I always wondered about those famous art colleges."

"CalArts? It was an experience."

"What kind of experience?" Barrows presses.

"If I had to say in one word, I'd go with 'pretty unreal,' actually."

Pinch joins the hunt, he and Barrows dogs on the scent of stupidity. "Unreal how?"

"Like, I don't know. Pretty trippy."

It occurs to Pinch that, unless someone takes control, they risk exchanging vapidities for the next half hour. "We'd like to hear how it was *studying* there. Could one learn, say, how to paint? Is that possible?"

"Painting is repetition at this point, right?"

"Are there life-drawing classes?"

"Maybe. But it's more free-flow. It's about finding your own subversion, right? You bring work in for crit, and see what gets born. But nobody's judging. It's pretty antifascist that way."

Pinch glances at Barrows, then at Marsden, as if to ensure that both are registering this gobbledygook.

Barrows asks, "Sorry, Temple, just to be clear, what do they *teach*?"

"Well, you can't teach art. You either fake it. Or you fake it. Right?"

"Temple's mentor was John Baldessari," Marsden notes. "He's the one who did that video piece *Teaching a Plant the Alphabet*."

"Does the plant get its MFA at the end?" Pinch asks.

Temple claps, laughing. "I dig that question." Other revelers are pulling at him, and he allows himself to be led off, with Marsden hurrying after. An adoring crowd closes around the new genius.

Pinch gapes at Barrows.

She shouts over the noise, "At least he's cute!"

"What are you talking about?"

"I'm not allowed to admire another man's looks?"

"If you must. But can't you have better taste?"

"Jealous?"

"Can't hear you!"

The next afternoon, Pinch delivers a hot mug of coffee to Marsden in bed, needing to denounce everything about yesterday night. "How," Pinch asks, "did you not fall over laughing at that horseshit?"

Marsden sits up. "You didn't like *anything*?"

"You can't tell me, Mars, that it was good."

"Who's defining 'good'?"

"You, usually."

"I still need to understand Temple's work better."

"Understand what? That's such a cop-out."

"It was an amazing crowd. And those weren't dumb people."

He's right: It was a cultured group. "It makes me lose hope in mankind," Pinch says. "But you have to admit, Marsden: That was *not* art."

"There's no doubt it was art. Like there's no doubt this is coffee. But is it good coffee?"

"How's the coffee, by the way?"

"Dreadful. But still coffee."

"No way Temple's work actually moved you."

"It made me laugh."

"Since when is that a criterion? And why would anyone laugh? It's for morons."

"Thanks."

Pinch withdraws the charge but not his overall claim. To proclaim *Piss Shit Fuck* as art? It *pisses* on the dedication of his parents, *shits* on the art Pinch venerates, and *fucks* everything he ever studied. "Or am I the idiot here? Am I that guy who, a hundred years ago, was saying modern art isn't art?" Pinch asks, *trying* to see the other side—yet only growing more incensed. "No, it's *not* like those days. This is different. There has never been a period like ours. Because yesterday was a hoax. Obviously so. My only explanation is you're so in love with that jerk that you can't see."

"Barrows thought he was juicy too."

"Don't be an idiot. Barrows saw him as a sociological study."

"Finding him cute was sociology?"

Pinch lights his pipe, puffing in anger, needing to cloud over his housemate's claims. He stirs up a growing recent contempt for Marsden, comparing him with Barrows: that she came from nothing and is hurtling toward accomplishment, whereas he—raised in luxury, ski trips to Aspen, vacation home in Muskoka, museum visits across Europe—passes his afternoons watching $3 double features at the Coronet. *I can't respect Mars anymore.*

Pinch's indignation, he decides, is *not* envy of Temple Butterfield, whom nobody will even remember in a few years. It's that Marsden isn't the same. Ever since Pinch got together with Barrows, Marsden has seemed sillier. To be flighty is charming when you're young. But eventually, you must attain something. *Barrows and I are going to. He never will.*

Marsden must have perceived the shift in Pinch's manner, for he repeats a pledge made only as courtesy in the past: that he wouldn't want to outstay his welcome in this house. After all, he's not even a student anymore! "Maybe I shouldn't be hanging around. If I've become a drag."

"I never said that." Pinch steps into the hallway. "I never told you to leave."

"No, no. I see that; thank you."

Pinch makes his exit—and Marsden decides to do the same, soon scouting for new lodgings. Around the house, they avoid each other. Pinch, gnawed by guilt, assures himself that success requires hard breaks sometimes. *This isn't coldness. It's maturity. Marsden fell too far back. He's part of my past now.*

On his last day, Marsden goes upstairs to offer farewell thanks. Pinch avoids eye contact, mentioning regrets about Marsden's departure—and suddenly he means it. Yet he neglects to ask for a forwarding address, and Marsden fails to offer it.


31


Barrows rips open a thick NYU envelope full of registration forms. "And so it begins!" They celebrate at the Blue Cellar Room, then march victoriously home, talking too loudly on his street, shushed by a neighbor peeping from a darkened window. Barrows is unable to sleep, eyes wide to the ceiling, chattering about next year. Pinch endorses every idea, exerting himself to appear normal. But days more pass before he can tell her. Actually, he can't. He just shows her his NYU envelope, which is small, containing a single page: "Thank you for your interest, but we regret . . ." He rushes through the ways that this isn't a disaster—there might be a waiting list.

"What about other colleges?" she says.

"I thought we were going there."

"But where else did you apply?"

He can't look at her.

"What? *Nowhere* else, Charles? Why?"

He takes a furtive glance at her and witnesses something dreadful: She is pulling away, watching him recede in the rearview. Her preparations must go ahead. She sends forms and references to the Institute of Fine Arts, confers with future professors. Pinch sits by the phone in his room, needing help. He has no idea what to tell Bear, but now believes NYU was correct to turn him away—it confirms what Barrows hinted—that his doctoral interest (Caravaggio) lacked inspiration, that he is out of step.

When he calls, Natalie is overjoyed to hear his voice yet senses something amiss. "I know you."

"You used to, yes."

"That's a painful thing to hear."

"Ignore that. It's not true."

"No, I think it is," she attempts brightly. "All the more reason to catch up. Actually, Pinch, I've been wanting to ask. Might I tempt you to pop over here before you disappear off to New York? I don't want to pressure you, but I can help with your flight."

"You don't have money for that."

"I've been saving up, hoping you might want to drop by," she says bravely. "You'd be so welcome. And bring your friend, provided you and she don't mind roughing it at mine! I'd be so happy to meet her. Or," Natalie hastens to add, "if it's easier, I could come there to Toronto? I might even see Ruth. She's been so generous to you."

"Not sure this is the time. I'm so busy right now."

"Yes, I feared that. Must be lots to do."

His breathing feels constricted, a rope cinched ever tighter around his ribs. *I couldn't be an artist, and now I won't even be a critic. I'm a pretender, a fake.* Pinch's worst fear rushes at him: *I'll never become my father, because I've always been my mother.*

"If something is the matter, Pinchy, I could come out there. Is there?"

He finds an excuse to end the call and immediately phones Bear. Pinch's voice transforms, upbeat and inquisitive. But he is unable to admit to his mess, eyes tightly shut as he prompts his father to talk and talk. Fortunately, Bear wanted to discuss something: the French cottage once owned by Cecil Ditchley, where the potter went bankrupt in the 1960s, at which time Cecil had offered it at a discount to Natalie, including his pottery studio. She was far too poor (and too unstable) then. But when Bear heard, he mailed a check, purchasing the place for his ex-wife's use, sentimental about "old Natty," as he called her. She has never once visited, the location being too remote. Nor has Bear. Which is why—between wives, at a loose end—he is off-loading the place this summer. Problem is, he can't speak more than menu French. "Which is where a certain multilingual son comes in handy."

Bear is sending travel expenses, including money for a first-class flight. Curiously, it's this detail—first class—that moves Pinch, like the squeeze of his shoulder that Dad gave when boasting of his son at the Petros Gallery. If only Barrows grasped that he isn't just another art history grad student but has actually dwelled in that world, was raised in it, lived among artists, could introduce her around. To hang on to Barrows, he must show her his most dazzling feature: Bear.

She is so deep in NYU prep that it's hard to discuss anything. "I'm going to France this summer," he begins.

"Great."

He nearly flares at her unconcern. Whenever he probes into their relationship status for next year, she is casual, vague, as if this were not the moment. Perhaps that's right. After all, he doesn't know what he'll be doing then or even weeks from now. "Sorry, Charles, I'm really busy right now."

He cringes at this belittlement but persists with talk of France. Barrows knows Europe only from reading and in art; the sole flight of her life was Edmonton to Toronto. As he knows, she longs to find her way there someday.

"You have a ticket already," he says.

"I'm not understanding you."

"With me. My father insisted," he lies.

"Bear Bavinsky wants to meet me?"

"He sent money for both of us to go." Pinch has calculated this: If he splits the first-class flight money, they can both travel, provided they do everything cheaply. "We'll stop in London first because Dad wants me to visit my mom. Hey, Barrows?" With false confidence, he adds, "You're going to Europe."

# London

## 32

Natalie stands apart from the pedestrians parading down Carnaby Street, her hair close-cropped and gray, bifocals dangling from a purple-silk ribbon. She mutters to herself, gaze tracking every approaching lone young man, briefly observing a bunch of catcalling punks, chains around their necks, wilting spiked hair. She has lost weight, seems rickety at her height, a loose T-shirt dotted with dried clay, jeans smeared with muddy hand streaks.

As Pinch approaches, he is unable to suppress a loving grin. "Mom."

She slips on her bifocals, nudges them off again, takes his arm. Without a greeting, Natalie leads her grown-up son a few steps—then halts midway across the crowded walkway and embraces him, fingers impressed into his back. She holds a second too long, looking at Pinch as if to conserve the image. Embarrassed, he chuckles and pushes back. And she's off again, leading him toward a vegetarian restaurant, informing him that she chose this because she didn't know what he eats nowadays.

"Maltesers," he answers as they step inside.

She looks back, a slow ripple of a smile. "I'm not eating. Just mint tea."

"Make it two."

At the counter, she knocks over their pot of hot water, then insists on cleaning the puddle, grabbing handfuls of the restaurant's paper towels despite the waitstaff telling her it's quite all right: "Really. Just leave it. Please." Natalie won't. The queue lengthens, everyone glowering at this kook on her hands and knees, wiping the floor. Pinch urges her to join him at a table. Finally, she obliges—only to realize that she left her plastic bag behind. She barges to the head of the queue again, pestering the staff, who rescue her bag from the bin—they had assumed her papers and notes were rubbish. Finally, she rejoins him, shaking her head. Pinch is exhausted already.

"You have to tell me," she says, toying with the teapot lid, "if everything is right with you. I've been worried."

"I'm fine. Tell me about you, Mom. You're selling at three craft shops now—let's hear."

After a pause, she concedes, "I'm all right."

"Your pottery?"

"What can I tell you? If you saw a ceramics fair these days, Pinch, it's such a muddle. You wouldn't know *what* you're looking at. Everybody's so bloody English—determined to be small, droning about salt-glazing and fiberglass. But I'm producing my sculptures, as I always wanted. Sometimes I think they're good. Except when I think they're god-awful. Depends which day. Which hour. Which second!" Flushing, she laughs, hand over her throat, twisting a chunky red plastic necklace.

"What are these new sculptures? I don't have a picture in mind."

"Calling them 'sculptures' is a bit rich of me." She shakes the salt dispenser onto a fingertip, tastes. "They're mashed lumps of clay, Pinchy. Gestural craziness from your crazy mother. *Un pasticcio*, a garbled mess."

"Don't make yourself sound so inept. People will believe you."

"Well, *I* believe me. No, I'm joking. You're right. I think they *are* decent, this batch. They're brilliant! How about that?"

When he turns his head to consider the "Soup of the Day" on a blackboard, her jollity subsides in the periphery of his vision only to reassemble when he turns back. "So you dare to make pottery without a function—what would Cecil say?" he jokes.

"Dear old Cecil." After his awkward visit to Rome, they fell out of touch for several years—Natalie cringed to recall her wretched state when he was there, how she misinterpreted everything. But they are back in touch again, and she still loves Cecil; he's still her supporter. "He's in Brighton now, still making the same terribly serious pots."

"Do you see him often?"

"When he can stand me. And your father? How's Bear? I marvel at that man."

"Same as ever."

"It's so hard to believe we were together. Don't you find? Anyway, the force of will in Bear is incredible. I envy him that. You need to be selfish as an artist—that's why it's so much harder for a woman." She pauses her rapid-fire stream, looks hard at Pinch. "I was at the craft shop the other day, and someone said, 'Natalie used to be married to Bear Bavinsky.' Another person went: 'Were you his muse?' I told them, 'When people say "muse," you know they mean "assistant"?' They thought me very bolshie, very women's lib." Fast, Natalie sips her mint tea, looks around as if everyone were staring. "But your father was an encourager of mine. It was Bear who bought my potter's wheel in Rome. Made me feel like a proper artist. I shouldn't forgive him for that! He inspires people, makes you feel you can. Sometimes, I wonder if that's fair, like when kids get told: 'You can become the president or an Olympic gold medalist! Just put your mind to it!' Such rubbish."

"You never told *me* I could be an Olympic athlete," he says.

"There are limits to what is credible, Pinchy."

He laughs. At first, Natalie seemed to blare her eccentricity. But this is a peek at his mother again, as if she were on the other side of a door and now leans out, and they see each other, know each other too well.

"I don't get why you always talk as if your career ended, Mom. You were just saying how well your sculptures are going. You can't doubt everything. You love your work, so it's worth it, right? You even loved Dad, right? Or you wouldn't have waited in Rome all that time for him."

"It was different in those days. I could hardly have returned to college in London while raising a baby, unmarried. At least in Rome, we had a place to live for free. But, of course, I was very keen on Bear." She smiles. "As your father liked to say, 'Natty, you're one in a million girls!' Eventually, I realized he meant it."

"You must've known he was like that. You two started seeing each other as an affair."

"But I was so young, Pinch. I didn't understand much of anything. And I was *so* unsure of myself. If someone told me I ought to do something, I figured they knew. What amazes me is I ever had the guts to tell Bear to leave. Seeing your father's face! Like a scolded little boy, poor thing."

"*You* broke it off?"

"I asked him to leave, yes. And immediately started regretting it. But it was impossible to back out. He got angrier and angrier, wouldn't listen to me anymore. I suspect he was ready to go himself. He shouted for a while, burned a few paintings, and went."

"Why burn a few paintings? Out of anger?"

"No, no. He just didn't want to leave anything substandard behind. Your Dad, as you know, is very worried about people seeing substandard work."

"Worried?" Pinch says. "Dad doesn't care what anybody thinks."

"I've never met an artist who didn't worry what *everybody* thinks. Or what are they doing it for? Some act like they don't care, but you can pick those out—they're the misanthropes. 'I'll hate the public before the public hates me!' Oh, poor Bear." A half smile. "I've never been able to get mad at your father. Why is that?"

"Because there's no malice in Dad. He's just that way. Like a huge ship, powering forward on his mission, and nobody can stop it."

"I see," Natalie notes, "that you're still very engaged with Bear."

He looks to the restaurant clock, irritated. Nobody likes to be understood without warning.

"I can't stick around for ages," he says. "But let's keep talking." He looks at Natalie and his spirits sink. She has skill and knows her craft. But he wishes she would stop hurting herself in this attempt to be an artist. It's so effortless for Bear, so beyond her.

"If you're in difficulty, Pinch, would you tell me?"

"I'm not sure."

"Well, what purpose do I have then? Really, though?"

"Lots of purposes." He fails to cite one.

"I saw you as a friend too early," she says. "I burdened you, like I burden all my friends. No wonder people run out on me. What do I offer?"

"That's stupid. When I was growing up, you were by far my closest friend." Only by saying this does he realize it's true. "And you achieved lots at a very young age, Mom. You uprooted yourself at, what, nineteen? Went all alone to London. I couldn't have done that."

"How *I* see it, looking back, is that I got myself into a predicament. I was pretending to be a grown-up. But I couldn't pull it off. Probably I should never have left Canada, should've settled down there, worked in a craft shop, married a nice accountant. I got so far into this artist impersonation that there's been nothing left but to keep it up."

"Do you regret having me when you did?"

"No," she responds with alarm.

"What?"

"Just that I think—I know—that I let you down. Terribly." She twists her necklace, trying to assert control over herself, slowing her breathing. At last she looks up, lips together, wet eyes blinking. "I keep having this feeling, Pinch. That I'm floating through each day. Like I'm here, but this isn't anything to do with me anymore." She indicates everyone in the restaurant, also nodding to the window over the street. "What people are busy with—eating or traveling or even just meeting someone fresh—that part of life is behind me somehow. I had my opportunities. Some went well, some less so. But I'm past that."

"You make it sound like you're a hundred years old. You're young still. And remember, Cecil said something like this when he came to Rome. Telling us how he'd put all ambitions behind him and felt much better for it. Right? Maybe it's a stage. That you don't care so much. It's healthy."

"And yet," she interjects, a light in her eyes, that of a younger self, "I *so* want you to see my pottery, Pinchy. I want you to tell me what you think. To say, maybe it's all right. I want approval. I still do." She shakes her head, touches her throat, forces a laugh. "When I'm dead, I'll probably be worried that people don't like my headstone!"

"Mom, you are doing much better. Seen from outside. You're working, throwing again, managing." He needs her to be okay.

"Of course, I'm doing well! My son is here from Canada—what else could I want?"

"That I don't run off, as I probably have to."

"As you must do. Run as far as you can. Don't look back." She smiles.

"When I fly back to Toronto, I go via London. Could I maybe visit your workshop then?"

"I would so love that."

"You can show me these famous sculptures of yours," he says. "We can have a proper talk."

She taps the scalding teapot, her fingertip leaping from the heat, then back, held in place. "I'd so value your opinion, as a fellow artist."

"Fellow artist? The last thing I made was your mint tea."

"You only poured it."

"See: I'm not even a tea artist."

Her eyes brighten again. "We're still friends, you and I."

Embarrassed, he chuckles, noticing all the people of his age around. "Actually, on the way over here, I was remembering our rides around Rome—going to Galleria Borghese on our rattly bikes. Me, veering into traffic to scare you."

With recollected anxiety, she touches her chest. "I know." But something distracts her. "I'm annoyed. I've left out so many things."

"Tell me."

"You need to go. We can discuss everything tomorrow."

"I'm not here tomorrow."

"But I'll talk to you anyway. I do every day. Did you know?" she tells him, returning behind her door of eccentricity. "I suppose you can't hear me talking from across the Atlantic. I wake up and say: 'Hello, Pinchy, what are *you* up to this morning?' Like when you were little in Rome."

"What did we discuss this morning?"

"I said, 'See you in a few hours!'"

The waiter deposits their bill.

"I'm sorry my girlfriend couldn't make it," Pinch says, looking away. "She had a meeting at the Courtauld, and it—"

"Yes, you mentioned."

Pinch sees that she disbelieves this, correctly so. He didn't want

Barrows to meet his mother, fearing that Natalie's strangeness devalued him. Now he is ashamed for that—yet still wouldn't want Barrows present.

Natalie's gaze sweeps across the restaurant, alighting finally on her son. "You need to go," she says, her hand—a slight tremble from the meds—on his fingers. "So, so much luck to you, Pinch."

He touches the top of her head—but is too upset and must stand in haste, unable to look at her. He mumbles thanks and is on the street, striding fast.

## 33

Barrows drives their rented Beetle onto a hovercraft across the Channel, then onward into France, motoring through the outskirts of Paris, he squinting at a map, directing them (very badly) toward their hotel near Montparnasse cemetery. The room is the cheapest available, a creaky-floorboards garret with a petrifyingly narrow balcony overlooking zinc rooftops. She passes an hour out there, gazing down, as he lies propped on the bed, puffing his pipe, observing her.

"What in hell are we doing inside?" she asks, spinning around. "We need to be *there!*"

With only two nights in Paris, they race through her itinerary. At the Louvre, she canters toward this painting or that, he accompanying, unable to study the art, only her. They return deliciously drunk to the hotel, she pawing at his belt, he watching as if viewing this from outside himself. On their last morning, they come downstairs asterisk-eyed and too late for the hotel breakfast, begging a maid for even a stale croissant (denied), then find a nearby bar and tear apart a *pain au chocolat*, dipping it in a shared *café au lait*, kissing hard outside, coffee breath, pastry tongues. "We already checked out of our room," she notes.

"In the car?"

But there's no time. They must reach Bear's cottage by nightfall to avoid the expense of additional hotels. It's nine hours by car from Paris, most of which she drives while he looks in puzzlement at the Michelin map in his lap, thinking of Cecil Ditchley, and of his mother, whom the cottage was bought for, and of his father too, who awaits them—the fact makes Pinch smile, erasing all worries. He regales her with tales of Bear, his artistic gambits, his rakish misdeeds.

"I must admit," Barrows says, legs on the dashboard (Pinch's turn to drive). "I've got mixed feelings about his work."

"Mixed how?"

"I don't know that I've ever loved it." She adds, "Keep that to yourself, please."

"No, I was planning to walk in there, thank him for flying us to Europe—then immediately point out that you consider his life's work pointless."

"I never said that."

"You're wrong, by the way," he says, grip slippery on the wheel. He wipes his hands on his corduroy trousers. "Have you ever met an artist, a really serious one, before?"

"Temple Butterfield?"

"Hilarious."

She pokes her finger in his ear, leans over, nips his cheek.

He dares a thought: *Barrows needs me to become what she will. So here's what we do. I come with her to New York and manage the unfashionable parts of her life—the cooking, the ironing, the cleaning. I want to be useful.* He looks at her.

"Eyes on the road," she says.

*And I can do independent research in my own time. There is a way out of this.*

"I'm sorry your mother didn't have time to meet up," Barrows says. "I'd have enjoyed that."

"What if I reapply next year?" he asks.

"To NYU? Of course. If you want."

"But what do *you* want?"

"I want you to tell me more about your mother. You keep changing the subject."

He claps his hand on her thigh as if to push down the surge of emotion inside him. There's a sharp turn ahead; he must return both hands to the wheel.

"Nearly there," she says. "Nearly Bear."

The roads keep narrowing: from highway to two-lane regional, to a belt of tarmac around the mountainside now. They lean into each turn, he hitting the horn in case another car races toward them, especially with the light fading. Finally, there: the roadside barrel, its staves splashed with red paint. He slows, turns in, the Beetle shuddering up a steep pebbly driveway.

The trip rushed by. He needs more time. More Barrows. Years more before they pull in. He yanks the parking brake, turns to her.

"About time!" Bear hollers, approaching through the dusky evening.

## 34

The painter, well into his sixties now, seats his two young guests at a long farmhouse table in the kitchen beneath hanging lamps circled by flies. Pinch talks in a nervous rush: how they'll need to find a real-estate agent in Prades tomorrow, must also tidy up the cottage for viewings, and look into the legal side of the sale.

"Nothing of the sort!" Bear interrupts. "I've decided to keep this pile of rocks, meaning you luckless rhubarbs came all this way for nothing. But there's good news. I'm compensating you with fine dining—fine as possible in this neck of the woods—and even finer boozing all week."

"Wait, what? You're not selling?"

"I'd be crazy to. Have you any idea how cheap booze is around these parts, Pinch, my boy?" Winking, Bear reaches for his pipe.

Barrows has never heard her boyfriend called "Pinch" and flashes him a quizzical half smile.

Bear resumes his account of coming here a few weeks ago and taking an unexpected shine to this dump. He has befriended a local butcher, and the lady at the *boulangerie*, and a Dutch couple who run a wine cellar. Foreigners dot this area, it turns out, mostly oddballs who drifted here for the cheap living.

"I always pictured Cecil completely alone," Pinch says.

"He was. The hippies and trippies didn't turn up till long after his day," Bear explains. "Now have a sip of this poison, will you?" He pours three overfull glasses of Côtes du Roussillon. From the first gulps, Pinch and Barrows ease into this rustic cottage, making merry with a coarse red, cold ham, crispy baguette, local butter.

"Why can bad wine taste so much better than the good kind?" Pinch asks.

"It's the company," Barrows responds approvingly. "The drink only tags along."

"Cheers to that, sweetie." Bear clinks glasses. "Know what else, kids? The very day after I get here, I just *got* to paint. Something in the mountain air. I drive breakneck to Perpignan for supplies and am working that very night."

"Me, thinking you needed help with the language!" Pinch says. "You probably get along better without French than I do with it."

"You deserve some credit, Charlie—you're the one convinced me to buy this place in the first place for your ma." He squeezes Pinch's shoulder, then turns to Barrows. "Always listen to this boy."

Pinch, cheeks burning, presses his nose into the wine glass, inhaling happiness.

Bear leads them on a midnight tour of the property, flashlight beam skimming the lawn, up to the fringe of the forest, then around his art studio, a structure in disrepair. The painter opens its door only a crack, points his light inside for an instant, the floor littered with Cecil's cracked pots, its air scented with clay dust and paint thinner.

"What are you working on?" Barrows asks, nodding at a large easel, the back of its canvas smudged with Bear's handprints.

"We'll never know," Pinch answers. "Nobody goes into Dad's secret chambers." To his father: "I'm impressed you already found someone to pose for you."

"These nutballs up here? They're fighting to sit. Problem is they're all smoking grass. Appointments mean nothing."

"I'd turn up on time," Barrows says.

"That so?" Bear says, expertly looking her up and down—a gaze Pinch has witnessed before.

As they all return to the main house, Pinch whispers to her: "His sitters pose *nude*."

"Oh, come on—he'd probably just paint my arm or ankle or something. Isn't that what he always does?"

"Even then, trust me, it's nude. There's a difference in how light reflects off fabric versus skin. It's how my father works."

"All right, kids, you get the run of the house. I'm camping in my studio for the duration. No arguing. It's a democracy up here, and two beats one."

"What if both of us vote for you to keep your house?" Barrows says. "We'll be fine. We're young."

"Won't hear of it." He speaks as one who prevails, and adds that all his work is in the studio, and he can't allow a couple of snoops to bed down there. "Not to mention, turp fumes'll rot your college-educated brains." He plants a good night kiss on Pinch's forehead, another on hers. "Been busting to see you two." He ambles off to his studio, crooning Sinatra for their benefit, a muffled medley of "I've Got the World on a String" and "Witchcraft" that persists until the lights go out up there, and it's all blackness except the firefly dots of vehicles creeping around the valley.

They awaken to a woman's voice. Pinch and Barrows peek out of the bedroom window, their cheeks brushing, both bedazzled by morning light. Bear is accepting a crate of apples from a middle-aged woman who speaks English with a Dutch accent. Overnight, a forested mountain grew behind the property.

Barrows opens the door to the back terrace and points to a gecko sunning itself on the flagstones. From behind, Pinch slips his arms under hers, cupping her breasts, hugging her to him. She twists around, licks his bristly cheek. "Starving."

"I'm not entirely edible."

So they wolf down ham-and-baguette leftovers while Pinch—his expectations about their future regenerated from a single night with Dad—drifts into embryonic-professor mode, telling her about Catalonia, how Basque Country lies to the west, Spaniards to the south, and how isolated terrain propagates obscure languages and dialects. In these parts alone: Anares, Gascon, Aragonese, Euskera, Occitan, Catalan.

A car kicks up pebbles and dust—the Dutchwoman driving away. Only then does it occur to Pinch that his father has no way of breakfasting—theirs is the sole kitchen. They hasten to his studio and apologize.

Bear isn't perturbed, just delighted to see them. In the cottage kitchen, he prepares a lavish midmorning feast of farm eggs and cheese and gnarled apples, which he slices with his Opinel penknife, wiping juice on the thigh of dirty jeans, his empty pipe poking from a hip pocket. Around noon, a bearded Swedish hippie arrives from a

nearby farm with his Irish girlfriend and her two kids from two previous hippies. Bear and they gab away, leaving Pinch and Barrows to
lounge on sun chairs.

"Light summer reading," Pinch comments wryly, nodding at her
paperback.

She lowers *The Gulag Archipelago.* "You should talk: *Syntactic
Structures?*"

"It's strangely fascinating."

At lunch, the Dutchwoman returns, bringing a magnum of *vin
ordinaire*, just as mouth-puckeringly tannic as the previous night's
red, and just as pleasing. Afternoon naps follow before Bear rouses
the kids with local sausages and *muscat doux* served in pottery mugs.
(Marsden always raved about the pairing of *muscat doux* with foie
gras, which he suggested they farm in the yard of the Annex house—
only required a willing goose!) Pinch smiles, but it fades. He's sorry
how matters ended with Marsden, that Pinch so coldly cut off a
friend of several years. Banish the guilt; too much at stake now. Each
day must go perfectly.

In bed that night, Barrows comments on how sociable Bear is. "Is
he sleeping with the Dutch lady?"

"Jorien? No, no. She's married."

"You noticed what time she drove off? *After* the afternoon nap."

He watches Barrows smoke a Virginia Slim, a wiseacre smile
cracking. *I completely love you*, he thinks.

"Diminishing returns, after a point," she is saying.

"What are?"

"When artists repeat early work, people say they're limited. But
if they innovate, it's 'lesser late work.' They get imprisoned by their
success," she says. "Hey, am I going to pose or what?"

"You don't really want to. Sitting takes forever."

"Maybe that explains why your father produces so little—not to mention all of his visitors, Pinch," she says, inserting his nickname as a tease.

"Don't call me that. It's what my mother calls me. And I promise, Bear is not gallivanting up here. If he has slowed his work, it's because we're around. But Dad is a machine. He works every day of the year. Trust me. I grew up with this."

"I didn't see stacks of canvases at the studio."

"Because he only just got here. And did you notice the oil barrel outside? He always has one where he paints. It's for burning paintings that don't make the grade. And that's nearly everything."

"Why? That's a bit extreme."

"It's smart. Dad's plan is to leave fewer than a hundred major works, each placed in major collections. He doesn't pump out factory products, like certain artists I could mention. Even fifty great paintings for posterity is way more meaningful than a thousand shitty sketches churned out for cash, like Picasso did."

"Okay, but how do you know Bear was painting before we arrived? Maybe he was busy seducing Jorien."

"First, because he said so. Second, because Dad doesn't busy himself with seducing. He does that in his spare time."

"You sound so pleased about it."

"Not pleased," he rejoins, chuckling. "I'm just worldly—unlike certain prim ladies of Alberta. Your prudish roots shine through."

She pushes him, laughing.

"Anyway, we saw at least one painting in the studio," Pinch notes.

"All I saw was the back of a canvas with hand smudges on it."

"Smudges from paint."

"True."

"Listen, I have this idea," he says. "I was thinking we could drive down to Italy. It's not that far."

"Didn't we come all this way so you could show off your Dad?"

"We came to sell a house," he says defensively. "And certainly not to pose for my father." But she's right. He brought Barrows here to display Bear to her and her to Bear. Only, she and Bear are getting along almost too well. Pinch is their connection yet feels himself shrinking from view. "If we go to Italy, I could show you around, impress you with my Italian. We can resume your lessons. Barrows?"

"Are you nuts? I'm having a ball," she says. "You go to Italy. I'm staying here with Bear Bavinsky."

## 35

Bear drives them to a nearby town for the weekly market, where farmers stand awkwardly behind portable tables loaded with local fare: wheels of cheese, *pain de campagne*, blood sausages. Behind them rise the Pyrenees, dogtooth peaks that inspire Barrows to pan across the landscape, inhaling crisp air. From a distance, Pinch watches Bear buying item after item, intent that the kids try everything delicious from around here. Speaking little French, Bear relies on pointing and horsing around, sharing uproarious laughter and backslaps with the vendors. Laden with purchases, he walks back to his son, places a few bags in Pinch's hand, throws an arm around his boy, and hands Barrows a few more bags, throwing his other arm around her, uniting the young couple, and leaving them to their intimacy.

"What's that amazing smell?" Barrows asks, peering into one of Pinch's bags.

He reaches in, breaks off a hunk of cheese. "Try."

"Won't he mind?"

"This is for us."

"He's so generous."

"I told you."

On the drive back, Barrows nibbles away, peppering their host with amiable queries about the life of an artist. At the cottage, Bear fetches an unlabeled bottle of red and distributes glasses. Pinch remarks, "That Basque guy selling the cheeses reminded me of *Supper at Emmaus.*"

"Reminded you of *what*?" Bear asks, chuckling.

"The Caravaggio, with that apostle spreading his arms. I used to look at that for hours back in my guarding days."

"What guarding days?"

"When I worked at the National Gallery. In London, with Mom."

"Oh, sure, sure."

"So," Barrows asks, "you're a Caravaggio fanatic like your son?"

"Dad is the one who introduced me to Caravaggio." He turns to Bear. "Remember? At Chiesa di San Luigi dei Francesi, when Birdie was visiting."

"Of course!" Bear says grandly, vaguely.

"Caravaggio *is* technically amazing," Barrows acknowledges. "Still, I can't help finding him a tad sterile. Each composition feels so staged. Those *tableaux vivants*—they all look, I don't know, like some amateur theatrical troupe."

"Oh, come on," Pinch says. "Yes, he posed his models. But there's stunning complexity in those compositions, also from a technical standpoint—that basket of fruit in *Emmaus*, just teetering there? Dad?"

"I hear where the lady's coming from." Pinch—who has revered Caravaggio *because* his father does—waits for Bear to add, "However..."

"However invaluable his contributions were," Bear continues, "I'd take Carracci over Caravaggio any day."

Pinch shuts his eyes an instant from surprise. "I remember you saying how absolutely anything a young painter needs can be found in Caravaggio."

"If a youngster asked me what to study, I'd be damned if I sent him to Caravaggio."

Pinch smiles in dismay. "I spent *years* copying Caravaggios."

"You painted?" Barrows says.

"Not seriously. But when we lived in Rome, Bear gave me the most amazing lesson once. All the basics in one afternoon."

"Were you good?" she asks.

"Terrible! Thankfully, nothing of mine survived. Dad advised me, quite rightly, that painting was not for me."

"I said no such thing!" Bear sucks the lighter flame into his pipe.

"Yes, you did," Pinch insists, fumbling for his own pipe. "When I was visiting you in Larchmont."

Bear leans back in his chair, nostrils flaring, smoke drifting out. He frowns, shaking his head.

"You did!" Pinch says, too fervently.

"You shoulda kept it up, dummy—a kid of mine could have done something special!" He takes Pinch's hand, dwarfing it, and gives a squeeze.

Pinch tunes out, distantly aware of Barrows inquiring about artistic process. With most outsiders, Bear refuses to talk shop, but he takes her questions, swilling wine and gesticulating in the smoky air. They both glance at Pinch, one after the other, as if he were an afterthought, then they resume.

"Is painting even part of the discourse?" Barrows is saying.

"What's a five-dollar word like 'discourse' mean?" Bear responds, sighing. "A person can't look at anything anymore without some fool telling him what it's 'supposed' to mean."

"Warhol says there's no meaning behind his art."

"It's the first time I've ever agreed with that donkey. The way it used to be, when a guy couldn't paint, he ended up a critic. Today, that guy, *he's* the artist!"

Pinch notices her smirk. His father is so outdated, and she sees him stumble.

"The way you talk, young lady, it's like any cockamamy new movement leads to a purer state. It's like Karl Marx talking."

"You saying modernism is a Marxist plot?" she asks, amused. "Because critics have suggested you're a reactionary. That Greenberg article about—"

"That piece was ridiculous," Pinch interjects. "And it was decades ago."

"Influential though," she notes.

"Look, here's a secret for you," Bear tells Barrows. "No great painter ever—not one—gave a damn about movements and manifestos. You think Degas sat around, sweating over Impressionism?"

"So what do you consider yourself part of?" she asks. "You're an island alone?"

"The truth is this: There isn't another artist around right now with my significance, not at this time," he answers. "When you see a Rembrandt, that is him on the canvas, him seeing. When I paint, it's the same. It's somebody else in the picture, but it's me on the canvas. Get that? Long after I'm under the dirt, I'll still be there. Nobody'll care anymore about some silkscreen of Marilyn Monroe or a dumb collage by that clown Bob Rauschenberg. What I'm working at is art. Not standing there like that lady who spreads her legs and pulls scrolls outta her jam pot!"

"Jam pot?" Barrows says, laughing. "So wait, I'm to gather that your motive is immortality?"

"Immortality ain't good enough for you?" He winks at her. "Hey, you sitting for me later?"

"Not sure your son is cool with the idea."

"Just because it takes so long," Pinch says. "And we're thinking of driving to Italy. Remember?"

"I remember saying I'm fine here. Or were you intending to bundle me into the car and start driving? Don't be so uptight, Charles!"

Flushing, he stammers, "I just didn't think you wanted to come to Europe to sit in a room."

"Who knows? Maybe I can write someday about the time I posed for the great Bear Bavinsky."

"Let's get to it then." Bear slaps his own thigh and stands.

Pinch, nauseated, sits in place, then stands in haste, following behind them. Each step up the boggy turf is a queasy softness under his shoes. In the studio, Barrows drops her sundress, kicks off her platform sandals, which land with two clunks. She straightens a strap of her ill-fitting bra, the cups caved over her small breasts. Pinch watches, frantic, mute. *These are the two most important people in my life. And they don't need me anymore.*

Barrows corrects a twist in the elastic of her panties.

"Steady there, tiger," Bear tells her, setting up his canvas. "Haven't even picked my paints, and the lady's already in her skivvies!"

"I don't mind lounging in my undies on a hot day. So long as you don't mind."

"I've seen worse sights."

Pinch tells her softly: "Maybe we should come back later when he's ready."

She ignores him, approaching Bear to watch him prepare the materials.

"Get comfy over on the drapery, sweetie," Bear says.

"How should I be?"

"Dad doesn't pose his models. You can sit as you like."

"Thank you, son of mine. And with that . . ." Bear looks to the door. "I don't work with an audience."

Pinch starts for the cottage—only to swivel around halfway, chest thudding. He speed-walks back. But Pinch can't just barge in. Saying what? He turns around again, quaking in place, looking toward the cottage. His heart is pumping overfast; he needs to be sick. *Did I drink too much? Come on—sober up. Think. My girlfriend is in there, naked, my own father inspecting her. Do I shove him aside? I can't.*

*But I can't wait here.* When a woman sits for Bear, Pinch knows, it's nearly a sexual act and often leads to one. He pictures Barrows where she is right at this instant. He bolts back to the studio, grabs the door-knob, and shoulders the door open.

His father kneels over Barrows, one hand on the ground by her neck, his face above hers, as if feeding on a carcass. They turn to Pinch without expression—they're otherwise engaged, Bear marking her place in chalk, Barrows still in her underwear.

"I was just . . ." Pinch says, breathless. "Maybe this isn't a . . ." His throat closes. Looking at neither, then approximately at her, he swallows hard. "Didn't you say before that you don't even *like* Bear's art?"

Cheeks flushed, she raises herself, resting on an elbow. "What are you talking about?"

"You told me that."

Enraged, she glowers at Pinch, who averts his gaze, looking to his father.

"Dad, if she writes about you, we don't know what she'll put in."

"Say what you mean," she demands.

"Just, on the drive, all that talk about Dad 'objectifying' women—would you publish that? It's my father's career on the line. You acted like he's some terrible retrograde artist, then posing nude now? Why? To be hung on a gallery wall someday?"

She stands, hands on hips. "Are you fucking insane?"

He can't meet her gaze. He looks at paint dots on the floor.

"If you can't accept me sitting, if you're that possessive of my body, be up-front about it."

"I didn't mean to have a big argument."

"Really? No?" She unhooks her bra, throws it at her pile of clothing. She pushes down her panties, lets them fall to her ankles.

"What are you kids arguing over?" Bear asks, indifferent to her nudity. "What do you mean, 'objectifying'? Not women's-lib jazz, is it?"

"Well, you *do* only paint women," she responds. "You're supposed to be this 'master of empathy,' who captures women so deeply. But a woman's hip is the sum of her? You've got to see how reductive that is."

"Could you put something on?" Pinch pleads, unable to look at her.

"Honey, I've been married five times, okay? Does that sound like a man who doesn't like the opposite sex? And I never painted a lady for the purpose of laying her. Hell, if I went to bed with sitters, it was to make for better paintings, not the other way around!"

"Some of your wives were artists. Including his mother. How did that go for her?"

Aghast, Pinch stares at Barrows. *I never put it that way; she's distorting this.*

Barrows adds: "The women's movement hasn't exactly landed in the art world, am I wrong? What's that line? 'When a woman makes dinner, she's a cook. When a man does, he's a chef.'"

"What in hell are you talking about?" Bear says.

"You're trying to hang some sort of slander on my father, on a lifetime of serious work."

"Actually? We're just talking," she says, as if to a moron, gathering her clothing, which she holds in a bunch before her. "Right, Bear? Or are you above the critical consensus?"

"That's exactly what I am. The only people who get tingles over what critics say is a breed of people known as critics."

"Whatever floats your boat, Mr. Bear. You and Rembrandt, gazing from your canvases for the edification of future generations, right?"

"Let me guess. You fancy yourself a critic someday?"

"I wouldn't mind."

"Well, tell me something, young lady. You ever seen the paintings of Gabriel von Max?"

"No, why?"

"Track them down. One I'd recommend is *Monkeys as Art Critics*."

"And that," she says, "proves my point."

"How so?"

"Because I never heard of the guy. He doesn't count now. And neither do you."

## 36

Once alone in the cottage, Pinch and Barrows fight in hushed voices. "I wasn't 'attacking' anyone. And he should be grown-up enough to handle it. Anyway, you seem to be the one who's offended."

"Don't tell me what he is or isn't," Pinch attempts, unable to keep up, unsure of his own views, just hanging on, terrified of what is happening, her every glance seeming to shout: good-bye. "We're enjoying *his* hospitality, remember."

"I'll leave then," she responds. "And, seriously, if you're incapable of discussing controversy without taking it personally, you will struggle in academia. You'll struggle at anything. The NYU admissions panel definitely got it right."

"Thank you. Thanks."

"I'm very sorry, but it's hard for me to respect a grown man who acts like a worshipful little boy around his father."

Flushing, he stands there, pointing at her, speechless.

"What is that supposed to mean?" she asks.

"Fuck you."

They lie in the dark for hours, neither able to sleep. Before dawn, she whispers: "I'm going."

"We'll discuss it in the morning." He pretends to fall asleep but is lying there, sweating, scrambling for a way back.

At breakfast, Barrows tells Bear that she needs to leave because of an emergency back home, though it's preposterous that she could've learned such news with no telephone out here. As she packs, Pinch stares at a window ledge dotted with dead bugs. "We came all the way here."

"I haven't forgotten that you paid for everything."

"That's not my point."

"Seemingly, if you pay the bills, I'm your chattel."

He slams the window closed, its latch shuddering, and points at her again, finger trembling. "You're insane."

She raises her eyebrows, as if to a third party. Barrows zips up her luggage. She lugs the suitcase outside, rebuffing his offers of help.

"You can't thumb a ride from here to Paris," he says. "Take the car, if you're going. But please, can we talk for a second?"

"We did talk."

"I lost my temper. I'm . . . I . . . I don't know."

She drops her suitcase on the gravel, looks at him, hatred draining away. "Don't swear at me again. Okay? Please."

He takes a half step closer. "Barrows, just—"

"Just hitting the road," Bear calls out, tromping down from the studio. "An early start is always best." He passes them, pops the front trunk on the Beetle, drops her suitcase in, and slams the hood, then hoists Barrows off the ground for a farewell peck on the cheek. Looking away, she expresses chilly thanks and slides into the driver's seat. She doesn't start the engine, instead staring through the closed window at Pinch, eyes wide: Can we talk?

Bear taps the roof twice, giving her a thumbs-up.

She starts the engine but remains in place, the exhaust cloud billowing. Pinch steps forward but is tugged aside by his father for a private huddle. "You, Charlie boy," Bear assures him, "are another *class* from that girl."

Slowly, the Beetle is reversing down the driveway, tires spitting up the stones and dust. Sharply, Pinch turns from his father, trying to catch her eye but only squinting at the glint on the windscreen. Bear waves at her in a semaphore sweep while addressing his son: "Better off without her, kiddo," he says, holding Pinch in a one-armed hug. "We're better off without her."

# Toronto

## 37

After flinging his suitcase into the house, Pinch sets out to find Barrows. When she drove away from the cottage, he had no way to reach her, so awaited their flight home, spending ten more days alongside Bear, who cavorted and socialized and never mentioned their departed guest. Each night, Pinch lay under the cottage rafters, head spinning from too much alcohol, tortured by the recollected spat and rehearsing what he'd say when he met Barrows at the airport. Once it was time to leave, he traveled by train and ferry back to Britain, almost forgetting that he had promised to see his mother. But he couldn't face that, couldn't bolster her, so he went directly to Heathrow. At the departure gate, he searched everywhere. "Sorry," the airline rep told him finally. "That person's name is not on your flight."

Her housemate answers the door, peering disdainfully over her glasses when he asks after Barrows. "Cilla isn't living here anymore."

"Where did she go?"

"If she didn't tell you, I can't."

"Did she leave for New York?"

"I'm not in a position to tell you that information." The door closes.

Pinch is back in his living room, clutching the briar pipe as tightly as possible, as if to crack the wood. In his other fist, he holds a set of keys from the cottage that he forgot to return, clasping them so the metal cuts into his palm. He extends his arm, gazes down it, measuring proportions, suddenly behind an easel in the Roman art studio, his paintbrush moving, its course seeming to precede his intent for an instant. He bites the pipe bit as if to crack his teeth, then searches for a Latin textbook, running through vocabulary lists, which strangely soothe him. He looks around. *Could take a coach to New York, find her at the department. What would my argument be? I need you. That's not a case; that's a difference of opinions.* "Whatever you like," he says aloud, addressing Barrows across the empty living room. "But this is a mistake." *For me. Not for anybody else.*

Soon, tenants will arrive at his house. He always pledged to leave upon finishing his studies. *To go where?* Pinch covers his eyes, wanting to erase himself. In agitation, he phones directory assistance to track down the number of the Institute of Fine Arts in New York then asks the secretary there how to reach an incoming doctoral candidate. They won't pass on private details like that. "You're not hearing my point!" He slams down the phone, telling the receiver: "Listen to what I'm saying!" He starts a letter to Barrows. But there was never any changing her mind.

He resumes his pacing, hemmed in by moving boxes. How can you be trapped by a future that hasn't happened? He studies the wall, then hammer-fists his stomach, wincing at each blow. He is saturated with hatred for someone who has nothing to do with this: Temple Butterfield, a fake who is far more consequential, far more important, far more successful than Natalie, than Pinch ever could be. *CalArts accepted an idiot like him. It'd have to admit someone like me. How hard could admission be? Very hard,* Pinch imagines.

He marches into the bedroom that belonged to Marsden. He needs his friend here. The last report was that he'd moved to Los Angeles as a studio assistant to Temple. Pinch tracks down a fellow member of Marsden's college entourage and learns the full account. Apparently, Temple made a video piece, *Fairy Dust*, featuring Marsden yapping to a fixed camera about various seedy affairs, childhood gripes, vitriol toward his family—punctuated by cocaine snorts and campy tears, all edited in jump cuts with the goal of a laugh riot. *Studio International* called Temple's venture into video art both "freakily hilarious" and "deadly serious," noting that its subject was "a real person" whose father was a member of the Canadian Parliament. In Ottawa, the Right Honorable Brian McClintock was shown excerpts of the film, which outed Marsden, prompting much of his family to disavow him. When Marsden returned to Toronto, he was ostracized even by his gallery friends there, owing to bitchy on-camera remarks mocking the Canadian art scene, calling it "easily a decade behind."

Reached by phone, Marsden sounds suspicious to hear from Pinch, yet agrees to a drink at the St. Charles Tavern. He arrives forty minutes late—hair platinum blond now, a hoop earring—and with two older friends: a mustachioed fiftysomething antiques dealer with mahogany tan, and a veiny muscleman in a lime tank top who keeps massaging his neck to banish a kink. These two stare through Pinch, swiveling around for cuter guys, then visit the bathroom to snort a few lines. Marsden, froggish eyelids fluttering, gazes across the table.

"I've heard the whole Temple story," Pinch assures him. "I wondered if you might like a little commiseration."

"And here you are to provide it. Just after the nick of time," Marsden says. "I assume you came to boast about something."

"The reverse. Barrows and I broke up. My doctoral applications went nowhere. I've got to leave the house soon and have no idea where I'll go. I haven't told my parents any of this. I'm kind of spinning downhill. My only hope is some obscure fellowship that I applied for because of a pushy professor. So, no: not here to boast." He picks at a beer mat. "I'd actually just like to erase all this."

"All what?"

"All the things I've misplayed. I'm sorry, by the way," Pinch inserts tensely, unable to make eye contact, clearing his throat. "I'd erase whole parts of me. Throw them off a building. Throw *myself* off a building."

"Oh, please," Marsden says, standing in disgust. "Please." He turns his back and joins his friends in the bathroom.

Heart thudding, Pinch holds still, humiliated. He stuffs a few dollars under the ashtray and takes a dozen steps along Yonge Street, fixing all attention on his feet to snuff out the shame. Someone calls his name. He turns, orienting to Marsden's voice.

"Jumping off a fucking building?" Marsden shouts, standing in the barroom door. "You are *never* doing something that stupid."

"I know."

"You're not allowed," Marsden says, choking up. "Okay? Because I said. Okay?" He pushes back inside the tavern, vanishing in there, lost in darkness for years more.

# Evenlode, Pennsylvania, 1976

## 38

Quakers founded Evenlode College almost a century before, but by the time Pinch arrives, little of that peaceable sect remains except in the name of varsity teams, The Quakes, whose furry mascot, Temblor, is everywhere on campus—sweatshirts, bumper stickers, coffee mugs, many of them themed with Stars and Stripes in this year of the American bicentennial.

Pinch explores his new college town, sidestepping flocks of drunken teens who stagger between a support system of frat houses, burger joints, drop-in clinics. Taking refuge in his one-bedroom rental, Pinch looks out the window, a church sign across the road: "Afterlife Guaranteed!" *Thank God*, he thinks, *that this fellowship lasts only nine months.*

He makes a showing at the department, introducing himself to Howie Zwinkels, a sociology professor with high-culture pretensions, who established the college's art history program in 1973. Vigorously, he shakes Pinch's hand, saying how he admires Bear Bavinsky. "Now I let you in on a little secret: All this rigmarole is nothing but a front for my wine club," he kids. "Imagine how excited I am to get an Italian speaker on board." He drags out a case of Tuscan reds and produces an Italian-language wine guide, which Pinch is compelled to read aloud. He translates so well that Zwinkels declares: "Forget this silly fellowship, Charles. Do your doctorate here!"

Pinch smiles politely.

"I'm not joking," Zwinkels says.

"Wow," Pinch responds, appalled. "Gosh. Maybe." Privately, he remains fixated on NYU, where he plans to transfer next year to join Barrows, even if she doesn't yet know. He'll require Zwinkels' reference to apply there. For now, Pinch must please the man. When they chat, he finds himself mimicking the professor's body language, arms folded, heel against the wall, accent shifting closer to Zwinkels'. After the weekly brie-and-Chianti tastings, Pinch closes the door to his one-bedroom, reading the church sign again.

After several weeks, he has a visitor, Widgeon, last seen a decade earlier, clinging to Bear's leg in Larchmont. Today, she's an overweight seventeen-year-old in an excess of makeup who is considering colleges for next year, with far more anxiety than hope. It was Birdie—a qualified vet now, married and living in North Carolina—who arranged this visit. She keeps Pinch informed on their extended family in irregular, funny letters. With typical snark, she explained that their half sister lacks smarts or a good education—might Evenlode be an option?

He escorts Widgeon around campus, shows her his office. "Any questions? Don't be shy." She shakes her head vigorously, as if he'd requested that she summarize Kissinger's strategy on China while performing a Nadia Comăneci floor routine. "Ask me anything, even if it sounds silly. Even if—" The office phone rings. Before answering, he tells her, "I keep getting calls for the last guy who was here." He picks up, saying, "Greg has left the department."

"Who? What?"

"Dad!" Pinch says. "How did you get this number?"

Widgeon hurries to her feet at the mention of their father.

"Dad, you know who's here with me? She came for a visit of—"

Bear says, "Your mother died."

For an instant, Pinch detaches, his eyes drawing in light, brain incapable of translating it; ears deafened, sensing only a plastic phone receiver; lips dry; hands cold; nauseous saliva under his tongue. He stares across his desk, Widgeon waving for her turn with Daddy.

"I'm sorry to say, Charlie, that she did it to herself. Stupid god-damn thing." Solemnly, Bear explains how he heard, that Cecil tracked him down through the Petros Gallery.

"What do you mean?" Pinch says, not able to grasp, or care, how Bear came to know. "What do you mean?" He opens his eyes wider for a clearer reality than this. The horror repeats, as if he weren't informed once but learns anew with each pulse of consciousness, falling from an airplane, spinning in somersaults down. "I don't understand."

Jumping in place, Widgeon beams at him. "Let me speak to Poppa!"

Bear states facts that accumulate like a highway pileup, nothing reaching Pinch, although the images will never leave him: "six days on the floor before they walked in . . ." and "a plastic bag over her head . . ."

When he puts down the phone, Widgeon is crestfallen. "Why didn't *I* get to talk to him?"

"Something happened," Pinch says, standing.

"Okay, but *still*," she says softly.

Pinch leads her from the department, points her toward the train station, unable to react when her angry tears brim. "I have to leave now?" she says.

"Sorry." Alone at his apartment, Pinch stands under the shower for so long that the hot water runs out, the spray thinning to a dribble—then pelting down icily. He gasps, not allowing himself to escape the cold. An hour later, he remains nude, sitting on the closed toilet, teeth chattering, this thudding horror. He covers his eyes with the towel, looks at the darkness. Natalie looks back, shrugs.

When he reaches her flat in London, Pinch washes all the dirty dishes, careful that no crockery touches, as if the slightest ding would crack him. He attempts to arrange a funeral but finds only a few numbers in her phone book. When he calls them, a few don't even recognize the name: "Sorry, *who* died?" Others feign distress and sympathy, clearly just wanting the gossip: "What happened exactly?" Finally, Cecil intervenes, asking if a funeral service is absolutely necessary. And so, Natalie is cremated. The urn awaits pickup.

After a few days, he forces himself to deal with her bedroom, on whose floor Natalie died. He opens her closet, dresses swaying. He gathers summer hats, empties her underwear drawer, pausing at the bedside table: her bifocals on the purple-silk ribbon. He opens a rubbish bag. But hours later, Pinch remains cross-legged on the floor, studying artifacts, nothing discarded. *What is my objective here? To respect her privacy? Or limit my pain? Or preserve something of Natalie?* Accomplishing one aim violates another.

Before this, he never took much interest in her pottery, so she never gave him any. Now he owns it all. Picking up one of her recent ceramic sculptures, he holds it under varied light, wary of doing it harm—his limbs don't feel wholly under his control lately. He envisages releasing the piece, watching it fall ever so slowly, smashing fast. He rests it on the floor alongside the others and lies beside them, watching her ceiling, hearing neighbors' footsteps, listening to her darkness falling.

He turns on a lamp and surveys the pottery forest. Her sculptures are not as he imagined, not quirky and disordered. ("They're mashed lumps of clay, Pinchy," she said last summer. "Gestural craziness from your crazy mother.") He presses his fingers hard into his throat, recalling that meeting, understanding it now as their last. These sculptures are not as she described—they're elegant arcs, the clay raw on one side, glazed on the reverse, slashed in stone green and pebble blue, each piece hand-built, eerily smooth, frail.

None of her works will sit in a museum, he knows. Natalie, toiling through the night, or building slow pieces at her solitary workshop, or looking at him from her potter's wheel in Rome—she was disregarded, and will remain so forever, among the billions whose inner lives clamor, then expire, never to earn the slightest notice. *What reason is there to care about any art if nobody but I will ever care about these?*

Cecil agrees to store the pottery that Pinch is unable to transport back to America. "Even without a funeral," Pinch says by phone to his mother's friend, "it'd be good to see you again."

"We must do that. In person one day."

Pinch wishes the old potter would invite him to Brighton. Cecil was her sole friend in this country. There is only silence on the phone line. "I feel that I need to talk about her," Pinch adds, "with someone who knows her. Knew her. Another time."

"I shall look forward to it, Charles."

Toward week's end, Pinch finally fills the rubbish bags, all in a hurry, trying not to view the contents, throwing in her bifocals; clay-streaked jeans and ragged T-shirts; an unfinished Iris Murdoch novel, her place marked with a ticket stub from a concert of Schumann piano sonatas on the night of her death, before she returned to this quiet room, hearing nothing beyond herself. On this same floor, she lay, tied a plastic bag over her head. He shuts his eyes. Plastic sucked in at each breath.

Outside, he lowers the rubbish into the metal bins with utmost care. But he can't leave it. He stands in place, mind stalled until a stranger passes and nods. Pinch nods back and returns inside, her purple-silk bifocals ribbon saved in his pocket.

## 39

Pinch returns to Evenlode with three pots (an early Natalie fruit bowl, a tea mug, a ceramic sculpture). He offered to send a few pieces to Ruth, but she was too upset to accept. When he informed her of Natalie's death, the line cut—she just put down the receiver. He called back, and she was shouting, too distraught to hear. "She wouldn't do this! She *would not* do this!" The line went dead again.

Back at Evenlode, Pinch resumes his studies, coasting numbly down the path to a doctorate. In the department, he agrees to any request, whether it's attending wine tastings or teaching freshman Italian classes. He acts cordial as a buffer against damage. During dinner parties, he looks directly at strangers, as he hasn't easily done since before puberty—yet his gaze is bland now, matched with bland smiles, never the slightest dispute, gaining him a reputation on campus as an insubstantial man.

Toward the end of that first academic year, he travels to Manhattan by train, needing to see Barrows. For hours, he crisscrosses Central Park, glancing over his shoulder for muggers, almost wanting one, which would excuse him from stepping foot inside the Institute of Fine Arts. But there is no mugger, only a drug pusher in bug-eye sunglasses and crop top football jersey watching him, plus couples bounding past in tracksuit tops and white shorts, part of the jogging craze. Distracted by watching the runners pound by, he realizes why he traveled here: He wants to tell Barrows about his mother and the inescapable image of Natalie on the floor in her London flat, which flashes through him during faculty gatherings.

If he tells Barrows, it'll sound like a bid for pity. Perhaps it is. He never even introduced them—if they had met, Pinch could justify approaching her with the news. But he was ashamed of Natalie. He halts. "I'm movin' here, dodo!" a runner barks, thudding past. Instantly, Pinch's pulse is fluttering, as if he'd been threatened with violence. He thrusts his hands into the pockets of his windbreaker, reminded that he has nothing to offer Barrows. He tucks his head down and returns to the train station.

In his second year at Evenlode, Pinch speaks rarely to his father, unable to deal with Bear's ego or to sustain throwaway remarks about Natalie. Pinch passes nights in the company of Martina, an Argentine grad student of comparative literature. A left-wing activist back home, she left Buenos Aires when the military took over, and she struggles with the American college lifestyle. After six months together, Pinch mentions Natalie's death, stating for the first time that both his mother and his grandfather took their lives. He sees her thinking: *You too?* Instead, she says, "Only happy words in this room." Things happened to her back home, and she cannot tolerate others' sorrows. He is with her to speak Spanish, to drink wine (even if she's the one doing the serious drinking), to sleep together sometimes—the pretense of connection.

Now and then, he drives to suburban Philadelphia to visit the closest major museum, the Barnes collection. He recalls what Barrows once claimed of its founder, that the man made his fortune from gonorrhea treatment and spat on paintings to wipe off bits he disliked. Pinch wonders if it's true and asks a guard, earning a blank stare. In Center City, he visits a giant new public sculpture, *Clothespin* by Claes Oldenburg, wondering if it's good, unsure what that means to him anymore. He watches people, creating thought-paintings: *Man Bores*

*Wife Who Wants to Read* or *Girl Shouting as Bus Pulls Away*. With a pocket-size Kodak Instamatic, Pinch lingers behind lampposts, snapping street shots, speed-walking from captured subjects. Once, he sneaks a picture of a hoodlum, only for the guy's crew to surround him, demanding what in fuck he's doin', until they realize he's just a coward and relent. The best photos—of bodies turning, eyes half closed, motives midway—Pinch enlarges. He pursues the instant before, or a fraction too late, the thinnest slivers of experience. Using a loupe, he studies strangers' faces, speaking aloud to them, copying their features in pencil-and-ink compositions so large that they become abstracted in his sketch pad. But these drawings irritate him: They lack everything, are balanced, complete; all human drives canceled. He scrunches each picture, jams it among the food scraps in his kitchen garbage.

After five years have passed at Evenlode, the seasons are too familiar to Pinch, as is his daily walk to the department. Freshmen still perturb him—they're incapable of walking properly, forcing him to slalom. In the mirror, Pinch detects a frown, believing he wasn't making one, only to recognize that this expression is now fixed on his brow.

Evenlode was to be a way station, yet he has remained longer than most of his peers. The grad students he met early, Martina included, have accepted academic postings elsewhere or took civilian jobs. Many have started families. More than once, Pinch has brought flowers to a maternity ward, which always recalls the day when Barrows' roommate went into early labor. How old will that child be now? Once, he and Barrows had a conversation under the bedsheets, he consenting to her plan for one daughter, an only child, which suited their ambitions. Whenever he passes a stroller, he peers in, wondering about these tiny humans. He'll sweep aside his comb-over and consider the limpid-eyed, bobbleheaded occupant of the stroller. Pinch wiggles his eyebrows, suddenly conscious of how his rubbery adult face must appear. "Hello, little one," he says, then a kindly nod to the parent and quickly onward.

To satisfy his doctoral adviser, Pinch loads his thesis with extraneous material about Venetians inventing flat crystal glass in the late fifteenth century, which increased the popularity of self-portraits; Lacan's theory of the mirror stage; Alberti's remarks in *Della Pittura* about the reflected face of Narcissus in water as a foundational myth of painting; Caravaggio's *Narcissus* as an allusion to mirror use in the High Renaissance. He will submit to any change sought, and composes letters of obsequious thanks—anything to escape here. He orders three copies of his bound thesis from a local printing press, mailing one to Barrows, an adjunct professor at Princeton, according to the bio on the back of her first book, *Losing Lily Briscoe: Women and Myth from Gentileschi to Nochlin*, just published by Yale University Press. The second copy he mails to Marsden's last known address in Toronto. The third he mails to his father, now living in Maine with his present girlfriend.

Pinch awaits the call, needing to hear his father's opinion on work that, years back, was initiated for Bear. This, Pinch knows, is why he persisted with his dissertation: for this solitary review. He will ask Dad if he should seek a publisher, a small press perhaps. Or he could set up as an independent scholar, outside the college ecosystem, so he'd stand apart, able to express unpopular ideas, like those he and Bear always talked about.

He hears nothing, so places the call himself. Bear's girlfriend assures Pinch that the package did arrive. "Still sitting here on the console table."

"Could you tell him I'd love to know his thoughts? As soon as he can—as soon as is feasible, given work." A week passes. Another. A third. Pinch orders himself to be patient. His mind keeps flipping back to this same subject. In bed, he rages over the wait. Finally, he calls Maine again, gets Dad on the line this time, talks about unrelated subjects—then shoots out his question.

"Kiddo, you should be proud as hell of what you've done."

Beaming, Pinch leans forward, then rocks back, reaching for the pipe. He grasps it, thrusts it in air, shaking his fist. "I'm so glad to hear this, Dad. I feel lightened, completely. I wanted to tell you: I've been thinking about your biography again. You have so many amazing stories. I could be your stenographer. It'd be a way forward for me. I'm sorry that I wasn't able to get into an Ivy League—I'm sorry about that. But you saw this piece of writing. And it was okay, right? What do you think? I'd come out there, if that works. Or we could meet elsewhere. Whatever suits you."

"Hold the line—Jenny's waving at me. What is it, sweetheart? Yeah, just finishing up. It's Charlie, the Italian one. Yep, that one. Ten seconds, babe. Charlie—you were saying? My undivided attention."

"So it was decent, the thesis?" He needs replenishing.

"Helluva lot of work you did. And solid work."

"There are loads of your ideas in there. Did you notice?"

"And I'm still waiting for my commission!"

In haste, Pinch lights his pipe, coughs. "And you saw the dedication?"

"Folks dedicate doctorates nowadays?"

"It was on the first page—you didn't see that?" He pauses. "Dad, I know you've been busy at the studio lately. But did you get a chance to read the whole thing yet?"

"Ah, what do I know about essays? What counts is that you celebrate tonight. It's a helluva accomplishment, what you did. You know, most fathers worry that their kids are doing too much celebrating at college. I worry you're not doing enough! You need to raise a glass to yourself, kiddo."

"I'm on my second mint tea already," Pinch says, attempting to play along, lifting his mug as if for Bear's perusal. "Drinking from one of Mom's ceramics, actually. It took me ages to use this. I've got tons of her pottery in storage with Cecil. Could I get him to send you a few pieces, Dad?"

"Poor Natty."

"You always liked her work."

"Whenever I saw your mother's art, I thought one thing: She wants to please, and it felt that way. No, her pieces were never really first class. That's why I always—"

Pinch hangs up, then raises the receiver, hand shaking, needing to smash the phone against the wall. But he's afraid. Of harm. Of damage. Of missing Dad's return call. In fact, Bear doesn't call back. Pinch was planning to propose moving to Maine and finding a place nearby, so they could start on the biography.

He pulls open the fridge door, hard enough that it slams against the cupboard, shuddering jars. Off cold shelves, he grabs at anything, gorging himself nearly to suffocation. Eyes watering, he dry heaves into the sink, grasps the metal faucet with both hands, rows it violently back and forth, unable to snap it. He punches the wall at full force, and howls from the pain. A dent in the whitewash. He hits it again, a red smear, his knuckles throbbing, dripping blood on the linoleum. He is unable to catch air. "Not done yet," he says, body quaking, eyes blinking. "I'm *not* done yet."

# Adulthood

OIL ON CANVAS

96 X 182 INCHES

Courtesy of the Bavinsky Estate

# London, 1981

## 40

Under thunderous rain, Pinch hurries down a muddy path, squelching after the elderly man who marches briskly ahead. "I'm getting a little soaked, Cecil! Could we take cover? If that's okay?"

Over the years, Pinch has often reflected on the noble hermit of his childhood, a man who plowed ahead with his pottery, irrespective of the world's taste. After Natalie died, they spoke by phone but didn't meet until today. Cecil arrived in his Morris Minor outside Pinch's rented flat near Belsize Park, returned the stored boxes of Natalie's pottery and said, "Shall we walk?" So they find themselves here, on an ill-judged hike across Hampstead Heath, during which Pinch has seen little but the back of the man's waxed Barbour coat.

Cecil veers off track, tramping toward the closest road, where he directs Pinch into a drab café, shakes off the raindrops, and points to a table. Tea arrives in chipped cups, the saucers slopping with milky brew. Cecil betrays no unease, but Pinch feels it, so tosses forth questions, each dropping like a dead fly between them.

"Is it even wetter than this in Brighton?"

Cecil sweeps aside gray-blond bangs, a plop of rain landing in his tea. "It rather varies. On the time of year."

Pinch copies Cecil, sweeping across his own hair as if readying for the school photo: a thirty-one-year-old teenager with bad skin and thinning locks, damp tweed jacket, pipe in breast pocket. He smiles, willing Cecil to mirror his warmth. Pinch is fond of this man who, in his small way, kept an eye on Natalie, no matter how difficult she could be. Pinch won't confess it yet, but this recent decision to move back to England was partly to assume his mother's bond with Cecil. For weeks, Pinch has awaited this meeting, needing counsel from the wise old potter, to hear how to salvage a bungled young life. Sitting opposite Cecil, however, Pinch speaks only of Natalie.

"What did you make of her work?" Pinch asks.

"She was quite skilled."

"Why do you think other people weren't interested?"

"Oh, there's very limited acclaim in ceramics."

"But she was good, right? People should have paid more attention to her work, no?"

For a spell, Cecil remains silent. His sight line sweeps above Pinch's head, as if a plane with a banner were dragging his response across the sky, though it's just a bug scuttling over the café window. "What *is* has never been what *ought*," Cecil answers finally. "You pose an is/ought question. When I was younger, I dabbled in 'oughts.' I have retired to 'is.'" He sips his tea soundlessly.

Pinch rests his jittery hands on the table, steepling his fingers, which he never does—only to notice that Cecil is himself making this gesture. Pinch reaches for the napkin dispenser, but finds Cecil's long tapering fingers doing the same. "Sorry—you first," Pinch says, embarrassed by this compulsive mimicry, so useful in acquiring foreign words, so obstructive in expressing his own.

"You had further questions? About Natalie?"

"I feel," Pinch begins, "I have this feeling that what happened with her involved me. In some way." Unable to look across the table, he gives a forced laugh.

"Oh, it's madness."

"What I said?"

"What she did. You can't dwell on it."

"That's all I can do."

Cecil wriggles higher in his seat, as if to signal an end to melancholy talk. "Tell me: What news of the great Bear?"

Pinch wants anything but to speak of his father. Cecil launches into reminiscences of that charming meal together in Rome, declaring himself awfully grateful to Bear for having bought that vast electric kiln at the cottage—not to mention having later taken the entire property off his bankrupt hands. "And he's as productive as ever, is he? And still represented by the Petros Gallery? Very fashionable place. How is Bear's press? Journalists must be a bore."

"Dad holds his own." *Why,* Pinch wonders, *must I reflexively puff my father? Has a single reporter approached my father in years?* When one of Bear's early paintings came up at a minor auction house last year, the lot went unsold.

"But how," Cecil persists, shaking the last drop of tea into his mouth, "how would you say his work is *selling?*"

Pinch rambles about the scarcity of museum acquisitions since the oil crisis, how private galleries care only about selling wall meat to financiers these days, and corporations are busy bejeweling their headquarters with slabs of Jasper Johns, Diane Arbus, Modigliani.

"Yes, yes," Cecil resumes, "but what does a good Bavinsky go for today?"

Pinch is taken aback. Why should Cecil, who chose a poor man's trade, lust at the pornography of another man's wealth? Perhaps *because* Cecil took the noble path, finding only hunger at its end. An artist's noble vision isn't enough, Pinch realizes. You must succeed.

And he reads the old potter before him with plunging clarity—that only manners brought Cecil here.

"Looks like the rain is stopping," Cecil remarks. Shortly, he stands, shakes hands, pays up. Pinch watches the waxed Barbour coat stride away for good. This cherished artist—requiring only his tools, caring nothing for the world's wants—he doesn't exist. Perhaps no such person ever has.

Readying to leave the café himself, Pinch glimpses himself reflected in the window, mud on his shoes, caked up the hem of his corduroys. Cecil was the last person to view him, so that man's impression holds sway: the son of my sad Canadian friend, an unattractive boy, testing my courtesy, so ferociously *wanting* something—wanting someone.

## 41

Pinch awakens with a start, breathing heavily, shaking off another nightmare about poverty. For years, he subsisted with the help of his grandmother, scholarships, teaching stipends. But he moved to London with scant savings, no job, no friends—and the expectation that Cecil would somehow resolve it all. Instead, Pinch has rent payments upcoming and a fast-dwindling bank account.

London itself seems harsher than he left it, with a thin surface of civility covering deep pools of aggression. During his decade away, there were race riots and power cuts, IRA bomb threats, everyone going on strike, from the gravediggers to the bakers to the hospital staff. The bad-tempered ripples persist, with Mrs. Thatcher pointedly extolling those who succeed, those with a ferocity for profit and the sharp elbows to achieve it—much the traits that Pinch lacks. Wandering around his neighborhood, he walks slowly, apprehensively. Then crossing the street, he must hurry across the roadway as drivers hurtle murderously toward him, perfectly willing to maim a stranger to make a point about the rules. Even the kids in polyester school uniforms disconcert him, marauding down the high streets, shrieking out as if to raise two fingers at the plodding grown-ups whom they must someday become.

Pinch will not ask for money from Ruth or Bear. He sends copies of a speculative letter to art history departments across southern England and Wales. Nobody responds. Checking the master copy of that letter, Pinch sees with mortification that he professed himself "moist grateful" for their consideration. And they moist certainly grant him none.

As a stopgap measure, he takes freelance work translating technical documents. The pay is low and tallied by the page, so he must work from first light, forking drippy fried egg between his lips, scanning his daily allotment. By dinner, he has done twelve hours, his only human contact the sound of footsteps from the flat above. When he bumps into those neighbors outside the building, he greets them with inflated cheer, hoping to precipitate a conversation. They nod, smile briefly, keep walking. So Pinch must take his companionship more stealthily, eavesdropping when on the Underground. He lingers amid the pub-leaving throng at a local chippie, handling a newspaper cone of breaded cod, drizzle-painted with tomato sauce, the malt vinegar wrinkling cryptic crosswords and editorials damning the miners.

By far his closest relationship is with the Bengali clerks at Imperial Foods, which he visits for pipe tobacco and Maltesers—all his daily pleasures and most of his meals derive from there. He chats with shelf-stockers, restores products misplaced by other customers, commiserates after a skinhead smashes the window and calls them "fackin' Pakis," which is geographically incorrect, Pinch notes, in addition to being disgusting.

When a new cashier is hired, Pinch makes his status at the shop known to her, asking after the owner by name. As she packs his items, the paper bag tips, a misshapen grapefruit lolloping down the checkout lane. He tosses it in the air (muffing the catch) and reads the name tag—"Julie M"—pinned to her orange jumper. She is distracted, and takes a pen from her apron, notes something in her palm. At the exit, Pinch pauses. "What did you write before? I'm just curious."

"Write?"

"In your hand."

She opens her palm for him to see. He approaches, squints at the smudged ink, which reads "gochut."

"What language is that?"

"It's . . ." She looks for the manager—not around—so digs into Pinch's shopping bag, taking out a jar. "That." Again, she displays her palm, and he makes out two faded words: "man**go chut**ney." Julie, a recent arrival to the capital from the north of England, hasn't tried this product or many others in the shop.

"Would you like to?" He twists the lid but grunts, reddening, unable to take it off.

Smiling sweetly, she insists he not bother. The expression transforms her. In repose, she was tired and middle-aged, but becomes a little girl when smiling. She must be around his age, perhaps a tad older, with caramel-brown curls framing confectionary eyes, a wide strong frame, soft without being curvaceous. Julie M is not beautiful. He experiences a rush of need for her.

Julie explains that she wants to be more adventurous, especially now that she works at Mr. Khan's shop. So that evening, he collects her outside Imperial Foods and leads her to a reserved table at the Taj Mahal, where Pinch explains the menu at length, only then daring to ask about her.

Hailing from a town near Newcastle, she moved south only

recently, after her marriage ended and she couldn't find work there. Pinch mentions having read newspaper articles about the dire situation in the north—that it's so bad mothers and wives are taking the train to King's Cross and turning tricks behind the station.

"We're not all on the game, you know," she says.

"No, God, no!" Pinch responds, mortified, neck blotching. "I didn't mean to suggest that. Sorry. Just meant how bad it is."

"I'd call myself lucky to have this job at Imperial. It's a foothold."

"A foothold for something else?"

"I hope so. Don't know what yet."

"What would you do," he asks, leaning forward, "if you could do anything?"

"Me? I'd probably read all day." If it has words, Julie tells him, she'll be at it, from a cereal box to a Dickens. She asks about his line of work, evidently impressed to meet a translator, which emboldens Pinch. She laments knowing only English and asks how many languages he speaks. "Could you say a bit for me?"

"In which one?"

"All of them."

He offers a few remarks in Italian, speaking with formality, saying it's a very pleasant evening, that he hopes she enjoys it.

"How do you go to sounding foreign like that?" she says admiringly. "Give us some more then."

He speaks a few lines in French, then Spanish, then German, braver as he goes, daring to say how much he likes her.

"What's all that mean?"

"It's just things from work."

"And you like your work then, the translating?"

"Depends. Can be a slog. But sometimes, yes. I like coming across words I never knew existed. That's the best part. There are tons even in English that I didn't know."

"Such as?"

"Absterge."

"That's not English."

"It means 'to wipe clean,' like you'd do with a wound before surgery."

"I would not!"

He laughs. "It's from Middle French, by way of Latin. Sorry, I'm getting boring. Throw a samosa at me when I do that."

"I should do, if you hadn't eaten them all, greedy bugger."

He suppresses the electric thrill of this—that he's dining with a woman, that he just asked her out, that she works at the best shop in London. *This had better go well or where do I buy milk?*

"But I'm mad," he adds. "Because it's not like I can ever use these words when nobody understands them."

She rises to find the toilet, her grin baring a gap between her front teeth. "Pardon me," she tells him. "I always absterge my hands before pudding."

Alone at the table, he continues to view her seat. *This is what I want to dedicate myself to. This.* After a mere hour in her company, he has lost any understanding of his years obsessing about art, posterity, failure. She seems truly intrigued by him. There's nothing cynical about Julie; perhaps that's it. He recalls a remark she made: "You survive off your wits." That recast in an instant how he perceived his entire life to date. Before, he had planned to badger more universities with applications. Seated here, he throws off that future. He'll take this future, even if he doesn't know what it means. *Me, alone in the world, braving it!* (Though he's emboldened to go it alone only by dint of *not* being alone tonight.) In a passing glimmer, he imagines sex with Julie: his hands on her hips, her breasts under the bra, his thighs against hers. *Stop that—too far ahead of yourself.* And here she is.

Over dessert, Julie speaks of her family, noting that she comes "from working people."

"Everyone is so preoccupied with the class system here," he says.

"You do realize that we've got a queen?"

"Yes, I often run into her waiting for the Tube."

Smiling, she nudges his spoon out of the way to reach their mango *kulfi*. "In this country, a person speaks two words and you know where they come from, what their schooling was. You're lucky, you are. You don't have that, with your nice American accent."

"Canadian."

"See? I didn't even know."

"Back when I used to teach, I always—"

"You were a teacher?"

"Only during my doctorate. Very junior classes on art history, plus Italian."

"So you qualified as a doctor too?"

"Not the useful kind. Not the kind that absterges." Flushed from lager and expectation, he looks directly at her. From his perspective, she has experienced a life so much fuller than his: raised three younger sisters and a brother; married a hard drinker, whom she supported by working as a cutter at a garment factory, where blokes gave the girls cuddles, like it or not; got divorced when Ben's boozing became too much; moved down here to London. By contrast, Pinch's life—so fumbling in his view—seems to Julie as sparkling and exotic as his foreign words.

"You're my bit of posh," she tells him. "And I'm your bit of rough."

## 42

Pinch's basement flat is small for two and would test another couple. But the better he knows Julie—her pudgy grin upon waking, her tone-deaf singing—the more Pinch is lifted from his crusty professorial manner. Often he praises her mind and criticizes the state education forced on her in childhood, implying that she could make more of herself. A person can still study at age thirty-four. When she enrolls at Birkbeck College, he deems this the relationship of his life—she esteems his view. After classes, Julie returns bubbling with big talk on big subjects, making insightful, innocent links among literature and sociology and philosophy. Listening rapt, Pinch feels his love galloping ahead. After a snotty man lampoons her question in class, Pinch orders her to ignore bullies like that. "You're the smartest person there by miles. I promise, Jules."

"He's actually pretty clever. Always talking about everyone's 'subjectivity.'"

"Subjectivity is just an underhanded way to attack other people. I'm sure *he* is entirely objective, right? He's preening for attention, I assure you." Pinch stops, sheepish suddenly. "Sorry—I'm frothing at the mouth."

"No, no, I'm enjoying the show." She smiles.

"Enjoy this then." He pulls up his shirt, slaps his gut. "Look at this monstrosity. How did I gain so much weight? I've become disgusting."

"Yes, but you're my disgusting," she teases. "You know, *I* wouldn't mind a big tummy."

"They're not hard to achieve. I call it the Maltesers diet."

"Like a pregnant belly."

"That's a bit insulting!" he says, laughing, petering out as he digests her remark. Julie delayed a family because of her ex and his drinking. She lost years because of that, and doesn't have endless time. He ponders the features of their child, but keeps seeing the daughter he's previously imagined: a little Barrows. He pulls down his shirt. "When you're further along with your degree, we can think of kids. If we took that step now, it'd be the end."

"Not the end of steps. Just a different one," she contends. "Charlie, don't think that I know nothing because I don't know Latin."

"Julie, everyone I ever met who knew Latin, me especially, knows fuck-all." He fetches a sausage roll from the fridge, eats standing, knowing why he rebuffed her. He loves Julie—but he isn't sure he accepts her. She isn't accomplished, isn't expecting to become important, which reinforces that he isn't, and won't be. Wincing at his disloyalty, he shoves the sausage roll back into the fridge.

"Grumpy?" she asks.

"Just some work things on my mind."

In the bathroom, he brushes his hair roughly across his balding pate, holds in his tummy as if an attractive stranger passed. He makes himself relax, looking directly at the reflection, jabbing his stomach with the toothbrush end, repelled by himself, needing Julie, though she is just on the other side of this door.

When her sister visits London, she wants to do a bit of Oxford Street window shopping without her kids, so Julie and Pinch take the two youngsters to the National Gallery, with Pinch acting as impromptu tour guide, pointing them toward famous paintings, explaining historical context, the tragedies and quirks of artists, embedded symbols, the technical choices that direct the eye or acknowledge predecessors. As Natalie once taught him at Galleria Borghese, he shows these kids to crouch before the pictures to catch a raking light, revealing outlines of the underpainting, where one discovers what the artists intended, in contrast to what they achieved. "And what a person intends is as important as what they achieve. Don't you think?"

"Are those mushrooms, Uncle Charlie?" the eleven-year-old girl asks, pointing at the foreground of the Wilton Diptych.

"Good eye, Liz. They were long thought, by people less sharp than you, to be flowers. But they've since been identified as aniseed toadstools and milk-caps—very rare medieval depictions of mushrooms, which appear much more frequently after fifteen hundred."

Bemused, the two kids run off to see a picture of soldiers fighting, and Julie goes with them.

Following after, Pinch considers her from behind, knowing her soft body beneath that dress, a secret knowledge—permission to her—that moves him, causes him to act sternly with the children at their next inquiry, because stern is the opposite of what he feels.

## 43

Bear Bavinsky has soured on matrimony. His latest ended in a divorce, with Elodie contesting ownership of his entire art production—the paintings he labored on for decades and kept, those that survived his scathing judgment, and which have held out all this time, awaiting a call from the great museums. Eventually she settled for a hefty lump of cash. But the close call unnerved Bear. He moved all his works to a private storage location in Europe, away from "the rats," as he refers to anyone who dares meddle with his hoard.

"I know you're not enthused about weddings right now, Dad, but could you be persuaded to attend one if you weren't the sucker in question? If it was me?"

"Charlie boy!" he responds, dropping the phone in enthusiasm, grabbing it again and apologizing. *Was that the first time*, Pinch thinks, *that Dad has said* sorry *to me?* "Happiest news I ever heard, kiddo! Congratulations, son! Who's the lucky lady?"

Pinch purposely kept details of Julie from his father. Now he pours them out, with Bear's enthusiasm serving to confirm his own, assuring Pinch that he loves her. After the call, he finds Julie doing the dishes and kisses her. "Let me finish. You call your sister."

Julie leaps off to do so, spreading the happy news. After rinsing the last knife, Pinch turns off the faucet and catches a snippet of her conversation in the other room.

"Not weak at the knees, Queenie. It's hard to explain . . ."

Pinch tries not to mind—he can hardly expect to stir a woman's passions! He knows what Julie likes about him: He's from a world more appealing than this dreary country, where her father is still fulminating about the strikebreaking scabs, her mum worries about the broken boiler, her brother spends his days at the new video slot machine in his local pub. Lately Julie talks about leaving England and setting up overseas; Australia maybe. He flips through the atlas in bed, and she tests him on capitals.

"Ouagadougou," he answers.

"How do you know that, Charlie?" She flicks off the light, not for romance but to dream open-eyed beside her foreign bloke.

A month before the ceremony, Pinch checks that Dad has his travel booked. Bear is finishing an important painting before flying over, and it's hard to know when he'll be done. It'd be crazy to buy a flight when there's a chance he'll be tied up. Pinch nods—he never entirely expected his father. "Either way, you'll be here in spirit. We'll raise a glass to you."

"A glass? Hell, a bottle at least! Here's what, kiddo: I'm sending over a case of champagne."

The event takes place at a register office with Julie's friends and family, plus Mr. Khan from Imperial Foods and a huge bouquet from Birdie, who is about to give birth in North Carolina, so can't make it. After the formalities, husband and wife step out into a drizzle, Pinch looking skyward, a droplet hitting his eye. He blinks, seeing Julie in a blur. "Nice weather for ducks," she says, and he lifts his new spouse off her feet, prompting her to wave theatrically, damsel in distress. Out of breath, he puts her down, presses his face to hers, the coolness of her powdered cheek against his warm temple.

"It's just you and me," she whispers.

"Well, for now," he responds, catching her eye.

## 44

A honeymoon is beyond their means, so they spend a week vacationing at home, starting with a fancy Italian meal prepared by Pinch. It'll be indulgence for days, with cakes and wine, reading in bed, sleeping late. He's a little embarrassed to have promised a case of champagne, which never arrives.

As the months pass, Pinch thinks more about having children of their own. In the past, when Julie hinted at starting a family, he dismissed the topic, speaking of finances: couldn't afford a baby, me as a freelance translator, you part-time cashier, part-time student. But lately, to himself, Pinch brushes aside all objections. He stops in the middle of the sidewalk, ruminating. Julie always depicted him as an intellectual of range and experience. Yet she is catching up—already, she knows plenty of professors more erudite and sophisticated than he. When she takes him on a trip to her hometown, he wants to treat her parents to dinner out. But it turns out that going for dinner strikes them as a showy extravagance. They only come to a shabby French restaurant to accommodate him, turning out in their Sunday best, worried about garlic, disliking most of the funny tastes. To make matters worse, Pinch cuts himself shaving before they set out, and the nick won't stop bleeding throughout dinner. When the bill comes, Julie's father insists on paying. This was *not* the agreement, but the man—in his early sixties, with a craggy face of a hundred—is offended by Pinch's insistence.

On the train to London, he recalls sitting beside Bear when they returned from New York City to Dad's wife and kids in the suburbs. He leans to Julie's ear. "I need to discuss something."

"In whispers?"

"Yes," he says, smiling. "Thinking about your nephew and niece."

"What about them?"

"Just thinking, I don't know." He pauses. "About a little person to join us." He leans back to see her eyes. "You don't seem overwhelmed by the prospect."

"We agreed: Not now."

"That was more than a year ago." His proposition—a source of doubt for Pinch until he spoke it seconds ago—feels like an urgent need now. "I wrote a list of baby names," he says, to lighten the mood, or perhaps cajole her.

"Charlie, I got so much studying ahead. You know that."

"Yes. Fine," he responds, hurt now. "I thought *you* wanted them."

"Don't put me on trial here."

"But you said that. No?"

"Can't I change my mind?"

"Then why did we marry?"

"When do I have time to do anything, even to breathe?"

"Can't we breathe on weekends?"

She doesn't laugh. Neither does he.

After this trip, they have sex less often. Each interruption to fetch contraception has become a weighted minute. Often they don't resume. Julie has taken a step away from him, which makes him step forward, which causes her to back off once more—a two-step that becomes more strained as the months pass.

"You were on the phone forever," he complains.

"Why do you hate it when I speak to friends?"

"Talk to anyone you like. Just, I thought we were going to watch something on TV. Forget it, Jules. Could you be quiet coming to bed?"

"Always am."

But he doesn't leave. "Meet me under the covers?"

"I'm doing homework, Charlie."

"Homework so pressing that you talked for two hours with Ben."

"That wasn't two hours. And what makes you think it was Ben?"

"Wasn't it?" he says, despising himself.

She and her ex-husband remain close—they grew up together,

and you don't forget that. He stopped drinking recently and is going through a vulnerable patch. When those two speak, Pinch hears her Geordie accent strengthening, her laughter echoing from the other room, the lights off in there. When he walks in, flicking on the lamp, she looks elsewhere, with reddest joyful cheeks.

He and Julie squabble nowadays, and they never used to. It's as if he were prodding for something—her ardor, her desire—that cannot come from pushing. When she suggests that he take a break from gray London, that he visit his father's cottage in France, it leads to their umpteenth quarrel.

"I'm *not* angry. But please, Jules, stop advising me. Okay?"

"I'm not advising you. And what's so bad if I did?" she says. "Your father would let you stay. And you'd do well with a break, rather than stuck inside this flat all day, translating rubbish about calculators."

"It's a computer manual. But thanks for the condescension." He adds, "Maybe both of us could go." He turns away fast, filling the kettle.

"I can't, Charlie. Can't."

"You could practice for your French class."

"France couldn't save the likes of me. Some brains don't absorb foreign languages."

"Not true."

"Actually, *you* should be a teacher."

"What is the point here, sending me off to my Dad's place?" he says, voice raised, wavering. "Getting me out of your hair? If I don't want to go, I'm *not* going."

"Just thought it'd be nice for you."

"*I* can decide what's nice for me. Okay?" He looks at her, his future deforming: disinvited from her body, from shared old age, from nicknames of convoluted origin. "Jules, we are not at the end."

She makes the tea.

He grabs a ballpoint pen, takes her hand, opens the palm, writes there. She reads it, looks up: "Can't, Charlie. I'm sorry. I don't feel that way."

With hideous clarity, Pinch sees himself: a pompous bore, a man he'd dislike. And he perceives the approaching solitude, closing around him. They both see it.

## 45

Pinch moves out and rents himself a second-floor flat in a scruffy terraced house in Earls Court. Within days, he is shocked awake—workmen erecting scaffolding over the front windows of all four rental flats, replacing daylight with metal poles and tranquillity with radio blare. He hides in the back bedroom, doing translations far from the workers' banter—and also to prevent them from seeing him. He's ashamed to stay inside all day without a single visitor.

Each evening the building regains its quiet. He broods over Julie, stabbed by perceived humiliations, loathing his pettiness. He lies in bed, unable to sleep, beleaguered by thoughts. *I, the same person hearing these gurgling pipes, will die. I'll be dead for infinity.* His mouth goes dry, palms clammy. He needs to squirm, to run outside. He remains still, breast shivering at each heartbeat. *Someday I'll hear nothing, see nothing. I'll be erased like a floppy disk. Before then, I'm imprisoned in this skull.* "You won't go away."

He reaches for the phone, dialing Bear. The call is brief—immediately, he perceives Dad's impatience at his low state. Pinch puts down the receiver, hearing his own breaths, sensing blips of distress. He gains perverse relief visualizing himself hanging there from the ceiling. After Natalie died, he wrote a long letter to Ruth, an affectionate essay about his mother. She never responded. *Nobody bothers to respond to me. I'm bitter. Bitter about everything.*

Pinch needs to hear another voice, any besides his own. As soon as Birdie picks up, he hears himself acting, matching her flippancy, skipping lightly over his separation from Julie, seeking reports on the extended family, including the siblings and cousins of whom Pinch is scarcely aware. Birdie herself is still in Durham, North Carolina, working part time at a veterinary clinic while looking after three kids with her husband, Riley, who served three tours in Vietnam and now runs his own construction company. Birdie is on the Left (the "Mondale/Ferraro '84" lawn sign is definitely hers), and he's far to the Right (the "Reagan/Bush" sign is assuredly his). She cares for pets and livestock; he cares for nails and rebar. Their differences were once a source of flirty heat. But now that it comes to raising kids, the sardonic exchanges don't end up in bed. Worse, his father's bullying, which Riley always spoke of despairingly, has become his own tyranny exacted on the household. As for Birdie's father, she is still raging at him. Bear flat out refuses to produce signed sketches for her—it'd be like printing money, she says. If he helped, she could leave Riley. Instead, she must keep her mouth shut and wait until the kids move out, which is years away.

"One of Dad's squiggles is not going to earn you big money, Bird."

"I heard a painting of his went for *forty grand* in New York last month."

"Not forty. Fourteen."

"Oh. Still. Fourteen thousand bucks is real money to me."

"Plus, that picture had a naked breast, which increases the price."

"Such a cynic, Charlie."

"It's true: the breast augmentation," he says. "That money isn't going to Dad, you realize, but to a collector—someone who bought Dad's art back when he was still selling it."

"Why doesn't he just get over that stupid no-sales rule?"

"Principles."

"Principles are peachy for them that can afford 'em."

"But Bird, how did you even hear about that sale?"

"I got approached by a dealer. What she didn't realize was, if I'd owned a Dad painting, I'd have sold it centuries ago."

"Who was this dealer? Eva Petros?" When Victor Petros died of a massive heart attack two years ago during Art Basel, his daughter took over. The Petros Gallery had parted ways with Bear by then but Eva is now doubting that breakup, especially with the fifties nostalgia fad. In the latest *Interview* magazine, Julian Schnabel was quoted as saying, "The painter who got me early is Bavinsky," describing Bear as "the greatest of the modern American greats." Not long after, that breast painting appeared on the secondary market, bought by Dennis Hopper, according to the *Village Voice*.

"Why, you know this person?" Birdie asks.

"I'm trying not to. Dad wants nothing to do with dealers, so I'm ignoring her."

"Do *you* have any of Dad's art?"

"I've asked him for stuff," Pinch lies to make her feel better. "But no dice." In truth, he would *never* consider bothering Bear for something. Only a few dozen of Bear's paintings are in private hands. All of these are Life-Stills, as the oversized portraits of body parts are known—the few that he sold early in his career, a practice that trickled to a stop by the early fifties. After, he kept everything deigned worthy, burned the rest. Nobody is even certain what Bear has been laboring at all these years, whether more Life-Stills or a new series altogether.

"He wouldn't give anything, even to *you*?" Birdie marvels.

Pinch is pleased by this remark—that Dad holds me in highest regard. Yet he despises feeling burnished by that, so he decides to help his sister and places a call.

"Hot damn, Charlie, it's nobody's business how I sell my work.

My own daughter, consorting with that Petros mob? You know that Victor Petros stole from me? Nine paintings I entrusted to that rat. And he sells them on the sly!"

"Did you report him?"

"How could I? The bastard gave me my percentage."

"So, wait—how was it stealing?"

"Look, I never approved those sales, Charlie. In my book, that's theft. They're all the same."

"Art dealers?"

"These relations of mine. Sniff a profit and—I hate to say it—they turn into goddamn rats."

For years, Bear has been gripped by the inheritance wars among Picasso's surviving wives and lovers and children, not to mention the tawdry recent case regarding Mark Rothko, whose gallery bilked his estate after he committed suicide. Such tales have caused Bear to consider taking one last wife, a special lady who'd be his posthumous custodian. "I cannot have my life's work ending in the sock closet of some idiot junk-bond tycoon, or with a rat like that Petros girl. You know as well as I do, Charlie: Bear Bavinsky never produced a thousand canvases a month."

"Everything you keep is carefully chosen." Pinch looks up at his ceiling, hearing himself slipping into the old relationship with his father, seconding every opinion, padding him.

"My paintings aren't for throwing around higgledy-piggledy," Bear continues. "When the big museums come calling, that's another matter. We accept those checks, no question. But if I let my kids turn the Bavinsky name into a bankroll—well, it ain't happening. Kills me that Birdie is stuck in a lousy marriage. But my work has to stand up, not be the payoff to some bum my daughter shacked up with. I won't be around forever. We have to get this right, Charlie."

Bear has long spoken about placing his art in only the most

important collections, but this is different. It's the testament of a man readying for a time after his own life and who interprets that demise not as obliteration but as a sort of paralysis, his body quiescent, his will alive. The absurdity of this, plus the callous remarks about Birdie, incense Pinch. *Heaven forbid we should want something from our lives—even after yours is done! Total allegiance is what you demand, with the hint that one of us might become your favorite. And,* Pinch realizes with self-disgust, *I won that contest. Few of Dad's other kids are even allowed his private phone number. But I kowtow. I'm his servant. So I was chosen.*

"Oh, I couldn't agree more, Dad," he says, heart thudding, wondering if Bear detects the sarcasm. "Not to sound over the top, but your paintings deserve *the* most prominent exposure. Venues fitting their stature. Suited to how they'll be understood in the future. Speaking as a former scholar, Dad, I believe fiercely that important art *must* be available for viewing by people of all stations. Not just those with extra white space on their mansion walls. That'd be fine if you were an industry like that heathen Salvador Dali. But that's not Bear Bavinsky. Never has been. Never will be. There's not enough Bear Bavinsky to go around!"

"Not enough of you *or* me to go around, son," Bear responds approvingly. "It's us two in this dogfight. Anyone disposes of my work for money alone, it's betrayal. Plain and simple. But you won't stand for it."

"Not while I'm alive and kicking. No, sir!"

"You know it, don't you, Charlie? You know. They are yours. My paintings. All I got. Not for the other kids."

"Where do you even have them, Dad?"

"At the French cottage. All my old pictures, right there in the studio. No rat will find that place. But when I croak, kiddo, I'm leaving you the keys. When I check out," Bear concludes, "I'm in your hands. You, my boy. You are the one."

Although Bear never realizes it, this is the moment when his son takes over.

# 46

Without telling anyone, Pinch heads to France. He is cantankerous throughout the drive, recalling taking this route alongside Barrows, plus Julie telling him to "freshen up" with a spell at the cottage. The pity burns into him still.

Pinch parks outside the cottage, slams the car door, marches toward the art studio, praying that these old keys—tossed in a suitcase pocket after his trip here with Barrows—will work. He tries them one after another, turning left and right, wiggling, shaking. The bottom lock opens but the second remains locked. He is at the end of hope, tries one last time—and the tumblers turn.

Dim morning light silhouettes Pinch. (It's dawn; he drove through the night.) Before him is the potter's kiln and an easel, as if Natalie were to one side, Bear to the other. But this is distinctly Dad's territory. Propped around the walls are Bavinsky canvases, front sides turned from view. This is what Bear has clung to; these are to be his legacy. More than two dozen huge paintings. Pinch turns, looking back through the studio door as if there were someone behind, spying.

After a minute at the entrance, he walks up the overgrown lawn, leaving the door wide open, purposely reckless (though petrified to do so). Fear causes him to hike faster into the woods. It's freezing, dewy, slippery. He has hardly eaten since departing London yesterday evening—just a fatty pork pie on the hovercraft. Shivering as he strides, Pinch speeds up to generate warmth, jogging now, gasping, pushing himself to go faster. *Stumble on a stump and you break your leg—that'd be the end. Nobody finds you here.*

In the closest town, he buys a ham baguette, and devours it on the street. Back at the cottage, he glugs a bottle of red wine, draining the contents in fifteen minutes, then tossing it out the window. The bottle lands silently on the grass. He finds a flask of Armagnac and downs that in large gulps, then storms back into the studio as if to punch someone, the location still infused with eye-stinging visions: Barrows sprawled on the floor, Pinch bursting in, disgracing himself.

He scours the place for something to give Birdie. Not a painting but something small, secondary and obscure—a piece he could sell on the sly. He finds no old sketchbooks, however, no napkin doodles, nothing extraneous. Bear is so controlling about how he'll be seen. Pinch kicks the air, nearly losing his balance, only now realizing how drunk he is. "All this fucking way for nothing." He wavers before the huge canvases, whose reverse sides are smudged with Dad's handprints, tobacco burns fraying the fabric. Pinch lurches at the closest painting, wiping *his* hands—still greasy from the sandwich butter—right there on the back of a canvas.

This fails to quell him, so he drags the canvas over, clutching the stretchers with one hand, pushing the rear of the picture with his other, jaw clenched, dropping to his knees to shove harder still, closing his fist now, knuckles twisting into the spine of the painting, the fabric taut, tacks buckling.

A pop: paint sprinkles, flaking down the front side. And Pinch falls back. He stands in haste, blood drained from his head, dizzy, ill, panicked yet still drunk enough for defiance. He tosses the painting aside. It falls on its face, banging onto the floor as he staggers away.

After a dry-mouthed slumber in the cottage, Pinch awakens in his father's bed, nauseated. At each step he takes to the bathroom, his brain shudders. He sits to piss, covering his eyes. He retains enough booze in his blood to wish that someone burned the whole art studio, that he could run away. He's also sober enough to decry his lunacy of five hours before, and to dread consequences. *What did I do?*

He runs a bath, looks furtively out the window. *What if Dad were to turn up?* Pinch sits in the hot water, sweat rolling down his forehead. He pulls at his hair, a blond strand coming off in his hand, floating away in soapy water. He digs his fingernails into his hairy thighs, scratching hard enough to incise red lines. *That painting is worth more than I'll earn in my life. It is part of art history. Or was.*

It occurs to Pinch that he doesn't even know *which* picture he ruined—never even turned it around. Barefoot, he hastens across the frosty lawn in a towel. He dries himself before entering. Teeth chattering, he walks toward the painting, picks it up, wipes away floor dust, and turns it around: an oversized picture of a woman's hands, a tangle of fingers, the image disastrously cracked, an entire patch missing, the underdrawing visible on stained canvas. But still, Pinch recognizes these hands: his mother's.

Like an insect in a matchbox, he paces back and forth across the studio. He shudders from the cold, yet throws his towel into a heap by the door. He keeps checking the damage, naked and crouching there, chewing down his fingernails. Each look sickens him anew. The canvas is distended where he rammed his fist. He finds pliers, picks off the bent tacks, frigid hands pulling the canvas tight—which only causes more paint to flake. In dismay, he grabs his hair, plier tips jabbing into his scalp. *Slow down!*

He returns to the cottage, puts on clothes, makes coffee—and returns to the studio. He places an easel beside the damaged painting. Arms quavering from caffeine now, he hoists the damaged painting, rests it on the horizontal tray, lowers the holder, screws the wingnuts tight. He flicks on a floor lamp, leaves it a few steps behind him. The shadow of his own head obscures much of his mother's hands. He keeps moving to reveal the extent of the damage, yet cannot get out of the way, condemned to his deformed shadow dancing before him.

*There isn't proof it was me. But why would a vandal break in, damage one picture, and of my mother? Then again, why would I do it?* "This is an actual crime," he says fearfully. From the rental car, he fetches his pipe, lights it, smoking hard. *Could a restorer save this? Once they know, I'm at their mercy.* When he was a museum guard, Pinch often ate lunch in the restoration department, permitted to observe— but from a distance. He hasn't a clue where to start.

A jar of Dad's paintbrushes stands on a table. Pinch leaves his pipe smoldering by the door, and he approaches a ruined patch of the painting. He has not painted since age sixteen. He takes a brush, dabs in the air—dry bristles poking nothing, testing the handle weight in his palm. *This is a violation. And Dad would notice. But what if I do this, and hide it, and he doesn't scrutinize this particular painting for a while? I never come back, I ditch the keys, and nobody ever knows that I was here.*

But no—Pinch cannot touch even a dry brush to the damaged painting. He drags a second easel beside the first, cuts and hammers together a blank canvas of the same dimensions. This way, he can practice harmlessly, perhaps even deconstruct the strokes of Bear's composition and test pigment mixtures on a blank ground, grasping how everything fit into the damaged area. Only then, perhaps, possibly, maybe, he could risk a touch-up.

By day three, Pinch is still engrossed in his practice canvas. He has sketched the entire painting of Natalie's hands. He has tested pigment mixtures. But something strange has happened. As Pinch toils away, time misbehaves, seeming not to move, then rushing forward, chunks strangely deleted. To know the time of day, he must step outside and look at the sky. *Is this Thursday yet? Saturday already?*

He visits the weekend market, driving too fast around hairpin turns, his gaze still back at the art studio, stirred only when speaking to the Catalan baker, addressing the man in an improvised blend of French and Spanish. At dinner in the cottage, Pinch recollects this exchange, easily his most vital in weeks. He folds himself a sandwich of that man's bread and another's *pâté de campagne*, alive to taste and sight (two flies circling above the kitchen table), reflecting on the potency of experience known only to oneself, which nobody else can ever witness, and heightened for it.

"All those cheeses," he mutters while chewing, walking in memory past market stalls, among merchants and shoppers, including a woman around forty who led two children by their hands. *"Est-ce que vous avez essayé leur cassoulet? Est-ce que vous le recommenderiez? Et un vin qui irait bien avec?"* he asks her now (at the time, he said nothing). *"Je m'appelle Charles. Enchanté de faire votre connaissance. Et les petits, comment s'appellent-ils?"*

On his last day at the property, Pinch dares to patch the damaged painting. He cannot know if his restoration is glaringly flawed—he left this so late and these are oils, so the paint won't dry for weeks; his new brushstrokes glisten. But he must leave, so drives at breakneck speed to Perpignan, buys replacement art supplies, then puts everything as it was, swinging open the studio door to test the sight upon entry. The place is suitably dingy, seemingly untouched, except for the fresh paint smell. He must count on Bear not visiting anytime soon.

Pinch lugs his practice painting outside and rests it by the oil barrel where he'll burn it. He touches the swaying flame of his Zippo to the back of his canvas. The thinnest smoke line rises—then he spits on his finger, pats out the smoldering dot. There isn't time to ensure that it burns completely to ash. Guiltily, he thinks of Birdie, for whom he made this trip, and for whom he has obtained nothing. A thought comes to him.

On the drive back, he is stopped at British customs. The officer points at the large painting lying flat in the back of his car. "What's that about, son?"

Pinch brushes aside an errant strand of comb-over, his hair specked with paint. "It's just a picture I did."

"What of?"

"Someone's hands, my mother's."

"Worth something?"

"No, no. Just a hobby."

"But someday," the officer says, winking, "we'll be famous, you and me, hey?" He waves Pinch through.

At the first stretch of open road, he steps on the pedal and hammers the steering wheel in excitement, inadvertently beeping the horn at a station wagon ahead. He drives up beside it, waving in apology; a sullen family glares back. Pinch returns to admiring the road, blinking at a low sun, taking jittery peeks in his rearview, seeing a fragment of his own face, aglow—and a painting in the background.

## 47

"Wait for Ms. Petros."

Four minutes pass.

How quintessentially New Yorkish of Eva to call, then place *him* on hold. But Pinch must accept it. He's been trying to reach her for days.

"So *thrilled* to hear your voice!" she says finally, as if they'd ever spoken before. Eva—estimating that the aging Bear nears his expiration date—has been sidling up to his kids, seeking to sell any Bavinsky art they possess. Annoyingly, his multitude of brats owns squat. As for Pinch, he always ignored her calls before. Until, suddenly, he can't stop ringing. Which is why she made him wait. "Please, dear," she tells him, "talk to me."

When Pinch does so, it's from a careful script. "I'll be honest," he begins (and this part *is* genuine), "my father would be furious if I sold this painting. He'd never forgive me. So I'm relying on your discretion. If we move ahead, this work can go *only* to a collector you trust as totally confidential, who'll hang it privately, never loan it out, or publicize the purchase. Is that possible? I mean, is that something you can guarantee?"

"Nebraska."

"What do you mean?"

"You ever heard of Mallard Dwyer?"

"Is that a kind of duck?"

"You! Are! Hilarious!" she says, not laughing. "Mallard Dwyer is a *muy rico* businessman from Omaha, or some such pointless berg. But here's the what: This guy—loaded as a result of his family's Big Ag holdings—turns up on my doorstep last month for guidance on buying. The reason for his sudden interest is a certain Judy-Lynn Mendez, whom you'll likely recall from *The Six Million Dollar Man*, where this highly talented young actress spoke two unforgettable lines in the role of switchboard operator. Afterward she tragically quit the business for holy matrimony to aforementioned old man Mallard. She brings the good looks, he brings the good life, including pretty pictures for their Omaha mansion."

Pinch—throughout the course of this discussion and several to follow—is meticulous never to state that this painting is actually *by* Bear. That much is assumed, but Pinch won't be caught on record saying so. When it comes to documenting the provenance, he acts haughty and impatient, playing the artist's weirdo son, declaring that he's had enough of all this absurd red tape. "Look, take it or leave it. I'm sorry."

Eva objects so strenuously that she hikes her commission to 50 percent. "Take it or leave it," she says.

He takes it, she takes it, and Mallard does too, informed that this is completely normal. After all, he's got the imprimatur of one of *the* galleries in SoHo. That's all you need, surely.

"How'd you do this, Charlie?" Birdie says on the phone, flabbergasted to find her bank balance rising to almost thirty thousand dollars after a mysterious transfer from a London bank account in her little brother's name. "What did you do?"

"Maybe squiggles on a napkin *are* worth something."

"Wait, this is from Dad? Why'd he do this? Shit, I don't even have his phone number to thank him."

"This isn't for talking about with Dad. Not with your children either. Not with Riley."

"Why would I tell *him*?" She adds in a whisper, "He nearly broke my nose last week."

"You serious, Bird? You need to go to the police."

"He's my sons' daddy. We just need to leave."

"And you will now. Right?"

"With this money, we're outta here. But wait, this is from you, Charlie? Or from Dad?"

"Does it matter?"

"It matters."

The transfer was the entirety of Pinch's cut of a $75,000 private sale, minus Eva's huge commission and expenses, plus bank fees and taxes. He explains none of this, replying only, "It's from Dad," wanting her to love the man again—or rather, knowing that she can't stop doing so, and that maybe this renders it less painful. "But you're not discussing it with anyone. *Ever.* Or I take it back. Okay?"

"However you're doing this, you saved me." She chokes up. "But Charlie, you're not exactly rolling in it. You don't need some of this yourself?"

"Hey, if *I* had cash like that, I'd only end up squandering it on my big sister."

She smiles, sniffs. "Love you, Charlie."

Afterward he sits on his bed, fizzing from gratification, excitement, fear. *Could I get arrested for this?* Fortunately, Nebraska isn't bristling with art appraisers who'd spot a questionable Bavinsky. Also, Mallard didn't buy this to flip it—he's establishing a collection, not dismantling one. The painting won't reappear on the secondary market for years. What's more, it was convincing enough to fool Eva and her staff. And none of them knows the original, so Pinch's copy didn't have to be perfect.

*But what if, when Dad next visits the studio, he notices the patched-over damage to the original? He still won't know it was me. And even if he figures it out, maybe I'd welcome that. I could point a finger in his face and say, "I did that, Dad. What's more, someone bought it for seventy-five grand. Yes, that's the record for a Bavinsky. And I hold it!"*

He yelps, drums on his knees. *A painting by me hangs in Omaha, Nebraska!* He shakes his head. To calm down, Pinch takes down an old Latin textbook and runs through verb tables, intending to dampen his thoughts by translating them into another language. But he keeps looking up from the page, preferring to hear his own mind for a change, petrified and electrified at once: *I even helped someone.*

In his closet, he finds the old orange jumper of Julie's, which he has adopted and wore on his recent venture to France. He presses his face to the wool—it's not her anymore, but the smell of charred firewood, paint, turpentine. And he is determined in a way unknown for years.

# 1985

## 48

Pinch walks around London unnoticed as ever. But for the first time, it feels like a choice, not evidence of failure. *Nobody knows what I am in secret, what I've done.* In Hyde Park, he looks benevolently at groups picnicking on hairy wool blankets, splashing wine and conversation. Previously he hated the showy joy of strangers. Now he'd like to fit among such people. And perhaps will. He has a plan, and is thrumming to start.

On his first day of the new job, Pinch steps past a knot of cigarette-puffing students outside the Utz language school, remembering the steps to lecture halls in Toronto. And it occurs to Pinch, perhaps for the first time, that he isn't a young man anymore.

This branch of the Utz chain is in Bloomsbury, a location calculated to harvest British Museum visitors after they've goggled at the plundered treasures of an empire shrunken territorially, expanding linguistically. The bulk of trade is teaching English to foreigners, but Utz also offers German, French, Chinese, Japanese, Spanish, and Italian—this final option employing Pinch, who will conduct classes by evening, private tutorials each afternoon.

Back at Evenlode, he taught an introductory Italian course, working off a rigid college syllabus. Yet Utz demands that its teachers not simply instruct but entertain. Consider yourself a cruise ship performer, one administrator told him. Some classrooms resound with sing-alongs, but Pinch's innovation is more sedate: an Italian-speaking-only policy in his classes intended to help pupils adjust to the sounds but that terrifies timid beginners, who sit there praying that he'll call on anyone else.

At first Pinch's classes flounder, students scowling, faith shifting to hostility. In some cases, he feigns a coughing fit and excuses himself to the staff toilets, where he hides in a stall, regaining composure. A single boneheaded student can undermine an entire two-hour session, as when Pinch asks Lower Intermediate to complete the sentence *"Non ho mai . . ."* (I have never . . .), and someone answers, *"Non ho mai toccato una scimmia"* (I have never touched a monkey), causing a pothead at the back to ramble about the monkey that resided at his parents' commune. "I loved that monkey. His name was Ringo."

*"Solo italiano, ragazzi!"* Pinch reminds them. *"Allora, Karen, sei tu la prossima. Per favore, completa la frase: 'Non ho mai . . .'"*

"What sort of monkey?" another student says. "My favorite is chimps."

"Chimps aren't monkeys. They're apes," a third student notes.

*"Italiano!"* Pinch interjects. *"Solo italiano, ragazzi!"*

Certain sessions do work, and Pinch grows addicted to that: It's like placing a child on a wobbly bike, pushing away anxiously—and she's off! On occasion, everything proceeds so well that class ends too soon. They'd all happily continue, were it not for the Mandarin teacher, Jing, who takes the room next, addressing him in one whip-crack syllable, "Chars!," as if to rebuke him for the travesty of his preposterous name, for the irrationality of English spelling.

A perk at Utz is that teachers may enroll in other courses for free. Pinch signs up for Advanced French, Advanced Spanish, and Intermediate German, sitting in each class with the textbook on his lap, stopping himself from answering the teachers' every question. When Jing next evicts Pinch from his classroom, it stirs a thought, and he becomes the newest pupil in Introductory Mandarin.

Pinch considers with fresh sympathy his fellow commuters on the Tube, reading of TV programs or talking of wallpapering the kids' room (but can we afford it?), of summer holidays (but can we afford it?), of schools (but can we afford it?). Arriving at work, he gabs with the janitors, who teach him phrases in Romanian. Then he marks assignments, pausing for lunch with fellow teachers or sneaking out for a stroll around the British Museum.

Dawdling before the Rosetta Stone, he contemplates a few attractive women he tutors, fantasizing about heedless affairs. At a novelty shop near Utz, he buys silly colored socks to wear in class—a conversation-starter perhaps, a wink to someone perceptive that he is not just a teacher here but something besides. On weekends, he prepares complex three-course meals, date-rehearsals at which he drinks a bit too much and eats a lot too much, scooping out a fourth helping of *tortiglioni alla barbara* and refilling his glass of rioja. "Don't mind if I do," he says aloud.

After a few months at Utz, he meets Julie for lunch, his satchel heaving with Chinese and German dictionaries. They must sign papers to finalize the divorce, and both intend to do so with civility. They've been in touch occasionally since he moved out, working through the shared paperwork. But this should be their last meeting. He imagined kissing her today; he even researched hotels around here.

Outside the restaurant, she greets him amicably, distantly, in a brown suit jacket with fierce shoulder pads, pleated trousers, silver hoop earrings. She graduates with her sociology degree soon, and he'd like to compliment her—to say, "You look so professional, Julie." But he doesn't want to intrude; often he feels she is stiff-arming him. Perhaps that's fair. He *was* overbearing, always there with advice, knowledge, "help."

They take a table at the PizzaExpress, which turns out to be an inappropriately peppy setting, a waiter swinging by to check in repeatedly, which forces them to fall quiet. Pinch longs to break her reserve, to reminisce about happily starving together when too poor to turn on the radiators, wearing socks and sweaters in bed. While she pages through documents, a strange thought passes through him, a counterfactual idea, that they did have a child together, a daughter, and she's alive somewhere—that Pinch and Julie are still together in that place, not coupled awkwardly at this restaurant but seated at a dinner table in their kitchen in Belsize Park, the three of them.

"Quite straightforward, not too complicated," he remarks about the typed page between them.

"Lucky," she says, "that we never did have kids."

"No, yes," he says, signing fast. "Absolutely. Yes."

## 49

As soon as the school holidays arrive he skips town, driving through France, windows down, air fluttering in, temperature rising as he travels farther south, cooling anew as he ascends into the Pyrenees. This time he informed Bear of the trip, priming him with concerns about burglars and squatters targeting seasonal properties. "I wouldn't mind popping over to the cottage, making sure all's well. You remember when I visited with Barrows? I stupidly walked away with an extra key! Just today, I happened across it in an old pair of corduroys. I could just let myself in, if you like."

"A key to my studio?"

"No, no—we were only in the cottage, remember? It's just a single key. But I can certainly try rattling the studio door, if you want. Make sure it's secure."

"Do that. Yes, fine—go, Charlie boy. Enjoy yourself."

Fortunately, why Pinch might volunteer to spend his vacation at a remote cottage off-season is a question that never troubles Bear.

Upon arrival he goes directly to the studio, checking the damaged painting. Now that the canvas has dried, Pinch's paint strokes blend in, the colors matching, except under closest view. And the retouched patch, considered without panic, isn't *that* large. He sweeps up floor dust, rains it over the surface, abetting the impression of age, and rests the painting where it originally stood, restoring it to the historical record among the collected works of Bear Bavinsky.

Relieved, he settles in to the cottage, then drives off for food, and onward to Perpignan for art supplies. When he opens the studio again, he clutches a pile of enlarged street photos—those he snapped years before in Philadelphia. On blank canvases he sketches out the fuzzy characters in the background of shots—strangers who become his sitters during these days alone on the mountainside. Pinch begins each picture clenched with tension, any dab containing the presentiment of failure—and the soaring possibility of its opposite.

When he painted as an adolescent, Pinch replicated his father's style (melded with Caravaggio, laughable as that seems now). Today he fumbles toward something of his own, negotiating color outward from a center point, tiny strokes, as if feeling through the void of each blank canvas. What marks his style is the deliberate inclusion of error: clots of red paint left untouched, black threads from hesitant bristles, stuttering lines in blue. From afar, faces emerge.

He finishes each session with aching shoulders and calloused hands, light-headed in the best way. He wonders what Natalie would've made of this—that he's painting again as she always wanted.

With a little wine in him, he amuses himself by leaving a picture in the easel and swinging open the door as if Dad were walking in, discovering it there. He plays through the scene, hardening himself to his father's commentary: "You want to please, Charlie, and it feels that way." Pinch imagines rejoinders, facts to decimate Bear: "You are so much less than you planned, Dad." But even mouthing this cruelty hurts Pinch. He'd never wound his old man, which is what Bear is now—old and frailer, no matter how he conceals it, laboring to appear just as ripsnorting as ever.

*But what if Dad saw one of my pictures and was impressed?* Pinch closes his eyes, shakes his head, jabbing his stomach. So hard to imagine. His irritation flares; he pours another glass. After a few more, he locks the studio and the cottage too, striding unevenly down the single-lane country road, leaning against fences whenever headlights whoosh by. After an hour, he reaches a public telephone in the closest village. He's phoning Dad to confess the sale—how nobody realized it was his, that it's hanging there still. *Nobody could tell the difference! You'll be gone someday, Dad, and I'll still be here.*

Bear's current wife, Lulu, answers. "Hey, Charlie. Poppa Bear can't talk right now."

"He's working?"

"Or what another person might call napping. Why couldn't I get the *young* Bear Bavinsky?" she jokes. "That's the problem with men. They wear out."

He makes a sound resembling laughter. "If you could tell him everything's swell at the cottage, I'd be most thankful." He puts down the phone and breaks into a blind run back up the winding tarmac, yodeling. If Bear had picked up, Pinch would've blurted the truth. Even in retrospect, the consequences chill him. He'd be banished from here. Pinch leaps, punches his fist in the air.

Before the drive back to London, he tidies the art studio with utmost care, concealing his intrusion, leaving it exactly as mucky and messy as it was, not a spot more. He fires up the kiln, slides in all six of the canvases he painted on this visit. He stands outside with his pipe, a twirl of smoke from his hand, a twirl from the studio chimney.

On the drive back to London, he keeps imagining those incinerated paintings on the asphalt that rushes beneath the car. They're pictures nobody but he will ever know. And that's how he wants it. Pinch returns to Utz replenished, full of affection for his students. He attempts silly jokes, and laughter bursts from his classroom. In the hallway he commiserates with fellow teachers, clucking in accord with their laments. "They're crazy to complain," he agrees. "Your course sounds excellent."

He is gracious because of his secret: that he isn't really a teacher. Yet this makes him smirk. *Me, a genuine artist! Yes, yes—an artist whose work hangs in the most exquisite collection in all of Nebraska!*

## 50

After a few years at Utz, Pinch becomes a personality there, his self-satirizing quirks drifting into shtick: the white Panama hat in summer, the smelly briar pipe, his necktie of turtles, the socks with double-decker buses. Often he lingers after-hours, perusing grammar texts in the library or writing down one-liners from his favorite joke book, slipping them into colleagues' mailboxes. When everyone has left, he strolls the corridors as if they were his, humming, muttering foreign phrases, sometimes even popping into the women's staff toilets simply because you aren't supposed to. He thrills at these unseen shows of nonconformity. One evening, before the mirror in the ladies room, considering his lamb-chop sideburns, Pinch mulls trimming them as per current fashion. Behind his reflection, a Chinese woman appears.

"Jing!" He spins around.

Bewildered, she retreats, the door closing after her.

He knows Jing only superficially from her Mandarin classes, and because she is married to Salvatore, a fellow Italian teacher who gives Pinch the creeps—part of why he's kept his distance from Jing. What irks him about Salvatore is that nobody seems to see what a phony he is, how the pretends to embody the stereotype of an Italian, bursting into opera during class, offering shots of *limoncello*, chirping *"Ciao, bella!"* to female students. But this guy, who claims to be Sicilian, was born in Wales to immigrant parents and speaks appallingly bad Italian. Nobody learns anything in his classes—yet everyone adores Sal! For a while he haunted Pinch's office, sitting without permission on his desk, yammering away in English. "I got this really hot bird in Intermediate. You seen her, Carlito?"

"No, actually. But I saw your wife in the hall earlier."

"Why you talking about Jing, mate? I'm telling you about this Katya bitch."

"And what Jing was telling me about Chinese dialects was so amazing."

"You're a knob." That was the last time Salvatore bothered him.

Pinch remains vexed that anyone could like such a fraud. *But, ah well—this is your day job. Who even cares about working at Utz?*

Apparently, he does. For, caught in the ladies room, he rushes into the halls, scanning for Jing, concocting a lie to preserve his job. He'll call it a blunder, beg her to keep it to herself. When he locates Jing, she's entering the men's room.

"If you use that toilet, I go here," she says matter-of-factly.

Smiling, Pinch returns to his office. *What an oddball she is.* Anyway, he seems to be safe. Until, minutes later, Jing knocks at his office door. "I am going outside to eat sandwich," she says.

"Good idea."

"You come?"

She leads him to a sandwich bar near Russell Square. Pinch orders only a mint tea, resenting this outing—he's only here to ensure that she doesn't plan to tell on him. At least he can use the occasion to practice Mandarin. Jing says nothing unprompted, so he asks about her life in China. Her family hails from Sichuan, but she grew up in the far west, Xinjiang. Her father, a professor of medicine, was ordered out there during the Cultural Revolution. Her mother, a well-bred doctor, was assigned to herd goats. Clandestinely, she educated Jing, teaching the girl a smattering of French and English and guiding her through the medical books left behind by her late father.

"What happened to him?" Pinch asks.

"Some students, they beat him to death," she says.

When Jing was grown, she undertook a long and punishing trek to London full of unstated indignities. She always intended to study medicine, but it never came to pass. This renders her current job at Utz both a triumph and a shame: better than she's had, far less than she should've.

Switching to English (Jing too wants practice), she says, "Chars, do you consider me a humor person?"

"I consider you a serious person," he says, believing this to be her desired reply, though it fails to satisfy her. "Do you consider yourself funny?"

"I like to be funny. Also," she adds, "I am ticklish."

"Not sure that counts."

"You laughed."

He reverts to Mandarin: "I have books of jokes in my office. I lend you one. I give it in your office."

She opens her soggy sandwich to inspect the contents, failing to notice that he is readying to leave. But his glimpse of her lonely dinner stops him. He sits again, as if merely having adjusted his underpants.

After their stilted dinner, the two become distant friends, bumping into each other in the halls after everyone else has vacated. Sometimes he tags along for her after-work sandwiches—he never wants one himself, but it's too sad leaving her to eat alone. Moreover, he respects Jing. She's the only other serious linguist on staff. This makes him increasingly uneasy about what he knows: that Salvatore is entirely unfaithful, constantly hitting on students. *Look*, Pinch reminds himself, *workplace melodrama doesn't concern me. What matters is at the cottage.*

# 1990

## 51

Pinch maintains loose contact with his father, speaking now and then, unsure what he feels about Bear Bavinsky nowadays. He does wish they could speak about painting—not so Dad would praise his art necessarily, but for the pleasure of a shared interest. Instead he inquires into Bear's ongoing work. "Are you keeping a lot of these pictures? Or most go into the fire?"

"If it went in the fire, why would I talk about it now?" Bear responds gruffly.

Pinch suffers a pang to hear his father's rebuff, but suppresses this. His main reason for these calls is to know when Bear will next invade the cottage, which normally happens for a few weeks during the summer, casting Pinch into panic that his father might notice something this time. Fortunately, Bear detests looking back at his own art—he has decided that the works preserved at his studio are sublime, and he can't risk reconsidering that view, so keeps the paintings turned to the wall. Pinch never rests until his father leaves the cottage again, at which point the place is his own. At any opportunity he may vanish there, always vague to colleagues at Utz. Fellow teachers, sipping coffee in the staff room, rib him for taking the same vacation every year. "Where *is* this glorious villa of yours?" they ask. "Why don't *I* get an invitation?"

Pinch looks into his Styrofoam cup, black liquid jiggling. A polite smile. He deafens himself to their banter, holding the scene before himself, converting their faces into shapes, colors, a flat composition. "If only it *were* a villa," he responds. "More like a heap of old stones!" Nobody needs to find that place, or know what becomes of him there.

Amid cycles of teaching and painting, Pinch turns forty. He deems it a meaningless milestone, yet is moved when his colleagues throw a surprise party, including a Tesco strawberry cake and two bottles of prosecco. The overtanned receptionist produces a gift certificate, bought on behalf of everyone. The card says "Happy 50th Birthday!," which is a little embarrassing; they make a joke of it. But he does look older than his years, with a hunch of which he is hardly aware, lacking anyone intimate enough to correct his downward trend. Only a few cross-swept strands of hair still intervene between his bald dome and the rain. A paunch juts over his belt, as if peeking off a high diving board.

Many more terms begin, and many more conclude, each time with a few departing students who request snapshots with him, promising to mail back copies from Tokyo or Cairo or Boston, or wherever their hard-gained vocabulary is to gently decompose. Now and then he falls for a woman in class and almost flirts. But he dreads being the creepy teacher—he considers Salvatore that, so becomes the sexless one instead.

Sometimes Pinch awakens from dreams in which someone was in love with him. He rarely remembers details, just a hollowness. He pushes his thoughts away from such nonsense and back to the cottage, considering techniques achieved last time, which he must replicate on the next. With the passing years, he attains a new vibrancy in his paintings, especially after putting aside the street photographs from Philadelphia and referring only to memory, eyes clenched then springing open to re-create faces from his past, not for accuracy but abstracted, recognizable only to him. Before leaving the cottage, he destroys all his latest efforts—it's strangely exhilarating, leaves his chest pounding.

Only once does he save a work from the flames—a woman's chin, which began as Julie's, became Barrows', and ended up as that of someone he hasn't yet met, perhaps will. He can show her, saying, "Isn't that *you?*" He hides the wet canvas in the attic, behind boxes of Natalie's old pottery, which he has gradually driven to the cottage, both for safekeeping and because this tranquil setting seems right for her art, alongside his.

For company in London he adopts two dogs from the Battersea animal shelter, fluffy white mongrels called Harold and Tony whose previous owner died. The man's body remained undiscovered for three weeks, but his pets were fine. "Not even hungry," the shelter employee tells Pinch, raising her eyebrows. "You put two and two together." As a result of such ghoulish rumors, nobody wants these dogs. But Pinch prefers outcasts, so takes them. Walking from the shelter he picks up the sniffly little dogs, their pink tongues hanging out, fangs glistening. One licks his hand with delectation. "No, boy! No!"

By the mid-nineties, Pinch can scarcely recall life before Harold and Tony, conducting long conversations with his roommates (doesn't matter in which language) and venting about work or the bruises of London living. Neither dog is overly bothered, which always makes Pinch less upset.

Then someone has sex—not with Pinch but with Mallard Dwyer. And everything changes.

## 52

Pinch is practicing Chinese tones in his living room, and his dogs are howling along, when an unfamiliar sound reverberates from the wall: his telephone. A paralegal is calling from Los Angeles with questions about Judy-Lynn Mendez.

"Who?" He is immediately on edge. She was the actress who married Mallard Dwyer, and who prompted him to start an art collection. But Mallard, it turns out, was caught in bed with an even younger starlet whom he met in the shoe department and befriended in the hot tub. The upshot is that lawyers are tallying assets, including a painting sold by the Petros Gallery. Apparently Eva directed the paralegal to Pinch, saying he would be happy to provide details on provenance.

Inwardly raging at Eva, he switches the receiver to his other hand, wiping his sweaty palm on the couch. "There's nothing I can tell you," he replies.

"Is there a number for your father possibly? He's living, right?"

"No."

"I'm sorry for your loss."

"You misunderstand. My father is alive. I just don't see any reason to let you harass him about a sale he had nothing to do with. He doesn't like to be disturbed. All right?"

"I hear where you're coming from, sir, but I do need to reach out to him."

"I've told you. There's no reason to bother him."

"Don't be abusive, sir."

"How was that abusive?" Pinch snaps, cornered by this twit, mind scrambling. "Look, call some other time."

"And you'll have his number then? I could call Monday."

"Fine. Fine."

For days, Pinch can barely sleep. He should've handled that better. *Do they already suspect something? Will they track down Bear regardless?* Pinch has never explicitly claimed that the painting was by his father. But that's how it was sold, and he took tens of thousands of dollars based on this. And he's inadvertently implicated Birdie too, by giving her the profits. He shakes his head, hand over his eyes. "What have I done here?" *Would it be possible to buy back the painting from Mallard and hide this whole mess?* But Pinch couldn't possibly afford a Bavinsky. Priced out of his own painting! He wipes sweat off his upper lip, the dogs watching.

"If I tell the truth," he informs Harold and Tony, "nobody will be understanding. This won't be okay." His only chance is to keep lying, and hope that closes the matter. He must confirm directly what he previously implied—that this was an original Bear Bavinsky, gifted to Pinch by the artist himself. It's better to gamble on that and hope Bear never hears of it than to let them ferret out Dad.

Blood pressure rocketing, Pinch signs the affidavit and faxes it to a law office in L.A.

"Coming through the machine as we speak," the paralegal confirms by phone. "Great, good. They can move ahead with liquidating now."

"Liquidating?" Pinch goes cold.

"Selling the work."

"I thought you just needed to confirm provenance for a valuation. You said this was just paperwork. Why didn't you mention it was for a sale?"

"Sir, you're being abusive again."

"How have I abused you? How?"

"I'm putting down the phone now."

For weeks Pinch jumps if anyone taps him on the shoulder. When the light on his answering machine blinks, he is terrorized, just circling it for days. When he finally listens, he finds a message from an American journalist who wants to speak in person; he's coming to London. Hands on hips, Pinch envisages his impending catastrophe. "Stay calm," he tells the dogs. *Just keep lying. What does this guy know?*

Pinch calls in sick, saying he's undergoing tests and won't be back at Utz until the following week. He drives through the night to the cottage, where he stares at the touched-up original of Natalie's hand, whose replica is now awaiting sale. Pinch glances at the other Bavinsky originals around him. He pulls out three more, turns them around—so powerful, Dad's art, so perceptive and honest. *As trying as Dad can be, as egotistical, he understands people, better than I ever have, better than Mom did, better than anyone I know. What if I just tell him? Might he understand? Would he say nothing, to save my skin? It's too much of a gamble.* If Bear becomes enraged, all manner of disasters follow—not least, this studio taken from Pinch's life. His heart sinks.

He turns on the kiln, heat emanating from the open doors, and drags over the original *Hands IX*, shoving it inside the inferno. He slams the doors, locks them. Pinch feels deathly ill. Back at the cottage, he avoids the sight of himself in the mirror, as he avoids the sight of smoke rising from the studio chimney. He turns the spigot on a wine box in the kitchen, fills a pottery mug to the brim, downs it.

What better option was there? If Dad were to learn of the Mallard deal, he'd go apoplectic, saying *Hands IX* was *never* sold—it's at a private storage location in Europe! If he came here and found the original, Pinch's affidavit would amount to criminal fraud. On the other hand, if Bear were to ever hear of the sale of *Hands IX*, and find that it's gone, everyone will assume Mallard's was the original. Provided that Bear never inspects the copy himself. Pinch grabs his own ears, shaking his head. If this falls apart, Bear will probably track down the name of the seller of *Hands IX* and find it was his own son. At least then, he can throw himself on Dad's mercy, explaining the mess Birdie was in—while making it clear that she had *nothing* to do with this. Better to plead before Bear than before a jury. Still, a dismal situation. He shuts his eyes, sickened. *Hey—there's no certainty Bear ever discovers this.*

Upon returning to London, Pinch arrives at the Ritz Hotel café to meet with the journalist Connor Thomas. The man's answering machine message had thrust Pinch into panic, but he proves a less intimidating presence in person, less newshound than artsy youth, a redhead with gelled spiky hair, a black waistcoat worn over a Nine Inch Nails T-shirt, torn jeans, burgundy Doc Martens. He clutches his Dictaphone as if it were an autograph book. "It's okay to tape this, Mr. Bavinsky?"

"Let's have a normal conversation first. Then we'll see. All right?" Pinch is curt, establishing himself as the adult. "You said on the message that you're researching my father. It's something specific?"

"So I'm hoping to confirm a couple of things. Nothing too tough. We love Bear Bavinsky at *Artforum*. I shouldn't say 'we,' like I'm on staff. I'm just hoping to contribute at this point. Technically I'm still in grad school. I believe you know one of my professors, Priscilla Barrows?"

"Oh," Pinch says, sitting up, "sure. That's a name from the past. She mentioned me for some reason?"

"Just that she dated Bear Bavinsky's son at college, and actually had an opportunity to meet your father once."

"Yes, that's all true. But look," Pinch says, "what exactly do you need? Does this have to do with Mallard?"

"With what? I'm just looking for background on your father's career."

"To what end?"

"A profile. We want to say how unjustly overlooked your father is," Connor explains meekly. "That's all."

"Bear is overlooked again? Isn't the consensus that my father is just another minor postwar painter?"

"Not in our books."

"You haven't spoken to him, you said?"

"I tried; no answer."

"Going through me is best. You did the right thing." Pinch is calming down. This kid is no threat. "Shall we get a proper drink?" He raises his arm for a waiter. "Normally, I don't like to say much about my father. But if it's just fact-checking, and for a student of Cilla Barrows, I'm willing to help. But not on the record."

"Oh, yes, I totally get that," Connor says, evidently delighted. "So basically, my interest is Bavinsky's recent works. All I've been able to dig up so far relates to his old stuff. I know about the early Life-Stills that he sold. And I know about the later Life-Stills that he kept off the market. Then there's all the rumors about his recent work, which nobody seems to have actually seen. That, for me, would be the mother lode. I'd *love* to get images of any recent paintings. I talked to his representation at the Petros Gallery, and they said maybe you'd help?"

"They told you that?" he responds, incredulous. "I'll tell you now: Nobody is getting images of Bear's new art." Pinch has studied all the Life-Stills at the studio in France, but has himself never viewed Dad's ongoing work; Bear has kept it strictly secret for years. Eva certainly has no clue. She doesn't even represent Bear. Perhaps she's hoping to tweeze out info herself, using this boy reporter as her proxy. "Let's stick to your background questions."

"Right, sure. So, like, my approach is how Bear Bavinsky is this lost modernist classic. The point I want to make, basically, is that Bavinsky is this proto-iconoclast following his own vision." He stops. "Why are you rolling your eyes?"

"Didn't realize I had. But I'm a bit wary of art journalism. Most of the time you guys reduce everything to jargon or to sales figures. Neither, in the case of my father, explains anything. If you want to make him look important in your article, you certainly shouldn't mention past sales, which'll be worse than any flash-in-the-pan star advertised on every other page of your magazine."

"Actually, the fact that Bear Bavinsky is not finance driven is what I plan to celebrate. Especially with everything going on."

"What's going on?"

"Money, everywhere. But honestly? The magazine is not market driven. If anything, the market follows us. Which isn't meant as an incentive. Which I know it wouldn't be."

Pinch chuckles: This journalist, pitching a tribute to the noble artist who is aloof to worldly rewards—while trying to lure the artist's son by hinting at higher sale prices! "I don't doubt your magazine's high ethics. But galleries do buy all your ads, right? Rather a coincidence that the articles end up reading like their wall text."

"Have you had a chance to look at us lately?" Connor asks delicately. "We're not like that."

"Let's hear your questions."

"Okay, so I know your father works mainly in Key Biscayne now, but he summers in France, right? Which is where you and professor Barrows went that time, correct? Now, where exactly?"

"The south of France. You can leave it at that."

"Cool. And, um, his new works? When will we see those? And are they Life-Stills? Or are they something new and different?"

To remain the gatekeeper, Pinch must assert an air of authority, as if he were his father's spokesman. "When I visit his cottage in France, the art studio is a separate building, and it's locked, and I respect that. That's as much as I'm comfortable saying."

Despite this scant assistance, Connor and the editors at *Artforum* piece together a story months later. The cover art is a 1962

classic (*Throat and Shoulder XVI*). As for the article, there's no mention of Mallard. It's fluff about Bear standing apart from other contemporary artists, escaping the post-Pop hangover and conceptualist
dogma, exactly as he once defied Abstract Expressionist dogma and
the color-field purists. The magazine extols his cult status among
those returning to figurative art, speaks of the enduring mystery
around his ongoing work these past decades, and concludes by calling him an "artist's artist"—that term of fatal praise, meaning no
normal person knows of Bear Bavinsky anymore.

But Eva Petros is not a normal person.

# 53

"Heavens to Betsy!" she says. "I am *so* relieved to get you." Prompted
by the *Artforum* article, Eva is planning an exhibition of Bavinskys
from private collections. She hopes to gather about half of the Life-
Stills that Bear sold early in his career.

"That is never happening," Pinch says, instantly on edge. He
needs people to *stop* paying closer attention to his father, which only
cranks up the risk that Pinch is exposed.

Eva covers the mouthpiece and hollers. "Felix, what's our latest
number on the 'vinskys?"

"Nine locked in," comes the muffled response. "Three more
likely, six maybes."

Eva returns to Pinch. "We're confident of at least eighteen. And
once word gets out about this show, serious collectors will be stran-
gling their grandmothers to get their art in this catalog. It'll be an
adrenaline shot to the valuations. Anyone who misses out is dumb
as shit. Needless to say, I would go weak at every pertinent joint to
add any Bavinskys *you* have put aside."

"Eva, I'm not having anything to do with this." Already she screwed him once, pointing lawyers in the Mallard divorce to him for the provenance of that painting, washing her hands of the problem and pouring the dirty water over him. Does she think that, when it serves her, people just forget?

"Hear me out, will ya?" she says, fake smile audible. "What we're hoping for, praying for, making goddamn animal sacrifices for, is an actual fresh contribution from the big Bear himself."

"Do you know how he feels about your gallery?"

"I know things weren't all smiles when he broke with us. But my papa was not himself toward the end. Point is, this is the moment to welcome Bear Bavinsky back to the Petros." She adds, as if parenthetically, "He still lacks exclusive rep, right? I find that fucking scandalous."

"Before I discuss any of this, I need to know what happened with Mallard. I thought we agreed—no, I don't *think*—you promised that the painting was going to stay in place. I told you I needed to keep that deal private. Now it's being sold somewhere?"

"Don't get your Calvins in a twist! Mallard's ex already sold it. And you know who bought it? Mallard himself. I talked him into it, made it clear that your father's work was only going up. We did the deal anonymously on his side, so his dearly jilted wouldn't revenge-milk him for a higher price."

"Wait, Mallard buys the painting from me, with you taking a commission. Then you sell him the exact same painting for a second commission?"

"So what? I'm a charity now?"

"And this show of yours, it'll include the Mallard picture?"

"That's looking like a no right now. He's still feeling a tad ripe about buying it through me twice."

"But the other Life-Stills you show—you're selling those?"

"Lordy, no. Most are loans."

"More charity?"

"Oh, you are so funny! Look, your father is of an age. I see his market heating up. And I want my name attached."

"He's 'of an age'?"

"I just want Bear to know he has a home here. We haven't forgotten him, never stopped worshipping at the Bavinsky altar. I *know* your dad will want to join forces. And I'm gonna track him down, by hook or by crook."

"No you won't," Pinch says, trying to stabilize his voice. "I'll phone him."

He makes the perfunctory call to Florida.

"They're fucking rats, that Petros clan," Bear says. "I'll sue them if they do this."

"On what grounds? You don't own those paintings. Anyway, don't worry: I'm blocking out all the stupid requests I can. But I wanted you to be warned. If anyone starts pestering you, just send them to me. Okay, Dad? Okay?"

"Why in hell can't they leave me alone? It's no wonder I don't show my stuff to these savages. All they talk about is goddamn Life-Stills that I did a half century ago!"

"And your recent stuff has moved on from there?"

"Where it moved is none of your concern," he answers coldly. "Now, are you saying I should give this tramp something to put on her walls? That seriously what you're proposing?"

"The opposite. I'd say do not respond, even if Eva finds you. Hang up on her. Ignore her totally. Do not talk with her, and she'll fade away. Don't engage with any of these rats. Agreed?"

"They are goddamn rats!" Bear concurs, sniffing. Pinch knows that sniff—his father inflating with pride. "And they sure are taking notice," he adds stiffly. "That kid yapping about me—what was it, Julius Schnozzle?"

"You mean Julian Schnabel? That was years back."

"The guy couldn't stop praising me. I'm his biggest influence. What a load of horse manure."

"Not that you listened."

"I don't give a flying damn!" he says, sniffing.

"Dad, seriously, I think you should keep away from this. We're agreed on that, right?"

# 1996

## 54

When Bear flies to New York to oversee the hanging at the Petros Gallery, Pinch is expected to be the artist's aide. This presumption—that he drop everything and rush across the Atlantic to serve the great man—causes Pinch to throttle a towel in his bathroom. Because he must go now. Partly, it's for self-preservation. But he has another motive, and tries not to dwell on it. It's the thought of his father—the man is well into his eighties now—doddering around there, tripping up, making mistakes. Pinch shakes his head: the long, loud effect of fathers.

Out of pride, he sets a condition before he'll attend. Bear must invite *all* his children to the opening—several have seen his paintings only in reproduction.

The gallery reserves the painter and son a suite at a stylishly underlit Midtown hotel, its employees as sleek as the guests, everyone dressed like hit men (hit men as imagined by Hollywood; lots of black Armani). Pinch winces apologetically to the check-in clerk when his father flirts with her. "I'd give you my room number," Bear tells her, winking, "but I figure you noted it down already." She laughs, for Bear is old enough now to find cute. And she perhaps noticed that his room is all-expenses-paid by a SoHo gallery that also left a mammoth gift arrangement of flowers, fruit, cheeses. This guy must be somebody.

In their suite, Bear dispatches the bellboy with a few bucks, closes the door, and slumps in an armchair, his forces spent at having acted as he once was, a front that he drops only around this child. "What does that say?" he asks, squinting at an itinerary left by the gallery. "Read it out for me, would you, Charlie?" Every item draws a sigh from Bear, who grumbles as if he's above such crap, though it's really because he's afraid of managing all this. Pinch promises to cancel everything that isn't mandatory. "Yes, can you?" Bear says with alacrity. "Please, do that, son."

Shortly Bear has nodded off in that armchair and must be helped onto one of the king-size beds for an afternoon nap. He is unable to get his shoes off, so Pinch unlaces them. Everybody gushes about how Bear never slows down—he's as driven today as when he was fifty! Because nobody is permitted to see this.

Dressing that evening, Bear blusters around the suite, cursing this palaver: to be trotted before art phonies, having to endure their imbecilic questions. Pinch stands at the perma-locked window, on the verge of confessing his forgery. What if Eva mentions the Mallard sale? She vowed not to, which means nothing. Pinch must prepare counterclaims. *Am I walking into a public disaster?* He stares down over West Forty-Sixth Street, remembering his last visit to this city, roaming Central Park, trying to summon the guts to see Barrows. That was right after Natalie died, when Bear told him: "Her pieces were never really first class." Pinch's outrage stirs anew at this man who rants behind him—those liver-spotted hands gesticulating, his dry lips flapping about the anguish of art-world attention.

During the town car ride to SoHo, neither of them speaks, each in his own funk. This will be the same gallery they visited together in 1965, though the neighborhood is much dolled up since then: yuppie pedestrians swinging shopping bags, gleaming storefronts, only a smattering of art spaces left. When the artist steps from the car, a welcoming committee awaits on the sidewalk: Eva ("Oh, let me kiss you, glorious Bear!"); a pretty publicist with orthodontically ideal whites ("You guys made it!"); and a bald gallery assistant in pink bowtie ("I am literally exploding with excitement right now"). To one side stands Connor Thomas, now on staff at *Artforum,* with ginger goatee and black eyeliner, long brown leather coat, and a red Manhattan Portage messenger bag that he clasps, dumbstruck before his idol. Everyone is gawking, not quite *at* Pinch, but near. It's intoxicating, people approaching Pinch with earnest whispers, knowing that he alone has the ear of the grizzled legend.

Eva leads them all inside the gallery.

"You folks are all gussied up. I shoulda worn my dinner jacket!" Bear exclaims, inviting only one response, which Eva deftly offers.

"*Your* only duty is to be Bear Bavinsky." She touches his arm. "Everything else—that's for us to worry about."

"Being Bear Bavinsky is a job I can just about handle." Winking, he stuffs a bolt of tobacco into his pipe.

"Ohmigod," the pink-bowtied assistant says, biting his lower lip. "So sorry: There's no smoking in here."

"Felix, I hope you are fucking kidding," Eva says. "Bear Bavinsky smokes wherever he likes. This is *his* house."

"Ohmigod, yes."

Next she calls over Connor, who wrote the catalog text.

"I'm so honored," he tells Bear, bowing. "I was thinking earlier how, for me, this is like meeting a figure from history."

"From history?" Eva retorts. "Bear is very much of this era."

"No, right, of course!" Connor sputters, blushing. "Just mean I can hardly believe it. Not that—"

"What *I'm* most jazzed about," Bear interrupts, heavy paw on Connor's shoulder, "is meeting the writer who did that helluva magazine piece. Point the kid out, would you?" Bear scratches his beard, glancing mischievously around.

Connor lowers his head. "You're too kind." He looks up. "I can't believe you read that. I'm so honored."

"You keep being honored," Bear quips, "then you'll run out of honor altogether, and you know where that can land a fella!" Everyone laughs to excess. "Word is, you wrote the program notes too, and a damn good job. Here's an idea. How's about giving me a guided tour? What do you say?"

"Wait, what?"

"The bum's name is Bavinsky, am I right?" Bear says, sniffing.

"I would be—"

The toothy publicist interposes, "Do not say 'honored'!"

"Humbled?" Connor ventures, and everyone laughs. "Can I be humbled?"

As Bear is led off by the starstruck journalist, Pinch nearly rushes forward to chaperone his father. But this should be safe: The Mallard painting wasn't included, thankfully—Eva is still trying to woo the collector back. And Connor himself knows nothing dangerous. When the two return from the impromptu tour, Pinch asks his father how it went.

"Tell you what, kiddo. A helluva set of pictures they rustled up. Damn fine."

Bear never did invite his other children. When Pinch realizes, he is highly annoyed. But guiltily, he is flattered too—he is the chosen child. He just hopes none of them hear about this event, which will convince them that he's trying to monopolize their father. Birdie has hinted that several siblings envy his access to Dad.

The gallery fills fast with guests, a sweaty jazz quartet bopping hard, the saxophonist's neck engorged as he rips a solo, although it's barely audible over the jabbering. The crowd—white faces, asymmetrical haircuts, interesting glasses—includes a group of youths, art-schoolers who scammed tickets and are making a rebel display of sitting on the floor, their hands around big glasses of free wine. One after another, renowned guests seek an audience with Bear, each of them raving not only about the paintings displayed tonight but about his contribution, how his art had inspired them. Most of the encomiums conclude with a version of "What are you working on now? And won't you put *any* of it into the market? Please do."

"Satisfy your public, darling!" Eva adds, handing Bear another flute of bubbly.

"Trying to bribe me with booze?" he says. "Because you can!"

She stands on tiptoes—a short woman in silver stilettos—and gives him a peck on the lips. "To buy *you* off, Bear, I'd try anything," she says, to whoops all around.

"They say Petros is an all-service gallery, right?" quips a snarky *Village Voice* columnist, everyone cackling, clinking champagne flutes.

Pinch stands a step apart, monitoring the scene. He takes out his pipe, feels for his Zippo. Everything is going far better than he feared. After all these hours of dread and vigilance, he allows himself a break, leaning against a bare white wall, sipping iced pinot grigio, surveying the crowd, noting that more than a few people are looking at him, knowing who he is: the middle-aged son—like a shorter, uglier version of Bear—who works as a teacher in London. If he had been born to another father, they would consider Pinch's achievements perfectly respectable. But relatives are judged relatively.

A sixtyish man in blue Oxford button-down, khaki trousers, and Rockport boat shoes, one hand drumming a fanny pack, the other gripping a glass of scotch, pushes through the crowd in the direction of Bear. An uneasy feeling suffuses Pinch. He delays lighting up, pockets his pipe, and hastens into the throng, cutting off the man's path. "Hi there. Can I help you?"

"You work here?"

"I'm assisting during this show, yes."

"The name's Mallard Dwyer."

After an instant, Pinch makes himself stand tall, forces a smile, heart racing as he shifts subtly to block the route toward his father. "What can I do for you?"

"Get out of my way for a start."

"Is there something that you needed?"

"I need to speak with Bear Bavinsky. Can you help with that?"

"Definitely," Pinch says, chest tightening. "What may I say it's about?"

"Just get the man's attention, will you?"

"But your question?"

"How is that your concern? All right, fine. I bought a painting of his. It shows some girl's hands. Now, I got this theory. Those hands are *more* than hands. Because I know art has meanings that aren't what you see. And there's that saying, 'Let me give you a hand.' Is that what Bavinsky meant?"

Pinch nods double-time, as if listening intently, sweat trickling down his brow. He wipes his upper lip, searching for any logical reason why Mallard may be disallowed from addressing the artist.

"I understand that the subconscious is important to artists," Mallard continues. "So is *that* what my painting is about? I want to hear it from the man himself. I paid good money for the thing. I got a right."

"All of Bear Bavinsky's portraits are painted from life, so I'm not sure the subconscious was central."

"Take my word, Bavinsky's highfalutin assistant. It's all the subconscious." He downs his scotch, places the empty glass in Pinch's hand, and pushes past.

Pinch launches himself before Dwyer again. "I'm sorry—it's not possible to just approach him. He doesn't like it. He's very shy." Bear's laughter booms from across the room.

"Take your hand off me before I snap it!"

"I'm not touching you."

"You just did. Out of my way."

"Wait, wait. Hang on. Let me arrange something exclusive for you. Okay? Privately with the artist, away from this crowd. I don't want anyone butting in when you're having your talk. I'll set it up, and be back to you in a few minutes. Okay? That's a promise, Mr. Dwyer."

Mallard, sucking his teeth, grunts as if to say, *I guess this is how leftie New York homosexuals operate.* He pushes back through the crowd to his trophy wife, who nibbles mousily around the crust of a tiny pizzetta.

Dripping with sweat now, Pinch pushes toward Bear, overhearing his father regaling admirers with an account of when Audrey Hepburn visited his studio in Rome and prevailed on him to sell her a Life-Still.

"Dad."

Bear doesn't hear. Pinch tries again. His father talks all the louder.

Finally Pinch grabs his father's upper arm, causing Bear to turn, livid. Pinch draws his father away from the others, saying dry-mouthed to Dad's hairy ear: "It's time to go. Okay?"

"What's that?"

Shouting: "The town car's still waiting outside! Let's make our exit! Okay?"

"Like hell!" He shakes off his son and swivels toward where Mallard Dwyer lurks. The Nebraskan shoots a quizzical look at Pinch: Now?

Pinch yanks his father back around, causing Bear to lose balance and clasp his son's windbreaker. Pinch grips Bear's elbow, holding firm when the old man attempts to shake him off. "I came all the way across the ocean. To help *you*, Dad." Teeth gritted, Pinch swallows. "And I am telling you it is time to leave. Now." Voice cracking: "Bear? *Now*. Enough of this. All right?" In desperation, he adds: "For God's sake! There must be a limit to how much fucking flattery you can take."

Bear looks right at his son, and it's among the most disturbing sights of Pinch's life: *Dad is frightened of me.*

Pinch drags his father toward the exit, gives a wave to Eva ("He's exhausted; talk tomorrow"), places Bear into the town car, jumps in afterward, shoving his father along the leather seat. "Back to the hotel, please. We're in a rush. Thanks."

As the car pulls into traffic, Bear says, "Where do you get off talking to me like that?"

"It was time to go. That's that. I decided it. Done." Pinch looks out the window.

"Goddamn unbelievable," Bear mumbles. "Never been . . ." His voice trails off.

After a few minutes, to cut the tension, Pinch points out where they stayed three decades earlier, recalling how he listened to a ball game in his room.

"Nope, we watched the Yankees on the TV," Bear says, more subdued.

"No, it was the Mets on the radio. You weren't there. You went back to the gallery. Remember?"

Bear frowns, puzzled, as if maybe, perhaps maybe? All this talk of *his* events, unrecalled.

"I almost phoned Mom, but I couldn't figure how to get an outside line, and thought I'd get in trouble for calling overseas. Who knows if I even wanted to talk to her." Pinch pauses. "Would be nice if there were a number to reach Natalie now. Tell her we're here together." He looks at his father.

Bear says nothing.

Up in the suite, the old man hobbles toward the bar fridge, takes out a lukewarm minibottle of Moët & Chandon. Stiffly he fetches two plastic cups, murmuring to himself.

"What's that about?" Pinch asks, still rigid with tension.

"A toast, I thought."

"To what?"

"To our dear Natty," Bear replies.

Pinch cannot respond. He nods, raises his plastic cup, too moved to speak.

## 55

On his next visit to the cottage, Pinch takes out the one painting of his own hidden in the attic. During the drive here, he was so jittery. But that dissipated the moment he emerged from the rental car, breathed this bracing winter air, walked up the path, unlocked the cottage. Safe here. Still, it's too dangerous to keep this painting. He gives a last look—a woman's chin—and takes it outside to burn.

That night he prepares duck confit, tasting directly from the pan, bubbles of fat spitting up his arms, gamy scent filling his nostrils, a fly buzzing somewhere in the dim kitchen. Each perception explodes inside him, then dissolves, experiences that are saved nowhere. He eats fast and lustily, then returns to the studio, painting until his focus blurs and there is no creaking forest outside, no loneliness, no time, only the bliss of action.

On his last day, he destroys all his new efforts too, distracting himself while they burn by leafing through a book bought at the Strand while in New York. He intended to read this during his stay at the cottage but hasn't managed a single page, just the jacket copy, which says the essays were previously published in *The Nation*, the *New York*

*Review of Books, October,* and the *Times Literary Supplement.* The author bio reads, "A professor at Princeton University, P. J. Barrows lives in New Jersey with her husband and two daughters." *Why,* Pinch wonders, *must they detail her family status? How is that relevant? Is it to flaunt the author's perfected life? Why not print, "Stunning intellectual of renown and she's got a winning spouse who probably runs marathons with his shirt off, an Ivy League lecturer himself—and did we mention their two adorable daughters, both cramming for exams they'll surely ace"?*

*I'm being horrible,* Pinch decides, whacking his thigh in punishment, which causes his dogs to run over and sniff the leg of his corduroys. *She has achieved a far more substantial life than I, and justly so,* Pinch thinks. Barrows had determination and rare talent. He wishes to boast of her to someone. What a muddled sensation: the success of one who didn't love you back.

A metallic clang in the kitchen. He leaps and the dogs bark. Only a frying pan that fell off the drying rack. *Why am I so on edge?* He survived the New York show. He looks to the ceiling, sighs, a shaky exhalation. Harold and Tony pant at him, tongues out.

"Your comments leave much to be desired," he tells them and stands by the window, darkness outside, the kitchen reflected, his eyes narrowing as if to draw a figure into focus: a tall young man in Toronto with wildly colored scarves around his neck, babbling flamboyantly, leading Pinch through underground bars, a squirrel under his bed. Gosh, that was more than twenty years ago!

On the night of Pinch's return to London, he travels directly to Utz, arriving after hours. His dogs bolt into Jing's office, where she is correcting homework. She emerges, a pen in each hand like tiny ski poles. "Do you eat dinner?"

"Pretty much nightly. You want to visit the sandwich bar of doom? I would love to, Jing, but I have my bodyguards to look after." He nods at Harold and Tony.

"I thought you are on holiday."

"I just popped in to do a little research. Actually, there's something I wanted to ask of you. I have to call someone, but don't want to do it myself."

"What I should say?"

"I like that you don't even ask who," he responds, smiling. "Okay, here's the situation. I'm trying to get someone's address, and I don't want him knowing it's me asking." Ever since thinking of Marsden, Pinch has wanted to find him again—their sad meeting at the St. Charles Tavern, when both were in such a desperate state, was the wrong ending. Pinch even wonders if Marsden might concoct a clever way to help him escape this constant worry about the forged painting. At the least, Marsden could be a confidant. But Pinch is picturing the Marsden he once knew, not Marsden as he left him. Anyway, Pinch is too shy to just call and ask for help. He will apologize in a letter.

He tells Jing, "I was looking up things on AltaVista on the staff computer, and it lets you read the white pages from different cities, including Toronto, where this friend of mine lives," he explains to Jing. "The problem is, I want to write, and it shows only his phone number."

She dials it, and covers the mouthpiece, telling Pinch, "I say 'flowers delivery.'"

"But don't give my name!"

While she talks, he hurries down the hall, shooing the dogs toward the staff room. He's so apprehensive these days, as if everything were ready to career out of control. He pulls at his fingers, fighting back an image that keeps intruding: Mallard Dwyer, slapping a scotch tumbler into Pinch's hand.

Minutes later Jing appears, holding a scrap of paper with Marsden's address on the back.

"Jing, you're a genius!"

That night, he takes out Natalie's portable red Olivetti and types a long letter, expressing remorse about the end of their friendship. He revises, striking out passages. He reads it again, crossing out still more. Finally, he is left with the opening and closing salutations. Even there, he's unsure of the tone. He balls up all the attempts and tosses them down the living room carpet for the dogs, which give chase and chew.

After classes at Utz, he visits the staff computer again and finds the phone number of a florist near Marsden's address—he'll bring to life Jing's ruse about that flower delivery. Pinch calls, ordering a modest arrangement to arrive anonymously. Soon a bouquet is presumably in Marsden's home, sowing mystery, which much amuses Pinch. To avoid detection, he waits a few weeks, then phones.

The voice that responds, however, seems not to be Marsden's— the man has a soft, slow delivery.

"Marsden?"

"Who is this?"

"It's Charles Bavinsky. Sorry, I'm phoning for absolutely no good reason. Except that I keep thinking about you recently, and rustled up your number. It's been ages. How are you? Is this a good time? Sorry, Marsden—is it okay that I called?"

"Charles." "So lovely to hear your voice again."

"And yours, Marsden!" he says, eyes welling up. "And yours!" Pinch coughs to disguise his cracking voice; he gives a hearty smoker's hack. "Where's my damn pipe?" He returns shortly and launches into loud chatter, asking for details about life in Toronto.

These days, Marsden works part time at the Art Gallery of Ontario, mostly doing photocopies for powerful people, which is fine, he explains. They know of his past problems and hired him despite all the gaps in his resume. He also volunteers at a Toronto charity for street kids, marching down the nastier alleyways with pamphlets on safe sex, shelters, needle exchanges.

"Isn't that dangerous?"

"You haven't seen me in a while. I'm pretty intimidating," Marsden says, in a voice utterly without threat. For a spell, Marsden explains, he became obsessed with weights, and bulked himself up with other means too. "Lots of supplements, and injections."

"Steroids? Really? Just to get strong?"

"To get beautiful," he replies. "I've been off for ages, but my body doesn't go back to normal."

"But you're doing okay now? In general?"

"Fine, yes. Given what I was up to, and when, it's a miracle that I'm still alive. The dreaded disease has spared me so far."

They talk and talk that evening. Pinch called for help and advice, yet he discloses nothing about his predicament, only asks questions and listens. Marsden is as candid as ever, but not showy anymore. Disturbing details emerge, and he never twists the tale to burnish himself. He feels no shame about failure—he never had that defect.

For a spell, he fell low indeed, even selling himself for a few years to pay for cocaine and amphetamines, prowling business hotels around King Street, downing a double amaretto in the lobby bar before 9 a.m., then heading to the elevators: upstairs for work. But that's the past, he says. "Hey, I was listening to the CBC the other day, and these critics were discussing your father. Apparently he's been discovered again."

"So I hear."

"I tell everyone at work how I was at U of T with Bear Bavinsky's son," he says. "And the rest of your family, Charles? You still see that grandmother in Montreal?"

"Ruth died a few years ago. An unhappy end, I'm afraid, given what happened with my mother."

"What happened with her?" Marsden asks, concerned.

"Gosh, really has been ages since we spoke." Pinch is never sure how to say this. Typically he says Natalie died of a long illness. But he tells the truth this time.

"I remember answering sometimes when she called from London," Marsden says. "I know you two were very close."

Pinch never considered it this way until hearing it. Natalie does accompany him more as years pass—when brushing his teeth at the medicine cabinet mirror, for instance, he sees her expression in his own. Or Natalie standing in his living room, looking at him; she shrugs.

"Did she explain why?" Marsden asks.

"In movies there's always a note. But hardly anyone leaves a note, it turns out. They leave an act." As Pinch speaks, her ceramics around the living room seem to light up. "I hate that you remember me avoiding her calls."

"I remember you talking to her."

"I feel guilty about what happened. Extremely."

"It's hardly ever somebody else. It's something inside the person who does it. I've met people like that."

"Should that be worrying to me in another way? My grandfather attempted suicide; my mother did it." He adds: "With my wild social life, I could walk offstage without the curtain moving, though my afternoon tutorials schedule would be a disaster!"

"Don't joke about things like that."

"I didn't mean it."

"So lovely talking to you, Charles."

"I'm so pleased I called you, Mars. Hey, do you ever pass through London?"

"World travel isn't in the cards, I'm afraid. On my wages, it's month to month."

"Well, if you find a pot of gold, you're welcome to crash on my couch."

"I will definitely consider it," Marsden replies, meaning, I definitely can't.

"Actually, know what? I've got school vacation in a couple of months, and I normally motor off to my dad's cottage in France. But what about this: What about you let me fly you here to London? You'd be helping me—I need your opinion on a few things."

"My opinion isn't worth an intercontinental flight. It's yours for the price of a phone call."

"No, this needs discussing in person. And honestly," he says, chuckling, "aside from my dogs, I've actually got nothing to spend my savings on."

"Except flowers."

"How do you mean?"

"That wasn't you?"

"What wasn't me?"

"Oh, nothing. Someone's been stalking me with flower deliveries. I don't know anybody that nice around here. Probably some creepy old loser."

"Not necessarily," Pinch responds, a trifle defensive. "I'm sure you have plenty of admirers."

"But no dogs, alas. What kind are yours?"

"They're two sons that people mistake for dogs. Come meet them."

"It's a generous offer. But I couldn't accept." As soon as they hang up, Pinch cancels his planned visit to France and resolves to buy his friend a plane ticket.


## 56


When Marsden emerges from Earl's Court Station, Pinch hesitates. His friend has the body of an ex-bouncer now, in a sweatshirt and jogging pants, face jowly, heavy pouches under his eyes. Pinch strides forward, touching Marsden's back in welcome. It's like clapping a stone column.

They're formal at first, both concerned that five days might be excessive. As thanks for the plane ticket, Marsden insists on treating at every meal, which causes Pinch—mindful of his friend's poverty—to divert them to the cheapest eateries, claiming each as a favorite. "It looks a bit greasy but it's *the* best fish 'n' chips in London."

Marsden notes that Pinch sought his opinion on something and wanted to speak face-to-face. But Pinch delays. How can he say it aloud?: *I've destroyed a major work of art by my own father. I've committed fraud. Everyone is going to find out.* He'll come clean to Marsden, but not yet. This visit is too important.

Mostly the two middle-aged men visit art museums—a decorated backdrop before which to restore their bond. Marsden wants to go to *Sensation*, an edgy show at the Royal Academy featuring contemporary British art, among which a frozen head made from the artist's blood, a dead shark mounted behind glass, and child mannequins with mouths like anuses and noses like penises. The boisterous young crowd is giddy and goaded.

"Pretty much all conceptual stuff," Marsden observes.

"Yes, I think that's right. It's not so much about making the pieces. The artist just has the idea. And, as they point out, even the Old Masters had apprentices paint large bits of their pictures."

"Fine, but the Old Masters did *some* bits," Marsden notes, a glimmer of his former contrarian self. "And they could have done the whole picture, time allowing."

"Well, all I know is that the worst British newspapers love denouncing this kind of art, which almost makes me like it."

Marsden stands on the other side of the glass tank, appraising the pickled shark. Peeping into open jaw, he says, "Is this good, enduring work, Charles? Or is it taxidermy?"

"I'm not sure 'enduring' and 'good' are the same thing, are they? As you can tell, I try not to have views on art anymore."

"Used to be all you had."

"You stopped drugs, I quit opinions."

"I still have a few. Including that this show is making me dizzy," Marsden says. "Window shopping at Fortnum and Mason?"

"Yes, the proper antidote."

As they cross Piccadilly, Marsden mentions Barrows, that they're still in touch. "Her husband is a lovely guy. They've got the cutest daughters."

"She's at Princeton, right?" he says, masking his surge of feeling, inquiring as if only mildly curious. "It's excellent when someone really worthy thrives. Don't you think? Feels like vindication."

"She'd love to hear from you."

"Maybe. But more about you, Mars," he says as the Fortnum & Mason doorman admits them to a paradise of marzipan fruit and chocolate pyramids. "Have you ended up happy?"

"Much better than I was, which is sufficient for now." Marsden lists a few goals. "One business idea is pet vacations for people who don't have pets. You'd pay to visit a farm and look after the animals. We'd assign each person a dog or cat or horse for the week. How does that sound?"

The idea lacks any of the bravura of the former Marsden. But this is a new person, and Pinch wishes to befriend him too, if only because they both knew that young man. "Pet vacations—I like it."

Upon departure, Marsden says, "I still don't know what you wanted my opinion on."

"Maybe it was just trickery to get you here." Pinch twinkles, taking out his pipe.

"Funny to see you still puffing that all the time."

Pinch considers the object in his hand, frowns. "I stole this from my father's tobacco box years ago, when visiting him in Larchmont."

"He never noticed?"

"I'm not even sure he's noticed that I smoke!" Worry lurches inside him. Because his friend is leaving? Pinch extends his hand. "Put it there."

Instead, the thick-armed guest embraces his small-shouldered, potbellied host. Shyly Pinch insists on his handshake afterward, and it persists at length, each man wanting an extra minute to express that this trip was important. Finally Marsden hoists his duffel bag, passes the Tube turnstiles, disappears down an escalator.

All the hurried pedestrians appear odd to Pinch, as if everyone in London had stilled these past five days, only to resume action now. On the street he holds a match over his pipe bowl, sucks down. After two drags, he removes the slobbery bit from his mouth, tongue buzzing, fingers yellowed. Crouching over a puddle, he taps out the tobacco, which hits the dirty water with a hiss. A smoke column rises, then is gone. Using all his force, he snaps the pipe in two and drops it in a rubbish bin. To a passerby he says, "I just quit smoking."

A week later he sends a lump of money to Marsden. It was just sitting in his account, doing nothing. What are savings for, if not that? Weeks pass, and he hears nothing. His concern becomes annoyance. Not even an acknowledgment? But a few weeks later, a seven-page letter arrives.

Marsden explains that he was too touched, hadn't known what to do, how to thank such an act.

"Don't thank me. It was a joy to do," Pinch writes back. "It comes with a sole condition. You're not allowed to pay it back. And a second sole condition: I need your help, Mars."

## 57

Worringly, Bear has moved the cottage and shows few signs of leaving. Normally he takes one trip there a year, a few weeks of summer break during which he cavorts and guzzles, rarely venturing into his studio. But he recently broke with his latest wife, and appears to be settling at the French property this winter, talking of staying permanently, even resuming his art there. Any day he might discover what's missing. Pinch can do nothing but wait.

"It's a disaster," he tells Marsden by phone, giving a variation on the truth, claiming that his crime was stealing an original Bear artwork from the cottage, then selling it to help his older sister. It feels too awful to confess that he drunkenly punched one of his father's paintings in spite, later burning it to hide the misdeed. He certainly isn't ready to admit to a forgery. That would mean confessing that he paints, a practice that feels too private, too fragile. Yet perhaps such qualms are immaterial now—Pinch might never again enter that studio. And without time in the mountains, standing before a blank canvas, trying to make something? *What else do I have? Couldn't Dad go anywhere but there?*

"What makes it worse," he tells Marsden, "is there's no phone line at the cottage, which means I can't reach Dad. I have no idea when— or if—he's leaving. Now and then I get him on one of his friends' mobiles. But for the most part, I'm left in this permanent state of fear. I'm only praying he's still half blind."

"Half blind?"

"Dad left his glasses in Florida. The last time we spoke, he still hadn't replaced them, so couldn't work. Not that blindness stops him driving on those mountain roads, which is insane. This whole thing is lunacy. I could see Dad freezing there. *I* know how to manage winter nights in that place. But am I supposed to quit my job and look after him now, his little assistant yet again? I'm not doing it." What's more, a leave of absence from Utz would be a risk. The chain is cutting costs, replacing experienced teachers with cuter, younger staff, which increases student enrollment. Among the latest hires is

Francesca, who hadn't taught a single Italian class before starting at Utz. Initially Pinch disdained the young botanist from Naples, who was immediately at his salary level. But she rose in his estimation by spurning the advances of Salvatore, then delicately telling Jing of her husband's serial betrayals. Ever since, Pinch has been most curious about Francesca. She's reserved, which makes him want to figure her out. In silly fantasies, he imagines taking her to the cottage—*without* Bear present.

"No, you can't be on a string to your father," Marsden concurs. "But why not hire a local to watch him?"

"It's hard to find anyone he'd accept, not least because Dad doesn't speak French."

"Didn't you say there are loads of foreigners around?"

"But how do I know they'll keep me posted? Bear would seduce them in minutes."

"Okay, here's the plan," Marsden says, clearing his throat, building to this. "I go."

"To be Dad's housekeeper? No way. That's way below you."

"My dear, you have no idea what's below me. And I want an adventure."

"Are you certain, Mars?"

Once assured about his friend's wishes, Pinch wires money for the travel and to buy a cell phone so that Marsden may relay regular updates—and so the two friends can plot how to ease Bear out of there. Upon arrival in France, Marsden tests his new Nokia, calling the spymaster in London. After this, Pinch hears nothing for days and grows increasingly frantic. Each time he tries the French mobile, it's the same message: network service unavailable. Late at night he panics about impending catastrophe and becomes exhausted and twitchy. Then, one evening, the display on his home phone lights up. He bursts off the couch, as do his woofing dogs, which leap about his feet, causing

Pinch to trip and fall to his knees. Wincing, he scrambles past the leaping Harold and Tony and grabs the phone.

"Six rings before you pick up? No way to treat your old man!"
Bear says over a hissing connection. "You know what happened
here, Charlie?"

"What?" Pinch responds with alarm.

"I found me a new roommate: this big queer."

"Don't call him a queer," Pinch says, eyes closed with relief.
*Everything's still okay.*

"Care to talk with your queer? He's right beside me."

"Hey, I'm really sorry about that," Pinch tells Marsden. "My father is somewhat out of date."

"Don't apologize! He recognizes an old homo when he sees one.
We're having quite a time here. Your father is really something."

"I know all too well."

"I'm horrified that you never introduced us, Charles. I feel de-
prived. Oh no—he's taking the phone back."

Bear yammers away, talking for two audiences, son and guest
(mainly guest). When the old man returns the phone in order to go
take a piss on the lawn, Marsden affirms that all truly is well. They've
even established a routine. Each night, after Bear's guests stagger to
their cars, the elderly artist—seemingly immune to booze—sets an
appointment with Marsden for the following morning. If they agree
on breakfast at nine, Bear is there at seven, looming over the leather
couch where Marsden sleeps, using the fireplace as his pretext for the
wake up. (Bear can't crouch to stack logs in the hearth because of his
bad knees.) Marsden arranges the wood, sparks a match—then is
summoned to drink coffee and hear the old man's ribald tales. For a
break each day, Marsden has assigned himself the task of hacking
a walkway up the hillside. With the weather warming, he'd like
Bear to get himself moving again—part of a strategy to eventually

persuade him to leave this property. But to reach the hiking paths in the forest, one must clamber up a hillside, which is beyond Bear. Hence, Marsden's staircase.

"Honestly, Charles, I'm enjoying myself. Your father has insane stories."

"He's in what I call his 'anecdotage.'"

"You say that, but Bear isn't exactly gaga. He needs his naps, yes. But he still spends a lot of time, ahem, on the job, so to speak."

"What's that mean?"

"Diddling a lady down the road, and I know this for a fact."

"The Dutchwoman?"

"God, no—she's ancient history. They're feuding actually."

"Yes, Dad specializes in feuds. You'll find half the locals won't say *bonjour* if you're linked to Monsieur Bavinsky. Who's the current lady friend?"

"Lady friends, plural. A German woman in Prades. And a French widow who keeps bringing yogurts. I'm telling you, Charles, it's a whorehouse up here. I keep asking myself how you became such a slouch in the love department with a father like him."

"A question I've asked myself more than once, Mars."

Bear's current nemesis seems to be the Catalan people as a whole. He has deemed them loutish and pigheaded after clashing with a local couple who sneaked onto the property to collect wild morels. Marsden has been commanded to procure donkeys to guard the land and, ideally, to attack poachers.

"I pointed out there's no such thing as a guard donkey. Then the Catalan couple turned up again, and Bear marched out there himself—remember, he's almost blind without his glasses, so I'm panicking that he's about to fall down the ravine. I run after, grabbing the back of his shirt while he's barking in broken French at these poor people with their mushroom baskets. They're talking about '*notre terroir*' or something, but your father can't understand. He's shouting: '*Parlez français! Parlez français!*' Meanwhile, the Catalan guy is going, '*Monsieur, je vous parle en français!*'"

"At which point you released the guard donkeys, which ran down the ravine and bit the marauding Catalans?"

"No, both sides just kept screaming. Which prompts an observation: Your father, who can't string together a sentence in French or Spanish or Catalan, gabs with everybody around here, while you—man of a million languages—have no interest in speaking to anyone!"

"*All* I want is to talk to people. I just have to find the right ones. And how will I know what language they speak? I must be prepared!"

Both laugh, neither certain if that was a joke.

What Pinch refrains from telling his friend is how trying life has become in London without the possibility of escapes to the cottage. Each day he feels smaller. "But no sign of Dad noticing anything missing from his studio?"

"That I know of? Nothing."

Another week passes, Pinch imprisoned at his flat, his job. This isn't sustainable.

When his home phone rings late at night, he rushes past his yapping dogs and picks up. It's Marsden, whispering, having stepped out of the cottage, ostensibly to get the firewood for tomorrow but actually zigzagging around the dark lawn for a cell-phone signal. "I'm such an idiot," he whispers.

"Why are you an idiot?" Pinch asks, heart pounding. "What happened?"

It's the staircase in the hillside. What began as whimsy, Marsden explains, drifted into obsession. He's been spending hours out there digging away, his palms a road map of dirt and blisters, nails cracked, joints creaking. Often, after toiling until dusk, he is scotched by a giant boulder, drops to the turf in frustration, hands on the soggy moss.

As if repudiating a lifetime of half-finished pursuits, Marsden has decided he *is* going to complete this.

Pinch interrupts, "But what happened? Is there a problem?"

"I kept leaving Bear alone during the day. He got bored. I came home tonight and found him wearing glasses. One of his lady friends took him to Prades to buy replacements."

"Which means he'll be going back in the studio now," Pinch says grimly.

"Worse. He's already started an inventory of his paintings."

"And he knows?"

"He's only just started. But I thought you should be warned. Charles, I'm so sorry. I messed this up."

"You couldn't be expected to watch him all day long, Mars. And he doesn't know *yet*. Maybe he'll get distracted and move onto something else."

"Or you could just tell him. Maybe you should? Oh," he adds, "oh shit."

"What? Mars?"

A muffled exchange follows.

"Mars?"

A deeper voice comes onto the line. "That you, kiddo?"

"Dad."

"What's the secret chatter about?"

"We were just catching up."

"I want to see you, son. Call in sick tomorrow."

"Come there *tomorrow*? Are you serious?"

"Fly out. Get a rental car. Get up here."

"Why, Dad? You have to tell me."

"Who says there's a reason?"

"Could you put Marsden back on?"

No answer.

"Hello, Dad? . . . Mars? . . . Anyone there?"

But the line is dead.

## 58

Pinch pulls over on a narrow French country road, delaying the last mile around the mountain, perhaps the final time he travels the route. He fumbles to open a bottle of water, takes a little sip, hardly able to swallow.

Minutes later he is there: his father walking from the cottage, Pinch hastening out of the car. Bear grips his shoulder, leans in. "Got a surprise for you."

When Marsden joins them, Bear leads everyone inside for a drink. Walking in his father's wake, Pinch stares hard at Marsden, mouthing, "He knows?"

Eyes wide, Marsden shrugs.

The two friends haven't spoken since that interrupted call—Bear has kept the cell phone ever since. In the kitchen he pours three hefty wallops of calvados into pottery mugs, plonking these on the long table. The old man dominates the conversation, even when instructing Marsden to recount his herculean labors on the hillside. Pinch sustains a polite front, toes curled. He needs to know why Bear rushed him here. Yet he sits there, nodding, and would listen for days if it'd delay his expulsion from this place, which feels so much his, invaded by their voices.

Realistically, he sees no way out. Even if Bear doesn't know yet, Pinch can't leave Marsden here indefinitely, spying on an old painter. Pinch envisages the revulsion on his father's face and looks down at the thighs of his corduroys.

Bear keeps topping off everyone's drinks. "The fire roaring, the booze flowing—what else could a guy want, save a few nice gals, hey? Though I can't speak for all of us in that department, am I right?" He shoves Marsden's thick shoulder, chuckling.

Smiling back, Marsden unlaces his boots and massages his sore feet, casting a quick nod to Pinch: Maybe everything is okay.

"I had this friend once," Bear says. "Helluva guy; tough as nails. Worked nights for the police down in Boca Raton. Interesting line of work. There's a real trick to it, he told me."

"Trick to what?" Pinch asks tensely.

"You never, ever accuse the guy," Bear replies. "He'll deny, flat out. And then you're screwed. Because he'll stick to that line, out of pride, if nothing more. Now he's in a jam, and so are you. The way to do it, my buddy told me, is don't ask the guy *if* he's guilty. You ask why. Because anything a man does, it can be explained. Give him a chance to make sense of it all, by his own logic."

They fall silent, the buzz of a fly.

Bear lights his pipe, the cloud thickening around his head.

He reaches for the calvados, pours the dregs into Marsden's glass. "That painting," he says.

"What painting?" Marsden responds.

"The one you took. Tell us what you liked about it."

Marsden sits upright, astonished. "That I took?"

"What I can't figure," Bear continues, "is how you got my studio keys. More impressive is that you whisked it away. Shows what a sucker I am without these specs on me." He takes off his glasses, places them on the table. "Wouldn't hurt to know who you gave it to. I'm assuming you sold it already. And you got your reasons. You needed dough. Or just like shiny objects. Hey, nobody's hanging you from the ceiling. Let's just hear what happened."

Marsden says, "I didn't take anything."

"You heard what I said before," Bear insists. "I'm looking to understand."

"Dad, he didn't."

"Go through my stuff, if you don't believe me," Marsden says.

"Of course you didn't leave it in your stuff! What do you take me for?"

"Dad, are you positive something's missing?" Pinch asks. "You know that for sure?"

Bear's chair legs screech back. He stands, pointing at Marsden, a forefinger so arthritic as to resemble a sideways twig. "You had your chance. Call the cops, Charlie."

"What are you talking about? No, Dad."

"You can tell them in French, goddammit. Why do you think I brought you here? Get the police, and I'll forget it was you who sent this rat my way."

Pinch stares into his sticky glass of liquor; he views the wood-plank floor. Somehow, he can't find the words for a confession. "Dad, *I* have keys." It's all he can say. Then: "That painting has been gone for ages. I needed help at the time." He will never mention Birdie—Pinch vows that to himself.

"Got to be kidding," Bear says, wincing as if force-fed a battery. "*You?*" He rests his pipe on the kitchen table.

"Bear?" Marsden interjects. "You said things can be explained if you hear a person's reasons. And he had reasons."

Bear turns vehemently to Marsden, as if his son weren't here. "Do you have any idea what that painting *was*? It was the guy's mother. His mother, Natalie, who took her own fucking life—who put a goddamn bag over her head!"

"I know what happened to her, Dad!"

"And he profits off *that*?"

"I didn't profit off it. This wasn't for money."

"Not for money? Oh, sure." Bear rears around, takes a step toward Pinch, jabbing his forefinger almost into his son's eyes, which are averted. "My whole life, I've been making something of my time on this earth. And you'd wipe that out." He shakes his head, bitterly disappointed, addressing Marsden. "He doesn't say a word to defend himself. Silence. Dead silence." Suffering the outrage afresh, Bear bellows at Pinch. "How *dare* you?"

Pinch's legs carry him down the driveway toward his car. His father bundles out of the cottage, Marsden alongside, a hand at Bear's elbow, ready to intervene. At the car door, Bear clutches his son's lapel, digs in his pockets. "Give 'em over!"

Pinch takes out a key ring, which Bear snatches away. "In *my* studio! Snooping around! Stealing from *me*! Who did you think you're dealing with? Who are you to me?"

Marsden, pulling the old man back, says: "Come on. You're upset. But don't go to extremes. You two are close. Don't wreck that."

"Close?" Bear says, shaking off the word.

"It's true," Marsden asserts. "It is."

"Not fucking 'close.' He's just the one I picked. Of all my kids, I picked that one."

"For good reason," Marsden says.

"Sure," Bear concurs. "Ever wonder *why*, Charlie? Look at me. You can't look at me?"

"I know why."

"Let's hear it."

"Same reason you chose my mother. Because nobody was as weak as us."

"Untrue, Charlie. Untrue. Not because you're weakest. Not for that. Reason I chose you, Charlie, is you were the genuine number. You know what I mean?"

Pinch shakes his head.

"Natty knew it too," Bear continues. "That Charlie's got something." He mimes the act of drawing.

Marsden asks what they're talking about. But it's father and son now, nobody else present.

"Know how many letters Natty wrote me? How talented you were, how you were really something else? Typical mother stuff, I figured. Then you bring that picture to Larchmont."

"Which you barely looked at."

"I saw it all right. When you and Carol were out, I go in the guest room, open your suitcase—almost the first day you were with us. I take out that rolled-up canvas, spread it out. And, well well well!" he says, fixing on Pinch. "Natty wasn't wrong. You had plenty to learn technically. But shit—you had something, Charlie: a style. Nobody can teach that. Gave me chills." He points. "You had something, Charlie boy. Something special. And *that* is why I chose you."

Perplexed, Pinch grabs his sideburns. "You told me I was terrible."

"Let's be clear, son. I said you'd never be an artist. And take a gander at yourself. Was I wrong? You honestly think I'd be tagging along to gallery openings of my own kid? Listen to me. Hear this. *You* work for *me*. Get it? You always worked for me." He claps his hand on Pinch's bicep, pinching hard. "And you dare steal? Get this: *I* win. You hear? I fucking win." He taps his pipe onto the grass, a tiny heap of smoldering tobacco, stamps it out. "Call the police, Marsden."

"I'm not calling anyone."

"Hell you aren't."

"I'm bigger than you. Forget it."

Bear lunges at Marsden, who easily holds him back. The old man loses his balance, then pushes back, shouting as he walks up the grass: "Off my property! Both of you! Now!"

"He's had too much to drink," Marsden tells Pinch. "Get out of here for a while. This'll be okay. We'll fix this. Just go for a while."

Pinch finds himself driving, heartbeat thudding in his ears, leaning into a bend in the road, sick drunk, out of sync, foot on the clutch, gearing down. At the nearest town, he jerks to a halt in a supermarket parking lot. On the steering wheel, his fingers tremble. He hears his own breaths and Bear's voice, shards of that man lodged in him.

## 59

Bear, who left his glasses back in the cottage, is stumbling toward the woods, barely staying upright on the uneven turf.

"Where are you going?" Marsden calls after him once Pinch has driven away. "Bear?"

"Where I goddamn please." His shoe hits a stump and he falls to his knees, swearing. Marsden hastens over, takes the old man's arm.

"Get offa me!" Bear snaps. "In my studio? Him? Looking at *my* work?"

It's not only Pinch who has lost control of this situation, Marsden realizes. Because Bear cares about this son. At the very least, he needs him. But he's gone too far. Marsden refuses to let it end like this—his own father rejected him years before and remains trapped by pride, unable to find a way back.

"Let's just take a breath here," Marsden says, helping the man to his feet. "Charles made a *huge* mistake. I'm not disputing that. He shouldn't have gone in there, or sold anything. But he regrets it, Bear. And he's your son."

Bear grunts, shakes his head, walking onward into the woods, each footfall unsteady. Marsden hastens along, a step behind. "This isn't safe, Bear. There's nobody to help you that way."

But Bear trudges on, grasping for the rope handrail of Marsden's stairs, pulling himself up, one step at a time. Marsden stabilizes the old man until they reach the top, where the hiking paths begin. Bear takes the ascending trail, past a disused mine and mouths of caves. Beams of sunlight thrust through swaying leaves, sprinkling coins over the undergrowth. "Get," he says breathlessly, "get the hell, the hell away from me!"

"We need to go back to the cottage. I'm serious. Bear, it was only *one* painting."

"You don't have a clue. 'Just one painting'? That's years of my life. Years!" Bear leans against a tree trunk, squinting, pained. "You don't have a clue. But my son, on the other hand? He, of all people—he knows. For him to . . ."

Marsden takes a half step forward, reaches for the old man's shoulder. He isn't shucked off. "Don't let this get out of control, Bear. You can't backtrack from a huge blowup."

"You're saying it's my fault?" He shoves off Marsden's hand. "What has Charlie even amounted to? Nothing. And he never will. What's he even do? Translating menus or something?"

"He's a language teacher," Marsden says, suppressing his anger.

"Oh, well, in that case! The kid is really leaving his mark!"

Marsden grabs Bear's wrist. The old man tries to pull free. "I've heard you telling every visitor here how your studio is some holy sanctum," Marsden says. "You fucking liar. You haven't done a minute of work the whole time I've been here!"

Bear struggles to get free, spittle bubbling on his lips, frothy dots hanging off his beard. "You-you-you—"

"Do you even *know* what art looks like anymore? That's why you don't let them sell your stuff. Because you're a mediocrity soon to be forgotten. You won? Really? Seriously?"

"I'll break you in two!"

Bear's threat—its absurdity—deflates Marsden. Abruptly, he sees this scene: a half-blind painter, traduced by his dearest son, bullied. While Marsden was following after Bear, watching that he didn't fall, the old man was just trying to get away—he was afraid, his ranting the last resort of a wounded animal. Marsden releases Bear's wrist. The old man falls onto his backside in the muck, ribs rising and falling, eyes hunted.

"I'm sorry," Marsden mutters, raising his palms in surrender.

Bear sits there, shaking.

"We need to cool down. Both of us." Marsden turns, exhaling slowly, walking a few steps to gaze over the path's edge, through trees that sink into the valley. The cottage must be straight below. He gives a tiny shake of his head, sighing in disappointment at himself. He hears a strange noise. "What?" he asks, spinning around. "What, Bear?"

The old man is on all fours, coughing, trying to lift his head. "The matter."

"What is?" Marsden drops to a crouch, a hand on Bear's back.

The old man stares, terror flickering in clouded eyes. "I'm not!" he wheezes. "Not done yet!" He fixes on Marsden, grips the younger man's sweater.

"Bear, you're okay," Marsden says, hiding his fright, for something *is* amiss. "Let's just rest. We pushed this too far."

Bear reclines on his side. His jaw closes, opens, like a beached fish. His eyes are fading.

"Bear?" In panic Marsden rolls the man onto his back, rests his ear to Bear's mouth. No warm exhalations; nothing. "Bear? Bear? Bear!"

Marsden learned CPR years before but struggles to recall the rules, seeing only scenes from television melodrama. He locks his elbows, attempts a few chest compressions. He pinches the old man's nostrils, blows into his mouth. In desperation he jams down harder on Bear's chest, causing a sinister crack—but a flicker of the eyelids, the focus returning momentarily to his gaze.

"That did something!" Marsden blurts.

He resumes more vigorously, checking between sets whether

Bear's breathing has resumed, studying the man's thin dry lips—a mouth that charmed sitters and enraged Pablo Picasso, that illuminated daughters and destroyed sons. Marsden blows a few more breaths, does more chest compressions; the old man blinks again. Yet whenever Marsden pauses for too long, life seeps from Bear's eyes. Marsden shouts into the forest for help.

What if he runs for help right now? He can't take the path they came by—it'd be ten minutes of descent, then finding the cell phone in the cottage, waiting for an ambulance, pointing the paramedics back here. No, he must take the direct route, forging right down the mountainside—he'll reach the cottage in around a minute, phone for help, sprint right back up, resume CPR. That could work. And Marsden *cannot* let his friend lose his father after that last exchange. They can still mend this.

He notes a gap between two pine trees, does a final set of compressions—again, the old man animates slightly. Marsden leaps up, dizzy for an instant, and he bolts toward the branches, vaulting over the path's edge.

Too late, he sees.

A ski-slope gradient plunges beneath, trees hurtling at him. He turns his shoulder, slams into a trunk, bangs past it, grabbing for anything, hands spiked by pine needles. He is picking up speed, grasping for any low foliage—and he snags a branch. The canopy swings overhead. He is hyperventilating, needing to vomit. Treetops drop away below him. There's no way back from this.

The tighter he grips, the weaker his sweaty grasp seems, his legs kicking for any solid earth. Whenever a boot tip hits mud, it immediately gives way. The branch he clutches quavers with his body, drops of melted snow pelting down.

*I'm about to die.*

He kicks out again, seeking anything firm. One boot tip bashes near-vertical mud. But if he lets go of the branch and tries to scramble upward, will his footing give way? The only chance is to launch in the direction of that foothold and pray that momentum flings his other leg forward, ramming it into the incline. If he hits a root, even a wet leaf, he'll slide down, somersaulting backward, spine snapping, skull cracked, lying in the cold wet forest, half-alive, devoured. *Erase that image!* But he can't: birds feasting on his brain. He plots and replots, palms losing grip. *Go!*

But he can't.

*Just go!*

His shin bangs into a rock, fingers claw the hillside dirt, and his thighs spasm. And somehow, he's there: on his knees, on flat earth—precisely where he was three minutes earlier.

Trembling, he crawls over to Bear, puffs another few lungfuls into the man, compresses his chest. Again life flickers in the painter's eyes. Marsden wipes the sweat from his face and rests his hand against Bear's hip, taking a shivery breath—whereupon he feels something under his fingers. A plastic antenna juts from the jeans pocket. It's the cell phone. Bear had it this whole time. That must've been why he was running away: to call the police on Charles.

Marsden battles to awaken the digital screen. Finally, the Nokia theme. And a signal. Frantically he opens the contact list, which contains only two entries: "Charles" and "Police."

His brain stalls, staring at gray digits.

Bear gasps, eyes desperate. His knobbly hand—which moved colors, which moved people—clutches a leaf.

Marsden looks at the cell phone again, and he stands. He glances down at the man, then back at the screen. "No," he mutters—then underhands the Nokia over the path's edge, into the void. The phone flips; it's lost from sight. After a few seconds, a distant *pop.*

"Enough," Marsden says, crouching beside Bear Bavinsky, his

knuckles resting soothingly against the painter's bearded cheek. "Enough of this life. It's enough."

## 60

Pinch sits in the supermarket parking lot, fogged from alcohol still, considering driving directly to the airport. But he must face what's happening. He starts the engine, turns back toward the cottage. When he arrives, he waits in the parked vehicle, braced for his father's wrath.

Yet he hears nothing. He gets out and perceives movement at the edge of the forest: Marsden, covered in mud, walking closer.

"Hey!" Pinch calls out. "Where's Dad?"

Marsden shakes his head, saying something about Bear collapsing, that nothing worked. Pinch can't make sense of it. "But where is Dad right now?" Marsden's response bounces off him. Pinch stands there, uncomprehending, saying, "We need to get help." He hunts in the cottage for the cell phone. "Have you seen it?"

"I don't know. Charles, honestly—it's too late."

A neighbor calls the emergency number on their behalf. When the paramedics arrive, a flurry of French conversation ensues, an ambulance in the driveway, a few nosy locals peeking around. Loud voices sound from up the path, men carrying down the body. Pinch glimpses his father on a stretcher—the last sighting. Marsden drives Pinch into town to deal with paperwork. Afterward, they hardly speak, hardly eat. Nothing seems appropriate.

Two days later, Marsden leaves. It's Pinch alone on the property. He awakens under his father's duvet, looks around the stone walls of the cottage, imagining this place before electricity came, back when the late Cecil Ditchley lived here, forced to walk an hour to the village for bread and meat, reading by candlelight, throwing pots on his kick wheel.

Pinch finds his father's glasses, still on the kitchen table, and throws them away. He unlocks Bear's studio, free to do so now, and surveys a cityscape of old brushes, its cemetery of mangled paint tubes. Dad, in his inventory, turned around every canvas—thighs, shoulders, throats. In the end, what did Bear think of all these paintings?

Pinch locks up and walks toward the woods, taking Marsden's stairs up the hillside, following the same muddy path where his father died. He steps over seedpods, dried pine needles, and plucks early wildflower buds, tucking each specimen into a piece of folded paper. A leaf floats down from a tree; it floats back up. "Lepidopterist" is the word that comes to Pinch—not "butterfly" or "butterfly collector," nor even an idea of the insect, just the word. *As that butterfly adapted to resemble a leaf,* he thinks, *so I adapted to resemble a language teacher.*

Nobody could find the mysteriously vanished mobile, so Pinch treks down to the village phone box to place calls—first to Birdie, so she may inform the rest of the family. Next, Connor Thomas, who agrees to write and circulate a news release whose purpose is to protect the Bavinsky clan from fact-checking reporters. Unfortunately, Connor fails to list all surviving offspring, causing the obituaries to cite Pinch as the only child. Bear's will appears to have read the same bulletin, for the entire estate goes to Pinch alone.

He learns this shortly before the memorial service in Key Biscayne and informs only Birdie. She—who arranged the event to unite Dad's children for the first time—advises Pinch to play dumb. Telling everyone risks souring the memorial. A middle-aged schlub approaches. "This is your brother Jeff, from Idaho," she tells Pinch. Jeff shakes hands, taking a name tag and a copy of the commemorative booklet, full of old photos of members of the Bear Bavinsky clan.

In total, Dad fathered seventeen children, it transpires, many of them in attendance along with spouses and kids of their own. Pinch looks along the buffet table; nearly every stranger is a blood relative. "Holy mackerel!" someone exclaims. "I got a nephew called Hannibal." More uncomfortable facts emerge too. Several of Bear's families overlapped, including a few wives. Three children have become painters (none with success), one is a struggling sculptor in Mexico, another describes herself as "a weaver and astrologer." Aside from Birdie, the only siblings whom Pinch has previously met are Widgeon and Owen. Widge never attempted to become Dad, but she did try to wed facsimiles, a series of shady charmers, which leads Pinch to wonder about her current hubby, a small-business owner who even resembles a younger Bear. As for Owen, he was expelled from medical school decades back and is still living off the wealth of his aged mother, Carol, while working on "a machine to cure diseases" that Widge is convinced will earn her brother a Nobel. Among Owen's many boorish traits is that he ogles every female in attendance yet refuses to speak with any.

In various guests Pinch discerns physical features of Bear. Several are of mixed races and some speak no English, which prompts Pinch to hasten over and interpret. During the service, siblings offer remembrances, most of which follow a pattern: slightly funny, slightly awful, plucky smile, throwaway conclusion: "But hey—that was Dad, right?"

To everyone who asks, Pinch diminishes his role in Bear's life. Yes, I sometimes had his phone number, but not always. Yes, I visited the French cottage, but it's hardly a villa. Bit of a dump: freezing, full of bugs, miles from anything. His relatives resent him, and they're not wrong to do so. For Pinch *does* consider his link to Dad more significant than theirs. He flashes to that final conversation with Bear. *Dad chose me.* Pinch's stomach drops. And his gaze falls too, fixed on the floor, all these strangers' shoes. *Dad picked me.* Queasily, he glances up, as if everyone could hear these thoughts.

"To speak frankly, Charles, I cannot understand why you cremated the body without consulting anyone. I do not get how that was okay."

"Sorry, Ivor. I didn't mean to upset anyone. I had to make a decision in the moment, and I was overwhelmed."

"But sprinkling Bear's ashes in France, without even checking what I thought?"

"Or what *I* thought?"

"Yeah, not cool, man. Not cool."

That night, Pinch and Birdie meet at the hotel, escaping their siblings for a room-service dinner of roast chicken and buttered spinach. "The thing is, a nicer person, an easier person, would never have painted like that," Pinch argues.

Birdie grimaces. "What bull! I know this is supposed to be a mourning period, Charlie, but I am going to speak ill of Dad."

"Why change the habit of a lifetime?" he jokes.

"You know I only bad-mouth him to you, right?"

"I know," he assures her. "I know you loved him."

"I was so busy trying to win an argument with Daddy that I hardly even think I met him. What pisses me off is I can't help smiling sometimes when I think of him, goddamn it! Mostly stuff from when I was little. He loved us when we were cute, right? Not so much when we developed opinions."

"Luckily that never happened in your case."

She snorts with laughter.

"There's this thing my mother always said about Dad," Pinch tells her. "Imagine if your neighbor was Leonardo da Vinci, okay? Only, he's an absolute pain in the neck. Complaining about noise, about the smell of your food, writing complaint letters that he slides under your door. He's awful every time you see him, whether you're sick, with a broken leg—doesn't matter. A nasty piece of work. But if you somehow knew what he was going to contribute to the world, how he treated you would seem minor. You wouldn't even mind. It's irrelevant."

"Wait, wait. Are you *seriously* comparing Daddy to Leonardo da Vinci?"

"Of course not; there's no equating artists. But Bear was significant in his way. The bad behavior only matters as art history now."

"Even if a man's important," she argues, "he doesn't get to live by different rules."

"Isn't society based on that premise?"

"Well, then I don't like society. And I didn't even like this thing today—not that a memorial is for liking. But I keep wondering what it was even for. Certainly not closure. And I arranged the damn thing!"

"The purpose was to see you again, Bird," he says. "Speaking of which, we need a toast. What do you say?" He raids the minibar, returning with a miniature bottle of bubbly.

As her plastic cup froths over, she sips fast and raises it. "To the worst best artist I ever knew," she says. "And to the son who takes over."

"I'm not taking over," he scoffs.

"Oh, you've taken over all right," she retorts, twinkling. "The question is, Mr. Bavinsky: What becomes of you now?"

# 1998

## 61

*Art in America* magazine runs an appreciation on Bear's life and career. The article, by Connor, is written abominably in Pinch's view, and rises to its preachy climax in the conclusion:

> When meeting him a few years ago, Bavinsky spoke to me of surviving the talons of Clement Greenberg, who mythically accused him of being a reactionary. Later, Bavinsky even overcame the embrace of *Life* magazine, whose photo editor published an image of a naked sitter. Gee whiz, shocking. Well, shocking for 1948.
>
> Throughout, Bavinsky painted "those meaty miracles," as collector Mishmish Shapiro dubbed them in a BBC documentary on her phantasmagoric life. Even today, viewing Bavinsky behemoths such as *Shoulder III* (1954) is to ask oneself: By what alchemy can an artist paint a *part* of the body and depict *more than the whole*? Spread your eyes over 1961's *Thigh and Hip XII* (*pictured, above right*). No feeling person can remain tearless when this painting is met with live. I use the word "live" advisedly, because the body almost literally moves off the canvas,

whose materiality is stripped more bare, one swears, than the unclothed model herself.

It is not only because of his unique facture that discussions of "a Bavinsky" envelop such auratic resonance, referencing both pictorial empathy and a depth of portraiture achieved by few during our current century. Bavinsky bypassed the tentacles of Pop Art and Op Art, Conceptualism, Fluxus, and Minimalism, and even bludgeoned away our fin de siècle anxiety, driving on through to the other side, untouched by the hype wafting from the coruscating distant shores of the so-called Art World. He was what only the greats have the courage to be: yourself.

As the marketplace grew more all-comprising, never did he fall into the maw of mammon. The only Bavinskys to sell in years have been those on the secondary market, notwithstanding demand, which has turned from lukewarm to scalding since his untimely passing. Taking advantage of these saunalike conditions, a private deal for *Hands IX* (1952) just netted almost a half-million dollars for a noted Nebraska collector, sources close to the Petros Gallery say. Representatives of Bavinsky's onetime dealer declined to comment on the record. But at the time of his death, Eva Petros issued a statement describing the artist as "an epoch in himself."

Well said. For Bavinsky never wasted time opposing frivolity in The Culture. His was the patience of ages. The road that he sailed renews every cynic's faith in authenticity, and in beauty, however we choose to define that evading quarry.

The screaming irony, of course, is that the so-called Art World is today thirsting to know what Bavinsky was fevering at during those decades in the wilderness. And, yes, the question arises—the wrong question, but a question of our times: Just how much will those paintings be worth?

A photocopy of this article circulates among the Bavinsky children, with the big-money sale by a Nebraska collector highlighted in yellow. Siblings keep writing to Pinch, saying Dad erred by leaving everything to one son who doesn't even have kids of his own to support. You need to share, buddy! To pacify them, he promises to hear everyone's views. Some want the paintings themselves; others insist the artworks be displayed in museums, as per their father's wishes; several don't care and just want money. Complicating matters, none understands the market or art institutions.

"Can't you put them up for auction? Have museums buy them, and we all make out good."

"Museums *can* buy at auction," Pinch answers. "But mostly it's private buyers. And you're subject to whoever bids highest. Which isn't necessarily the museum of your choice."

"So we sell private to the museums we like; the top ones."

"But they have to want to buy. And you're reliant on dealers who have priorities of their own."

"Donate them?"

"What you're perhaps imagining is that I'd hand the paintings over, and they'd go up on the walls of MoMA or wherever. But most of what major museums have is in storage. The likely outcome is I'd give away the paintings, and they'd end up in crates. We have a lot to think about."

"How come you keep saying 'we'?"

"Because I want to include all of us in this."

"Then tell *us* what paintings you got! I still don't know, man. What's to stop you selling on the down-low and never telling nobody?"

"That's the last thing I'd do. I'm just asking for a bit of patience. Lots of people are involved here."

"Lots of people are getting old and dying with jack shit! Is that what Pops intended? Let's fuckin' sell, and split it, bro!"

What Pinch fails to mention is that he has already approached a few museum directors, but nobody will consent to a restricted donation—not for an artist like Bavinsky, who would constitute a decent addition but is hardly the megastar to boost attendance figures. Moreover, everyone is wary about so many disgruntled Bavinsky children. Who wants to accept midmarket artworks, when they could all end up in court?

Most nights upon Pinch's return from Utz, his answering machine light blinks with messages from relatives. "Charles, an update on your plans. Call me back."

But Pinch doesn't know his plans, with the inheritance or anything. He keeps circling around his final exchange with Bear, when Dad implied that Pinch himself could've been a serious painter. That career is beyond him now—the gatekeepers of art are hardly yearning for a schoolteacher in his late forties with little charisma, less hair, not a single show to his name! He tries to laugh, but his spirits plunge—this life has hardly been his own.

There is a flip side, however. During his Tube ride to work many mornings, ruminating over what in hell to do with his father's art, Pinch clenches his eyes shut and sheepishly remembers something. *Bear Bavinsky liked how I paint.* He imagines compositions for his next trip to France, and ponders inviting someone to the studio. When she views his paintings, he'll consider the side of her face, anticipating her response. *Let her like it.*

It's his Tube stop. He leaps to his feet, beaming just to imagine.

## 62

Students stream from her classroom, chatting loudly, calling farewells back to Francesca. In the hallway Pinch stands aside, nodding greetings to a few familiar ex-pupils. When they have scattered, he approaches her classroom, glancing around to ensure he is alone. He takes a deep breath and raises his hand to knock—just as Francesca emerges.

*"Che colpo!"* she exclaims, hand on her chest, and tucks back her hair, long and black in springy curls, her round face broadening when she smiles, causing him to do the same. Francesca, who is twenty-nine, finds herself in a peculiar position in London. She left Italy in frustration with the lack of opportunities and the incivility, but is now employed not merely to teach the Italian language but to embody British fantasies about a carefree nation she never knew. In private, she is cutting about the follies of Utz, which allows Pinch to be the same. They've grown friendly, perhaps even fond of each other, especially since Salvatore quit.

Everyone assumed that Pinch would take over as the Italian department chief. But the promotion went to Francesca. Briefly, this stung. But he accepted her suitability: bright, popular, organized. Also, Pinch hasn't stepped foot in Italy since his teens (though he sometimes claims otherwise to students). His sense of modern Italy derives from reading *La Repubblica* most days, which enables him to speak journalese about bribery scandals in Milan or the burlesque of Berlusconi, though he remains prone to comically outdated slang, which entertains Francesca immensely.

*"Scusa, perdonami,"* he responds for having startled Francesca, and touches her arm in apology, amazed that he's doing so. Pinch commands himself to channel Dad: chin up, a wink. For weeks he has wanted to make an advance. Alone at Bear's cottage, dealing with the French bureaucratic consequences of death, Pinch contemplated her daily, seeing himself driving Francesca around the area, explaining the local language groups, showing her the market, providing tasting boards of local cheeses, matching them with local

wines ("Of which I know a tad too much," he joked on his own in the car). When walking into the woods, he wondered whether, as a botanist, she could give a proper tour of his land. *She'll stay in the cottage, and I'll take the studio. Unless. Unless.*

But each morning back at home in London, the bathroom mirror has dissuaded him, a reminder that he's so much older than she, chubby, bald, frumpy. So today, he forwent his reflection, which explains the mussed hair and bad shave. The pretext for standing in her classroom door this evening is a long-standing promise. Francesca is moving into a larger office—that of the departed Salvatore. Pinch pledged to help her move her furniture, and he has kidded about lifting dumbbells to prepare. She keeps demurring, worrying that it'd be too heavy. Perhaps the janitor should do it?

"I will not be deterred, Fra!" he tells her now, and marches toward her old office, where he stands before the bookcase, estimating dimensions with his arms.

"We should take down the books first, no?" she notes.

Grinningly, Pinch waves this away—he's all bravado tonight, not least because of something amusing he'll show her: a dried lump of paper in his pocket. At the cottage he picked wildflower buds to show her, folding them into a sketchbook page on which he jotted questions as a conversation-starter. Once home, he stupidly laundered those trousers, flowers and all! He'll show her the lumpen result, adding, as if in passing, "You have to come see the place yourself. It's amazing. What do you think?" For now he smirks at her bookcase. "Not too hard for a tough guy like me!" He rolls up his sleeves, jokingly flexes an aging bicep.

"Don't hurt yourself, Mr. Schwarzenegger," she says, grinning, taking a step closer.

He meets her gaze. Switching to English, he says, "I've been busting to do this," and leans in to kiss her.

"*Oddio!*" she cries, recoiling as if he were contagious. She hooks the thick curls behind her ear, unable to look at him, adjusting a framed picture of a man on one of the shelves. "I'm sorry, Charles. I'm engaged."

"What? Oh, you completely misunderstood," he insists ridiculously, throat flushing crimson. "I was reaching past you to take down some of the dictionaries. After all, you're far too tall for me to kiss—I couldn't reach, even if I wanted to!"

"Don't worry about it."

"I wasn't worrying. Just as point of fact." He gives a nervous cough. "I'm here to move furniture."

"Forget that, Charles. The janitor will do it. Really. Thank you, though." She fills a Bankers Box with papers as a way to conclude the excruciating exchange.

"Isn't even heavy," he says, legs apart, grasping one side of the bookcase, then the other. As if to tighten his grip, he shifts about, unsure how to give up.

"Charles, it's much too heavy with the books still in. I'm not joking."

"Oh, it's not even full!" He tries again, vein bulging in his forehead. "I'm going to get this." He holds his breath, straining, grunting, then slaps both hands underneath a shelf for leverage.

"That's not stable!"

But he is lifting it; he's managing—until the shelf flies up and volumes of the Enciclopedia Zanichelli crash down, bashing into him, her desk, the floor. She squeals, for the entire shelving system is coming apart. A vase falls, smashing on the carpet, glass shards everywhere, water seeping from downed irises. Dictionaries on the higher shelves shower down. Pinch raises one arm to sustain the falling bookcase, the other to protect himself, hardcovers cascading onto him.

"Charles! Stop! Please!"

Finally, to save himself, he darts away, inadvertently barging her into the hallway, the shelving clattering down behind them, her possessions smashing onto the floor, an office wrecked in seconds. He lands on his knees, and pain shoots from his spine. He clasps the sweat-soaked back of his shirt. He cannot breathe.

Above him, Francesca holds her breast, which he inadvertently elbowed. She hurries into the office to collect the smashed photo of her fiancé. Pinch tries to stand, but the back pain knocks him back down.

"Charles, I think you must go," she says, in English. "Okay? I must clean."

He tries to rise. Another bolt of agony. "Sorry," he says, wincing, "I can't move. Something with my back. I'm in serious pain."

She helps him to his feet, as if he were a senior citizen. Fighting down a scream, he shuffles out, insisting that he's better now, just fine, though inwardly obliterated by nerve damage so agonizing as to erase her voice, almost erase his shame.

At the end of the corridor, he turns, is out of view, and lowers himself, holding his breath until he lies on the coffee-stained carpet, blinking up at white fluorescent. He holds still, praying nobody comes. Minutes later he overhears Francesca speaking with muted horror into her desk phone, then locking up her office for the night and leaving.

A half-hour later, footsteps approach. Jing stands above him. They have not spoken much of late—Pinch has been dealing with his father's death; she with the demise of her marriage. With much difficulty, she helps him to stand, then leads Pinch outside to flag down a black cab. She insists on accompanying him home. Neither speaks during the ride. "We are both working late again," she says finally, on the fold-down seat opposite him. "We are the outcasts."

He reaches over to shake her hand, but the movement tweaks his spine again. He grips her fingers.

"Almost home," she tells him.

Jing offers to help him inside, but he declines, claiming that the drive did him good. Alone, he inches up the entrance stairs, struggles for the house key in a tight pocket, and makes it inside his flat, the dogs snuffling his trouser legs. He can't even crouch to pat them. He stands there, cringing to recall an hour ago. *So pathetic, still trying at this age, like the last middle-aged man on the dance floor.*

*That,* he decides, *was my final attempt. Enough. Enough of other people. All I need is my cottage: Disappear there, stay within the borders of a canvas. That is my company.*

# Old Age

OIL ON CANVAS

64 X 150 INCHES

Courtesy of the Bavinsky Estate

# 63

Afternoon tutorials start in seventy-two minutes, but Pinch remains in bed. Exerting his stomach muscles, he wills himself upward but only howls. The torture originates in his spinal column. But people are waiting. He cannot stay here. *Get up!*

With a shriek, he forces himself vertical and punches the bedside table—except that hurts too. Pulse racing, he is rendered mindless, in primal distress. He holds still, tries to catch a breath, and proceeds to the nightmare of dressing.

His walk to the Tube station is normally eight minutes. Today he needs almost forty, each footstep an act of self-harm. Pedestrians push past, grumbling, taking him for a daytime drunk. On the train platform he tenses his muscles, unable even to wipe perspiration that rolls down his bald pate, halting in an eyebrow—then slithers ticklishly down the bridge of his nose.

The train doors open. Crowds shove in all directions. He edges inside, clasps a pole with both hands, the metal slippery under his grip. The carriage lurches forward. He takes strangulated gasps at each bump.

Pinch expected his pain to recede when he got active. But he shouldn't have traveled. *I need a doctor.* While in line at the pharmacy, he swallows four ibuprofens, dry. Before the first tutorial, he takes four more. They numb him only slightly, alarm messages still arrowing to his brain.

"Everything all right, Mr. Bavinsky?"

"Yes, yes, Monique."

"Do you have a fever or something?" she asks, shifting her chair away from Pinch, who is dripping.

"No, I'm fine. *Cerchiamo di parlare in italiano, d'accordo?*"

He makes it through the day and home, where Harold and Tony leap around his ankles, needing dinner. He can't stoop to upturn the can of dog food into their bowls. "Sorry. Later." Breathing with as little expansion of his lungs as possible, he unbuttons his drenched shirt. His shoulder muscles are a solid block, so taut that his neck shivers. After an hour-long effort and many yelps, he is lying on his bed.

By dawn, Pinch has not slept and is bursting to pee. This is unlike yesterday, when movement was only unbearable. Today he seems to have lost executive control, pain overriding volition. "I'm stuck," he mumbles, picturing an insect pinned to a board. *I am the source of these thoughts. Why am I saying them aloud?* "Stop that." His words emerge with a gust of breath, lowering his rib cage, causing fresh violence to his spine. Shivering, he inhales, smelling his own sweat.

*Not yet fifty, and I'll need a wheelchair.* He moves his eyes to the left, right, up, down. *Locked-in syndrome—now that would be suffering; this is not. Come on—get up!* Failing, he screams out.

The cordless phone is too far on his bedside table. But if someone calls him, he could lunge in that direction, perhaps knock the phone off its base, which will connect the call. Then shout for all he's worth.

The day passes. Nobody phones.

*A human bladder is like a balloon,* he reassures himself. *Can it explode like a balloon?* "Prior to the invention of aluminum tubes," he says to distract himself, "artists kept paint in pig bladders. Oh, screw it." He pees on himself.

The dogs are seated at the base of his bed, looking quizzically upward. He hears only their panting. "If nobody saves me and you're hungry, boys—get stuck in!" He chuckles, trying to suppress it. "Only, *after* I've snuffed it. Agreed? Boys?"

And the phone rings.

Whimpering, he jabs toward it, shoving the bedside table. The phone wobbles. It teeters. And it plunges from sight onto the carpet. He shouts his predicament, does so thrice, wondering who hears. *Please don't be a telemarketer.*

Two hours later, someone is fiddling with the lock to his front door. He recognizes the voices of Jing and his landlord, a bizarre mix of unrelated parts of his life. Immediately he downgrades his fear from existential to social. *Are my trousers stained? Will they smell urine?*

His landlord grimaces, but Jing appears unbothered. She takes control, calls the ambulance, demanding that they drug him before attempting a move. She is formidable. "Oh, right," Pinch mutters, disappearing into the fog of a serious painkiller, "you studied medicine once."

He needs only a day in the ward. The doctor prescribes analgesics and muscle relaxants, and speaks of a possible operation. Edgily, Pinch explains that he drives long distances, *must* visit France regularly. *Can't be trapped here.*

"Listen to your back," the doctor says.

Once home, he finds himself on that same bed. He lies in a drugged torpor, replaying the humiliation in Francesca's office, squeezing his eyes shut to blacken the event, which runs on a loop.

Daily, Jing stops by to walk and feed the dogs and to pick up his groceries and tidy. She expects no gratitude and ignores it when offered. Once, Pinch is in a bleak mood and snaps at her, deploring himself afterward. The next day she returns, seemingly unbothered, claiming to have nothing better to do after work. But she does have another concern: Salvatore is demanding a big settlement in the divorce, claiming she forced him out at Utz, which is nonsense. He's pushing for her to sell their marital home and pay him a lump sum, probably so he doesn't have to work anytime soon. Jing bought that place with her own money, and resides there today—she'd be cast from her own house.

"I hope you don't mind me saying this, Jing, but your husband disgusts me."

"Thank you."

"He doesn't even speak Italian. Did you know that? It appalls me how few of our colleagues take languages seriously. I know hardly anybody else who takes advantage of the free classes."

"I'm doing Beginner French."

"We're almost the only ones. Nowadays," he adds bitterly, "the main reason people get hired at Utz is they're good-looking."

"It is lucky," Jing comments, "that they do not have this policy when we apply."

He laughs, then winces. "Don't be funny, please."

But he finds very few causes of amusement. His infirmity drags on. Each night, he lies rigid in bed, in the clutch of pain.

"Do you need me to come over there?" Marsden asks, calling from Toronto.

"I'm fine."

"Could you do something to distract yourself? Your dad said you painted before. Couldn't you get back to that?" Marsden asks. "I could send you a set of pastels or watercolors. Let me. You should, Charles. You should do this."

Pinch boils at the suggestion, which he takes as patronizing, an allusion to what Bear said during their final exchange. Pinch wants to retort that he's not some pitiful amateur—*a work of mine once hung in Nebraska of all places!* But in his current state, to characterize himself as a painter would be absurd. Nothing sadder than those who declare themselves artists when not a soul cares what they create. Effort and humiliation feel so close. "You're trying to cheer me up. You're trying to be kind. I know, Mars. But it's having the opposite effect. Actually, I should probably go."

When the phone rings minutes later, Pinch snatches it up, needing to redo that conversation. But it's a disgruntled sibling, bullying him for details about the will. Pinch ends the call in haste, turns off the ringer, lowers the volume on the answering machine to zero.

In coming weeks, the tape clicks on at all hours. He is besieged by those savages. He pictures them breaking into his cottage, bashing down the door to the studio, pillaging everything, smashing Natalie's pottery. In the shadows of his bedroom, Utz students are snickering as he enters the classroom and fellow teachers are gossiping: "He threw himself at Francesca! Revolting, right?"

He turns on the bed, punishing himself by torquing his back— immediately repenting, begging his pillow, surrendering anything. *Let them slice me apart; just stop this.* The orthopedic surgeon remains so cautious, telling him to wait and see.

Eventually Pinch does improve slightly and is able to distract himself by reading his Advanced Latin textbook from university and by leafing through the daily papers (*La Repubblica, Die Zeit, Le Monde, El País*), which Jing collects from a local newsagent. When Tony falls ill ("In solidarity with me," Pinch says, stroking him), Jing transports the dog to the veterinary clinic. He never returns. Harold cannot manage without his lifelong ally. The animal sleeps all day and doesn't last till year's end. Pinch wasn't present to comfort either of his dogs when they were put down. He won't forgive himself for that. He cannot stop imagining them, each there alone, looking around for him.

Eyes brimming, he lies on the living room floor, studying the plaster medallion on his ceiling. He distracts himself by eavesdropping on the married couple who moved into the apartment below and used to have intrusively loud sex, until it was their newborn making the late-night screams. Pinch still hasn't figured which language that family speaks. Someday he hopes to meet them and to say hello to their little kid, whose feeding times and sleep times he knows through the walls.

One morning he ventures outside for a slug-slow shuffle around the block. When returning to his building, the woman from the apartment below is struggling to hoist her pram up the stairs. Pinch stands there, so wanting to help, explaining at length about his back.

"It's not necessary!" she says with a brisk smile, face red as a tomato, the sobbing baby needing milk, not this chatterbox neighbor. She shoulders the building door open. It slams behind her. She calls out from inside: "Sorry! No free hands."

Sometimes, Pinch conducts tutorials at his home for longtime students, among them an aging ex-boxer who works for the London Underground and is studying Italian to keep alert as retirement nears; a thick-eyebrowed Catholic sister aiming to make the case for nuns' rights at the Vatican; and a stockbroker who, having survived a brain tumor, is learning every Lorenzo Da Ponte opera libretto.

Jing schedules the tutorials on Pinch's behalf, intending to raise his spirits. But they demoralize him. At Utz, his status derived from mastery in the eyes of his pupils. When they view his shabby flat, witness him moving around like a man of ninety, he senses himself shriveling in their perception.

At his next meeting with the surgeon, she finds enough progress to rule out an operation. "You will always have pain, but it can be managed. Who doesn't have a war wound or two at your age?"

"Not sure it qualifies as a war wound," he says, buttoning his shirt. "I got this running from a falling dictionary."

When a nurse signs him up for a hearing test, as mandated for those his age, the results are worse than average. Nothing to worry about, she says.

"Nothing for *you* to worry about," he responds lightly. "They're not your ears!" If one faculty is deteriorating, others must be in equal decline. His body is decomposing from the inside—he keeps seeing the image of an apple rotting within its skin.

He looks at the cordless phone, intending to call Marsden. They haven't spoken often since what happened at the cottage. But Pinch longs for that voice now. He picks up the phone but there is no dial tone—somebody is already on the line. (He forgot the ringer was off.) It's one of his siblings' lawyers.

"I haven't sold any of the paintings. Stop contacting me!"

"Excuse me, Mr. Bavinsky, sir, according to legal records there was indeed a bill of sale. From your name to the name of a Mr. Dwyer of Omaha. Occurring back in—"

Pinch slams the phone onto its base, the impact reverberating through him. Widgeon too is hounding him with requests for money to expand her business selling handmade greeting cards and candles online. And Birdie asked in a letter if something will go to her kids, noting that Bear never even bothered to meet them.

"What I think," Marsden contends when they speak, "is just dump all the paintings on the market. Bear himself was doing an inventory, right? Perhaps he was thinking of selling."

"Why are you pushing me, Mars?"

"Because I can't stand that you feel obligated to him. Sorry—it's not my business. But I hate it."

Pinch is ashamed to admit that he's clinging to these paintings. If he cedes control, what has he got? Everything feels like more than he can manage, from washing himself, to the thousand phone messages, to opening mail. He's on disability leave, but the school won't tolerate this indefinitely. He dreads returning there. Everyone at Utz has become so young, and they're all more accomplished than he. His students talk casually of stock options and postings abroad. They brag of weekend getaways to Prague and check flashy Motorola flip phones. Previously, he always thought: *None of this matters; in secret, I'm an artist!* But away from the cottage for so long, he can't understand why he ever went. His attempts at art seem the height of futility.

As a boy in Rome, he once calculated that when the Year 2000 arrived, he'd be a half century old. Thankfully, he never pictured his true millennial New Year's Eve—fireworks fizzing outside, the muffled countdown of revelers in adjacent flats, his murderous rage at them, at everyone, even Marsden.

*Why*, Pinch wonders, *have I become so angry? Because of the pain? There are pharmaceuticals involved too. Or was I always this way, detesting those who outstrip me, at school, in university, in painting?* He thinks of Temple Butterfield, that great artist. *I'm so petty, hating people who don't even think of me. The truth is that I have achieved what I deserve.*

## 64

The new century begins with fanfare, the world marching toward ever more democracy, economies growing infinitely, the Internet guaranteeing better versions of everything. On a distant sideline, Pinch observes, buried under misery—until something unexpected happens: He wakes with almost no pain.

Gingerly, and withholding belief, Pinch steps around the flat, testing this resurrected body, repressing any expectations, until they culminate in a sob of joy and a defiant stamp on the ground—only to chastise himself for forgetting his neighbors and their sleeping baby. *Still, this is amazing. Is it real? Will it stay?*

He parts the curtains, peeking at dawn. *I could just go outside. But it's too early.* He's become fearful of hoodlums, having no ability to protect himself. *Now? I'd punch those druggies in the nose!* He tries to calm down, but cannot stop this jittery high. *The pain will come back. Be careful.*

Instead, he kicks a pile of unopened letters, months' worth, and halts to see familiar handwriting among the scattered envelopes. He stoops, atrophied thighs shaking, and flops onto his backside. He rips open the letter, finding condolences about his father from Cilla Barrows. She found him through Marsden, and is saying—or rather, she *said*; this is from ages back—how much she has come to admire Bear's work, and that she shudders to recall her callow self in France. She inserts a gloss of her past quarter-century: publishing books, teaching, raising a family. "I still owe you money for our European vacation," she writes. "How much was my share?"

On Natalie's old red Olivetti, Pinch types a response, with warmest greetings and a jokey summary of his own life, adding the email address that the Utz school recently forced on everyone. "P.S. Absolutely no need to pay me back."

After breakfast, he ambles at a slow but acceptable pace to the Earls Court post office. Who was ever more elated to stand in an eleven-person queue? He chats to the adorable Jamaican granny working the wicket, Pinch gabbing away, as he's seen others do. How angry that used to make him! Now he can gripe about *his* back and *his* doctor. "Well," he says at his leisure, "must be off, my darling!" Everything has an exclamation point today!

Chattering to himself all the way home, he recalls Natalie's manic spells, when she bounded around the art studio in Rome, and worked on pottery through the night. He always cautioned her to slow down. "Oh, enjoy your highs!" he tells her now. "Why didn't I let you? Am I older now than you ever got? God, I think I am."

He ponders Bear too. To succeed as an artist demands such a rare confluence of personality, of talent, of luck—all bundled into a single life span. *What a person Dad was!* Pinch decides that perhaps he himself had ability too, but this was insufficient: He lacked the personality. The art world was always beyond him. For the first time, he accepts this.

And he longs to tell someone of his painless state. After hesitating, he phones Jing. Might she come out for a drink?

The pint of lager looks huge on the pub table before her. He buys Jing a packet of prawn-cocktail crisps, then gobbles them himself, laughing to notice he has done so. He rises to buy more. "Look! I can get up and down!" When she tells of putting her house on the market to satisfy Salvatore's greed, Pinch becomes indignant. "That's terrible! You know, *I* should just buy the house," he says. "Listen—what if we did a deal privately? You'd save, I'd get a mortgage, pay you a good price, and you could pay off that idiot without losing your home. I'd actually like to own property in London."

"Slough."

"That's almost London."

"My house is very cold, Chars."

"I specialize in cold houses." Thinking of the French cottage, he smiles. The absence of that place is what made him crumple this past year, perhaps as much as the pain itself. And he can return there now. "Look, I could rent your house back to you, so you'd get to stay as long as you liked."

"It's too big for me alone."

"Then I take a wing. Why not? I need to move—I associate my place with Harold and Tony. I'd welcome a change." Suddenly he doubts his own stream of promises. Does he, a man in his fifties, want a housemate? Does he want it to be Jing? Then again, if she speaks Mandarin around the house, that'd be useful. But does free language tutelage justify the purchase of a house?

He's distracted again, grinning about that letter from Barrows—nostalgia overcomes him. He claps his hand upon Jing's and gives a hopeful squeeze.

## 65

When fully sober, Pinch prefers to simply lend Jing £10,000 to pay off her grasping ex-husband, rather than buying a charmless house in Slough. But there is fallout from his high that night: He left a tipsy voice mail for his landlord, giving notice, quite rudely too. Sheepishly, Pinch called back, but his flat had already been promised to someone else. Until he finds a place, Pinch must lodge in a spare room at Jing's house.

On his first day back at Utz, he and she take the train into central London together. Francesca greets him warmly, explaining that she had to hire another Italian teacher in his absence. "Don't look so worried! You still have the same number of hours."

"Yes, great." He lowers his head. "Thanks."

He sits at his office computer, struggling to learn the new Utz software suite, when he discovers a pleasant surprise: an email from Barrows, who is insisting on restitution for their long-ago trip to France, estimating her debt at $2,000. This is a ludicrous sum, he emails back, warning her not to send a penny. If she does, he'll never buy another of her books.

*Priscilla Barrows <pjbarrows@princeton.edu> wrote:*

Charles,

You read my books? Apologies! I'm boring the hell out of you (not to mention my six other readers).

—CB

Tom Rachman

*Charles Bavinsky <charlesbavinsky@utzlearning.com> wrote:*

Dear Barrows,

You have nothing to apologize for. I do buy your books, but confess that I've started none!

Yours sincerely,

Charles

*Priscilla Barrows <pjbarrows@princeton.edu> wrote:*

Ouch. How come?

—CB

*Charles Bavinsky <charlesbavinsky@utzlearning.com> wrote:*

I was afraid that I might be mentioned. (I'm only joking.)

Yours,

Charles

*Priscilla Barrows <pjbarrows@princeton.edu> wrote:*

Ha! ☺. We have a saying at Princeton: "Have I read it? I haven't even taught it!" My books are basically cultural takedowns in which I linger over phrases like "subversive sociality." Avoid! Avoid!

*Charles Bavinsky <charlesbavinsky@utzlearning.com> wrote:*

You used a smiling face. I don't know how to do that on my machine. If your fellow academics knew that you put smiling faces in your letters, you would be a pariah.

P.S. How do you do smiling faces?

*Priscilla Barrows <pjbarrows@princeton.edu> wrote:*

They're "smiley" faces not "smiling" ☹. I'd refer you to the essay on email etiquette in my last book, BUT

SERIOUSLY, which you bought and wisely failed to read.
And, no, I'm not telling you how to do smiley faces.
You'd only abuse the privilege.

Love, Barrows

In less than three weeks, their email correspondence has surpassed the ease of communication they achieved during nearly a year of dating. It's so much easier to connect when you cannot touch.

Finally he deals with his clogged answering machine, a full ninety-minute audiotape. To his alarm, he missed a number of calls months ago from Marsden, who was worried about the protracted silence. But most messages are from irked relatives or attorneys. Early in the tape, they are only menacing. As the messages progress, the same voices issue dated cautions. They're questioning the will, impugning his behavior, demanding to view what he possesses. This mess is closing in.

In the months ahead, Pinch consults with lawyers at length—before conceding that he might have to abandon these paintings or face bankruptcy from legal fees. Another fear is that the French authorities might discover that he inherited paintings in their territory, which could land him in tax hell. It'd perhaps also trigger tax claims in America and Britain. Nope, there's no way to retain the art. Yet he can't accept handing it over.

When emailing with Barrows in recent months, he often lampooned his small life as a language teacher. He did so with genuine amusement because he's demonstrably something more—in charge of serious artworks, of a foreign property, of the Bear Bavinsky legacy. All that makes him almost important. And they say he must surrender that.

# 2002

## 66

During the next school holiday, Pinch drives too fast through France, the highway lane stripes whipping underneath, as he whooshes past gas station turnoffs and countryside. Once in the studio, he contemplates his father's paintings; the twenty-six Life-Stills that Bear hid here and that Pinch inherited. He passes two weeks alone, occasionally dashing out to buy food and supplies. On his last day, he hikes down to the village pay phone to call New York. "I don't suppose you could fly out here in a few months?" he says into a crackly line.

On the agreed date, Pinch returns once more to the cottage, finally hearing a Hyundai Getz struggling up the driveway, engine coughing, the tires spitting pebbles. The parking brake cranks and out steps Connor Thomas, in a pink polo shirt with collar popped, cargo shorts, Teva sandals. "Oh wow—I'm actually here," he says, looking around.

Pinch leads his guest to the kitchen, where a Life-Still rests against a table leg. Another even larger Life-Still is flat on the tabletop; a third rests against a wall. "Nobody else has seen these, Connor. Nobody ever, except Dad, me—and now you. What do you think?"

Eyes bugging, hands clasped behind him, Connor gapes, neck

straining like a chained dog. "I had *so* hoped it'd be this." He leaps
from one Life-Still to another. "Dare I ask, Charles? Are there more?"

Pinch hesitates—then nods, prompting a squeak from Connor,
whose attention returns to the art. He crab-walks the length of
the table, leans toward a canvas for close inspection, clutching his
thighs. "Awe. Like, real awe. And Bear's studio was here, right? Can
I peek?"

"Let's hold off on that."

"Right, totally. I'm getting ahead of myself. Wow. I could seriously faint." For show, he gulps a few breaths of air and fans himself
with his hand, then fixes on Pinch. "Perhaps I'm speaking out of turn
here, but aren't you crazy to keep these here? It must get damp and
cold, no? There could be a fire or a theft or anything."

"This is where Dad always kept them. The safest place in the
world. Nobody even knows where this place is."

"Except me now. Something goes missing, and you can send the
*gendarmes* to hunt me down!"

For a chilling instant Pinch hears his father barking at Marsden
to get the cops up here. Then Pinch is back, smiling at his guest,
waiting for Connor to detect the obvious flaws in these three paintings, all of them copies that he produced during his last visit. When
the man figures it out, Pinch will confess to the prank and bring out
the authentic Bavinskys, which they can compare for amusement
(and for the presumed flattery Connor will offer his host). But amus-
ingly, the supposed Bavinsky expert finds nothing untoward, bubbling with worshipful remarks, each of which is like a firework of
elation inside Pinch. He smooths over a few long strands of hair,
readying his confession. "Connor?"

"Charles, I need to thank you for selecting me." He bows with a
hand-twirling flourish. "These paintings are *un*believable."

"I was going to say something."

Connor is not listening, beguiled by replicas.

"I was going to tell you." Pinch stops. *It'd make Connor look foolish to expose him suddenly like this. Do it delicately later.* For now, Pinch can't help basking. "You know, I just realized the time. Pretty late for this part of the world. If we're going to eat tonight, we should find a restaurant."

"Who needs food when my eyes are feasting on these?"

Pinch smiles, feeling like a twit for his jubilation from a charade. He drives Connor to Vernet-les-Bains, promising "*the* best restaurant anywhere around," though Pinch has never eaten out when visiting the cottage. The place turns out to be empty, with an unctuous manager who presses on them every piece of fish and game in urgent need of dispatch from the kitchen.

"Those pictures are in my head now," Connor remarks, stabbing at his rabbit stew.

Pinch fills their glasses again from a carafe of Côtes du Roussillon, taking a long sip to ready for his confession.

Connor holds up his glass, gazing at the ruby liquid as if art itself sloshed around in there. "I'm seeing them everywhere I look." He clinks with Pinch, who takes another bracing gulp.

"Before we get into further discussion of what you saw today, Connor, I need to mention something. There's a larger reason I invited you out here," he says.

"I'm intrigued."

"Well, I wanted to propose something. A bit more than your just writing one article."

"Don't keep me hanging!"

"Connor, I'd like you to consider writing a book on Bear Bavinsky, the official biography. I could give you exclusive access to all there is. Everything." Pinch dips a nub of baguette into his glass. "What say you?"

"Emphatically, yes!"

Pinch swallows the winey bread, swipes a napkin across his lips, sits higher. "My Dad had mixed feelings about putting his work out there, and he's not around to state a preference today. So I need for us—not just me, but you too—to take on that mantle. Essentially, what I'm saying is: I want to invite you to work alongside me on this."

"I am speechless."

"Tomorrow I'm going to show you all the Life-Stills that Bear left me. And here's the tough part: They will not be together again. Probably ever. Hard to say, but I'm giving them away. All of them. Bear's other children do deserve something."

"Hold your horses, Charles. Is this what Bear wanted? 'These works should be in major collections.' That's what he always said."

"I know what he said," Pinch replies, a little testy. "You tell me the alternative then." Pinch sees his father shouting at him outside the cottage, jabbing a finger at him, saying, *"You* work for *me."* And Pinch recalls phone conversations during university, when Bear dangled the prospect of collaborating—always in the service of his art. *But it's mine now. You* work for *me, Dad. Without meaning to, you ended up working entirely for me.*

Pinch taps his fork against a serpent of entrecôte fat curled across his plate. "What am I supposed to do? They're relentless, my family."

"Do you have to give in?"

"Off the record, Connor, there's no way for me to hold on to these. I'll lose them anyway if I fight this."

"Why not donate them to the French state before anyone can stop you; get them displayed somewhere edgy?"

"Who can guarantee the French state wants them? And once I declare these works, they'll tax the hell out of them, and I lose all leverage. No, my plan is this: You study them over the next few days.

Gradually, quietly, I drive them to London in the coming months. Probably it violates export-license rules, but I won't be profiting personally. Once I get them all home, a clever lawyer can reinterpret Dad's will so every Bavinsky child gets something. Tax liability then becomes the concern of each individual. I realize that means most of them will sell, and the paintings will be lost to the wind. I don't love knowing that. But if you can think of an alternative, say so."

"I find this heartbreaking. Also for what it must be doing to you."

Pinch nods sadly, stroking the tablecloth, breadcrumbs jumping. "All I can do is encourage them to sell to reputable collectors."

Driving them back to the cottage, he grips the steering wheel tightly, needing to sober up, needing to come clean. The next morning, Pinch brings out genuine Life-Stills, twenty-three of them—but cannot resist infiltrating his three replicas among them. The contrast seems obvious to Pinch. *Doesn't this guy see?*

"Your father was a genius," Connor declares. "Truly."

Over the next days, Connor takes notes and photographs, and tape-records their conversations. Pinch hides his nerves, awaiting the moment to admit what he's done. He's going to climb up to the attic, where he's hidden the three originals, and lug each down in turn.

Delaying this, he cooks a meal for his guest while Connor rambles away. The journalist alternately moons over the wizardry of Bear and frets about his flight home. Last year, he stood in line at a Starbucks on the Upper West Side, ready to order his grande latte, when the first plane hit. Unfortunately, bombing Saddam into oblivion is the only option, he now argues. Otherwise, what? Risk dirty bombs in Times Square next? "Don't get me wrong. I hate and despise Dubya with a passion," Connor says. "But myself, as someone who lived the attacks, I can tell you that there's no negotiating with terrorists. A guy like George Bush, who's not plagued by mental quandaries—maybe he's the right man for the moment. You know?"

Standing over a bubbling pot, Pinch offers meaningless grunts, accepting the role of bumpkin that Connor has evidently assigned him. And out here, clashing civilizations does seem like another planet. The aroma of shallots and white wine rises from his copper saucepan, swirling steam dampening Pinch's brow, his spirits climbing with it toward the ceiling.

He *will* confess. *I cannot let this go too far.* If he were to allow his fakes to get out, they'd be detected. And if nobody noticed? What would he gain? Sure, he'd get to keep the originals. And that means much to him. But he could never show them—they'd be prisoners of the attic until Pinch was someday found out. *No, no—it'd be insane.* Yet he is bewitched by the momentum of this. He lowers his head toward the saucepan, eyes closed. *You could be charged with a crime, if this got out of hand. You'd lose everything.*

*Lose what exactly?*

On Connor's last day, the man stalks about the cottage, studying the paintings for the last time. He leans in for a hug, which Pinch awkwardly consents to. The journalist bids farewell, squashes himself into the Hyundai, and remains silent until he's driving down the mountain—at which point he shouts out the window: "Got me the start of a fuckin' *book*, baby!"

## 67

When the shippers arrive outside Jing's house, their boss marches in and measures the painting, calling in two assistants, who wordlessly pack the artwork and lug it out to their truck. They claim there's no seat for Pinch, so he follows in a black cab, pressing his face to the partition window to keep the delivery truck in sight. "Too late to get out of this?"

"What's that, mate?" the cabbie asks.

"No, nothing, nothing—the traffic."

The movers pull up on Euston Road, bundle out the painting in its protective casing, haul it into the lobby of a skyscraper. They cannot locate the service elevator, so grumblingly proceed up an emergency stairwell. Pinch hastens alongside, which irks the two grunts, who say nothing, only glower at each other. On the fifth-floor landing, their boss calls for a water break. "Hot today," he tells Pinch, wiping a rag across his forehead. "Hope you getting yourself a pretty penny for this picture."

"I'm giving it away to a relative."

"That's family for you," he responds without interest, nodding to his crew. "Right, gents. The onward march of time. On one, two, three—hup-we-go!"

When they reach the lawyers' office, a Petros Gallery representative awaits to check the painting and confirm its condition while a solicitor hovers with documents. Pinch sits in a deep leather chair, arms folded tightly across his midriff, squashing his gut. Too anxious, he stands, gazing from the floor-to-ceiling window overlooking BT Tower and cranes. Staring down, he chews his nails, muttering. In the glass reflection, he catches the solicitor rolling his eyes at the Petros Gallery rep—they've probably been warned about Bear Bavinsky's son, the oafish teacher who arrived out of breath in white Panama hat, dress shirt untucked, armpits soaked because he stupidly took the stairs with the movers (notwithstanding a physique that cries out for automated transport). No matter—everyone here is far more concerned with the art than with the artist's offspring.

After an hour, all is done. "Can I leave?" Pinch asks.

"Not only can you, but you must," the solicitor responds with a fawning smile. "Enjoy your day, Charles. All is in order. Signed, dated, soon to be delivered."

On the street, pedestrians stride past him; vehicle noise from Euston Road drowns out his frantic mumbles. "It's done," he says, queasy, pinching his tummy. When he rolls his aching neck, the Panama hat falls, skittering down the sidewalk. He runs gracelessly after, catches it under his shoe and stoops, dusting off the brim, puffing from exertion. He makes himself stand fully upright, forcing his spine straighter, and plonks on the hat, pulling it down as if hiding from pursuers in a Casablanca bazaar. *I did this. I just did this.*

He emits a little laugh, and glances up, dazzled by the shiny skyscraper, where they are right now, admiring a forgery. "It's done now," he says. "Done."

## 68

While the sale is pending, Pinch suffers torments at work, locking himself in his office, head between his knees, sitting up only to check and recheck his email in-box, convinced that someone is about to twig. He whispers a rehearsal of excuses: "What happened is, I must've mixed up *my* copy with the original. It was a mistake." He sits there, leg jiggling, computer keyboard bouncing. Checks his in-box again.

When an email from the Petros Gallery arrives, he goes cold. He cannot open it. Pinch speeds down the hall to the staff room, initiating a preposterous conversation with one of the German teachers regarding pencil supplies. "At the very *least* they should provide sharpeners."

He stands in his office again. He opens it.

The sale went through. No problems. None.

Pinch punches the air, wincing at a twinge in his spine. But he's okay. He hurries up the corridor, tittering like a moron. *Those art-world idiots! The oh-so-perceptive critics! The empty-headed collectors! No one could tell the difference!* Of course, the provenance was unimpeachable, direct from the Bavinsky estate. Plus, this is a work of mid-tier value, unlikely to merit the price of a forensic examination. And who'd suspect Pinch himself, when he isn't profiting from the sale? Certainly nobody believes that he'd be capable of anything this skilled. Best of all, the Petros Gallery and its buyer are now implicated: Eva endorsed this as authentic, while the Abu Dhabi collector (and his high-paid team of advisers) staked their connoisseurship on the purchase. Everyone involved gained a motive to forever insist this is the genuine article.

Over the coming months, Pinch transfers ownership of his two other forgeries to two other siblings. When the remaining sisters and brothers hear of Pinch's secretive gifts, he is mobbed with demands, threats, and offers to drop pending lawsuits. Gradually he sets about satisfying them. Many complain that he *still* refuses to produce an inventory of the entire estate, or let anyone select their artwork. Above all, they loathe how he distributes these paintings: with legal strictures, endless papers to sign—and how he drags it out! Clearly the guy cannot let go. What they don't realize is that Pinch cannot act any faster—he must still produce their paintings. And with Italian classes to teach too!

Whenever Francesca can spare him, even for just a long weekend, he makes haste to the cottage. No time to drive through France anymore. He flies to Toulouse, hires a car at the airport, guns through the mountains, all while prepping brushstrokes in his head. Once in the studio, everything slows. He scrutinizes his father's paintings, deciding which is next. Once copied, the original goes in the attic behind the boxes of Natalie's pottery. Decades from now, when Pinch is old and gray and beyond worrying about incarceration, perhaps he'll reveal this scandal and find a grand museum to take Dad's originals. Everyone will fall down with laughter.

For now, he labors in a nervous thrum, knowing that each additional fake ratchets up the chance of exposure. Among the scariest parts is his drive back to Britain, when he must break every speed law to arrive for work, sometimes nodding off for an instant on the road, a still-wet painting in the back of his car, which he rented in Toulouse but expensively returns in London.

Fortunately, Jing works long hours, so he can sneak the latest artwork into the spare room where he sleeps. He collapses on his bed, inhaling glorious paint fumes all night. When the canvas is dry, he ages it with floor dust and diluted coffee and pipe smoke (never letting himself inhale). Everything would be simpler if he could carry out his counterfeiting at a flat of his own, but the travel costs have eaten into his savings—a modest rent to Jing is all he can afford. But it's richly worth this poverty. Every sale is an injection of euphoria: It's vindication, even if nobody knows.

When next toiling at the studio, Pinch glances across the floor for his dogs, which are not there, nor anywhere. Pausing, he runs through the people (including both Harold and Tony in that category) who have liked him, wondering why they did—not in self-pity, but to understand. He raises his paintbrush, looking from an easel with the original to an easel with his imitation, a woman's slender waist taking form.

He stops for lunch, slapping a handful of pâté into a slitted half baguette, drops in a few cornichons, and munches right there, seated on the studio floor, washing down each mouthful with glasses of a deliciously dismal local red, which mellows the fierceness of his joy. He reaches out, as if to tap his mother's hand. "I told you, Pinchy," Natalie tells him. "You are really very good."

# 2007

## 69

After four years, each half sibling has received at least one painting. To outward appearances, they are flogging Bear Bavinsky's prized Life-Stills—held for decades by the artist, previously unseen in public—to the highest bidders, among them a Bulgarian wrestler (crime boss), a Malaysian baby-bottle billionaire (mass polluter), and a pharmaceuticals heir from Sweden (her art collection kept at a tax-dodging Geneva warehouse, among boxed-up Chagalls, Modiglianis, Picassos).

Pinch's slow distribution of these forgeries has an unintended consequence: The art market is tantalized. Each sale sets a Bavinsky record, meaning those siblings to whom Pinch provided paintings early (the most deserving or most litigious) earned considerably less than family members at the end of the line. When the final Life-Still sells for $2.4 million, it's a sum so large as to terrify Pinch. At these prices, future buyers will check the paintings closely. Then again, what is there to find? The provenance is impeccable, while the pigments and brushes are those that his father used.

When Utz closes for the Christmas holidays, Pinch packs his luggage, reminds Jing that Natalie's immortal cactus in the kitchen requires no water, and he is gone. That night, he flops onto Bear's bed at the cottage, watching a fly circle under the rafters. *Maybe I'll remember this sight in a prison bunk!* He chuckles, sinking into reverie, imagining Barrows' admiration and of Marsden's amazement.

"You think I ignored you, Mars, when you said I should paint again," he tells the room. "Guess what?"

*But, no. I can't speak about this.*

He sighs, and sighs again, as if oxygen might inflate his mood. Lately his spirits have sunk. After all those efforts to placate his relatives, Pinch has copied and distributed everything and is left with nothing but a stack of Bavinsky originals hidden in the attic, which nobody can know about. And now what? His siblings aren't even sated.

Downstairs he leafs through a copy of that commemorative booklet from Bear's memorial service that includes reproductions of old family snapshots. Many of the kids are pictured when small, most eager, none smiling. Throughout childhood, Pinch longed for a team to join, full of best friends, as siblings were in the movies. To a degree, Birdie was that. The others all resent him. *Dad always kept us apart, put us at odds. Was that on purpose?*

A memory surfaces, perhaps his earliest: standing in Bear's studio in Rome by the copper bathtub, which was scalding to the touch. Dad rising from the water, the man's thick wet warm hand on his son's head for balance, rough fingers pressing down, Pinch's little shoulders tightening, his eyes looking up.

Everybody knows that Bear Bavinsky painted long after those days, well into old age. But nobody knows what.

Time to show them.

## 70

Next summer at the cottage, a black Porsche Cayenne growls into view up the driveway. At the kitchen window, Pinch raises his hand in acknowledgment and hurries out to greet his guest. Connor—the once-gelled ginger locks shaved to stubble—exits the vehicle, wearing a sports jacket with skull embroidered on the back, skinny black jeans, and black cowboy boots, with whiffs of boutique cologne emanating. "So awesome to be here again. I've been stoked this whole drive. You're not letting me down, right?"

Laughing, Pinch looks to the pebbly ground, taken aback by this familiar tone with which Connor seems to declare his elevated status since they last met here, six years before. Today, he's an influential writer and critic, successful enough to rent this luxury car. He steps ahead of Pinch, letting himself into the cottage. "What you got, my friend?" he asks, sitting at the long kitchen table.

From the next room, Pinch carries in a canvas on stretchers. Both men consider the painting; neither speaks. Pinch steps out again and returns with a second picture. "A small sampling," he says, watching his guest closely, "of the late works of Bear Bavinsky. These are them." He presses down a loose strand of hair. "What everyone's been asking about for years. And you're seeing it."

Connor flings off his burgundy skull jacket, as if to better study the artworks, which are part of a startlingly different series than the Life-Stills. In those, Bear never portrayed any face, as if a gaze threatened to wrest the painting from his control. These two paintings—each an enlarged physical detail of the sitter, still employing the pugnacious Bavinsky brushstrokes, his swirling reds and violets—here, his subject is the face, pictured too close, staring at the viewer as if trapped by the borders of the canvas.

"Who *are* they?" Connor asks.

"Before I get to that, what do you think?"

"Before I get to that, who *are* they?"

"But you like them?" Pinch asks.

"I'm still taking them in. But what I want to know is why you didn't put these out there earlier."

"I'm not sure he wanted them seen. I'm still not sure. Before we go further, Connor, could you just tell me what you think?"

The journalist crouches before the first painting, taking his time.

"Needless to say," Pinch adds tensely, "you're evaluating these in strictest confidence."

"Meaning?"

"Just that, for now, this is all off the record. You're here as a fellow expert."

"I *am* writing about these. I flew all the way here."

"And I paid for your flight, Connor. I was clear that I just wanted an opinion."

"Hey, you do know what I do for a living, right?"

"We're just assessing these," Pinch says, voice wavering between rage and fear. "I need to know if they even merit showing—and not just because they're by Bear. But because they're good. If they are. So are they?" Pinch toys with his Panama hat, which sits on the table. "Sorry—I'm passionate about these pictures."

"No kidding."

"Look, maybe you're not the right audience," Pinch says, scrambling for a way out of this. "You don't seem to get them, which is a pity. Because I think they're valid. Or I thought they were."

"You are so protective of your old man."

"This is silly, Connor. I haven't decided what's going to happen with these. If you're unimpressed, I don't want you going home and writing something negative about my father's final artworks, which he labored over for years and years. If it's best they remain private, then they need to stay that way."

"Listen, man, you got to make your intentions clear next time, if you have, like, terms and conditions."

"I *was* clear."

"Uh, not so much. But hey, you're keeping more than these up in this joint, right? Tell me there's more than these two."

All afternoon Connor takes notes, seated at the kitchen table, leaping up to check the paintings, a mysterious smile lurking. By late afternoon he raps on the table, announcing that he must dash: dinner with friends in Perpignan. "Anything to avoid the dive you took me to last time."

That night Pinch cannot sleep and repeatedly gets up to study the paintings. *Apparently they're wretched. Clearly, I have no taste. I can't judge anything.* By morning he is exhausted, worn down—and determined to clear the air with Connor. He brings out another of the late works and prays for a better response. Around noon Connor arrives hungover. For a fresh start, Pinch asks about Connor's flight over here. "No terrorists on board, I'm glad to see!"

"What's that mean?"

"Last time you were here, you kept saying how with your luck there'd be terrorists on the flight home. Remember? I was cooking for you, and you were saying how Saddam Hussein needed to be taken out. You don't remember that?"

"Um, I was totally against that war."

"Oh," Pinch says, hesitating. "Look, I didn't mean to go down that rabbit hole."

"I was never for the war, okay? Not to be rude here, but can we get to work? If you're making coffee, I could seriously do with one."

As happened the day before, Connor snorts with amusement when studying the paintings. Pinch stands back, infuriated.

"Any reason you're staring at me?" Connor asks. "Kinda distracting."

Pinch would murder Connor to undo this humiliation. But there is no reversing. When this guy viewed forged Life-Stills six years ago, he venerated every one. Because they fit; those were in the expected Bavinsky style. Yet these are shit. How can he even say? Connor has no judgment of his own. He admires what one is supposed to. These paintings are not what he knows, so he turns catty, elevating himself above the artist. *These* pictures, he'll say, are just minor late works.

*So absurd,* Pinch thinks, his fists clenched. *If Bear were present, standing beside these paintings, everyone would love them. That is the problem. It's me here.*

71

Back at Utz he writes a cordial email to Connor, trusting that the journalist had a comfortable voyage home—and ensuring that they're on the same page about *not* publishing anything about these works.

> *Connor Thomas <artspeakeasy@gmail.com> wrote:*
>
> Charles,
> Talking to a bunch of publications.
> —CT
>
> *Charles Bavinsky <charlesbavinsky@utzlearning.com> wrote:*
>
> Connor,
> I'm sorry to read this. Even if you didn't love these
> paintings, I hope you'll be kind about my father's last
> works. He wasn't young then, and his sight wasn't great.
> But I must leave it to you.
> Regards,
> Charles
>
> *Connor Thomas <artspeakeasy@gmail.com> wrote:*
>
> Charles,
> I still love Bear. Just not sold on these . . .
> —CT

Pinch rereads that reply. *What is Connor implying? He's not sold on them? He can't be questioning the authenticity, can he?* On the verge of panic, Pinch types out a response.

*Charles Bavinsky <charlesbavinsky@utzlearning.com> wrote:*

Dear Connor,

I would be most grateful to see a copy of this article in advance of submission. If there are factual errors, I can let you know.

Sincerely,

Charles

Pinch keeps checking his in-box. Later that day:

*Connor Thomas <artspeakeasy@gmail.com> wrote:*

It doesn't work that way. No peeking. Ciao.

In his room at Jing's house, Pinch paces, shaking his head. He has lost control of this—that is what petrifies him. He digs up a phone number for the Petros Gallery, cringing at the idea—any interaction with Eva makes his skin crawl, especially when he needs her.

"So great to hear from you!" she responds, voice fading as she leans off-mike to steal a drag from her assistant's cigarette.

Pinch responds with insincere warmth of his own before moving to his purpose. Thrilling news: Bear left behind other artworks; a series painted toward the end of his life that Pinch has recently shown for the first time.

"To another dealer?" she asks with revulsion, as if handed a sandwich of live pigeon.

"I showed Connor Thomas. That's all." Hesitating, he adds: "But, Eva, how do you feel about this? To know there's another Bavinsky series around."

"Delighted!" she says, meaning "furious," because Pinch approached that tin-eared typist before her. "I *do* wish you'd let my team handle the reveal, dear! We'd generate a way bigger splash. We've got a publicity department for things like that!"

"But, Eva, you don't represent the estate," he says, softening this with: "Plus I wouldn't want to impose on your team. I can only imagine how busy you are."

"Next time, just call! No expectations. Even to say hi. You could *never* impose on me, dear."

He bristles to be patronized as "dear," especially by someone so much younger. But he must play along. "The reason I'm calling," he proceeds, girding himself for this, "is that Connor has me concerned. He seemed oddly negative about these works. No idea why. I'm afraid that I made a mistake, that I should have locked them away forever."

"Well, that is not the answer. Anything by your papa—a spitball, a paper airplane, for Christ's sake—bedazzles me. I mean, the Life-Stills are *the* American masterpiece of the twentieth century."

For the first time in weeks, he bursts out laughing. "You think that, Eva?"

"I worship the Life-Stills without equal. But I'm going to love this new series the same. How to choose? I'm Solomon now? As for Connor, screw that a-hole. Show *me* the stuff, not some hack. My job is to look and love. And will I ever! Truly, madly, deeply."

How she flatters! As if vanity trumps reason. Perhaps it does with artists. In truth, her pseudo-enthusiasm boosts Pinch a little.

"Why can't people just celebrate greatness?" she continues. "That is what's wrong with our culture. I'm almost serious about that."

"But if Connor is casting aspersions," Pinch goes on, mouth dry, "then what *I* worry is that people might take a second look at the Life-Stills you sold on behalf of my siblings."

"A second look?" Suddenly icy. "How?"

He clears his throat, a fake cough to buy a few seconds. "Connor won't let me read his piece, so I have no clue. But I'm worried that his article could be pretty nasty. And if he says your gallery sold bad Bavinskys, he's accusing *you* of bad judgment. Almost implying that you misled clients. That's insane, obviously. But I know how important credibility is to your job."

"Oh, please. I have credibility coming out of my ass."

"I just thought you might want to check in with him," Pinch says, feigning calm, "so he's not saying something wildly incorrect. Or libelous. Or just stupid. He should know there are consequences."

"What consequences do you have in mind?"

"That's not for me to say. But if someone smears you, I imagine your friends in the art world might turn their back on that person. If his article dents the resale value of Bavinskys, that's sure to affect you in the future. Right? Which'd be so unfair, given how much you've helped raise his reputation. But I'm just talking, Eva. I don't understand that world."

"Clearly, I need to see these late works."

"Connor took photos."

"Leave this with me."

In agony, Pinch waits. No word from Eva. Nothing from Connor either. Weeks later, he calls the gallery again.

"Did Felix not email you?" Eva says. "Me and your journalist buddy chatted. He told me where his rinky-dink story is going."

"Somewhere obscure?"

"Actually, he landed the *New Yorker*," she says. "After you and me talked the other day, I got in touch with an editor friend at the mag and arranged a meeting for Connor. The two of them hit it off big time."

"Eva! What the hell! Why did you do that? What do they have, a million readers? And why would they even publish him?"

"He's got a scoop, wouldn't you say?"

"What scoop? What's he writing? Eva?"

"Patience, dear."


## 72


On the day of publication, Felix phones. "Eva said to read it aloud."

"The whole article?" Pinch snaps. "Couldn't you summarize? I'm really on edge here."

"Eva said read it aloud."

"Okay, okay. But please, start."

The feature is called "Hunting Bear," with the subheading, "The Hidden Truth of an Artist's Legacy."

Pinch scarcely processes what he hears, not least because Felix reads in bewildering upspeak: "After the sexualized shoulders and legs and arms akimbo that established the Bavinsky brand, his crepuscular efforts prove more naked still? The face itself is his nude here? Eyes, stripteasing before us? We stare back?"

"Felix, are those questions in the original? Or are you just reading it like that?"

"Reading it like what?"

"Just go faster. Please."

The prose is abysmal, the pacing turgid—it's a personal history starring Connor Thomas, rhapsodizing about a lifelong (since Princeton) love for the works of Bear Bavinsky, then his feelings upon meeting the great man and his angst over the painter's estrangement from contemporary art. At first Pinch is mentioned only in passing. But the article keeps circling around him. *Wait for it.* He shuts his eyes, hardly breathing.

"You ready?" Felix asks.

"Just get to it."

"I'll put you on with her now."

"Felix! Finish reading it!"

"That was the finish."

Eva gets on the phone. "You likey?"

"Eva?" Pinch responds. "That was nothing. That was Connor finding the paintings, like some kid detective. Which, parenthetically, is *not* how this happened. But nothing negative."

"You need to trust me, dear."

"How did you talk him around?"

"I didn't talk anybody around. I looked at his photos, and I explained what we had here: 'Those are fucking gorgeous, you dingbat.' He could either see what I saw, and be at the vanguard. Or he could not see it, and be a bonehead when everyone else starts raving."

"You liked them?" Pinch asks hungrily.

"Frickin' gorgeous! I told that *dummkopf*," she continues, "that writing about a bunch of 'problematic' art or whatever he thought—that's a nonstory. But single-handedly discovering unknown masterworks? That'll get serious play, as I proved, putting him in touch with my girl Friday at the mag. A dumbass like Connor just needs a little steering."

"Eva! You're amazing."

"*Awwww*," she purrs. "Valentines right back atcha, dearie."

"But you honestly liked them? From those photos?"

"Anyone with the slightest taste would fucking drool."

Pinch always considered Eva's defining trait to be insincerity. Yet now that she approves of his art, he finds ways to respect her: She's experienced, influential—she was listed in *ArtReview*'s Power 100 last year, dammit! She's an opinion maker. *And I*, he thinks, *am a total hypocrite. But a hypocrite who can paint!* He closes his eyes tight, opens them, pupils dilated. "Eva, there was this one bit in the article I didn't get. Where he quoted you, it said the Petros Gallery represents the Bavinsky estate. Which isn't technically true."

"Um, seriously?" She slams on the cold again. "What have I been doing here?"

"No, right—you've represented us superbly. There's nobody else I'd want to do the job."

"Yay!" Warmth restored (and contract on the way). "Here's what I'm thinking: these new pieces in a miniretrospective celebrating Papa Bear, tying a bow on the legendary history between our two fathers. I'm thinking the inaugural for our new art space in Bushwick, what I'm calling Petros 2.0. You psyched? And, later," she adds, "if you care to test the market with these, that can happen. *Ça va?*"

They sign off, and he smacks down the phone receiver, beaming at the ceiling of his room, imagining Eva at her desk in the gallery, loathing him. Another appalling estate, she'll think, and take it out on Felix.

<br>

## 73

When the Petros Gallery announces its show *Bear Bavinsky: The Faces*, the interns mail out embossed invitations with the artist's initials printed back-to-back, **ꓭB**, Intended to resemble the number 88, which is lucky in Chinese culture—Eva is looking to the Asian market these days. Her publicists seed considerable media interest, soliciting an arts-section story in the *New York Times* that speaks of "a first look at the long-rumored treasures by a 20th-century American master." This prompts coverage in lesser organs: ad-heavy art mags, bankrupt big-city newspapers, dutiful wire services, snarky blogs.

Pinch arranges an advance viewing for the Bavinsky children. At

Bear's memorial, several of them spoke with dejection about how Dad never invited them to a single show or allowed them to visit any of his studios. Eleven of Bear's children make the trip to New York, and are herded together for brief remarks from their brother before entering. "Over a lifetime of painting, Dad produced two main series, just a few dozen major works in total. That's all, from thousands of paintings that he started, nearly all of which he destroyed," Pinch says. "For those outside our family who care about art, the Life-Stills mean the most. But the paintings in the next room, I think you'll find, mean something specifically for us. To each of you." He nods from person to person.

"If the show is for us," a sibling quips, "I assume we get to keep the paintings, right?"

Eva breaks in, promising wine and canapés, leading the Bavinsky offspring into her new postindustrial Brooklyn gallery.

Once inside, the siblings stop short. Because, on the walls, it's them. Not thighs and throats of unknown women but Bear's family, each member depicted in a separate portrait, their faces from years before, looking out as if at the painter himself. *Birdie, Age 15* is especially upsetting. If Pinch shuts his eyes, he can hear her weeping outside the Roman studio. Inscribed in each face is harm that Bear inflicted. The series is a late message from their father: He never forgot them, no matter how it seemed; he knew that he'd wounded them. The paintings are remorse made visible.

Pinch stands there, rigid with anxiety, stuffing himself with salted peanuts from his cupped palm, flung in bunches into his mouth, as when a boy at Mishmish Shapiro's party. He's avoiding the sight of the portraits. (It's difficult with eyes staring from every canvas.) Instead he watches his siblings, all of whom stand before their own image. Pinch imagines others walking around this gallery: Natalie and his grandmother Ruth, Mom with her back to him, turning, raising her eyebrows at him, smiling. He smiles back, choking up, and looks for an exit. Outside, he looks at the brick frontage of Petros 2.0, emblazoned with Murakami-inspired graffiti mural. Someone taps his shoulder.

"That stuff is by our father?" Birdie says. "For real?"

Briefly, he is caught out—then realizes she means this as awe.

"When you see what he accomplished, what he left behind," Birdie continues, "maybe he *was* right how he acted. Would it be better if he'd shown up for softball games, only to die without doing what he knew, *knew*, would be so great? It's bigger than us. Bigger than us, Charlie." Moved, she sniffs.

"Happy. Just am." He hugs her, then steps back shyly. "A rare squeeze from your little brother."

"More of those!" she commands, wiping under her lower lids, avoiding the eyeliner. "Oh, Daddy! The art was so much better than the man."

## 74

Through the coming weeks, the culture pilgrims file into the Bavinsky show, reveling in the work of a painter who is both satisfyingly obscure to the masses and pleasingly wicked in character. Nobody wants a well-behaved artist.

In a press release, the Petros Gallery declares that attendance broke all previous records. It says this of all its shows, but the claim is almost true this time. Articles about the Bavinsky revival invariably cite Connor Thomas, "who is completing the official biography of the artist." All the publicity prompts a bidding war for his manuscript, leading to a seven-house auction and a juicy advance. He has become the definitive voice of Bavinsky studies, and uses his role to lavish praise on "the Faces," as the late series has become known.

When Connor phones with research questions, Pinch can't resist: "I'm so glad you came around to these paintings."

"Ohmigod, they were always amazing. I was only absorbing how radical they were. Given his facture. You know?"

Pinch doesn't know. But he supposes that this is how culture works: The taste-makers call something important until it becomes so, making themselves important in the process.

"This bankers' association in Frankfurt is paying me to talk about the peacemaking powers of art, whatever that means!" Connor boasts. "Eight thousand bucks for a half-hour gabfest. *And* they're flying me business."

Neither Pinch nor Connor delves into that awkward time at the cottage. The journalist behaves as if they're old soldiers together, while Pinch dutifully provides any answers required: Bear's views on other painters and aesthetics generally, where he lived when producing particular works, plus Pinch's own reminiscences, insights, speculations. When Connor shows him a draft of the manuscript, Pinch finds his own words ventriloquized throughout. There's also plenty that he never knew.

For example, how wealthy his father's family was. Not simply "in the furniture business," as Bear said, but owners of the largest such enterprise in the Midwest, including factories, warehouses, distribution centers, which he left behind to pursue the life of an artist. He inherited a small fortune when his father died in 1938, which explains why Bear never fretted about making a living. "Live as if money doesn't exist, kiddo, only choices!" Somehow Pinch hadn't questioned how his father afforded such an expensive motto.

Connor also unearthed that old story about Bear jumping from his schoolhouse window to see if he'd fly. It seems to be true, confirmed by medical records: both legs and four vertebrae fractured, a body cast from age seven to nine. Connor excerpts a 1978 interview with *Der Spiegel*, in which Bear mentions undergoing numerous surgeries in childhood, stating that he still suffers intense back pain at the easel and that the discomfort worsens with age; to paint has become excruciating. Regarding that childhood accident, Bear told the German magazine:

> It was three stories up, and I expected the fall to last longer. If my head hit first, I would have been finished. My nurses gave me hell for picking off the dressings, but I liked seeing the scars. Later I heard that many important people spent their childhoods as invalids. Jack Kennedy, Edith Piaf, Lionel Barrymore, H. G. Wells. It's useful to think you're going to die. If it doesn't wreck you, you do what you want afterward.

Also new to Pinch are stories of Bear traveling around Europe after the war. He spent a period in northern Spain, not far across the border from the cottage. During a two-year fellowship in Rome, Bear was expelled for bringing "questionable women" into a work space granted by the American Academy. In internal academy documents, Bear is recorded as describing the women as "artists' models," saying that if they also happened to be ladies of the night, well, there's a rich tradition in painting women of that trade—ask Manet, Toulouse-Lautrec, Schiele. The administrators didn't agree. So he took a dingy studio down the hill in the shadow of Regina Coeli prison, converting a former grain depot into his art space, later the home of his third wife and their only son, Charles.

Other biographical snippets catch Pinch's attention too: His father was engaged in a torrid affair with Mishmish Shapiro. And Dad moved permanently to Italy, not from love for his family there but from antipathy for contemporaries in New York with whom he'd fallen out—hostilities that cost him a place in various landmark shows, including the 1959 *Documenta* exhibition in Kassel and the Guggenheim show of sixty-four American painters in 1961.

Bear then abandoned the family in Rome and returned to New York because of pressure from his dealer, Victor Petros, a man famed for the quip: "Success in art is fifty percent timing, fifty percent geography. The rest is talent."

After Bear fell out of fashion in the sixties, he endured years of personal doubt, womanizing compulsively, drinking to medicate his knee and back pain. "When an artist disappears for this long," Connor writes, "it is rarely a tale of mirth." After decades of anguish, the biographer says, the late portraits mark Bavinsky's redemption.

History will never know that Bear was simply blocked: painting and burning, painting and burning, unable to believe in what he created anymore. Not a single genuine work survives from the midsixties onward—around the same period that Pinch went to Larchmont.

In Connor's manuscript, two anecdotes particularly amuse Pinch: that the young Bear—caught by his first wife with a lover—had staged a wrestling match between the two women, and that Bear had once ordered Natalie to shear off her hair before he painted her to gauge the exact shape of her head. Connor interviewed Marsden for the chapter about Bear's death, and these chestnuts must have come up. Pinch refrains from correcting either yarn. His intent is not for the biography to be accurate, but to be indelible. The only part Pinch asks to change is a line describing one of Bear's sons as "a onetime would-be painter who ended up teaching Italian."

"I'm a professor of Italian at the Utz School of Language in London," he tells Connor. "Actually, no—make it 'an Italian teacher at Utz.' I'm not a professor."

"Drop the painter bit entirely?"

"I bet you wrote a couple of sonnets as a teenager, but you'd feel pretty silly if someone referred to you as 'the would-be poet.'"

"Point taken. For now and ever, you are the Italian teacher."

## 75

Among those who attend the Faces show in Brooklyn is the noted academic and author Cilla Barrows. In an email she raves to Pinch about what she saw. He rereads her note, a bolt of joy each time. "You should have told me you were going!" he responds. Back when he composed letters on paper, he didn't exclaim constantly. But something about online exchanges turns his prose into musical-theater dialogue:

*Priscilla Barrows <pjbarrows@princeton.edu> wrote:*
Tell you? How come? Is there a VIP lounge at Petros?

*Charles Bavinsky <charlesbavinsky@utzlearning.com> wrote:*
If only! So you really liked it?

*Priscilla Barrows <pjbarrows@princeton.edu> wrote:*
Muchissimo. Thoughts of Sickert, Lucian Freud, Soutine
as always.

*Charles Bavinsky <charlesbavinsky@utzlearning.com> wrote:*
Dad hated to be compared, but those are all great
painters!

*Priscilla Barrows <pjbarrows@princeton.edu> wrote:*
Let's just agree the paintings are very Bavinsky. It took
me a few decades, but I get Bear Bavinsky now. I can
even boast of having once met the great man.

*Charles Bavinsky <charlesbavinsky@utzlearning.com> wrote:*
You even dated the great man's son!

Why does anyone reach out to an old flame? It's never entirely innocent. He sees her in their Paris hotel room, lying on the bed, her shirt off. Pinch shakes his head, partly to rid himself of a sexual image while at his workplace, partly because he and Barrows erred—we should be together still. He reads her message again, whispering to the screen, "I painted those. Barrows? That was me."

## 76

Pinch always planned to sell the Faces to whichever Qatari royal or Kazakh mining mogul or Italian fashion house owner bid the most, irrespective of how distant the paintings ended from public view. Actually, the farther the better. It was safer that way. And he wanted none of the profits, having always planned to split the money among his siblings—a reparations fund from Dad. Anyway, that was the idea.

But Connor, intoxicated on attention, takes it upon himself to contact museum directors, reiterating Bear's oft-stated wish for prominent public display. Donation is a distinct possibility, Connor says, implying that he can arrange that. When he announces during an NPR interview that the Faces are destined for major public collections, Pinch is caught out. He contacts Eva, counting on her to slap down Connor. But she shocks Pinch by favoring bequests too. Museum placement is a stamp of approval for any artist, inflating the valuation of all the Bavinskys in private collections, most of which her gallery sold, and many of whose owners (prompted by Eva) are itching to test this ever-hotter market. Pinch cannot intercede without seeming to violate his father's lifelong directives.

So he delays. The Faces sit in storage with the Petros Gallery. Pinch wakes in the middle of the night, stomach in knots, getting up to reread emails on the subject. Jing, who knows little of his predicament, is an unexpected oasis. What he always feared about a houseshare—that she'd intrude when he sought privacy—has not come to pass. He is the one who moseys from his bedroom, checking if she's around. He can tell just by listening: the tick of laptop keys, or the distant murmur of phone conversations in Mandarin. Jing has quit teaching and started a tourism company, catering to wealthy Chinese visiting Britain. Several nights a week she leads coach trips to Oxford, Bath, Blenheim Palace. She's doing well, with five employees and an endlessly trilling mobile. When he asks about her workday, he hears of comical tourist mishaps and marvelously peculiar requests. He and Jing watch TV together too, mostly BBC documentaries about wildlife. Lacking Western physical reserve, Jing provides him battering massages, digging her thumbs into his pressure points to prevent flare-ups of his back pain. She also takes his pulses—not only of the heart but of the liver and kidneys too, though Pinch's understanding of anatomy suggests that those organs do not palpitate. Still, he lets her prod and tweak, and invariably feels sturdier.

Yet Pinch is more frail than others in their late fifties. Worry about a relapse of his back problem causes him to avoid vigor, and he hasn't exercised through dog-walking in years. People are always encouraging him to replace Harold and Tony, but he cannot. Making for the train station each morning, he treads tentatively along the sidewalk, dampening each step by wearing clunky white running shoes, which gives the impression of an elderly man, especially with his threadbare beige corduroys, ragged tweed jacket, and Panama hat.

One evening, Pinch is quizzing her about her one-time medical aspirations in China, curious as to why she never pursued that line of work. To his surprise, he discovers that she was political back in China, and that it destroyed her chances of serious study.

"You were a protester?"

"No, no. Nothing important."

"But brave?"

She laughs, looking down. "No, no."

Smiling, he watches her. "Jing at the barricades! I wouldn't drive a tank at you!"

She frowns at him.

"I meant that in admiration," he says. "Sorry, Jing. Not to make light of anything. Really. I'm useless in that department—never defended anything but stupid opinions about art. You know that I've never voted? Isn't that terrible?" he says. "Listen, I'm making a decision. Right now. Okay? The second half of my life will be full of activism and . . . What's funny? The idea of me with a protest sign is a bit hard to imagine, granted. At the very least, I'm giving more to charity."

"I buy goats for a village in Niger."

"You do not! Do you? Jing, you're so much more decent than I am." Forehead creased; disappointed in himself. "I want to march in a rally. Something meaningful. Keep me to that. Jing?"

She reaches out as if to touch him, then appears to change her mind. Theirs isn't that kind of relationship. They resume language practice. She is teaching him Sichuan, while he corrects her English idioms.

"Chars?" she asks later that night. "What is the difference between 'jug' and 'jar'?"

He's reading, so responds distractedly. "Pretty much the same."

"I'm going to bed. Do you want me to leave this door ajug?"

77

After mixing pigments at procrastinating length, Pinch loads his palette, approaches the easel, his bifocals swinging on a length of purple silk. He stands to one side, moves to the other. Beginning a new painting has always scared him. It's worse now. The critics admired something he did. And strangers—queues of people waiting to enter the show in Bushwick—are standing behind him too, peeping. Should he recapture what pleased them? Or attempt what *he* wants? He remembers that nobody cares what, or if, he paints at all.

*What,* Pinch wonders, hands on his hips, *if I confessed?* He imagines interviews—people asking why he chose to depict what he did, why it meant so much to him. In this fantasy he sweeps aside all complications and lawsuits and criminal charges. As the dream dissolves, consequences glare at him. *I am well and truly stuck.*

As if outside himself, he glimpses this painter, here before his easel. *Bear never once painted me. Dad certainly didn't want me saved for posterity!* And Pinch himself has never done a self-portrait, only depicting his legs and elbows and hands when young. *Well, it's bad enough seeing this gargoyle mug in the mirror each morning!* He smiles. *Actually, I could bring a mirror into the studio.* He has a better idea—not to replicate his looks, but to paint the person who has happened to be Charles Bavinsky.

He presses the tip of his sable brush into a shiny blue knob of paint, swipes the laden bristles across the center point of the canvas. Gingerly he proceeds outward, his nose close enough for its tip to become flecked with color. Many hours later he retreats, bashful to have painted himself. His gaze drifts down the shaft of the paintbrush, halting at his tight fingers. "Artists shouldn't question," Natalie once said. "We should just do, like ants."

"Why am I talking?" he asks the studio. "Only me here."

But he finds solidarity here, linking himself with all those quiet types who looked upon blank surfaces with expectation, those who mark objects to erase themselves, who dissolve in the bliss of work. Pinch raises his brush, leans forward on the balls of his feet, floorboards creaking. From the corner of his eye: all these painterly tools, a kaleidoscope of colors, his companions. *Is that tragedy? That the*

*peaks of my life are entirely inside? Other people—those I so craved—*
*mattered far less than it seemed. Or is this what I pretend?*

As the tide of sadness flows closer, he returns to work, misplacing himself there, though it's his own image taking shape before him. After a measureless stretch of time, he wipes his brushes on rags, drops them into the turps jar, and sits beside the spattered boom box on the floor, clicking a CD into action. His father required bopping jazz to work, but Pinch cannot hear music while painting. Only after.

He lies on the studio floor, fingers laced behind his head, knuckles pressing with pleasant soreness into the wooden boards, his entirety absorbing Schumann's *Kinderszenen* op. 15, no. 1. *"Von fremden Ländern und Menschen."* He inhales the paint fumes, his breath quickening, eyes stinging. He sits up, glances around: a blurred, joyous sight.

# 2010

## 78

It is entirely sensible when Pinch and Jing—he nearing sixty, she nearing fifty—initiate a sexual relationship. She's matter-of-fact about the human body, and her bluntness amuses him. They continue to sleep in separate rooms, however. Intercourse is just something that happens when it suits both parties, like her bruising massages. Equally, they have reached genial accord about running the household: She vacuums and gardens, never squeamish about snipping slugs in two with the secateurs; he does their laundry and irons, even if he's falling behind lately, so weary all the time. These past years have exhausted him. For once, he should try a proper vacation, catch up on sleep, not just race off to France. He ponders this an instant. *Never!*

"Did you bring down the napkins?" Jing asks.

"Yes, yes." But he hasn't, so opens the cupboard, reaching for them. She laughs to have caught him out. "I'd done it in the future!" he protests. "The future past. Hey—I invented a new verb tense."

They often share meals; it's harder to shop for one. "If you're cooking tonight, make something horrible, so I don't overeat again," he says. "Look at this abomination." He lifts his shirt to expose his paunch.

"You're thin."

"Hey, don't minimize my gut," he replies. "I put a lot of work into this." Yet she is right—he's trimmer with age. "Lack of exercise clearly agrees with me."

When they're splitting dinner one night, he burns his tongue on the chicken soup. The injury takes ages to heal, with the annoying side effect of causing him to salivate constantly, which makes him thirsty, which makes him glug water, which makes him pee. He is reminded of his water-drinking contests with Barrows, so sends her an email, which proves awkward when his situation takes on a different shade.

A visit to the doctor places Pinch on the wrong side of that window between the healthy and the ill. "I quit years ago. My father was the heavy smoker—perhaps I inherited this from him," Pinch jokes, without amusement.

"It isn't something you inherit," the oncologist replies. "As I tell all my patients, three out of four people will suffer from cancer over the course of their lives. Given enough time, it's the natural state of cells."

"I don't find that particularly comforting."

The oncologist speaks of Kaplan-Meier curves, how each case is different, that we're talking about a range here.

"Thank you for explaining that," Pinch says, so terrified that he clings to manners.

"Twelve to thirty-six, if you're asking for a number."

"Months," Pinch adds, smiling to appear cavalier. "That's quite a range!"

"My colleague can run through what's next."

When Pinch walks from the hospital, he is unable to register sounds, perceiving other pedestrians as silent beings, who step around him. He needs to tell someone, a particular person: Marsden. The time difference makes it too early to call, and writing this in an email would be wrong. So Pinch carries on with his day, which passes in a slow blur: tutoring at Utz, evening classes, exchanges with colleagues, his tongue—the enemy now—darting about in action, then inert on the train home. *I was lenient with my students. Why did the diagnosis produce that effect?*

Jing knows the test results were today. Hearing them, she poses myriad smart questions, none of which occurred to Pinch at his appointment. He ought to feel gratitude for her interest but is detached, imagining other patients confronting a case like his completely alone. There was probably someone like that in the waiting room today. Never does Jing doubt his diagnosis or urge a second opinion, as others will. Nor does she panic. This is the situation.

"It's good I know you," he says.

### 79

The operation is gruesome and not worth dwelling on, he informs Barrows by email. Pinch says he'll need months to retrain what remains of his tongue, but this proves untrue. Within weeks, he can speak very slowly and with a lisp, which strangers take to be mental impairment. To avoid such exchanges, he avoids talking, except with Jing or medical staff.

For a man who spent his adult life teaching people to communicate, Pinch is unbothered to become mute. With others yammering all around, he eavesdrops and comes to an opinion: Only a fraction of speech transmits word meanings; the bulk is entirely social—to console, ingratiate, jockey. He writes down his own remarks, keeping pads and pens everywhere. This has a condensing effect. Hand gets tired, brain gets to the point.

Pinch discovers something more. He had lazily assumed the Chinese to be a stoical people and had attributed this to the population size—too many souls to indulge in sentiment. But Jing, even with her medical knowledge, sobs when he displays his butchered tongue.

This angers him. He must consider her now, alongside everything else. Yet her fragility protects him too—he can only pity himself when alone, and she rarely leaves him.

For distraction Pinch flips through Natalie's old pottery manuals: technical guides about glazes and strident manifestos by Bernard Leach. He hates never having taken up pottery. *Why did I overlook this? I'd probably love it. Mom tried to show me. Well, that's decided: I'm learning it, the second I improve a little.*

After dark, the night terror descends, a cold finger against his breastbone. His eyes spring open on blackness. *Such a mess that I'm leaving. And I am leaving.* He hears house sounds, a distant police siren—all this will continue, *as if I'd never been.* He distracts himself by visualizing every room at the cottage. *All of Dad's originals, still in the attic. I must admit what I did. What can anyone do to me now?*

He lies still, trying to control his breathing. In through the nose, out through the mouth. Slower. The dread returns, that demon touching his chest.

By morning he assumes his bright manner. "You know what they say?" (With Jing alone, he speaks shamelessly in his slobbery way.) "When it comes to dying, nobody got it wrong yet!"

"You're not dying."

"Not if I don't have to." He pokes her arm affectionately, joshing more than ever, gaining a warmth for people that he never before experienced—he's become curious about strangers, and forgiving too. Pinch so wishes that he'd been this way all along.

## 80

He speaks often of the cottage, although a trip is inconceivable while undergoing treatment. He transports himself there by learning Basque. "The word for 'sandwich' is *'ogitarteko'*!" he informs Jing.

"Isn't that fantastic? Listen to this: '*Hizkuntza bat ez da galtzen ez da-kitenek ikasten ez dutelako, dakitenek hitzegiten ez dutelako baizik.*'"

His childhood nickname derived from Basque, he tells her. When Bear was traveling around northern Spain in 1947, he discovered a local bar food. When his next newborn arrived, he took to calling him "little *pintxo*," which became "Pincho," which settled into "Pinch"—how Natalie always referred to him.

"I need to be in my cottage." *At least once more. Dad's paintings just lying there. I can't leave it like this.*

"You want to go talk with Basque people?"

"Don't know if I'd talk to them. But I could find them at the market and listen."

"What's the point learning, Chars, if you never talk?"

"The point? More words!" His medication-dulled eyes glint. "More!"

His trip keeps getting delayed. The oncologist says: "Treatment first, then travel. Maybe next summer. That's the plan—next summer we get you to that cottage. Sound fair?"

## 81

When Pinch is readmitted to the hospital, Jing asks for a list of people he'd like to speak with by phone. He has so few to suggest. He's been in regular touch with Marsden and Birdie since they heard of his condition. But he wouldn't mind hearing from Julie again. After decades of life, that's it: Marsden, Birdie, maybe Julie. He leaves out Barrows—he's ashamed for her to know, as if dying early were a form of failure.

"Not too bad here! Could be worse!" Pinch tells Julie when she phones. He asks after her niece Liz and nephew James, recalling the memorable tour they all took around the National Gallery. "Fun, that was."

"Gosh, I'd entirely forgot that. Well, Elizabeth lives in London now, works in marketing, though she's on maternity leave now. James does something in tech—do not ask me what! He's got *four* little ones, believe it or not."

Pinch longs to say: Do those two remember me? I was fond of them.

"I was really just calling to thank you, Charlie."

"To thank me? I didn't do anything," he says, exerting himself to hide the lisp. "You're back living in your hometown, back with your first husband—seems I had no effect at all!"

"I owe an awful lot to you. I had no confidence before, which *you* gave me."

"All I did was encourage you, which somebody should've done long before."

"I'm up to all sorts of things with my life because of you. Ever so grateful, Charlie."

After hanging up, he holds on to the phone, other hand flat on his chest over pictures of Harold and Tony. After those two died, he was distraught—couldn't speak their names for a couple of years. Nowadays he studies their photos at length. They make him laugh.

*So fast gone, isn't it. Was I anything?* What anguishes him most is not that he didn't succeed, but that he didn't experience more: other lovers, intrepid trips, peculiar foods, a daughter and a son, both grown, returning to see him. "How nice you could come! Sorry I'm not at my best. Take a seat—there's space on the edge of the mattress. Tell me, what have you been up to of late?" When young, Pinch considered human connections the refuge of those who couldn't make art. *Or is art just the refuge of those who cannot connect?*

Work colleagues drop by, including Francesca, who brings a stack of grammar books, knowing they will divert him: the brand-new Italian, German, French, Portuguese texts, all pilfered from the school. "Courtesy of Uncle Utz," she says.

He reaches for his notepad, writing, *"Molto gentile. Grazie."*

Nearly without exception, the colleagues who visit are women. The male teachers can never make it, which hurts him, although he never lets on—he always replies cheerfully to their text messages.

One man who does appear is Marsden, turning up alongside a diminutive companion with tweezed eyebrows and carefully trimmed beard, as groomed as a French formal garden. Privately, Pinch thinks of Rob as Marsden's sidekick but doesn't use that term, knowing it sounds dismissive. As it happens, he immediately warmed to Rob, who has sensitive gray eyes and, despite his size, is always in everyone's way, apologizing excessively ("So sorry!"), only for another person to tap him on the shoulder, setting him off again, like a well-dressed pinball.

Marsden and Rob flew in for the week to help Pinch with his return from the hospital. They make an excellent team, supplying all Pinch's favorite treats—not least, plentiful Maltesers. Rob compiles a list of vegetables that are supposedly cancer-fighting, and discreetly adds them to Pinch's diet. They place flowers around the bedroom and bring out his favorite art books. Each day, they interrogate Pinch on any desired comforts and, no matter how obscure, track them down, always in the most lavish version. When he can't eat, they consume his favorite meals in front of him, which is heavenly for Pinch.

"I just realized something incredible, Marsden!" Pinch kids. *"You* were the love of my life! Did you realize?"

"You even sent me bouquets in secret."

"Me? I never!"

Everyone laughs—in medicated delirium, Pinch can be extravagant. But he is at ease around them and speaks as himself. Among the worst aspects of illness (with ample competition) is the incessant talk of illness. Instead they discuss music and films and old days in

Toronto. When their departure approaches, Marsden and Rob announce their intention to stay on—they are clearly needed here. But Pinch declines. Jing is worse at caring for him, but she's in tatters over his current state and suffers when she finds nothing to do.

Tensely Marsden packs, repeating aloud everything they must do before the taxi arrives. Rob bids farewell and waits downstairs. Marsden and Pinch are left alone.

"You have to let go of my hand at some point."

"You mean it doesn't come off?"

"It's become quite attached to me."

"I feel the same way."

## 82

When Pinch asks Birdie if she had a comfy flight, she can't remember. It's too shocking to see her brother like this. Throughout her four-day visit, she avoids him, finding things to go out for, rushing to the kitchen at any opportunity to wash dishes or clean the fridge shelves—anything. On her final afternoon, he forces a conversation. He wants to settle a few things, needs to apologize for not having stood up for her when she visited Rome, for trying to be Dad's favorite. But when he approaches any subject, she keeps interrupting, not allowing this to be the last conversation—it's not the last anything!

"I'm not sure *when* I'll die, Bird, but I'm certain it'll be this that kills me."

She changes the subject, talking of when she picked up her new little brother at the international school in Rome, eating ice creams in those gorgeous piazzas, little Charlie translating her flirts with Italian boys.

"What funny times!" he says.

"I love how you maintain such high spirits, Charlie."

"Because this conversation is for you, Bird. I won't be here to remember it. And I need to get this in your memory in the right way."

"Oh cut that out! You ain't going nowhere!" She hurries on to a discussion of the Faces show in New York. "How great that was," she marvels. "Our dad."

## 83

When Barrows hears about Pinch's sickness from Marsden, she emails immediately. "I'm doing a talk at the LSE in a few weeks. Could I see you?"

He hesitates. *I'm so hideous now. Who cares? I do.* As her visit nears, Pinch reads the alarm in people's eyes. *Oh, stop fretting about how everybody sees you!* He recalls his excitement of younger years when meeting with Barrows. *I've missed her. Missed a lifetime in her company.*

They must have a long talk when she comes. But he sounds moronic. Well, she can talk; that'll suffice. Suddenly he needs Barrows to know—she, whose opinion matters more to him than anyone's—he needs her to know that she adores an artist, and it's me.

Barrows sends increasingly detailed messages: I'm about to leave New York, just arrived in London, checking into the hotel, will be at your place around midday before the conference opens, so looking forward. By email he explains how to find Jing's house, sending instructions three times. "We can have lunch and talk. I might have to just listen sometimes!"

Jing goes to her office to leave Pinch and his friend in private. An hour before Barrows arrives, he props himself up in bed, bravely refraining from painkillers to keep his mind clear. As arranged, the front door is left unlocked so she can let herself in.

*When I tell her about the paintings, she'll see that I achieved something with my life. Even now,* he thinks, shaking his head, *even now, I need to impress Barrows!*

"Hellooooo?"

"Here! Up here!" he calls out, cringing at his slobbery voice.

*Clomp, clomp* up the stairs.

"Hey, it's you," he says, chest tightening. *Yes, yes, that is Barrows. Hair still long, entirely gray now. She doesn't dye, and good for her— natural, dignified.* "Forgive the sight of me," he tells her. "I look like a ghoul. It's the chemo. Does it to everyone when you're on this dose." (Untrue; they stopped his chemo weeks ago.) "I should keep the lights low so nobody has to see!"

"You look fine, Charles."

"Fine is one thing that I do not look. But thank you."

She pulls up a chair.

He asks her to speak of her conference, which relieves him of talking for a while and allows him to muster saliva. He scarcely hears, so preoccupied is he with this imminent confession. He'll go over everything, explain what he did, how and why.

Speaking of her own work, she is distant, pleased with herself. *Was she always like this?* Barrows keeps diverting back to the subject of Bear. "I was thinking of our crazy trip to France," she says. "At the time, did you realize why I was going there? I think you did, right? My big notion of writing something about him."

"About my father? No, I wasn't aware."

"Didn't you sort of bring me for that reason?" she responds, an arch smile. "To show off your famous father?"

"Did I? Maybe."

"Anyway, I never got enough material. Because of that argument."

"What was our argument even about?" he wonders, aiming to shift to warmer matters.

"About you being obnoxious, if you don't mind me saying."

"Oh," he responds, taken aback. "Yes, it probably was. Anyway, I'm sorry to hear that. Actually," he adds, interrupting her, "I'm very sorry to do this, Barrows, but could you possibly go?"

"Are you not feeling well?"

"Very much not. But that's the norm. I don't mean to be rude. And I know I am. But it's a matter of urgency—I'd quite like to be alone. And my time is limited these days. Sorry; I shouldn't be doing this."

She rises, gathers her belongings. "I traveled quite a ways to get here."

"No, you're right. I apologize." He looks directly at her.

She leans down. A kiss on his cheek.

"I wish you such good luck, Barrows."

That night, Jing asks how it went with his friend.

"Quite well." And he means it. Pinch isn't downcast about the meeting. He is relieved. Because Barrows was not the person he imagined. Anyway, not that person to him. Not anymore.

## 84

Jing enters his bedroom. Pinch reaches out, eyes shut, seeking her hand. He urges her to sit on his bed and describe his dogs.

As her words reverberate, he drifts into fevered sleep. Phones are ringing, the house bustling with policemen—he wakes, inhaling turpentine, smelling Bear's clothing. He sniffs again, the dust of Natalie's clay, dirty doorknobs, her gray fingertips. *How amazing my mother and father were! All those years, all their bullying doubts, all in the paltry hope that strangers might someday stand before their work and look, probably no longer than a few seconds. That's all they were fighting for. What driven lives!*

And his own life? Viewed at any point along the way, it seemed to Pinch to have so little direction. But from the present vantage, what happened feels inevitable—not because events were beyond his control but because they were within it. He couldn't have been other than he was. That doesn't hurt anymore. Just another ant, marching up and down.

Or is this the painkiller talking? He smiles in the dark, unsure if the thin light framing his curtain means almost morning or nearly night.

He recalls a conversation with Natalie when, in sullen adolescence, he read her a line of German philosophy that claimed evil outweighs good by a comparison of "the respective feelings of two animals, one of which is eating the other." Natalie recoiled. That, she retorted, overlooks so much: sensory experience, change, ideas, and a few allies (how few!), all of which combine into more than the waiting darkness. Don't you think, Pinchy?

"I brought you a leaf," Jing says, placing it on the bedspread.

He opens his eyes, takes it by the stem. "Lepidopterist," he says.

"What language is that?"

"Just a language in my head."

Noticing Pinch's eyes flutter closed, she tiptoes away.

"I have a question," he says, or believes that he says. "Why is that leaf so beautiful? Why does one thing contain beauty and another doesn't? The park, it overwhelms me." (He says "park" but means "back garden.") "Almost makes me cry to look out that window. But those concrete flats over the fence actually make me furious. Not that nature is better than artifice. Because art *is* artifice. Sorry, what was the question?"

"The question is: Why should a leaf be beautiful?"

"Because it has healthful associations? Or because, within our primal selves, we associate color with plenty? Might that be it?"

"But why find beauty in a painting? And how can an abstract be so affecting?"

"Or a piece of pottery, for that matter," he adds.

Silence interrupts him; it holds.

He yearns for beauty. More. The art books around him—he doesn't care to view them. Lately he finds the sublime in unpretty faces. He could watch them for years. Natalie was right: Life *is* thrilling.

*Must get to the cottage. Must.*

Charles Bavinsky outlives his father by little more than a decade.

# Portrait of an Artist

HAND-BUILT ABSTRACT CERAMIC,
SPLASHED BLUE AND RED GLAZES,
INCISED LINES

16 X 9 X 6 INCHES

Courtesy of Xiao Jingfei

# 2011

## 85

Upon learning of Pinch's death, his siblings contact the Petros Gallery. They know their brother's plan was to bequeath the Faces to museums. Can that be canceled? Everything depends on Pinch's estate. His sole beneficiary is someone named Xiao Jingfei. Wait— what? This must be a mistake. It turns out to be the woman in whose house Pinch lodged during his final years. Was this some sleazy affair? Did she manipulate their half brother when he was sick? In any case, this is an outrage—a stranger controls *their* legacy.

Complicating matters, tax officials are meddling, with the French, the Americans, and the British all making claims to the inheritance. And one big question hovers over everything: Are there more paintings?

A lawyer counsels Jing to immediately conduct an inventory at the cottage where the deceased apparently stored his father's art. If she finds nothing, fine. But if she gets lucky? "You realize how much a Bavinsky goes for these days?"

Jing refrains from answering—or admitting that she has no idea where Pinch's cottage is. She does own a set of scratched old keys, however, and considers asking Birdie for the address. But perhaps that sister is allied with hostile family members. Instead, Jing approaches another of Pinch's final visitors, Marsden, who mentioned living at the cottage for a spell.

"You can come and show me?" she asks by phone. "I pay for your flight. Okay?"

They meet at an airport outside Barcelona and drive north into French Catalonia. Marsden's transatlantic haze is intensified by the strangeness of returning here. He attempts to converse with her, but most exchanges falter. "Interesting," he says, "how Charles studied grammar right till the end."

"Chars liked preparing."

"But what for, at that point?"

"It's good to study."

They drive up the mountain in silence, united by someone who doesn't exist.

"Scary to think what we might find," he remarks, looking at her.

Gripping the wheel, she slows into another hairpin turn.

86

He guides Jing around her own property, pointing to the art studio and the woods behind. In the cottage kitchen, dead flies dot the tile floor. The shelves are stacked with domestic pottery, stamped on the underside with the hallmark "C.D." Upstairs, the bed is made, linen humid, whiffs of potpourri. Entering each room, they flick on the lights with anticipation, as if someone might lie there, sit up, staring at them.

On the bookcases are battered thrillers, guides to the Roussillon in English, and a notepad so old that when Jing takes it from the shelf, pages flutter to the floor. It once belonged to Cecil Ditchley and contains glaze formulas in elegant cursive of the kind that nobody can produce anymore. They also find a copy of the Bavinsky memorial booklet, along with Pinch's bound thesis on Caravaggio, with Bear's notes jotted in the margins, even though he always claimed never to have read more than a few words. Marsden rests the Caravaggio thesis on his palm—he has never read this. He recalls staggering up the stairs of that shared home in Toronto, Pinch frowning at his desk at this housemate with a bottle of booze in hand. That isn't a happy memory, for they were growing apart. The indolent and the industrious cannot stay friends. But such distinctions are trivial now. Their affinity on the steps of the Sidney Smith lecture hall proved truer than any rupture.

Marsden flips open the thesis, stopping at the dedication: "To the two great artists of my time, Natalie and Bear." Marsden smiles. He slides the copy into his bag, calling out: "No paintings over here. But don't abandon hope. We still have the studio to check."

They walk out into a drizzle, quickstepping up the soggy turf. Jing fiddles with the two locks on the studio door. Inside, she flicks the light switch but they remain in darkness. She turns on her smartphone flashlight, its beam picking out matted brushes, twisted metal paint tubes, a table splodged with hardened slugs of color. But there is no art except an unfinished picture on an easel: a face shown overly close, viewed at invasive proximity, forcing its subject—a youth—to turn away, as if edging off the side of the canvas.

"That could be worth something," Marsden says.

They can't risk carrying it back to the cottage through the rain, so leave it for now, locking the studio.

"Well, that's pretty much everything," Marsden concludes. "There's storage space in the attic, but it's junk up there. Old boxes of his mother's pottery. Nothing of value."

The low clearance in the attic forces them onto their hands and knees. Her phone light illuminates dusty cardboard boxes of ceramics, many in tissue paper, a few cracked. Marsden unwraps a long-necked vase, reads the bottom, signed in the clay: "Natalie."

He shows Jing. "Lovely, don't you think? Is that glaze blue or green? It's so dark up here. Gosh, there's tons of pots. Not sure what you'll want to do with them all."

She angles her light above the boxes.

"It's rafters that way," he explains.

But the sweep of her beam halts.

"Holy shit," he says.

It's so cramped that they cannot reach the other side without first removing all of Natalie's pottery. Marsden is touched by how gently Jing treats it, lifting pots from the disintegrating boxes, cradling each piece down the stairs, notwithstanding their shared impatience. "Nearly there."

They approach the rafters, raise the tarpaulin. Stacks of paintings. "Oh my God."

"Let's bring them down first," Jing says, maintaining outward cool, but stiff with tension.

With utmost caution, they transport each canvas into the kitchen. Marsden—leg jiggling—counts them. "Twenty-six here. All Life-Stills. This is insane, Jing." With her permission, he scrutinizes a few. "Wow. Just, wow."

But gradually something troubles him. He checks another painting. And another. "I'm a bit confused now," he says. "Okay, this requires a small admission. When I was here with Bear, I did something a bit naughty. One afternoon, I found his keys left in the cottage door. I went to return them to him, but noise was coming from upstairs—he was with a lady friend. So I tiptoed away. I had this key ring in my hand. Actually, the same one you have. And I found myself sneaking into his studio, which was strictly off-limits. I was just curious. And I saw a bunch of these Life-Stills. Which is what's confusing me."

"Why is that confusing?"

He does a Web search on her smartphone, bringing up an image that looks identical to the painting before them. "See that? A hedge fund manager bought this picture." He finds an image of another painting in the kitchen. "Look, this is a *Vogue* shoot—this painting is in a mansion in Saint Petersburg." After repeating this with several others, he turns to her. "Hate to tell you, Jing. These are copies. It did seem a bit too good to find original Bavinskys dumped in an attic. I'm sorry."

"Maybe Bear made two of each painting?"

"Bear hardly kept *one* of each painting. These are copies. And, I'm afraid, not worth a penny."

## 87

They're famished, so they lock all the doors and drive to the nearest village for lunch, where the only restaurant is a drab pizzeria. They take a table by the door, chewing crusts, a downpour outside, an occasional car whooshing by. Neither says much, yet they have become closer by dint of their shared hope and shared disappointment. "Tired," she comments.

He smiles, nods.

When she returns from the toilet, he watches her approach, feeling so fond of Jing for her kindness to his friend. She was terribly in love with Charles, Marsden knows, and is sorry that his friend never let himself fully reciprocate. "The unfinished painting on the easel— did you make out the face?" he asks her.

"Chars?"

"I'd need to see it under proper lighting, but I'm pretty sure, yes.

I knew Charles when he was not much older than that. What's odd is I have no memory of seeing *that* painting here."

"Bear did it after you left maybe?"

"He died before I left." He wipes his hands on a serviette, pausing, seeing Bear lying on the mountain path. "Come to think of it, that portrait couldn't have been done in the studio. Bear didn't paint the Faces here."

"Yes, yes, he did."

"You're wrong, Jing. I was living here. And they weren't around."

"But Chars always brought them back from the cottage."

They keep eating, neither tasting now.

"I have a scary feeling again," he says.

"Me also."

They drive fast back up the winding hill. The paintings are untouched, which almost surprises them—their focus made it seem as if the world were converging here. The cloudburst is over, so they lug the unfinished portrait into the kitchen. "Yes, it's Chars," she acknowledges. "As young man."

But Marsden is occupied, studying the reverse sides of various Life-Stills, which are smeared with threads of tobacco and manly handprints. Marsden turns to her, agape. "Holy fucking shit, Jing. *These* are originals."

"What do you mean?"

"These here. These are real."

"But you say Bear only does one of each picture."

"That's true. Is it possible that the ones people bought, that *those* are copies? Is that possible?" he says, flushing from excitement. "And who came out here obsessively, Jing? Who was the only person?"

"So that is Chars' painting, hanging in Saint Petersburg?"

"They all are. I *bet* you!" He claps, jubilant—but is still jittery, still running through the consequences.

Jing walks into the living room, trying to digest this. She pauses

at the memorial booklet, its pages paint-spattered, folded at reproductions of family snapshots. These photos are curiously familiar,
including one of Birdie at age fifteen. Jing searches online for images
from the Faces series. She starts shouting for Marsden. "Look! Come
look!" The Faces paintings aren't identical to the memorial photos.
But they were clearly inspired.

"I'm telling you," Marsden says triumphantly. "*I* saw Bear's late
days. The man was terrified to work. He had his trademark style,
and was resting on it. There are no late works by Bear Bavinsky."

"The late works of Bear are the early works of Chars."

"They're his late works too," Marsden remarks sadly. "Well,
you're a rich woman, Jing. All those collectors who bought phony
Bavinskys might sue the sellers, but that wasn't you. It was his siblings. I guess they might sue the estate. Come to think of it, you'll
have lawsuits. Still, in my view, you have every right to put these on
the market."

"What about the Life-Stills that Chars painted?"

"Oh, it'll be a huge scandal," Marsden says, delighted. "When
your originals hit the market, there'll be insanity. What a comedy!
Hey, do you think Charles cultivated that pompous journalist, Bear's
'authorized biographer,' to pull this off—to have an expert at the
ready to verify all his fakes? Or is that too crafty? Jing, you have *no* idea
the stink this is going to cause." Rubbing his hands with glee, he finds
a Cecil Ditchley teapot and a box of loose Darjeeling. At the stove he
tests the gas tank, which still has fuel, and makes them a brew.

Jing leans over her steaming cup. "What I do now, you don't tell."

"Is that a question?"

She approaches one of the original Life-Stills, lifts it, and drags it
toward the front door.

He stands, bemused. "Whoa—it's raining outside. Jing? Jing, stop!"

But she persists, pulling the painting by one side, which causes
him to grab for the other side, lest a decades-old masterpiece be

dragged along the soggy lawn. He keeps telling her to stop, or at least explain herself. She keeps moving, saying only: "You'll see. You can see now." She back-kicks open the unlocked studio door and drops her side of the canvas on the floor. "This machine? What is it? Fireplace?" She points to the kiln. "How do I turn it on?"

"Hang on, Jing. What am I supposed to not say anything about?"

"I burn them, all the paintings."

Blinking double-time, he scrunches his face. "Jing, *this* is an original. Apologies—I thought you understood. We're talking millions of dollars, each one."

"I understood."

"Then I don't."

"If I sell these ones, then the paintings that Chars did, all around world, they come down. And the museums that are putting up the Faces, also by Chars—what happens?"

"Okay, fine. But you cannot just destroy original works of art. These are the rare few that Bear saved. He kept them back for years and years. These are part of art history. You can't. I'm sorry."

"Chars' paintings go in the museums," she insists, kneeling by the kiln, struggling with the latch.

"You're not doing this," he repeats. "If you want to honor Charles, remember that he spent years guarding these paintings."

"How I can turn on this machine?"

"I'm not showing you. Sorry. I won't."

## 88

Marsden strides fast toward the woods. *This woman is nuts.* He scrambles up the subsided remains of his staircase in the hillside, pausing at the beginning of the hiking path. He is panting; his pulse won't slow.

The forest rustles. The remains of that old Nokia must be in there somewhere. Could've been his own remains rotting there.

*Why,* he wonders, *am I so upset with Jing? Because what she's suggesting is a violation! I will not allow it. But why not? I'm supposed to maintain the integrity of art history? As if there weren't thousands of forgeries all through the great museums!*

He kicks a tree trunk. "Charles," he says, turning to see his friend. *How can you not be here?* On the snowy steps before class in Toronto: "We're smoking Cuban cigars today, my dear Charles. Come admire us. And apply your body heat. We're ice cubicles, and it's for you alone to save us." Marsden presses his knuckles hard into his breastbone, to drive back the grief. Then he smells smoke and swivels around. It's billowing from the studio.

He starts running, nearly losing his footing, skidding to a halt before the oil barrel, which is flaming from kerosene. Jing stands in the studio doorway, trying to drag out the Life-Still.

Marsden blocks her way. "You're *not.*"

She tries to barge past, but he needs only a half step to deflect her.

She tumbles, losing her grip on the canvas, which he grabs. She hits the grass, gasping, winded from the fall. She hurries to her feet, nearly in tears, raising a muddy hand against him, as if to ward off violence.

"You think I'd hurt you? Never. Ever." He offers his hand.

"They're mine. I am allowed to do this!"

But he closes the metal lid over the barrel; the flames peter out. He places the Life-Still back in the studio and walks past her, back to the cottage.

Before the kitchen table he stands, hands on hips, staring down at these genuine works. He runs his fingers over the rough fibers of the back of a canvas, which is smeared with charcoal where Bear Bavinsky once wiped his hand. "I'm *not,*" Marsden mumbles. "This is insane."

Glancing around the kitchen, he recalls a scene just outside, Bear—eyes wide with rage—shouting at his son: "*You* work for *me*. Get it? You always worked for me. And you dare steal? Get this: I win. You hear? I fucking win."

Marsden looks at the ceiling—then pushes out the cottage door, striding back through the rain, finger leveled at Jing, who sits in the studio doorway. Yet he bypasses her and stoops before the kiln. "This," he says, "is how you turn it on."

She meets his gaze, the briefest confirmation, and drags over the painting. Marsden stands at the far wall, staring fixedly away, wishing he could ask his friend how you make something of such beauty. Behind Marsden, she grunts from exertion, struggling to fit the large canvas inside.

"I'm not helping," he tells the wall, then rotates. He takes the painting, stamps on one stretcher beam, which cracks, then does the same to the other side, folding it with ease, cramming canvas and wood inside. "We're doing them all?" he asks. "If you say yes, I might be sick."

Together they carry in every other Life-Still, moving in haste, dragging them up the lawn. Side by side, they kneel at the kiln, sweat drops splatting onto these last-century originals, which Marsden kicks and snaps apart, leaving her to ram them inside. He works fast, needing this to be over.

When every Life-Still is inside, he slams the kiln door, locks it. Looking pointedly at her, he says, "I did *not* do this."

"I didn't too."

Through the peephole they watch as the temperature rises. Canvases curl. Elbows, hips, thighs—they yellow and burst into flames. Smoke rises up the chimney, spiraling over the valley.

They return to the kitchen, spent. Jing raises her clunky tea mug, clinks his.

"To Chars," she says. "Artist."

"To Charles!" Marsden affirms, voice cracking as he looks to the ceiling, blinking fast. "Best of artists!"

Before leaving the property, Marsden pockets a Cecil Ditchley mug—a token of this place, where he will never return. The lone object Jing takes home is that unfinished self-portrait of Pinch pictured as a youth, back when he believed he'd endure, that strangers would know of him someday.

Jing keeps that painting under his bed in the spare room. At times, she takes it out. Never for long. Just a look.

# London, 2018

## 89

On the twentieth anniversary of Bear Bavinsky's death, the first major retrospective of his work is organized at Tate Modern. Marsden and his longtime partner, Rob, close their Prince Edward County bed-and-breakfast for a few days and fly to London.

The museum is holding another show too, *Selfie Shtick: Autofictions of the Contemporary Canon*, where once-snarling, now-domesticated Young British Artists have chosen works by their personal friends, including huge plastic dog feces by a Taiwanese sculptor, computer-generated images of a Czech artist known for dressing up as Disney characters, and even a video series by Temple Butterfield. The exhibition has won rave reviews, so Marsden expects everyone to congregate there, allowing for a peaceful inspection of the Bavinskys.

But he is wrong. Crowds are trooping into *Bear Bavinsky: The Body Politic*, with throngs gathered before all of the paintings, which are ranged across eleven rooms. Many visitors take photos with their phones, wanting evidence of their proximity to greatness; others stand frozen with audio guides, learning about the artist's private life: the opulent childhood in St. Louis, his precocious rebellions and wartime traumas, the fierce debates at Black Mountain College, the scene in Greenwich Village, his travels through bombed-out Europe, years in the critical wilderness, his volatile relationships with women, most notably his third wife, Natalie, now recognized as the painter's muse, demonstrated by her appearance in so many of the Faces series. For context, the curators included a vitrine of eight ceramics by Natalie, marked "Courtesy of Xiao Jingfei," whom visitors assume to be a tycoon collector.

The first rooms contain Bear Bavinsky juvenilia: childhood sketches drawn in a hospital bed, already showing promise; slapdash portraits from his army days; early experiments with abstraction; his unique style, approaching its consummation in the mature works that dominate subsequent rooms, including a triumphant display of eighteen Life-Stills from private collections, plus fourteen of the Faces, which were lent by museums.

According to the catalog, the Faces have all entered prominent public collections, owing to the tireless efforts of the Pulitzer-nominated biographer Connor Thomas, who has made it his mission to accomplish the lifelong wish of Bear Bavinsky. The museums didn't pay full valuation, instead covering outstanding taxes and fines owed by the estate. Today the Faces reside in the permanent holdings of the Musée d'Art Moderne in Paris, the Menil Collection in Houston, the San Francisco Museum of Modern Art, the Norton Museum of Art in West Palm Beach, the Art Gallery of Ontario, the Moderna Museet in Stockholm, and the Gemeentemuseum in The Hague, among others.

In the final room, Marsden hesitates by the exit, not willing to leave. Rob is curious to peek into *The Selfie Shtick*, so Marsden returns alone to the beginning of the Bavinsky exhibition, renting an audio guide this time. The narration speaks of Bear as "the embodiment of that old slogan: art for art's sake." He toiled for decades without caring what the public thought; he scorned money; he dedicated himself to a singular vision.

*Why*, Marsden wonders, *are these myths still recited about artists? It's probably lucky that Charles never became a painter in public. They'd have demolished him. Rather, they'd have ignored him. He lacked the personality, which is so much more important than any audio guide dares say.*

Instead, this one cites "the erotic absence of the Life-Stills," noting that "from the sixties onward, a frequent claim against Bavinsky—strenuously denied by the artist—was that he was an aesthetic reactionary, and to some, a misogynist." But, it hastens to add, Bear redeemed himself in the purest way: through art, as shown in "the undeniable humanity of his Faces series."

Marsden smiles. Bear gains his glory in the end! Though this isn't quite the end. There's fifty years hence, one hundred, five hundred, all diminishing toward that everlasting instant when nothing by human hand remains. But today, Bear is triumphant: strangers speaking his name, estimating his prices, dreaming of his objects on their walls.

For a minute, the crowd clears. Marsden is alone in the room, standing before Pinch's paintings and Natalie's pots. He urges his eyes to hurry, to absorb this, to save this sight.

Gradually other visitors drift in. He takes a last glance around, presses "Play" on the audio guide, and proceeds toward the exit. "From these masterpieces, Bear Bavinsky speaks," the narration concludes. "Even today, even beyond the grave—from these paintings, truly, we know him."

# Acknowledgments

My gratitude to those who generously contributed to my research with conversation, books, or lessons, including Haidee Becker, Milton Gendel, Jacob Burckhardt, Peter Miller, Alvin Curran, Rosemary Donegan, Charlie Hill, Edmund de Waal, Sue Salies, Peter Rockwell, Robert Cook, Nina Berson, Ian Mader. Here in London, warm thanks to Natasha Fairweather and Max Edwards; and in New York, Elyse Cheney and Alex Jacobs. Also, Andrea Schulz and Emily Wunderlich at Viking. Jon Riley and Rose Tomaszewska at Quercus. Michael Heyward at Text. My valued friend Patricia Reimann at dtv. Lasting appreciation to Aldo and Margherita for kindly allowing me to write at their home in Puglia. To Carla for helping me decipher the art world, and Gideon for bottled deliveries. My most-valued art appraisers: Clare, Jack & Samuel. And my first Italian teacher, Ian Martin. Lastly, my love to Alessandra and the Chooky.